Xavier Wallace

SHAW RECLAMATION

JEFFREY + WALLACE

ISBN: 9781764141284

ISBN (eBook): 9781764141291

JEFFREY + WALLACE PUBLISHING

www.jwpublishing.com.au

XAVIER WALLACE

www.xavierwallace.com

Xavier Wallace

Xavier Wallace was born and raised in regional New South Wales, Australia. He attended public primary and high schools, before studying business at the University of Newcastle. He worked in Canberra for the Australian Government in both the public service and politics for over a decade. He has a Master of Politics and Public Policy from Deakin University. Xavier's interests include politics, government, national security, media and communications, philosophy, ancient history and mythology. He is an advocate for equality and human rights, including LGBTI+ rights. Live music, thriller novels and action movies occupy his time outside writing and work. He loves spending time with his family and friends, and his groodle, Atlas.

Xavier Wallace is the author of the Max Shaw spy thriller series.

Dedication

For my aunts, uncles and cousins.

Acknowledgements

When I was in primary school, Year 5 from memory, I wrote a speech called 'My Family'. It had some fun lines in it roasting my immediate family, but it also didn't spare my extended family from the public grilling. Like most roasts, it came from a good place. A place of love and endearment, and a constant desire to laugh.

It wasn't until I was at university that I realised my family was the odd one out. I thought everyone grew up knowing their aunts, uncles and cousins. In fact, I thought they probably lived around the corner from each other, went to the pub together and even packed up and trekked away on annual holidays together. But sadly most people don't know or have anything to do with their extended families, and those that do often wish they didn't.

My extended family is very close. My cousins and my sister and I grew up more like brothers and sisters. And, my aunts and uncles were like extra mums and dads, often coming to sporting or academic events to provide me with encouragement and praise or being on hand to give me a bit of discipline if needed or even to give me sage career counsel.

I'm the odd one out. I no longer live in the same city, but the others all still live at home and spend a lot of time together. I love going home to catch up with everyone for drinks, dinners and normally a lot of laughs. And yes, we do all actually go on holidays together, every year, to the same place – for over forty years (for some of them anyway).

And, the crew is constantly expanding as more second cousins are added! They are all growing so fast and becoming great kids. I'm thrilled to get to spend time with them and hear about their adventures.

I want to thank you all for your friendship, love and support over the years. I look forward to coming home again soon for a few beers and even more laughs!

The Max Shaw Spy Thriller Series

Shaw Vengeance

Shaw Initiation

Shaw Confrontation

Shaw Intervention

Shaw Reclamation

Shaw Salvation

SHAW RECLAMATION

By Xavier Wallace

Fifth Novel of the Max Shaw Spy Thriller Series.

Prelude

The ancient theatre of Epidaurus was packed with scholars from across the globe.

The magnificent wonder of the ancient Greek world was abuzz with excitement as the academics spoke to each other and waited for their presenter to take the stage. It was early in the evening; the sun was setting casting glorious pink, purple and orange patterns across the sky.

A modern stage had been set up on the antiquated and weathered stone where the original concrete stage had sat for generations. Large projector screens hung from either side of the stage on black backdrops and a much larger display sat perfectly centred behind the stage.

There were speakers in various sizes lining the stage even though it was said you could drop a coin on the ancient stone at the front of the theatre and it could be heard throughout, thanks to its incredible acoustics.

Upbeat music was playing, rumbling in the space and adding more energy to the assembled crowd.

The stage was subtly lit, but as the night moved in and the first stars started to appear, two Hollywood style searchlights came on stretching their beams up into the heavens. They swept back and forth, only getting more intense with each minute that rolled by.

The first three rows of the theatre had been reserved for journalists who were taking their seats and readying their microphones and notepads as their cameramen set up in long rows halfway up the theatre's slopped, auditorium styled seating area. Some of the cameras were already rolling, their bright lights shining to help capture the moment and beam it live to audiences around the world.

"Ladies and gentlemen," a strong male voice boomed over the crowd to the delight of the masses who all took their seats.

"Please welcome to the stage the Chairwoman and Chief Executive Officer of A&A Enterprises, Isabella Lyadova!"

The crowd all rose to their feet and cheered and applauded as the screens all flashed in unison to reveal the A&A Enterprises logo. The A on the left had an ancient Greek god wielding a bow and arrow. The figure was Apollo and he came out from behind the letter at the crossbar and was shown from the waist up. The god on the right A was in a similar position and she was wielding a sword and shield. It was Athena. Their gold armour shone brightly then faded to white matching the '&' symbol as the two As took on their golden glow as if the metal had liquified and run into the letters.

The screens on either side of the stage held the logos and glowed brightly, as the main screen changed to a camera feed from the centre of the theatre. The footage followed Lyadova onto the stage to more thunderous applause from the crowd.

As she got to the centre of the stage, Lyadova nodded her thanks to the crowd and smiled broadly, taking in the accolades. After a full minute, she raised her hands.

"Thank you," Lyadova said, motioning for the crowd to take their seats. "Thank you very much. What an amazing welcome. Thank you all for being here. Welcome to Epidaurus!"

"This theatre was built at the end of the fourth century BC," she said, staring down the lens of the main camera. "It is completely symmetrical and still to this day stands as a masterpiece of human achievement and of enduring beauty. It was built as part of a sanctuary to the Greek god Asclepius, the god of medicine. I chose this location for this very reason. I believe what the world needs now is a dose of good medicine. A cure for our aches and pains. A prescription to relieve us of our ailments and a way to rid our world of a crippling disease."

"The disease I refer to is not a medical condition, but rather an increasingly isolated and disconnected world," the powerful CEO said as she paced to one side of the stage. "Our world has been suffering. War and terror are on the rise, not only between nations, but within our own countries. Civil wars are rising up, bred from ignorance and intolerance. Generated by the enduring battle between those who have power, money and privilege, and those that don't. Spawned from a lack of compassion and a lack of knowledge."

"Too often people hide behind the veil of ignorance," Lyadova stated as she turned and started for the other side of the stage. "Too often people are too quick to react and forget to use their judgement and foresight. Too often people are denied the chance to learn and grow. But today that comes to an end. Tonight, I am here to announce A&A Enterprises' latest project – I call it Alexandria 2.0."

The screen in the centre changed to a series of sweeping camera shots from inside an enormous server room. It stretched for hundreds of metres. Row after row of gleaming black servers with colourful blinking lights and blue neons. Those images were followed by paintings and sketches of an ancient building in Egypt.

"The Library of Alexandria was created to collate the knowledge of the known world," Lyadova said, returning to the centre of the stage. "It was said to have held up to four hundred thousand scrolls from across the empire and was seen as a place of academic study, of knowledge transfer and of learning. A way for the best and brightest to collaborate, share and debate ideas on everything from philosophy and military strategy to religion, health, governance and everything in between. While the ancient Library of Alexandria had these lofty goals, it was also a way to project power and influence, and to use knowledge to gain the upper hand over the empire's enemies."

"Alexandria 2.0 is the realisation of the original library's goal to be a repository for the world's knowledge," Lyadova said, returning her gaze to the centre camera. "But the difference is that instead of collating information to use as a tool against others, A&A Enterprises will make it free for every person on this planet to access and use. Every scholarly paper, every textbook, every religious text, every artwork, map, artifact, sculpture, poem, novel, documentary, historical location, will be catalogued, stored and made available to anyone who wants it. We will work with every museum, library, university and governments around the world to build the collection, digitise it and store it forever. We will do three dimensional renders of ancient and important sites from across the globe to give people full access. And, through our virtual reality technology, you will feel as if you are there, walking the halls of our shared history, our shared world."

The crowd in the theatre rose to their feet and applauded as a young man dressed completely in black walked onto the stage carrying a tablet computer which he passed to Lyadova then left the stage.

"With this tablet, I will start the countdown to our future," Lyadova said, pressing the palm of her hand to the little computer screen unlocking it. "But first, I want you to meet someone."

"Good evening, Isabella," the same voice said over the speakers. "How can I help you?"

"Good evening, Apollo," Isabella replied, looking up and to the right as if speaking to a higher power. "Tell the people who you are."

"I am Apollo, the librarian of Alexandria 2.0."

"What is your role, Apollo?"

"I exist to build, collate and catalogue the greatest archive on Earth, on your command. Once completed, I will maintain the collection, update it when new works need to be added and be the virtual assistant charged with helping people navigate the archive to find the information they are seeking."

"Apollo is the future," Lyadova said, returning her gaze to the camera. "He is artificial intelligence. He scans the internet for content which he then catalogues. If the item is free, he will copy it into our servers. If it is protected or copyrighted, he will make a payment for the item. If he needs to, he will contact the owner and arrange terms and payment for the item. Once the terms are agreed, he will transfer it and store it for all time. A&A Enterprises will also start funding research and academic activities throughout the world. I am personally donating more than half of my fortune to build this project and another quarter to fund ongoing research. Tonight, I will give Apollo the order and he will start building our library. In fourteen days, Apollo will be available to the world."

The crowd rose to their feet and applauded.

"A&A gets its name from Apollo and Athena," Lyadova said as the logos flashed onto each of the screens again – the gold running back and forth between the letters and the gods. "Apollo was the god of knowledge and Athena the god of wisdom. Tonight, I am here to announce that through Alexandria 2.0, A&A has finally realised its goal and will provide the world with a single, free, independent and verified source of information at the click of a button. It is only through learning, sharing and collaborating on academic and creative grounds that we – not as a nation or even a group of nations – we as the human race, can come together to build our knowledge and wisdom for the betterment of our world. We are in this together and can only succeed if we cherish what we have. If we appreciate and understand our history. If we learn from each other and build not only our tolerance, but our acceptance of the things which make us different and, more importantly, the things which we all have in common. It is time for the world to come together and it is my hope that through having access to all of this information, we can all learn, grow and realise our potential."

"Apollo," Lyadova yelled over the loud applause of the crowd, again speaking up to her right. "Build the archive."

"Yes, Isabella," the hyper realistic electronic voice said over the speakers. "Starting the build. Estimated time to completion is thirteen days, twenty-three hours and fifty-nine minutes."

Chapter One

He collected his metal tray and held his place in the line, inching ever closer to the servers.

When he got to the head of the line, he sat his tray down on the metal rails and slid it along as he walked. One by one the servers ladled food onto the tray. At the end of the line, one of the men behind the counter gave him a bread roll and a sealed cup of water.

He turned back to face the cold concrete dining hall with its icy steel tables and chairs which were bolted to the floor and its grey walls with their chipped paint.

He walked among the scattered men. They came in all shapes and sizes. Some were big, gruff looking guys covered in scars and tattoos, while others looked like businessmen, neat and tidy hair, and unblemished skin. The businessmen sat in silence by themselves eating their breakfast, not daring to look up. The gruff men were loud and yelling insults at each other, while taunting the businessmen and the guards.

He walked on, moving away from the crowds. Row after row of mostly empty tables stretched out before him, until he reached the far end of the room. He marched left to the corner and took the seat with his back to the wall, so he could watch the room. It was an occupational requirement, before he was thrown in this hellhole, to know exactly who was in the room as well as the location of the exits and any weapons he might need to use. Having his back to the wall also meant he could not be jumped from behind in a surprise attack.

Scheveningen Prison was once a gaol for resistance fighters and prisoners of war by the occupying German forces. It was now home to torturers, war criminals, murderers, and genocidal dictators and their henchmen. The businessmen and their gruff fellow prisoners were a mix of each of these categories.

Max Shaw had been there for over four months, awaiting trial at the International Criminal Court.

The former Australian Intelligence Service or AIS agent and head of field operations was six foot three and the months in prison had done nothing to diminish his massive muscular frame. In fact, other than reading and sitting staring at the wall, there was not much else to do but train. So Max woke at five o'clock every morning, as he had since his first day of training at the Wool Shed, AIS's secret training base in regional New South Wales. He used his cell as a training ground. Push ups on the floor, elevated push ups and dips using his concrete bed, squats, lunges, burpees, sit ups and shadow boxing, and he often used his bedsheet to do pull ups with the sheet tied to the cell door. All before breakfast.

Max had found himself in the prison, after being the subject of rendition by the British Government and two months of intense torture and questioning. One day out of nowhere, Max had been whisked off on a prison transport plane to The Hague in the Netherlands.

He was on trial for torture, war crimes, murder and the assassination of two world leaders. He was charged with acting without authority on foreign soil and he was facing life in prison.

Max had met with his lawyers on multiple occasions. Evidently the British had been compelled to turn him over to The Hague when someone started questioning his whereabouts. The Australian Government had applied pressure on both the British and the Americans to find out what had happened to their best agent.

Max knew the only person with enough drive and credibility to ask the right questions of the right people and get a result was Blake.

Vice Admiral Blake 'Hermes' Smyth was the recently commissioned head of the Australian Intelligence Service. He was the man with all the secrets and the man charged with keeping Australia and its allies safe. He was trusted by the most senior politicians on both sides of the aisle and was fast gaining a reputation on the international stage as one of the world's most reputable and efficient intelligence agents.

He also happened to be one of Max's oldest friends and in the days leading up to his capture by the British, Blake had become Max's partner.

They had been together walking down a sidewalk in Washington DC when Max had been captured. Blake had been shot in the leg as Max was bundled into the van and it sped off. The thought of the incident still angered Max all these months later.

He was also bitter and angry about the rendition. The British Government should have been thanking him for taking out terrorists on their home soil, including a couple of high-profile politicians and aristocrats who had been plotting against the British people. But instead, they chose to whisk him away, then throw him in a hole, before sending him off to The Hague.

Not only was his treatment the cause of his anger, but Max was also upset because he had just started to pull his life back together and make a fresh start with Blake, and when he was shot Max felt helpless. He couldn't defend him and he felt sick in the stomach thinking about Blake being in any pain. He also knew Blake's anguish would have continued, even as his leg healed, trying to find Max and find out who took him and why, and then trying to work out how to get him back.

As head of the AIS, Blake had a growing number of agents with him at any one time to serve as his bodyguards. As the van had sped off on that Washington street, three of his guards came to his aid while two others gave chase. They followed the van to the airport and recorded the plane's serial numbers and departure time, and sent it through to AIS to track.

By the time Blake got to the hospital, he knew the plane was one of MI6's and he started making calls. He also called the White House which had just awarded him and Max medals for thwarting a terrorist attack on American soil. The American President, Amanda Torres, had given the flight clearance, but refused to admit she knew Max was onboard.

Blake was readying an assault to rescue Max, but he was ordered to shut down the operation by the then Australian Prime Minister, Bronwyn Ferguson, who was worried it would irreparably damage the relationship between Australia and the United Kingdom, and potentially with the other Five Eyes countries. Ferguson had recently been removed from office for her perceived weakness and her collapsing poll numbers.

Max simply was not worth the risk. Not to the Ferguson Government anyway.

So Blake set about finding information and building a case which could be used behind the scenes to pressure the British and secure Max's release.

Two months after Max's rendition, Blake presented the file to the British and they panicked. Blake had uncovered their whole rendition program, including locations, numbers and names of those being held without trial. They knew that if Blake presented the information to The Hague they would be undone. So instead, they flew Max to The Hague and levelled charges against him to take the moral high ground, to let justice have its day and bring spy craft to the surface.

The British Prime Minister, Timothy Birmingham, made a speech at Westminster pledging to disband MI6 and roll back the country's covert intelligence apparatus, claiming it was an antiquated throwback to a time where the world was at war. It had no place in modern society and he would be entering conversations with the Five Eyes intelligence countries to discuss the UK's withdrawal from the controversial treaty.

The Americans and Canadians had joined the Australian Government in trying to get Max's case thrown out, given the secrets which could be exposed. They did not want the world to know how close it had come to war and collapse, and they certainly did not want the world to know how they managed to fight off their enemies using the intelligence agencies. They also believed that as an intelligence agent, Max was legally doing the job he was legally authorised to perform.

Max and his colleagues around the world had to get in the mud and wrestle with the worst of the worst. To succeed they needed to use the terrorists' own tools and tactics against them. They had to do unthinkable and unspeakable things to achieve their mission and their enemies were just begging to exploit their weaknesses, including turning their own countries against them by exposing their tactics.

Birmingham had continued on his crusade and had exposed the Five Eyes and some of their tactics. He forced global intelligence agencies to defend themselves to the very people they were fighting to protect. He had set off a public backlash which was threatening to bring on civil war within western nations. And he was using Max's trial as a catalyst.

Max, known in The Hague as Witness S, could gain his own freedom if he provided the court the information it required on the operations of the AIS and Five Eyes treaty. There was growing speculation the court had been infiltrated by rising and former superpowers who were keen to expose the West. Max refused to provide any information and told the court he had no idea what they were talking about.

Max sat playing with his food with his plastic fork. It looked atrocious, but he didn't have much choice. He ate thinking about the day ahead as he noticed two men checking him out from the other side of the room. They were from the gruff section.

He calmly scooped up another mouthful, pretending not to see them.

The two men made their way over to him as he took a swig of water to wash down the gruel.

"Morning, fellas," Max said as the pair arrived. "Enjoy your breakfast?"

"We have message for you," one of the men said in a heavy Russian accent.

"I don't want to hear it."

"I think you will change mind when you hear."

"Who is the message from?"

"It is from Kremlin."

"The Kremlin has a message for me?"

"Yes."

"Well, what is it?"

The Russian and his comrade jumped the table, tackling Max from his seat and pinning him to the ground. The Russian climbed on top of Max and started pounding on him, punch after punch, as Max tried in vain to block the incoming blows.

"The message is start talking or this will happen every day until you either dead or wish you were dead," the Russian said in a staccato between the punches.

"Well, errand boy," Max said, grabbing his attacker's hand and blocking a punch, "I have a message for you to take back to Mother Russia. Tell that arsehole that he will never break me and I will never talk."

Max threw his head forward and broke the Russian's nose, then kneed him in the nuts. He felt the big man go weak and capitalised, throwing his own series of punches, each connecting with his assailant's face. One after the other he punched and grappled until the Russian was on his back and Max was on top.

As Max went in for another hit, the second man slammed Max's metal meal tray into the back of his neck and shoulder.

Max stopped and turned to face his new attacker. He was a much shorter and weaker looking man than the Russian. Max jumped to his feet and grabbed the little man by the neck, lifting him off the ground and punching him twice, then he threw him against the concrete wall in the corner. He hit with a thud and cowered into a ball afraid to look Max in the eye.

Max felt his legs go out from under him as the Russian swept his own leg into the back of Max's knees. Max fell as the Russia staggered to his feet. He came running in to kick Max, but Max caught his leg, rolled onto the Russian's planted foot and drove his elbow and the back of his arm hard into the Russian's kneecap. He kept rolling up the leg as he was pushing down on the knee, until he felt it break. The Russian screamed in pain and let loose a string of expletives in Russian.

Max got to his feet as the Russian bounced on his good leg, reaching out to the table for support.

"You broke my leg," he said through the pain. "You will pay for that."

Max leapt off his left leg and drew back his right fist, before slamming it into the Russian's face. He landed and crouched before springing up and throwing a violent left hook into his stomach. As the big man buckled over, Max grabbed his head and threw his knee into his face. He was out cold before he hit the ground.

"Be sure to pass on my message," Max said as a bunch of security guards arrived.

The guards grabbed Max and started to drag him away.

"You'd better deliver the message," Max yelled to the little man still cowered in the corner. "I'm not sure your friend heard me."

Chapter Two

Max had been returned to his cell.

It was painted in a blue tinged grey. Everything was grey. The walls, the roof, the metal bars, even the concrete slab which rose out of the concrete floor to form a bed.

The bed had a thin mattress which was more like a mattress protector than an actual mattress. If it wasn't for the cold, Max would have just slept on the concrete and not noticed the difference. He had slept in some terrible places over the years, from deep bushland, to caves and even some dive hotels when he was on the run in some of the worst areas of the worst cities on Earth. All considered, the concrete was fine.

The toilet was made of stainless steel and had a basin and taps built into the top of it.

Max washed his knuckles and rinsed the blood from his mouth in the tiny basin, then sat on his bed, lost in thought.

The Russians, the Chinese, even some European countries hated the Five Eyes treaty and the western world's intelligence systems. But that hate was nothing in comparison to that of terrorists and their state backers. The system spent every minute of every day trying to stop them from realising their goals of a global caliphate and the destruction of the infidels, and ultimately the complete destruction of the west.

The British Prime Minister, Timothy Birmingham, was a risen messiah for those that felt democracy and capitalism may have run its course. He had clawed his way to power promising sweeping reforms to government. He promised to scale back defence spending as well as overhauling the intelligence system. He was looking to dramatically increase welfare spending and taxes on the wealthy and middle classes.

In his youth, Birmingham had been a member of the UK Communist Party, but he realised quickly that was never going to cut it with the broader population and switched parties. He was still trying to shake off the communist labels, but somehow had got through to people by promising jobs and equality. It sounded nice on paper, but delivering was going to be difficult. Right wing commentators were ropeable and each night took to the screens to ask how he could have been elected.

Max was shocked by the recent announcement Birmingham had made on withdrawing the UK from the Five Eyes alliance and ending the country's military support for various wars and peacekeeping missions being carried out with allies around the globe.

The Five Eyes treaty had served as the backbone of the UK's security for decades and the special relationship they had with the United States was at a low not seen since the Revolutionary War. He was making a huge mistake and that upset Max more than the fact Birmingham was using Max as a political prop.

For years Max had worked undercover as a political adviser in Canberra. It was a job which had given him access to domestic and international travel without raising suspicions while he was actually working for AIS. His experience in the corridors of power had left a bitter taste in his mouth for politicians, especially populists like Birmingham who had no clue how the real world operated.

There was an electronic buzz and the lock clicked, opening the sliding metal gate on his cell. A guard walked in with a no nonsense look on his face.

"It is time for you to get ready," the guard said. "You have five minutes in the bathroom then you are to report to the guardhouse where you can get changed."

"Got it," Max said, getting up from the bed and heading for the shower room.

The shower room was a large, tiled, open space. Rows of shower heads hung from long metal pipes running the length of the room. Each shower head had a metal chain which you pulled down to turn on the water. There were no hot or cold taps, it just came out somewhere on the colder end of the spectrum. On a winter's day, like today, the water was like ice.

Max used the thin, watered down body wash the prison had provided in big pump bottes which were bolted to the walls, and let the freezing cold water run over his scarred and batter body.

Max showered briefly and dried, then headed for the guardhouse where a new suit was waiting for him. A dark navy blue from a tailor in Sydney and a crisp white shirt, with a blue tie which had thin red stripes. There was a new pair of dark brown R.M. Williams boots, and Max's watch and rings were sitting on the bench.

There was a note in his lawyer's handwriting pinned to the lapel. In simply read, *From H.* Blake's AIS callsign was Hermes, *H.* Blake had sent him a new suit for his first formal appearance at the International Criminal Court.

Max smiled and got dressed before being handcuffed and escorted to a waiting motorcade. There were four police motorbikes and three SUVs. Max was placed in the rear of the middle SUV in the line-up.

Max watched the beautiful city of The Hague on the North Sea roll past the window. Like other parts of The Netherlands, the architecture was fascinating. Rich red brick walls framed with white borders and feature pieces, like balconies and architraves. Arched doorways and windows of the older buildings occasionally gave way to more modern glass structures and large treelined parks and public spaces.

Most of the trees were bare, their leaves long gone thanks to the biting winter winds. Those with leaves were patched with a light dusting of snow. The front yards and gardens, and the sidewalks were similarly covered by the fresh powdery snow.

Cars parked in the street looked like they had been sculpted out of the snow, as they were completely covered.

People walked along the sidewalks in long winter coats, with scarves and gloves, while some wore beanies and hats to keep the warmth in.

Max was thankful for the SUV's heating which was working perfectly.

Eventually the motorcade peeled away and left Max's SUV to enter the grounds of the ultra-modern criminal court.

The bollards lowered into the ground and the big metal gates swung back to let the vehicle onto the grounds.

There were protesters waving placards and banners in protest to the global intelligence system Witness S had come to represent, thanks to Birmingham. Witness S was now one of the most controversial men on Earth thanks to the rising fear and spread of bullshit Birmingham and his supporters were pedalling. The Americans and their other allies, including Australia, had successfully argued to have Max's identity shielded; it would never be released, even if he was found guilty, much to the upset of Birmingham and his supporters.

The ranting mob tried to get close to his SUV, but were stopped by local police holding them back. The blacked out windows meant they could not see him, but he could see them. Most of the banners he could see were calling for him to hang or rot in gaol, while others were calling for MI6, AIS and the CIA to be shut down. Max had to admit some of the signs were quite impressively made and some were even quite witty, but most were negative and he turned to look out the other window.

Max couldn't help but feel upset at the sacrifices he and his colleagues around the world had made to give these people the very freedoms they were now expressing. They had no idea how many times the agencies they wanted closed had saved them from devastation.

On the other side of the car, a similar crowd had assembled. They too were yelling and shouting, but not at him, they were protesting the other protesters. They held up signs calling Witness S a hero and demanding his immediate release.

The rival groups were at fever pitch, ready to explode at any minute and the local cops were struggling to keep them contained.

The car managed to make its way down the concrete driveway which was lined with black light poles as the gate and bollards again closed off the grounds behind it.

The International Criminal Court building was made up of five large rectangular blocks, the largest of which sat in the centre with two either side. The structures were strikingly different to the city in which they sat. They were modern box-like concrete and glass buildings protruding from a long three storey structure which ran the length of the property. Randomly scattered across the building, blinds in the windows had been pulled down which made the whole place look like massive irregular chess boards.

The SUV pulled up in the large concrete square outside the main towering glass and metal framed building. Max was rushed through one of the stainless-steel turnstile doorways surrounded by guards and into the foyer with military precision. The guards had constructed a small shield to protect his identity from the paparazzi with their long lens cameras who were gathered with the protesters at the gate.

Max was ushered into the main court room. There was a raised panel for the justices at the front of the room with five high back black leather chairs awaiting their arrival. In front of them was a row of eight computers for the officials and court clerks.

The rest of the room was divided into two with three rows of computer lined desks on both sides facing the middle. The whole room was lined with a mix of white-washed wood panels and acoustic panels in light green and grey muted pastels.

Behind the room there was an elevated observation room on the second floor. The glass panelling stretched up a couple of storeys, allowing the enclosed auditorium full view of the court.

In the centre, at the rear of the court, was a single table with chair and computer monitor for the witness.

The United Nations logo and the court's formal name was written in both French and English on the front of the justices' long bench. The whole thing screamed power and authority.

Max took his place behind the witness table and his lawyers forced the guards to remove his handcuffs. The room stood as the procession of judges made their way into the court room. Everyone took their seats when commanded, ready for the proceedings to start.

"Ladies and Gentlemen," the lead justice Winston Stafford said. "The court is now in session. I remind all present that the witness is to be referred to as Witness S and anyone found to have breached the anonymity afforded the witness will be held in contempt and prosecuted. Today's hearings are in-camera and accordingly the cameras and sound equipment in the court are only for use in the court and are not being broadcast to protect both the witness and the national security of the countries which will be referred to during the proceedings. The gallery at the rear of the court is made up of officials from the relevant countries and is not open to the media. We are here today to discuss the evidence gathered by the prosecution and to determine if the case will go to trial. Can you please read the charges?"

An official at the front of the room stood and held up a folder.

"Witness S," the official stated, "is sitting as both a defendant and a witness. He is a defendant charged with multiple counts of crimes against humanity and war crimes, including wilful killing, torture, inhumane treatment, wilfully causing great suffering, destruction and appropriation of property, denying a fair trial, unlawful deportation and transfer, unlawful confinement, taking hostages in armed conflicts. All of which constitute significant breaches of the Geneva Conventions. He is also charged with non-armed conflict crimes in violation of article three of the Geneva Conventions, including murder, mutilation, cruel treatment, torture, outrages upon personal dignity, taking hostages, sentencing or execution without due process. He is also serving as a witness to these crimes, carried out by himself, his agency and partner agencies on behalf of the Commonwealth of Australia and allied nations, including the United States of America, the

United Kingdom, and the Dominions of Canada and New Zealand."

"These are very serious allegations," Stafford said. "Is the prosecution ready to proceed should the case go to trial?"

"Yes, Mister Justice," the prosecutor said, standing. "We have had the opportunity to discuss this matter with the relevant countries and with the witness. With the court's permission we are seeking the right to issue subpoenas to over one hundred and thirty witnesses, including several former and current world leaders."

"How was the court informed of these allegations?"

"The government of the United Kingdom referred the matter to us."

"And the witness, how did he come to be in custody of the court?"

"Again, the British Government captured the witness and handed him over to the court."

"The United Kingdom is a party to this trial."

"Yes, Mister Justice, the government has indicated their full support for the trial and stand ready to present their own history of abuses against the Geneva Conventions and international law."

"They are willingly subjecting themselves to trial?"

"Yes. The Prime Minister himself has provided a statement. If it pleases the court, I am happy to read it and enter it into the records?"

"Proceed."

"It reads, 'I, The Right Honourable Timothy Birmingham MP, Prime Minister of the United Kingdom, do swear to attend the International Criminal Court to provide evidence in the matter of Witness S. I do also undertake to provide the court with the history of my country's involvement with the so-called Five Eyes intelligence alliance. It is my hope that by bringing these matters to the attention of the court and laying them in the light for the world to see, that together we can reshape our nations to better serve the people. My government stands ready to assist the court and I have instructed the Departments of Justice, Home Affairs and Foreign Affairs to provide any and all information required. I have also directed the heads of both MI5 and MI6 to participate in the trial and to provide any information requested.'"

"Have the other countries issued statements?"

"The United States has provided a statement refusing to cooperate and has indicated their strong opposition to such a trial as both a stunt and a risk to not only its national security, but global security. The statement indicates it will be seeking to take action to terminate the trial and abolish the criminal court in the United Nation's General Assembly should it continue. New Zealand and Canada have simply said they will provide representatives, but nothing further."

"And Australia?"

"The Prime Minister of Australia has provided a statement, which I am happy to read to enter into evidence."

"Please go ahead."

"It reads, 'I, The Honourable Roger Duff MP, Prime Minister of Australia, commit to supporting our agent, known as Witness S. We do not dispute the alleged activities and will strongly argue that not only are these activities necessary, but they are encouraged by my government as a robust deterrent to both state and non-state actors from committing crimes of terror against my nation. The work of Witness S and the Australian Intelligence Service, often in support of their sister agencies in allied nations, is vital to our national security and to global security. I do not apologise for it and will never apologise for it. The International Criminal Court's mission is to bring justice against those accused of committing atrocities, but I ask, where was the court when terrorists detonated a nuclear device in Perth, Western Australia? Where was the court in stopping similar devices from exploding and killing millions in San Francisco and London? Where was the court when a terrorist took possession of a deadly chemical weapon and a nuclear submarine and threatened global destruction and the death of billions? It was sitting idle, waiting to punish the very person who stopped those attacks from unfolding. Did he bend and break the rules to stop those attacks? Yes, without question, but he did so at the behest of my country and within his legal authority. Without him the world would be a vastly different place, especially for the billions who would be dead and those of us who would have been left to fight over whatever was left. This trial is a sham. We should be pinning yet another medal on the witness, not parading him around on the whims of a recently elected populist who does not fully understand the ramifications of his decisions. I also question the means and arrangements made to have our agent transferred to the custody of the court. He was subject to rendition by the very nation now claiming the practice as wrong. Something does not add up here and the court needs to strongly consider the context. I am sending the head of the Australian Intelligence Service, Vice Admiral Blake Smyth, to testify on our nation's behalf. I have declassified various mission files and have asked Vice Admiral Smyth to provide the court with the examples of how this agent and others like him have thwarted terrorism here and abroad, and to provide a further statement on my behalf on the future of Australia's participation in the International Criminal Court.'"

"Does the defence wish to enter a statement?"

"Mister Justice," Max's chief lawyer said as he got to his feet, "the Australian Prime Minister's statement goes to great lengths to help put our case, including that the witness acted within his legal authority. If the court has issues with the laws of Australia, then the appropriate action would be to question the country, not my client. We would add that the media attention and protests being unleashed throughout the world, including at the front gate of this very court, stand as a testament to this trial being nothing more than a political football which does nothing but seek to damage the witness and risk national security for political gain. I would ask the court to strongly consider throwing out this case, taking into account the statements from the three world leaders. It is clear there are other issues at play here and the witness should not be made the scapegoat for the actions of these states, let alone have the court's good reputation tarnished as a political tool, rather than a symbol of justice. It is not fair to the witness and the case should be terminated immediately."

"I appreciate your consideration of the court's reputation and your passionate defence of your client. We will take these matters into consideration. Is there anything else you would like to add?"

"Yes. This morning my client was attacked by two inmates at the prison. The men are Russian and came bearing a warning to my client. They told him to start sharing his secrets or they would continue to harass him and they threatened him with violence. The court must urgently consider his immediate release. Clearly, there are people involved in all of this who could bring about serious harm for my client or, God forbid, they may assassinate my client. For his safety, I ask the court to consider this immediate request."

"I was made aware of the incident. While I agree there may be evidence we need to consider of third party influencing and witness intimidation, I would draw your attention to the fact one of the antagonists was rushed to hospital after your client assaulted him. I believe he is well skilled to defend himself, should the need arise."

"You cannot be serious! He should not have to defend himself. He is a high-profile witness and should be in the care of the court. I move for an immediate mistrial."

"I thank both the prosecution and the defence for their statements. We will take these matters into consideration. Before we deliberate, I wanted to give the witness an opportunity to make a statement. Would you like to say anything?"

"Mister Justice," Max said, standing, "for years, I questioned the role I was asked to play and the tactics used to defend the innocent and defeat those who sort to unleash disorder and death. But during my career, I have come face-to-face with some of the world's worst terrorists. People who sought to use, among other things, chemical, biological and nuclear weapons against our people simply because they wanted money or because they had a different god. These people and their organisations operate in a world without your rules and without what I am sure is your strong passion for justice and sense of humanity. You can hold your rulebook up to them and ask them to act accordingly, but not only will they not care, they would sooner put a bullet between your eyes for even questioning their actions than live by your rules. The only way to beat these people is to get in the weeds with them, get down in the mud with them and take the fight to them on their level. We should never kid ourselves, there are bad people in the world and they need someone willing to match them and use their tactics against them to stop them. Whether it is a rogue state or a lone terrorist, the only way that you get to sit there and ask your questions, then go home to your family, is because of people like my colleagues in the intelligence world bringing order to those who prefer disorder. I don't deny some of the things we do are brutal and it would be fantastic to never have to employ them, but sadly this utopia does not exist. I operate in the real world and I make no apologies for taking action to save people from heartache and death. And, I have personally suffered, as have countless other agents. The collapse of the global intelligence system is exactly what the terrorists and our enemies want, and it would dishonour the sacrifices of everyone who has shed blood, lost their life or had their world turned upside down by the loss of a loved one. Without this system in place to protect us, I hate to even imagine the war and wave of terror which would follow."

"I thank the witness for his statement. My fellow justices and I will now consider the information and evidence provided to determine if the case will move to trial. It will take us several days to reach a determination. In the meantime, the witness will continue to be held at the Scheveningen Prison. The court stands adjourned until further notice."

With the bang of the gavel the pre-trial hearing ended and Max was whisked back out of the court, into the waiting motorcade and back to gaol.

Chapter Three

Lyadova sat at her antique wooden desk. It was exquisitely craved from a dark brown timber. It was made to look as if the tabletop was resting on four trees. Each of the legs was sculpted to resemble the trunks with a wider base and veiny roots near the floor, thinning as it rose until it reached the desktop where it fanned out again. Its branches were woven into the support panels and stretched across to join each other in a beautiful leafy canopy. The canopy illusion stretched up into clouds which ringed the desk, framing it. At small intervals were engravings of the ancient gods. Zeus and Hera sat in the middle on their clouds, with the others evenly spaced leading to the corners.

It was an amazing feature piece in an otherwise modern and sterile office made of hard white walls and glass panels under white neon lights. It had a brutal, stiff looking sitting area with square uncomfortable furniture. There were no personal effects in the office. The walls were blank and false panelling hid bookcases and other normal office equipment.

On her desk was a clean, sharp lined, brand new laptop. It had no cords at all and instead drew power from the metal base plate it was sitting on. The screen itself was completely clear and transparent. A guest in the office could see what was being displayed, albeit from the back.

Lyadova was watching various news clippings compiled by A&A's media team. The sound was beaming around the office from a series of hidden speakers in the roof and walls.

"In other news, it has been three days since the Chairwoman and CEO of A&A Enterprises, the world's largest technology company, Isabella Lyadova initiated her Alexandria 2.0 program," the reporter said. "While the announcement has been widely acknowledged as a ground-breaking initiative in its sentiment, it has been met with mixed reactions."

The footage cut away to a series of vox pops from around the world.

"I think it's great," one man said. "I'm an academic and I know how useful this resource will be for all fields of study. And just today, Apollo, the program itself, contacted me to arrange funding for my latest research on genetic sequencing. I'm really excited by it."

"I was on holidays with my family at the Louvre in Paris," a middle-aged woman said. "The goon squad from A&A turned up and pushed their way in with their cameras and started filming every artwork and the building itself. It meant we missed out on some of the exhibits because they were closed. It really wrecked out holiday. No, I do not think it is a good program. People should get off their butts, come out and experience these things in person. Get away from their computers and experience real life!"

"This is yet another example of major corporations stealing our identities," one aggravated young man said. "As if it wasn't enough for them to track our locations and invade our privacy, now they are vacuuming up knowledge itself. We must rise up against this new threat. F[bleep]k you, Isabella!"

"World leaders have mostly welcomed the idea behind Alexandria 2.0," the presenter said, returning to the screen. "However, they have almost universally agreed that there are issues with privacy, piracy, information security and intellectual property rights which need to be worked through. Well, they'd better work quickly. The program is already running and we are only days away from the date, given by Ms Lyadova, for the world to be granted access to the mega database. Only time will tell. We will keep you across developments as they come to light."

Lyadova sat thinking about the news clips, but was interrupted by a small screen which popped up on her laptop. It was her assistant.

"I am sorry to interrupt," Elias Laskaris said, his voice cracking slightly. "I have *him* on the line for you."

"Pull yourself together," Lyadova said, dismissively. "He is just a man. Put him through."

Laskaris disappeared and a new window opened on the screen. An older man sat staring at the camera with piercing blue eyes. His office was covered in wooden panels and adorned with numerous trinkets and gifts, including an impressive solid gold dagger which hung on the wall under a huge wall ornament.

"Privet, comrade," Lyadova said, warmly greeting the man in Russian.

Chapter Four

Max was into his second hour of training for the morning in his small gaol cell. His legs were stretched up onto the concrete bed and he was doing push ups. He had noticed over the last few days how fast his repetitions were becoming. Prison had one upside: he felt like he was back at peak strength and fitness.

There was a familiar electronic buzz and the metallic click as the door to his cell unlocked and slid to the side. A portly old guard stood in the doorway as Max continued his push ups.

"You have a visitor," the guard said. "Get up and follow me."

"Who is it?" Max asked as he lowered himself to the ground and held the position.

"Do I look like your fucking social secretary?"

Max turned his head and looked the guard up and down. "It would probably be a step up for you," Max said, "but I'm not sure you'd have the brains for it."

"What's that supposed to mean?"

"Case in point."

"What?"

"Nothing," Max said, pressing up and getting to his feet.

The guard walked into the cell and handcuffed Max, before leading him out through the corridor.

Four cells down from his own was the Russian who had attacked him the previous morning in the mess. His mouth was wired shut and he was wearing a large metal brace holding his head straight. It stretched up from his shoulders to a metal headband with cheap looking foam on the inside pressing against his forehead. A second set of wires were extended across to his bottom jaw and teeth. He was also sporting an off-white foam neck brace.

He glared with anger as he saw Max walking past and got to his feet. He grabbed the door of his cell and rattled it in anger, letting out a frustrated and furious growl through his locked teeth.

"What's that for?" Max asked smugly as he pointed to the neck brace. "To stop you licking your stitches?"

The guard let out a small laugh, before prodding Max in the back.

"Keep walking," the guard said, taking a moment to hit his baton on the Russian's cell gate. "And you settle down."

The Russian tried to say something, but it was too muffled to understand. Max just smiled and walked on.

The guard led him into a holding cell, cuffed him to a metal bar which was bolted to the table and left the room.

Max sat in the room on the cold metal chair waiting for over an hour.

The room was painted in the same blueish grey, thick from years of coating over the existing layers of paint.

He was not sure what was taking so long or why he was being held here, or who his mystery visitor was. He let his mind wildly speculate, but all he wanted was for Blake to walk through the door.

When the door finally opened, he was surprised to see the man before him. In all the random thoughts he had run through his head in the hour he had been sitting there, about who could be visiting, this man never featured and for good reason.

Max had not thought about him since the moment he had thrown him through a plate glass window. Ten years ago.

The door closed after the guard told his guest he would be waiting outside if there were any problems. The visitor walked over and took a seat opposite Max. He drew deep breaths as if he was recovering from a long gym session.

Max's cold eyes locked with his.

"I was hoping for a warmer reception," Andrew said, nervously stroking his long greying beard. "It was a long time ago, Max. I hoped you were over it."

"I don't easily forgive scumbag criminals," Max said, coldly.

"Look where you are sitting, Max. I fucked up. I know it. I admitted it and I did my time."

"So what? All's forgiven?"

"You threw me through a fucking window and I nearly bled out!"

"You're just lucky security got there before I got my hands around your throat."

"Isn't that exactly why you are in here? Taking matters into your own hands. Whatever happened to protecting the system?"

Max flinched forward towards Andrew, but the handcuffs caught his hands. Andrew jumped back and raised his hands in surrender.

"Okay, okay," Andrew said. "That was a stupid thing to say, but please, Max, I admitted what I did was wrong and I went to gaol for five years. For what it is worth, I don't think you should be in here. Without you the country and big parts of the world would be very fucking different to what they are now."

"What are you doing here?" Max asked, cooling his temper.

"I need your help."

"You have got to be kidding me."

"You are the only person I trust," Andrew said, looking down. "And the only person I know here."

"Here as in The Netherlands?"

"As in Europe."

"I am the only person you know on the whole continent? How the fuck were you a spy for so many years?"

"I was the guy at the computer, the man in the chair, not the man on the ground. You guys were the ones with all the local contacts. Plus, my list of friends shrank pretty dramatically when I went to prison."

"Understandably."

Andrew looked around the holding cell with incredulity and gestured towards the walls as if to remind Max of where he was.

"I know," Max conceded. "Got it. So, let me humour you for a minute. What help do you need?"

"Thank you, Max."

"Don't thank me yet. As you have pointed out, several times, I am in gaol awaiting trial for war crimes among other things. I'm not sure how I am going to be able to help you do anything. If I even choose to help you at all."

"Please, Max. It is a matter of life and death. I need your help."

"Calm down," Max said, reassuringly. "Just tell me what you know. Start at the beginning."

"Have you heard about Alexandria 2.0?"

"I heard something on the radio about it yesterday morning on my way to the court, but that's it. Can't say I really understood it."

"I forgot you're not really a tech expert."

"That's why we hired so many analysts and computer nerds like you. I have other skills, but I get by if I need to with technology."

"I'm having horror flashbacks to briefing you when the new tablets arrived. God, that was painful. You don't get tech, do you?"

"Yeah, yeah, all right. I'm not that good with technology. So, explain it to me. What is this Alexandria 2.0 project about?"

"You like ancient history, right?"

"Yes."

"Well, you will know Alexandria in Egypt was once home to a massive library. The dream was a place for all the world's knowledge to be stored."

"I'm familiar with it, yes."

"Well, this is the digital version of that. One sole source and storage place for all the world's knowledge. All electronic, accessible to anyone with a computer."

"Okay, so a bunch of university professors can share information and students can learn for free. Sounds fine by me. Why should I care?"

"Because that's just the public relations spin. The truth is the program is designed to do a lot more than that."

"Like what?"

"Like harvest intelligence and defence secrets. Like conduct corporate espionage. Like destroy other organisations to create the largest monopoly on earth with its fingers in every pie. Basically, making it indispensable in everyone's lives."

"Back up. Did you say harvest intel?"

"Yes."

"How can they do that? The intel agencies have the best IT systems on Earth."

"Well, that's the thing."

"What did you do?" Max asked as Andrew lowered his head. "How do you know they are doing this, Andrew?"

"I helped them build it."

"Oh, for fuck's sake. How could you be so stupid?"

"I didn't know that was their intention. I found out later. Much later. Too late, honestly."

"So, what did you do?"

"I was hired to build their firewalls and parts of the AI system. Given my experience, they were keen to have me and they were willing to look past the whole gaol thing."

"That's not a surprise given what you've just told me. They are fucking criminals."

"I swear I didn't know, Max. I'm here, aren't I? Trying to fix it."

"You built a military grade firewall and AI program capable of defeating our systems?"

"Yes, but I didn't think they would use it like this. I built it solely to defend them. I didn't know they would reverse engineer it to use it like they plan to."

"Well, you got one thing right. You didn't think."

"I'm sorry, Max."

"Why did you come to me with this? What can I do? I'm stuck in here."

"I need your help. I need you to stop the program from becoming fully functional."

"Why didn't you call AIS?"

"Well, that's the thing. Apollo's first mission was to attack the telecommunications systems. He is tied into everything and listening to everything. Like Echelon on steroids. That's how I found out about their plans and the Russian's involvement. If I contact AIS, they will know, and they will kill me before help arrives."

"The Russians?"

"Yes, The President himself signed off on the operation."

Jesus. If he gets access to our systems, we'll be practically defenceless."

"That's why I'm here."

"When does the system start attacking the defence and intelligence systems?"

"That is the last phase. They will harvest information from all over the internet for the next few days and weave their way into millions of businesses servers. Apollo will duplicate himself and when he is everywhere, he will then be strong enough to simultaneously attack the intelligence agencies worldwide and they won't know where he is coming from because he won't be in just one place. My best guess is that by Tuesday he will be ready."

"Him? He? It's a fucking computer. Why do you call it him?"

"Apollo is as close to real artificial intelligence as it gets. He has a voice and, Max, I have to say he is incredible."

"It. It is about to take down global intelligence systems and start a war with Russia we might not win, and you're sitting there pissing your pants in excitement. What is incredible is how fucking stupid you continue to be."

"Max, we only have a few days."

"I might not hear whether my case is being thrown out until the end of next week and that's not to say it even will be. I can't really see how I can help stop something by Tuesday."

"I don't know who else to turn to, Max. She might sound like a caring global citizen, a philanthropic goddess, on the television, but Isabella can't be trusted. We don't know where her loyalties lie and what she intends to do with all those secrets. We can't let her get her hands on that information or give it to the Russians."

"I need some time to think about it. Can you give me twenty-four hours?"

"Thank you, Max. I'm staying at the Marriott. I'll come back to see you tomorrow morning."

Chapter Five

Andrew was led from the holding cell by a strapping young guard in a crisp uniform, leaving Max deep in thought in the holding cell.

The pair wound their way through the rolling corridors, the various electronically controlled gates and across the surprisingly lovely grounds of the old prison.

In the security hut by the main gate, Andrew signed out and collected his possessions, before heading out into the street. He took a moment to tie his shoelace and gauge his surroundings. He couldn't see anyone looking at him, so he got to his feet and made a beeline for his hire car.

It was a new Ford sedan. A new, bright yellow, Ford sedan. The ostentatious vehicle pulled away from the kerb and headed towards the main part of town.

Andrew checked his mirrors, constantly vigilant, trying to memorise the vehicles around him to see if he was being followed.

In the township, he doubled back on his route a few times and drove in random patterns, weaving in towards his hotel.

When he was satisfied he wasn't being followed, he turned onto his hotel's street and parked at the front door.

He grabbed his bag and went to get out, but spotted two men in dark trench coats inside the lobby. They were standing like security guards by the door, but Andrew had seen them before and it wasn't at the hotel.

They were from A&A.

His heart started to race when they were joined by a tall masculine woman in a long white trench coat. She had short blonde hair which ran on a diagonal from high on one side of her face, over her eye and down below her ear on the opposite side. It was shaved on the high side and at the back, almost back to the skin. She had broad shoulders and a no nonsense look on her face. She gave the two men the order to move out, but as she was putting her reflective aviators on, she spotted Andrew. She immediately whacked the closest guard with the back of her hand and pointed at Andrew, sitting in his bright yellow car.

The two men drew their weapons and started walking briskly towards Andrew. He locked the doors and started the car.

One of the men raised a silenced pistol and fired it in Andrew's direction. It shattered the passenger side window as the car lurched forward.

The bullet grazed Andrew's arm.

He reached over and felt the wound. His hand was covered in blood and he panicked. He hit the accelerator and sped off into oncoming traffic. He narrowly missed a truck as he wrestled the car into his lane, clipping a small smart car and sending it into the adjacent lane. The smart car was T-boned and crumbled by a pickup truck.

The accident closed the street as the woman in the white coat punched the man with the gun in the face. In was unclear if it was in frustration because he missed the shot or for the fact that he had drawn his pistol in such a heavily populated area.

Either way, she wasn't happy.

The three of them marched quickly to their black Opal sedan and drove down a side street to loop around the accident.

For over thirty minutes, they drove in a grid pattern searching for the yellow Ford until one of the men spotted it, parked in a side street. The driver reversed back and turned down the road where Andrew had parked to check his wound.

Andrew had been wearing a long-sleeved business shirt over a T-shirt, under his jacket. He had removed the jacket and business shirt, and torn one of the sleeves off the business shirt. He used it to bandage his wound. As he was about to put his jacket back on, he saw the black Opal pass, then reverse back at the end of the street.

He tossed his jacket into the passenger seat and hit the ignition. The Ford sprung forward and took off down the street.

He was breathing hard and could feel his heart pounding in his chest, as he saw the Opal give chase.

The two vehicles raced through the streets of The Hague. Andrew was an analyst during his time at the AIS, not a field agent, so he was not trained in defensive driving. He was used to driving a computer, not a vehicle at high speed in a busy city. He sideswiped a blue hatchback, bouncing his car and showering the road with plastic and glass.

He swore as the Opal smashed into the back of his car and shattered the back window. He swerved wildly trying to keep control of the Ford.

Andrew checked his rear-vision mirror and saw one of the men raising their pistol. He ducked down and the bullets started flying. He was zig-zagging the car down the street bouncing it wildly off parked cars and trying to give his chasers a harder target to hit.

When they sped out across an intersection, Andrew held his breath hoping no cars were coming in either direction. He looked left and right, back and forth, in a frenzy. Luckily there were no cars or trucks.

He breathed a sigh of relief as his car shot through the intersection and down the new road. In his mirrors he could again see the Opal zeroing in on him. He kept watching the passenger, who had reloaded his pistol and was getting ready to fire again, but then he saw him start yelling at the driver and put his hand up on the dashboard in a brace position.

Andrew was confused, but then looked down and through his own windshield to find a bus reversing out into his path. He pulled hard on the wheel and slammed on the brakes, and the car instantly responded, but it was too late. The passenger side of the bright yellow Ford slammed into the rear of the bus. It hit off centre and the engine bay was torn off as the metal safety beams bounced out, having absorbed the shock.

The Ford stopped in its tracks.

The front of the car drove down and crumpled, as the rear of the vehicle lifted off the ground, before the whole car bounced back in the direction it had just come.

The bus slid slightly in the opposite direction as the back and some of the side windows shattered.

Andrew's Ford bounced hard, then rolled gently against the gutter. Smoke and steam were billowing out from under what was left of the hood, as petrol and oil started leaking onto the ground. All of the windows were shattered and Andrew was unconscious, laying on the airbag. Blood was pouring from his nose from the impact of the airbag, but he no doubt had other injuries too.

The crew from the Opal had managed to stop their vehicle and get out. The two men rushed to Andrew's car and it took the two of them to pry open the damaged door. They cut away the curtain airbag and found their wounded prey.

They dragged Andrew out of the vehicle. One of the men reached in and grabbed his bag and mobile phone which were wedged between the seat and the dashboard.

The men put Andrew's arms around their necks to shoulder his weight and rushed forward to their vehicle. Andrew's feet dragged across the tarred road until they got him to the boot of their car.

They dumped him into the trunk and slammed the lid, before speeding off to the confusion and intrigue of the growing number of pedestrians and passers-by who were starting to gather.

Chapter Six

Max woke at five and had spent two hours training in his cell.

As he did his last push up, the alarm sounded throughout the complex and the cell doors opened. He went out into the corridor and when instructed, walked with the other inmates to the mess hall for breakfast.

As usual he had taken a position in the far corner with his back to the wall so he could watch the room. A few of his fellow prisoners cautiously eyeballed him, but looked away when he locked eyes with them. They had seen what he had done to the Russian and were not going to run the risk of crossing him.

Sunday mornings were slightly different at Scheveningen. Inmates were allowed some free time in the morning to watch television or read, or have private time for prayers and worship if that was their thing.

It certainly was not Max's thing. He was sitting in the mess hall on his cold metal bench seat where he had been since breakfast. It had been three days since his visit from Andrew and he was anxious. He had expected him to arrive at the prison on Friday morning, but the day passed without a visit. By lunchtime Saturday, Max was starting to worry something might have happened to him. But today, he was almost certain something was wrong.

One of the guards brought in a stack of papers and magazines, which a couple of the inmates grabbed to get a taste of the outside world.

Max leant with his back against the wall thinking when he overheard a conversation at a nearby table.

"Apparently, it happened on Thursday," the older man said, lending over the paper. "There was a car chase through the city and a bunch of gunfire. Ended in a massive crash when the car getting chased slammed into the back of a bus. I miss the action, don't you?"

"Jesus, yes, how many dead?" the other man asked.

"Well, that's just the thing. People saw the driver get pulled out of the car and thrown in the trunk of the chase car."

"Now that I do miss. The fun of a grab like that in broad daylight. Jesus, the excitement. I miss it."

"Me too."

"So, did they find them?"

"Not yet. The government is getting smashed with questions."

"I bet."

Max got to his feet and walked over to the two men. They both nervously looked up at him.

"Can I please see the paper?" Max asked.

"Sure," the older man said, trying to sound confident.

He handed over the paper and Max saw the smashed yellow sedan and damaged bus on a closed down road in The Hague. He read part of the article.

Police say they have not yet been able to track down either the driver or the occupants of the second vehicle. They say the second car, a black Opal sedan, was found on the outskirts of town burnt out. Police have confirmed they found shell casings in the vehicle. The casings were nine millimetres and likely to have been fired from a pistol, perhaps a Glock. The man pulled from the crashed vehicle is described as a bigger man with a greying bushy beard.

Max saw the time of the incident and the description, including a detailed description of the clothing the man was seen to be wearing, and knew it had to be Andrew.

His thoughts swirled in his mind. For the first time since he arrived at the prison, he felt trapped like a caged animal. His natural instinct was to dive into the crisis and find out what had happened to his former colleague. It was true they had a rocky history, but that didn't mean Max would want him dead.

Max remembered the day he had thrown him through the glass window. Blake had been running an internal audit of the AIS's staff following a major security breach. They knew at least one mole had been planted in the agency working against them. Blake led the team and Max carried out the interrogations and the arrests.

It was a cold winter's day in Canberra when Blake and Max had met to discuss the latest findings of the investigation. Blake presented Max with hundreds of files which showed an analyst had been siphoning money out of the AIS's accounts. One point two million dollars had been stolen over a two year period. It had started in very small amounts, but had grown larger and larger in the recent months.

The evidence all pointed to Andrew.

Max was furious. He marched out of the meeting room and down into the large open planned mission room of the AIS bunker. Three AIS security guards approached Andrew from the far side as Max came in behind him. He was sitting at a desk in front of a large computer screen and he stopped typing as the room fell silent. All the nearby analysts and agents had stopped working to watch what was happening.

Andrew looked up and saw the guards, then spun in his chair to find Max only a foot behind him. Max's expression was of pure distain and anger. His cold eyes pierced right through him.

Max grabbed Andrew by the throat and dragged him to his feet with one hand.

"You've got some explaining to do," Max said, pushing the analyst back hard against the desk.

"What are you doing, Max?" Andrew choked out, trying to pry Max's hand from his throat so he could breathe.

"You know exactly what you've been doing. Did you seriously think you could get away with it?"

"Get away with what?"

"Two years. One point two million. You son of a bitch. How many people could have been put at risk because you were skimming off the mission funds?"

Andrew's eyes sank.

"That's right, you arsehole. We know what you did."

Andrew tried to fight his way out of Max's grip, but he was far too strong. He tossed Andrew to the ground with one hand.

Andrew stumbled and rolled hard into an office chair, as their colleagues stepped or rolled back away from him. He grabbed a desk to try to pull himself up, scrambling forward on his knees. Max grabbed his head and pushed it down hard, flat against the desk.

"Please, Max," Andrew said. "I'm sorry, I would never hurt anyone. I didn't put anyone at risk. I just borrowed some of the extra money that wasn't being used."

"We use it all," Max said, only inches from his ear, "and we are constantly asking those arseholes in Canberra for more money so we can stop terrorists. You put all of it at risk for your own selfish needs and desires."

Max grabbed him by the back of the neck and shirt, dragging him up to his feet, then threw him forward. Andrew stumbled again and rolled on the hard carpet. He got to his hands and knees, and reached out for one of their colleagues, pleading with them for help, but was left wanting as his colleagues turned away from him.

Andrew got to his feet and turned back to face Max. Shaking and erratic. He was clearly thinking of something, his eyes were darting from side to side. He looked panicked.

"Don't even think about it," Max ordered.

"What choice do I have?" Andrew asked as he turned his back on Max and ran towards the elevator.

But he didn't even get close. Max wheeled him in before he even got to the end of the room. He latched hold of Andrew again by the neck and back of the pants, and picked the big man up and tossed him head first through the glass window of the nearest conference room.

The glass shattered inward and dropped all around Andrew. He was bleeding badly from a number of wounds. There were large slivers of glass jutting out of his skin and the more he rolled around in pain, the deeper they drove and the more lacerations he got.

Max knew he wouldn't try to run again.

Max turned back to the rows of shocked colleagues who were all standing and watching him.

"Get back to work!" Max ordered, scattering the crowd.

Max tossed the paper back to the other two prisoners and walked back to his cell. He spent the rest of the day trying to get his lawyers on the phone, but the guards were being more difficult than usual.

For the first time in his time there, he started to think about how he could break out. He thought about all the corridors and rooms he had been in. Thought about the layout of the prison and pieced together a rough blueprint in his mind. His training meant he had carefully logged all of the guards and their movements, as well as their weapons, and the layout of the grounds, from the first minute he had been inside.

He figured it was not impossible, but as close as it could come. Improbable was a better term.

Max's plans were put on hold when the nuggety guard came back to his cell door. He had another visitor.

Max breathed a sigh of relief. Maybe the man in the paper had not been Andrew after all. He could go back to Plan A.

Max was led across the prison for the holding cell. This time he took even more careful mental notes on the guards and complex, and the guards' patrol patterns. He saw the snipers in the towers and felt the realisation and doubt at his chances of escape with them still in place.

He took his seat on the far side of the table and the guard cuffed him to the metal bar again, then left the room. Max settled in expecting another long wait, but was pleasantly surprised when the door opened within a few minutes.

He was even more surprised to see Blake walk into the room.

"Just give me five minutes," Blake ordered and Max saw his lawyers hold their positions in the corridor behind Blake.

Blake closed the door and walked over to the corner of the room. He took out a small coin like object and reached up, placing it on the side of the room's security camera. The little red light went off as Blake walked around the table and embraced Max. The pair held each other for the longest moment then kissed passionately. Blake placed his hands on either side of Max's face and they stared lovingly into each other's eyes. Blake rested his head against Max's.

"I missed you," Blake said.

"I missed you too, Blake," Max replied. "It's great to see you. What are you doing here?"

"I was called to give evidence, but I don't think that will be necessary now."

"Oh really? How come?"

"Well, I will let the lawyers go through it properly with you, but it looks like the case will be thrown out. The Prime Minister has signed an order threatening to walk away from the international court system if the case goes ahead and he has convinced the Americans, Canadians and Kiwis to do the same. The US has made good on the promise by circulating a motion in the United Nations' main committee which would have the court disbanded. It is a warning shot, but it looks like it has worked. We got news this morning that the court was dropping the case."

"That's great news."

"Yes, it is. Finally, you can come home."

"And not a minute too soon. I need to talk to you."

"What is it?"

"Andrew Rixon was here a few days ago."

"Rixon. Why? What could he want? I thought he hated you?"

"He's been working for A&A. Designed their IT systems, including the AI. Apparently, it's all a front. They are going to make a move against the Five Eyes and other global intelligence agencies."

"What? How?"

"It gets worse, he thinks the Russians are involved. Sukhanov himself. Andrew thought he was building them a firewall, but instead he helped them build a program to get around our firewalls."

"Jesus. It's already running. Lyadova is all over the news."

"He said the program will be ready to start the attack on our agencies in the next couple of days."

"What did he hope you could do from in here?"

"He said I was the only person he knew and could trust in Europe. The thing is, Blake, I believe him. He was scared and clearly trying to make some sort of deal."

"Where is he now?"

"I have no idea. He was supposed to meet me again on Friday morning, but he didn't show. I just read about a car chase and a crash in the city. The attackers bundled the driver, who fit his description, into their boot and drove off."

"Why didn't you reach out?"

"He said that A&A were watching and listening. That they had already hacked into global communications networks and he couldn't risk it. I have been trying to contact the lawyers since I saw the news, but I couldn't raise them."

"They have been in meetings for days trying to secure your release."

"Good. So, when can I get out of here?"

"In a couple of days. There will be a hearing either tomorrow or Tuesday to dismiss the case."

"That's too late, Blake. The attack will start on Tuesday."

"Leave it with me. Talk to the lawyers and let me make a few calls. I will start gently looking into all this, starting with trying to track down Andrew."

"Be careful, Blake," Max said, squeezing his partner's hands tightly. "These people are powerful."

"We've faced worse. And, I have an increased security detail now. They are all our people. I personally vetted them. I am constantly surrounded. I will be well protected."

"Well, even so, with the Russians potentially involved, you need to watch your back."

"I'll be fine, Max," Blake said, reassuringly. "I'll be there for the dismissal and we can leave together and sort all of this out."

"Thank you, Blake. I really did think I was going to be thrown in some hole for life and never get to see you again. I can't have that, Blake. I love you too much."

"I love you too, Max," Blake said, and the pair kissed again passionately, before a knock on the door interrupted them. "I'd better let the lawyers in. Stay safe. See you at the court."

"Thanks, Blake," Max said, pointing to the camera. "Don't forget that. Be careful."

Blake smiled and nodded, before grabbing the coin off the side of the camera. The little light came back on as Blake smiled and walked out of the room, pocketing the small digital interrupter.

Chapter Seven

The Chief Justice of the ICC, Stafford, sat in a lavish hotel restaurant. It was intimately lit with warm flickering candles. Crisp white linen lined the tables and chairs, with gleaming glassware and highly polished gold cutlery. A small bunch of native tulips sat in the centre of the table, precisely placed. They were perfectly cut with white petals and had a sweet smell, just perceivable over the smell from the nearby kitchen.

The restaurant was in an older style building, giving it a closed in, but homely feel. A roaring fireplace was warming the room and the flickering flames helped build the cosy atmosphere.

The restaurant had some private rooms towards the rear and was frequently visited by wealthy European travellers as well as officials from various nations visiting the courts.

He was sitting in a private room at the back drinking a glass of chilled white wine in a long-stemmed glass. He smelt the wine and took another sip. It was crisp and dry, and he let the flavour coat his mouth.

There was an expensive painting of a man with a long white beard standing on the bow of a Viking longboat as his troops rowed in the background. The walls were covered in similar smaller paintings of the Viking era. There was even an impressive painted shield, which looked medieval, hanging on the far wall. It was adorned with various runes.

There was a soft knock on the door.

"Yes," Stafford said.

"Justice Stafford," the waiter said. "Your guest has arrived."

"Please show him in."

"Yes, sir," the waiter said, holding open the door for his guest.

"Hello, Winston!" the guest said, walking into the room. "This is a lovely place."

"Can I get you a drink, sir?" the waiter asked.

"I would love a pint of whatever the best local beer is you have on tap."

"Not a problem, sir. Here is your menu. I will be back with your drink in just a moment."

"Great, thank you."

The door shut and the pair shook hands.

"It is good to see you, Sir David," Stafford said.

"Please, it's just David behind closed doors," he said.

Sir David Maher was a member of the British House of Lords and the chair of the judiciary committee. Maher and Stafford had grown up together and went to Oxford at the same time, both studying law. They had both worked in various courts as lawyers, then judges.

Stafford had a real interest in international law and made the move into the international law courts over a decade ago, while Maher had chosen to pursue a career in politics.

The previous Prime Minister had appointed him to chair the committee as a consolation prize after turning him down for a role in Cabinet. He had spent the following months undermining the Prime Minister and government, and eventually he endorsed the then opposition leader, Timothy Birmingham, during the election and switched parties.

"What are you doing in The Netherlands, David?" Stafford asked, taking a sip of his wine, already knowing the answer. "I am not sure meeting with you is such a good idea at the moment, given everything that is happening."

"That is, of course, why I am here, Winston," Maher said. "The Prime Minister is about to announce that I will be joining the Cabinet as his Attorney-General."

"Congratulations," Stafford said as the waiter entered and sat Maher's foaming beer on the table, before raising his wine glass. "To your success."

"Thank you," Maher said, raising and clinking their glasses, "and to yours, my old friend."

"So, you came all this way to celebrate your promotion?" Safford said, smirking.

"Not exactly," Maher said, taking a large sip from his pint before sitting it down on the table. "The Prime Minister knows we go a long way back. He has asked me to come and discuss the case you are presiding over."

Chapter Eight

As it had done before, Max's motorcade travelled through the streets of The Hague to the International Criminal Court and Max was rushed inside to the jeers of the protestors in the street.

Max was feeling good. Following Blake's visit on Sunday, he had met with his lawyers and they were confident he was going to be released at a hearing during the coming days. They showed him all the paperwork and records they had made, and he couldn't help but feel an overwhelming sense of happiness, and frankly, quite a bit of relief. He was getting out and could get on with his life. But, most importantly, he could finally settle down with Blake and enjoy some time together. He was eager to get away from the prison to reclaim his freedom and his life.

But he knew he had something to do first. He had spent all afternoon Sunday thinking through mission plans on how to track down Andrew and get to the bottom of what was happening with A&A.

He couldn't walk away from the world of espionage, not just yet anyway.

Max walked into the room in the suit Blake had bought for him. He smiled warmly when he saw Blake in the viewing gallery behind the glass above the rear of the courtroom.

The court was called to order and Max turned back to the front of the room, as Stafford and the other justices came into the room and took their seats.

The officials read the case details and everyone in the room took their seats.

"Good morning, everyone," Stafford said. "I remind the court that today we will be announcing the outcome of our deliberations. Our decision is final and not subject to debate during today's session. Have the two parties had the chance to meet and discuss terms?"

"Yes, Mister Justice," Max's head lawyer said. "We are ready to proceed."

"Thank you," Stafford said, shifting his notes around. "My fellow justices and I deliberated on the matter of Witness S and his appearance here as both witness and defendant. My fellow justices agreed with the defence and have indicated their support for the witness to be excused from the court. I was of the same opinion, however, it has come to my attention that several nations have become involved in trying to force the hand of the court. This court is an independent body and will not be dictated to by world powers. In fact, we exist to combat such forces. Those who seek to manipulate behind closed doors, rather than in the open for the world to see. To safeguard the reputation of this court as an independent arbiter on the world stage, I have decided that the trial shall go ahead."

Max turned back to look at Blake who was standing with both hurt and anger on his face, his normal poker face letting go as his happiness turned to upset.

Max just nodded to Blake to let him know everything was okay. To keep him calm.

"Mister Justice," Max's lawyer interjected. "This is not what we were told. We were informed the court would be releasing my client today and I would ask you to hold to your word."

"Sit down!" Stafford shouted as the other justices looked on, confused. "I will not be interrupted. I said at the start of the proceedings that this was not the forum for debate."

"If this isn't the forum for such debate, then when and where is?"

"Silence! One more word from you and you can join your client in prison."

"Mister Chief Justice," one of the other justices said, "forgive me, but this is not what was agreed. We determined that the matter would be thrown out. I would ask you to consider my learned friend, the defence attorney's position."

"It has been decided. The case will go to trial and, if the facts stack up, Witness S, will be free to go. However, there is a significant question before the court and that is how will it respond when under pressure from nations to force its hand. We cannot allow it."

"That is a matter for another forum and has nothing to do with the witness before us. There are other methods to pursue this."

"I thank my learned colleague, but I disagree, and the case will continue."

Max's lawyer looked furious, but he held his tongue. The protesting justice looked to her other colleagues, but they just shook their heads. She would need to take the discussion offline and hold talks outside the court.

"The trial will commence in one week's time," Stafford said. "Until then the witness will remain behind bars at Scheveningen Prison. Today's session is now closed."

Stafford hammered down his gavel and the justices all left the room. Max noticed the justice who had spoken on his behalf protesting and questioning Stafford, but he just ignored her and walked out.

The guards came over and handcuffed Max. His lawyer came over as Blake disappeared from view in the upstairs gallery.

"We had a deal, Max," his lawyer said. "I don't know what happened. We will get to the bottom of this."

"Mr Shaw," the prosecuting lawyer said, walking over. "I am sorry. I am not sure what happened. We had made a deal with your lawyer. We will work together to try to sort through the matter."

"Thank you both," Max said, "but something doesn't feel right here. Something is wrong. Did you see the other justices? This was news to them as well."

"Leave it with us," his lawyer said. "We will do what we can."

"It could be weeks before I'm out, right?"

"It could be months, Max, depending on how we go with the justices and procedures of the court."

"It's too long," Max said quietly to himself.

"What was that?"

"Nothing," Max dismissed his comment as the guards started pushing him for the door.

Blake arrived and walked beside him.

"I will figure out what happened, Max," Blake said. "We will get you out."

"I'm sure you will," Max said, "but it might be too late. Did you find Andrew?"

"I was able to see some CCTV footage of the car before the crash. It was definitely him. Our team tracked the various vehicles and we think we have a location. I was hoping you could lead the mission, but I'm going to have to do it now."

"No, Blake," Max said, stopping in the corridor. "You can't do that. It's not your job anymore. Let one of the others do it."

"We don't have anyone close enough. We need to move today."

"Get moving," one of the guards said, shoving Max in the back.

"Fuck you," Max replied. "Hit me again and it will not end well for you."

The guard laughed and pushed him again. Max turned back and headbutted the guard, busting his nose. He staggered and swore, but the other guards grabbed Max and started dragging him fast towards the motorcade.

"Don't go in, Blake," Max yelled back over his shoulder. "Get someone else!"

Blake didn't have time to reply. The guards threw Max into the backseat of the waiting SUV and closed the door.

Max looked out the window to Blake as he stood in the grand glass entry way of the International Criminal Court and pleaded with his eyes for Blake to do as he asked, but he could see the resolve in his eyes.

Something just did not feel right about all of this and Max couldn't shake the feeling he had deep in his stomach. He had learnt very early in his career with the AIS that his gut was the best judge of a situation and it hadn't steered him wrong yet.

He sat in the rear of the vehicle as it pulled out onto the main road and started speeding off towards the prison.

He couldn't wait for weeks or months for the lawyers to sort the mess out. He needed to get out now.

Max felt around in his pocket as best as he could with his hands cuffed behind his back. Slowly he dragged the note, *From H*, his lawyer had attached to his new suit from his pocket. He pulled it in behind his back and slid the attached paperclip off and straightened it. He worked the clip into the lock on his handcuffs and began picking it.

When his first wrist was free, Max slowly moved his hand around, careful not to arouse the guards' attention. He freed his other wrist and reached for the passenger seat guard's pistol.

"What the fuck?" the driver said.

Max looked up at the driver expecting to have been busted going for the gun, but instead he found both guards staring out the windscreen at a smoke trail streaking across the sky.

Max knew exactly what the smoke was trailing behind.

"Stop the car!" Max ordered as the small rocket propelled grenade exploded when it collided with the car in front of them.

The car was hit on the driver's door and flipped it off the road. It rolled onto its roof, completely engulfed in flames, as a black and red cloud of smoke and fire rose into the sky.

There was no way anyone would have survived.

Max heard gunfire behind him and turned to see two SUVs pulling up alongside the third car in their motorcade. It was assaulted from both sides by violent volleys of bullets from machine guns. The windscreen and windows cracked and were covered in blood as the driver and other passengers were riddled with holes.

"What the fuck are you doing?" the guard whose gun he had been going to steal asked, seeing Max's hand free from the cuffs.

"They're not with me," Max explained, "but, you're going to need me to help. If you want to live, you need to give me your pistol."

"No fucking way!" he said, drawing the pistol and aiming it at Max's face. "You will just shoot us and escape with your crew."

"They are not my crew," Max said, leaping forward and removing the gun from the guard's hand in a quick, almost effortless motion. "If they were, you would be dead already."

Max turned around and smashed out the back windscreen with the butt of the pistol, then opened fire on the closest SUV as the trailing vehicle from the motorcade sped up the gutter, out of control and smashed through the shopfront window of a local delicatessen.

Max's first shot went wide as his own car hit a speed bump at pace. He bounced, slamming into the roof, turning back to face the driver.

"A bit of warning next time would be good," Max stated, before turning back and firing again.

This time the bullets found the front windshield. A tight grouping of three bullets hit the driver in the face and neck. The vehicle lost control and drove into a parked car, stopping it dead in its tracks, showering the street with glass and plastic as fuel poured out of both cars and ignited. A massive fireball exploded into the air with a cloud of thick black smoke.

The chase car opened fire on Max's car. Bullets slammed into the boot and what was left of the back window. Max crouched down trying to avoid the onslaught, returning fire occasionally when he had the chance.

He ducked up from behind the backseat and fired until his pistol ran dry. The bullets all hit the windscreen or bonnet of the chase car, but they didn't seem to have any real effect, other than to cause the vehicle to swerve trying to dodge the bullets.

He lowered himself again behind the seat.

"I need a clip," Max said to the guards.

"I don't have a spare," the guard said.

"Here, take mine," the driver said, reaching for his own pistol.

As he unclipped the pistol from his waist and went to pass it back to Max, his face exploded, spraying the windscreen with blood and he fell forward in his seat against the wheel. His deadweight stomped down on the accelerator and the car raced off.

"Jesus Christ!" the other guard said in sheer terror. "What are we going to do?"

"Drag his foot off the accelerator and take the wheel!" Max yelled. "And give me that fucking pistol!"

The guard wiped some of the blood from the windscreen so he could see, then struggled to pull the driver's leg off the accelerator.

"Watch out!" Max yelled, but it was too late.

The guard had been distracted by the driver's leg and had taken his eyes off the road. A small truck was on the street ahead of them, travelling slow, fully loaded with soil.

Max wrapped his arms into the seatbelt on either side of him as the guard tried to steer the car away from the truck, but he pulled too hard.

The car was accelerating hard given the driver had pushed the pedal to the floor. When the guard turned the wheel, the vehicle swayed then lifted from the ground as the front tyre caught the roadway, then hit a deep pothole, and the momentum carried the rear forward.

It rolled.

It went up and over its roof three times, before slamming into the back of the truck in a cloud of dust and smoke.

Max's arms felt like they might pull out of joint as the car tumbled then came to a sudden stop.

He groaned and blinked, lucky to be alive, but he didn't have time to think about it. He heard the SUV pull up not far from his own crumbled vehicle.

He untangled his arms and rolled his shoulders to assess the damage. Everything was working. He was dazed and shaken, but it was time to move.

Max rushed forward looking for the driver's pistol. The other guard was out cold.

Max's top half was in the front of the cabin, leaning over searching the floor, when the door opened and two men grabbed him by the legs. They dragged him out of the car and he rolled onto his back as he hit the bitumen.

The two men looked down at him and the last thing they each saw was one bullet each from the barrel of the driver's gun.

The two men fell to the ground beside him. He got to his feet as two more men climbed out of the SUV. He sprinted around the truck using it for cover as the two men opened fire. The soil in the truck puffed as the bullets pounded in.

Max fired around the rear of the truck at the two assailants. They returned fire, hitting the truck and the soil. The three traded shots until Max finally lined one of the men up and put a bullet in his head. He dropped to the ground as his stunned comrade watched on. Max lined him up, but he dodged away at the last minute and the shot went wide.

Max's pistol clicked empty, so he tossed it onto the ground. He looked around for anything he could use as a weapon as he heard the man getting closer.

Nothing.

The machine pistol swung around the back of the truck. Max grabbed the guy's wrist and pulled it away from himself as he moved to control the shots.

Two shots went off, but thankfully missed Max. He grabbed the guy's wrist tighter and elbowed him in the face, then wrestled the gun from his grip and shot him in both knees.

The attacker dropped to the ground screaming in pain.

"Who sent you?" Max asked.

"Fuck you," the man said through pain and tears as he clutched his knees.

Max put the last bullet through his right hand and into his right knee, irreparably damaging both.

"Okay," he screamed in pain, "I work for Isabella Lyadova!"

Max's brow furrowed on hearing the name of the CEO of A&A Enterprises.

"Why does she want me dead?" Max asked.

"They are covering their tracks," he said. "You spoke to the IT guy. I guess you know too much."

"Where can I find her?"

"Paris."

"Thanks," Max said, turning his back on the dying man.

"Are you going to help me?" he asked. "Please, I told you what you wanted to know. You promised."

"I didn't promise you anything," Max said, turning back.

The man pulled a knife with his good hand and lunged for Max, but he was too fast. He kicked a lever on the side of the truck and the tray quickly rose up and dumped a couple of tonnes of dirt on his screaming attacker.

When the dirt settled only his knife welding hand remained in the clear. Max saw it go limp as the guy suffocated under the dirt.

Max took the knife, putting it in his belt, then quickly checked the other attackers for anything he could use. He also checked both the surviving guard from his motorcade and the truck driver to see if they were okay.

Satisfied they would both survive and hearing the approaching sirens, Max made a decision. He couldn't go back to gaol, not now they had tried to kill him. Not now they had confirmed Andrew's story. Not now he had a mission.

Max jumped into the idling SUV and drove off.

Chapter Nine

Max dumped the car and made his way on foot to an ING bank branch.

"Goedemorgen," the concierge said, "hoe kan ik u helpen?"

"Goedemorgen," Max replied. "I'm sorry it's been a while since I spoke Dutch. I need to make a withdrawal."

"Yes, of course, sir. We can help."

"The only thing is I was mugged on the street and they stole my ID."

"That will not be a problem, sir. I can help. We just need to verify your identity in our system. Please follow me."

The man led Max to a computer terminal and asked a series of questions. Max was using an alias he had set up years ago. Max Symonston, accountant, Melbourne, Australia.

"Yes, here we are, Mr Symonston," the banker said, pulling a face when his photo appeared.

"I've grown my beard and hair since this photo was taken," Max said as he looked down at his clean shaven face and tight haircut, in the photo of him as a much younger man, both of which were dramatically different now.

"Yes, I see. I like it."

"Well, thank you."

"It is my pleasure, sir. Now, how much would you like to withdraw? Your current balance is one hundred and forty-seven thousand, two hundred and fifty-two US dollars."

"I think ten thousand will be enough to see me through. Can I get that in euros?"

"Excellent, I will get it for you now. Please just confirm the withdrawal by placing your finger on the scanner."

A green light flashed on the screen and the banker smiled, before rushing off to the tellers at the rear of the branch. Less than three minutes later he was back with an orange envelope and a receipt.

"Here is your money, Mr Symonston," the banker said. "Is there anything else I can help you with today?"

"Yes, can you please point me in the direction of the Marriott Hotel?"

"But of course, it is only four blocks north of here. Cross in two blocks and take a left."

"Thank you," Max said, shaking the man's hand.

"You are welcome. I look forward to seeing you again. Vaarwell, adieu."

"Have a good day and thanks again," Max said, smiling broadly as he placed the envelope in his jacket breast pocket.

He made his way to the Marriott, taking a circuitous route to check for tails. He stopped at a café and had a coffee. It was rich and strong, and delicious, but he guessed that anything would be after months in gaol.

He paid for the coffee then strolled down the street as if he had no cares in the world, blending in.

When he reached the hotel, he walked straight over to the counter and greeted the check in attendant.

"Yes, hello, I'm sorry," Max said. "I stayed here last night, but I have a problem with my room and I need to speak to a manager please."

"Is there something I can help you with?" the attendant asked.

"No, I really must speak with the manager. Can you please go and get him or her?"

"Yes, of course, sir," he said, walking off towards the office.

As soon as he was out of sight, Max spun the computer monitor around and grabbed the keyboard. He searched for Andrew's details in the system and got a room number. He turned the monitor back around and dumped the keyboard back over the desk, and headed for the elevator. The doors closed as the attendant and his angry supervisor arrived back at the now vacant check in desk.

Max took the elevator to the fifth floor and walked along the corridor looking for Andrew's room. Three doors away he saw the cleaning cart and looked around for the cleaner. She was in the room opposite. She walked out and said hello, before rummaging around in the cart for supplies. Max saw the swipe card on her belt and when he got close enough, he pretended to trip on the vacuum, kicking the hose into the wall for dramatic effect.

As he fell, he grabbed the key card and it broke free from its holder.

The cleaner was very apologetic and helped him to his feet. He told her it was nothing, he was just clumsy and it happened all the time. Not her fault at all. She seemed relieved. He smiled and told her to have a good day, then turned to face Andrew's room.

He used the cleaner's access card and the door unlocked. The cleaner nodded and smiled one last time, before he clicked the door closed between them.

Andrew's room was covered in clothes and looked like it had been ransacked. He guessed he was not the first to check out the room. He looked through the papers on the table, but there was nothing there, then he checked the draws and cupboards.

Nothing.

He found Andrew's suitcase and checked the pockets. He found Andrew's ID card from A&A and pocketed it. He checked the lining of the bag, but there was nothing there. He was about to move on when he wondered if Andrew had been shown the handle trick.

Max pushed down on the suitcase's handle button extending it out, then held it in and yanked the handle completely out of the bag. At the bottom of one side, Max saw what he was looking for, a small hole cut out like a square version of a breach you found in rifles.

Inside the breach, he found a USB drive.

There was no computer in the room, but the television had a USB port, so Max slid the drive into the available slot. The screen came to life and Max used the remote to scroll through the pictures.

Andrew was right, Max wasn't very technically savvy, but he knew the photos he was looking at were indoor fields of computer servers which seemed to go on for miles. Each series of photos was followed by a map with a pin indicating the location of the server. Andrew had been doing his homework. There were a few other files, but the television could not open them.

Max pulled the thumb drive out and pocketed it. He was about to leave when he heard movement at the door. Someone was coming in. He silently climbed into the cupboard and watched through the slots.

"Please wait there, sir, while I check the room," the man said as the room door closed behind the new entrant.

Max spung out of the cupboard and pushed the man into the wall, holding his stolen knife against his throat.

"Who are you?" Max asked.

"Agent Shaw," the man said. "I am Casey Reardon, head of security for Vice Admiral Smyth."

Max relaxed straight away and let go.

"Is he here?" Max asked.

"Yes, sir," Reardon said. "He is in the corridor. I'll get him."

"Thank you and sorry about the knife."

"That's okay, sir. As far as I am concerned you are still the head of field operations and deputy head of the AIS. You're my boss, so I'll just chalk it up to a training exercise."

"Thank you, Casey. I hope to be back at work very soon."

"I think you already are. Good luck and Godspeed, sir."

"And to you."

"The room is clear," Reardon said, walking out into the corridor. "Agents Porter and Greene hold the corridor. I've got the door. All other agents, hold your positions."

Blake looked at Reardon curiously as the other two agents walked to opposite ends of the corridor.

"I figure you could use some privacy, sir," Reardon said, opening the door for Blake.

"Thank you, Casey," Blake said, not understanding until he saw Max standing in the room.

The door clicked shut behind him and he embraced Max and they kissed.

"I saw the news about the motorcade," Blake said, "and I thought the worst. Until I saw the unlocked handcuffs and paperclip. The authorities think you escaped by killing your guards."

"Did they not see the other vehicles in the motorcade and the bodies in the street from the attackers' crew?" Max asked.

"Yeah, but they couldn't put it all together. I'm helping with IDs and analysis."

"Good. Thank you, Blake."

"Of course," Blake said, sitting on the bed next to Max and putting his hand on Max's.

They sat there silently for a few seconds, before turning and passionately kissing each other. They ripped each other's clothes off and made love, tenderly. Taking time to remind themselves of each and every detail of each other's body.

Max found the scar in Blake's leg from the bullet wound he received the day Max was abducted from the street in Washington. He gently kissed it and traced it with his fingers, memorising every detail, before kissing up his body until he reached his lips.

They held each other for a short period and for that moment it was as if the world outside had paused and their problems vanished.

The pair showered and got dressed, while Max showed Blake the thumb drive contents.

After they reviewed it, he handed it to Blake.

"I'll go through it and start working up some plans," Blake said, pulling on his boots. "But first we have to check out the warehouse where we think they have Andrew."

"No, Blake," Max said, "I'll check it out. You can't be seen to be doing this sort of thing anymore. Plus, your security team will be a bit conspicuous."

"You can't do this alone."

"Yes, I can and to be honest, at this point in time it is probably for the best. I'm going to get Andrew back, if he is still alive, then I'm going after Lyadova in Paris."

"Paris?"

"Yeah, the guy under the pile of dirt gave her up."

"She was behind the attack?"

"Yes. Apparently, I know too much."

"You need some back up, Max. I'm coming with you."

"No. Get word to anyone we have in the region and send them in to help, but you need to stay here and pretend we haven't spoken."

"I'm going to be the first called by the hearing and the police, for sure, now you've allegedly escaped."

"I know. I'm sorry for all this."

"Don't be stupid. I will always have your back. Let's go get Andrew than you can go to Paris."

Blake walked for the door not waiting for Max to protest again.

"Reardon," Max said as they walked into the corridor. "I need a favour."

"Yes, sir," Reardon said. "What can I do for you?"

"I need you to take Blake back to the embassy. He can't follow me or go to the warehouse. Am I understood?"

"Casey works for me, Max. They go where I like."

"I know. I love you, Blake, but you need to trust me. Talaria."

"No, Max," Blake protested on hearing his emergency security codeword.

Talaria was the name given to the ancient god Hermes' winged sandals. Simply saying the right codeword triggered a security detail to take action to protect their protectee. In this case, on foreign soil, on hearing the word talaria, the team would rush Blake 'Hermes' Smyth into lockdown at the embassy.

"Talaria," Reardon repeated into his comms unit without pausing.

Agents Greene and Porter spung into action at both ends of the corridor and came running for Blake. They grabbed him by the arms and rushed him off towards the elevator.

"Max!" Blake yelled.

"He's going to be pissed about that," Max said, "but it had to be done. I can't put him at risk."

"I understand, sir," Reardon said. "I'll do my best to talk him down."

"Thank you," Max said starting off for the staircase.

"Agent Shaw," Reardon said.

Max turned back to face him.

"Here, take this," Reardon said, handing Max his silenced pistol. "Good luck."

"Thank you," Max said, smiling appreciatively. "I look forward to working with you when this shit is all over."

"Oh, you owe me, I'm going to cop it," Reardon said, laughing and jogging off after Blake.

Max pushed open the fire door and took the stairs down, before bursting out into the sunlight.

Chapter Ten

Max took a looping walk back through the city weaving his way towards a parking lot he had seen earlier.

En route, he found a small sunglasses shop and purchased a new pair of reflective Oakleys. Next door he purchased a burner phone. It was a recycled smart phone with a new sim card which he loaded up with credit.

A few blocks later, Max walked into a camping and disposals store. The store owner gave him a quick nod as he entered, then went back to his television. The rugged looking man was watching some sort of outdoors adventure type show.

Max wandered aimlessly through the aisles like he had all the time in the world. He found a new duffel bag and a black carbon hunting knife, as well as some cable ties and rope which he placed in a carry basket.

He headed down the hunting supplies aisle. He picked up a solid metal Maglite torch and placed it in the basket with some massive batteries to run it. At the far end of the aisle, he found a camouflage jumpsuit. It had flecks of greys and white, as well as some blacker squares, ideal for European winters. He pulled one of the larger suits down and hung it over his arm.

Max started back towards the counter when he found a small multitool which included plyers and a screwdriver. He tossed it in the basket and walked down to the counter.

He placed the basket on the counter as the owner looked him up and down. It wasn't often men in tailored suits came in to buy camping supplies. Max just ignored the look and bundled the purchases into his new bag as the man scanned them.

The television behind the counter cutaway to a live feed from outside the International Criminal Court. A lectern was set up and it was covered with microphones, all wielding an array of local and international news service logos. The commander of the local police force walked up to the lectern.

Max tried to act uninterested as the breaking news banner flashed onto the screen with its scrolling news feed.

"Good afternoon," the officer said. "My name is Luuk van den Berg. I am the commander of the Korps Nationale Politie. I am sorry to have to report that this morning, Witness S, who is on trial at the International Criminal Court for war crimes, escaped police custody. We are appealing for witnesses to come forward who may have seen a number of cars speeding through The Hague, ending with several crashes throughout the city and a number of fatalities."

The man serving Max stopped and turned back to the television.

"At this stage, while I will not release details," van den Berg said, "I can tell you we have several men who were found with gunshot wounds and are likely to have been killed in incidents unrelated to the serious car crashes."

Max knew what was coming and looked around the shop for a distraction. He found a lighter and some chemical fire starters.

"Excuse me," Max said to the shopkeeper, holding up the items. "Sorry to interrupt. How much are these?"

The man turned back to face Max as the police officer on the television held up a crude police artist sketch. It was deliberately vague around the eyes and mouth, but it perfectly captured Max's long dark hair and spartan-like bushy beard.

"This is the man we are looking for," van den Berg said, holding the picture up as the cameras all zoomed in on it.

The shopkeeper turned back towards the television as Max slammed a small hammer down on the counter, causing him to flinch and turn back.

"I'll take this too," Max said. "How much do I owe you?"

"Four hundred and seventy euros," he said and held out his hand as Max counted the money out onto his palm.

Max placed five hundred euros into the man's hand and grabbed his duffel bag full of supplies.

"Keep the change," Max said as he quickly marched out the door.

The store owner paused momentarily to look at the cash and shouted a thank you after Max walked out. He smiled to himself at the large tip which was certainly out of the ordinary. He pocketed a fifty euro note, rounding it up, and turned back to the television.

His smiled faded quickly when he saw the screen and after a full minute of watching van den Berg's press conference, he reached for the telephone.

Max was at a full sprint with the heavy duffel bag over his shoulders. He ducked down a side alley and when he was sure no one was watching, he used a skip bin to jump the concrete fence of the carpark.

He wandered around the parking lot until he found a relatively new BMW X5 with its bold masculine bonnet and grill, and sloping sporty rear end. It was normally not the car he would choose to blend in, but given the suit, he might have looked out of place in a normal sedan.

Max tossed his duffel up onto the bonnet and removed the multitool he had just purchased. He found the screwdriver and took the screws out of the licence plates. He did the same to the car parked next to it and swapped the plates over. An old blue Opal sedan was now sporting the white BMW's plates. He took the Opal's plates over and screwed them into the BMW.

He pulled out the smart phone he had purchased and within a minute had accessed a secure AIS server which Blake had set up years ago. It was off the grid and only a select few agents even knew it existed. It was a place to store mission data without having to directly access AIS to shield it from viruses and attacks, especially when operating outside Australia.

Fortunately, it was also a place where agents could download specific applications they needed on missions, like file decryptors, fingerprint scanners and in this case, basic hacking tools.

Max downloaded the app he was looking for and opened it. There was a drop-down box which he pressed with his finger and a list of car makes fell down. He found BMW then navigated through the models until he found X5 and pressed it.

Signal one, flashed on the screen, followed by *signal two*, then *signal three*. On *signal four*, the BMW's blinkers flashed, its cold blue lights illuminated and a small beep sounded as the doors unlocked.

Max grabbed the duffel and climbed into the driver's seat. He tossed the bag onto the passenger seat, then went back to his phone. *Please enter signal number*, appeared on the screen with a keypad. Max hit four and the phone started sending out signals again. On the fourth go, the car started. Max registered the fourth signal and stored the information in the app, ready for next time.

He pulled the shift into reverse and backed out of the park, then selected drive and sped off, out of the carpark and into the street as the sound of police sirens filled the air.

He calmly turned the SUV onto the street where the camping store was located and saw the police swarming in as he drove past.

None of the police officers even looked in his direction. He smiled to himself and drove on.

Max had been on the road for well over an hour when he finally arrived in Antwerp, Belgium. He drove through a quiet suburb on the outskirts of the city and found a motel which rented rooms by the hour. The engine shut down when Max parked the car in the motel carpark.

He grabbed his bag and headed into the lobby. It smelt like a hundred years of cigarette smoke and the walls were stained yellow, confirming the source of the smell. The older woman behind the counter wasn't surprised to see a man in a suit; she was used to men from the city renting rooms to spend an hour with a local hooker. She didn't ask any questions just pointed to a sign that quoted the hourly price. Max handed her enough for three hours even though he wouldn't be there that long. She handed him a key with an oversized plastic tag and he headed out to find the room.

The room was just as bad as Max had predicted, but after months in gaol and many more in a cycle of rendition between cold dark bunkers throughout Europe in British custody, it wasn't so bad. It too smelt like smoke and ash; the curtains and bedspread were stained and faded.

Max clicked the door shut and turned on the television. The local news was reporting his escape too and the authorities were trying hard to bat away the incoming questions about how this could happen or that could happen. Max almost felt sorry for them, but then remembered they were hunting him for crimes he had not committed. It was self-defence and as for the ICC trial, well clearly something was not right. He had been told he was going to walk away a free man, but Stafford had broken his word. Max wanted to find out why, but first he had work to do.

He undressed, rustled through his duffle then walked to the bathroom and studied himself in the mirror. In the months the British had him captive, he had hardly eaten or trained, and he had lost weight, but in the recent months at Scheveningen he had been training hard and eating again. He was still thinner than ever, but his muscles were defined and firm. He felt surprisingly good.

He studied his face. Over the last few years, he had grown accustomed to his longer hair and beard, but sadly the police sketch and description drew on both as standout features.

Max grabbed a nearby bin and sat it in the basin then pulled the brand new, razor sharp, black carbon hunting knife out of its sheath. He tossed the leather cover onto the benchtop and took hold of a clump of his beard with his left hand, then with his right, cut the hair as close to the skin as he could and dropped the handful of hair into the bin.

He worked his way around his jaw line and down his neck, removing the beard.

When he was satisfied, he turned his attention to his hair. It had been pulled up in a high bun for court. Max grabbed the topknot and sliced it away. His hair fell down over his forehead and eyes, like a nineties' boyband member, as he dropped the bun in the bin. He grabbed the fringe and cut it free, before working his way to the back.

Max took the bin out of the sink and poured the hair into the toilet and flushed it. He didn't need the cleaner or the owner getting suspicious.

He ran the hot water in the sink and put his head under the faucet, wetting his remaining hair and beard, then put the plug in and filled the sink. He took one of the small soap packets and tore it open. He lathered his hands up, then rubbed them all over his head, chin and neck. He grabbed his knife and carefully shaved his head and removed his beard.

When he was finished, he cleaned the knife and re-sheathed it, then rinsed the sink and climbed into the shower. He had nicked himself more than once and the small cuts stung under the piercing hot water.

Max put his suit back on and adjusted himself in the mirror. It had been well over a decade since he had seen his face without a beard. He rubbed his hand over his smooth face then over his bald head. It was going to take some time to get used to, but for now at least it would give him some form of anonymity.

He gathered his things, hit the unlock and start buttons on his mobile app and the big BMW roared to life in the carpark. He pulled the motel room door shut, leaving the key in it with its big plastic tag swinging in the breeze.

Chapter Eleven

Andrew screamed in pain.

He had spent over a day in the onsite infirmary in a medically induced coma following his crash into the bus. A full medical team had checked him over and surprisingly he was only suffering from a fractured arm and some swelling with minimal internal bleeding. The doctors had operated to relieve the swelling and drain the blood, and they had adjusted his arm and put it in a thin cast to try to stop him making it any worse.

They left him in a coma on request of the woman in the white coat. She did not want to risk him and his friends wrecking their plans. They were too close to their goal and her superiors would not tolerate another incident.

But she had just found out, Witness S had escaped custody and was on the run. She had found a visitor's tag to Scheveningen Prison in Andrew's bag among the assorted items he had squirreled away.

She eventually ordered the doctors to bring him out of the coma and when he was conscious, her two goons had strapped him to the metal chair he was now sitting on. His hands were duct taped behind his back. His feet were firmly planted in a steel bucket and water was lapping at his shins and calves, and there was a jumper lead clamped on the top lip of the small drum. The other end was firmly biting the outlet on a car battery. The second outlet also had a lead hanging from it. The red rubber covered wire ran across the floor and up into the rubber gloved hand of the driver from the car which had chased him in The Hague.

Andrew knew the men as Leonid and Alexei. They worked for Nina, the woman in the white coat. All three were Russian, former special forces, and the personal bodyguards of Isabella Lyadova.

Alexei was holding the jumper cable. He was smiling from ear to ear, getting some sick pleasure out of Andrew's torture.

He was a tall man, thin, almost sickly looking. He had on a pair of black jeans and black Doc Martens boots which were laced halfway up his shins. He had a shiny silver studded belt on with an oversized belt buckle and just before he had started torturing Andrew, had removed his tight black T-shirt revealing his gaunt frame. His abs and chest were covered in tattoos. Ravens, vultures, crosses, skulls, death with his sickle and other deathly scenes were scrawled all over his body and down his arms, all stopping just short of where his collar and cuffs would end to obscure them in other settings. He was wearing a thick brown rubber welding glove.

But the most alarming and disturbing image was in the centre of his chest. The tattoo was done to look like his chest cavity had been torn open with jagged edges. Ribs, heart and lungs had all been painstakingly done in graphic detail. But in the centre of it all was a hammer and sickle which had been woven into the internal organs, like it was as important as his heart or lungs. Veins were clearly shown attached to the communist symbol and they looked like it was pumping its power throughout his body.

"Please, no," Andrew pleaded.

Alexei turned and looked at Leonid. Leonid was a massive lump of man. Easily six foot six and over one hundred and thirty kilos of mostly muscle. His shoulders and arms were huge, and his T-shirt sleeves had been cut or ripped to accommodate his bulging biceps. He had blond hair cut short on the sides and back, with some length in the top, while his face was perfectly clean shaven.

He nodded to Alexei.

Alexei smiled and turned back to Andrew. Without a word, he sat the end of the jumper led on the side of the bucket. Electricity shot through the cables, bucket and water, and through Andrew's body. He convulsed and violently thrashed about, until Alexei removed the cable.

Andrew slumped in his chair, sweating and drooling.

"Now, Mr Rixon," Alexei said, holding the lead only inches from his face. "Who did you meet with at Scheveningen Prison?"

"Are we seriously doing this?" Andrew huffed. "He was just an old friend."

"Why is he in prison?"

"Same reason I was, got caught doing the wrong thing."

"What did he do?"

"Same thing I did. Defrauded the government."

"You do not go to Scheveningen for fraud. Try again."

Andrew said nothing; his eyes darted around as he tried to come up with a better line.

"Did you visit Witness S?" Alexei asked.

"I don't know who that is," Andrew lied, lowering his head.

"Your body language would say otherwise, Andrew. You see, the world does not even know who Witness S is, but today he escaped. He fled after the International Criminal Court ruled that they would pursue the case."

"Is that so? Well, I don't know who he is, so I can't help. Let's just forget all about this and I'll go back to work, this is too much. I'll just forget you did this to me."

"Are you playing games with me?"

"No! No, God no. I'm just saying, this is nothing and we can just forget everything and pretend it didn't happen."

"What is in it for me?"

"You want something? Money? How about money? I can get you lots of money."

"It is tempting, but I am a man of my word and I promised to do a job on you."

"I don't know anything. I am just the IT guy. That's all I'd like to say."

"That is bullshit and we all know it. Since you are not taking me seriously, I might have to find another place to clamp this lead. Maybe your nipple or your nose or maybe I will clamp it down on one of your balls and walk away."

"No, please."

"Tell me who you met with."

"I can't tell you. Why are you doing this?"

"Why?"

"Yes, why?"

"Because it's my job and what I was ordered to do."

Andrew said nothing.

"Fine," Alexei said, dropping the lead beside the bucket, narrowly missing it.

Andrew flinched as it hit the concrete. Alexei walked over to Leonid who handed him a small pocketknife, then he walked purposefully back to Andrew and cut away his pants and underpants, leaving him exposed.

"What are you doing?" Andrew asked nervously as Alexei closed the blade back into the handle and tossed the knife back to Leonid.

"I am going to clamp this lead to your scrotum," Alexei said, picking up the lead and holding it above Andrew's exposed groin. "Unless you want to tell me who you met at the prison."

Andrew gritted his teeth and said nothing, but the fear in his eyes was showing. He was panicking and trying without any success to hide it.

Alexei sighed and lowered the lead. The metal grazed Andrew's balls and a jolt of electricity hit him and burned the exposed dry skin. It was only on for fractions of a second, but it was enough.

"Okay, okay, okay!" Andrew yelled, terrified and in pain. "I'll tell you. I met with Witness S."

"Who is he?" Alexei asked.

"His name is Max Shaw."

"How do you know Mr Shaw?"

"We used to work together at AIS."

"What is he doing in prison?"

"He is being set up as the fall guy for war crimes and torture committed during and after his time with the AIS."

"Why did you go to see him?"

"I thought he could help get me back to Australia and maybe get my old job back."

"What is wrong with your current job?"

"Seriously?" Andrew asked, raising an eyebrow and almost laughing. "No one would ask that."

"What is so funny?"

"Nothing. Nothing is funny and nothing is wrong with my current job. I wish I had never brought it up."

"What else did you tell him?"

"Nothing. I just asked for his help to get home."

"You didn't tell him about your work here?"

"No. No, I swear to God."

"You can swear to me, but right now I just don't believe you."

"This wasn't the plan!"

Chapter Twelve

Max pulled the car off the highway and into a section of bushland.

He drove down a long winding dirt road for a few minutes before turning and driving deep into the overgrown forest. The branches scratched and clunked on the metal and glass as the luxury SUV pushed deeper.

As Max drove into the dense bush, the foliage and snow shielded the big car from the road.

He shut off the engine and climbed out. He took his suit off and changed into the camouflage jumpsuit. He was happy with how it blended into the dry wintery scrub.

There was some snow lying on the ground and in the trees, and the late afternoon air was brisk. Max wished he had bought some warmer undergarments in the camping store.

He clipped his knife to his belt, grabbed the silenced pistol Reardon had given him, checked it over and chambered a round. He slung the bag over his shoulders, then started making his way through the bushes.

Through the overgrowth, Max sighted the security fence and its various sweeping cameras. It was about eight feet high, topped with razor wire. It had various warnings about keeping out, at intervals on the wire panels. There were two men with assault rifles at the door to the main building.

The building itself did not really look that impressive from the outside considering it supposedly housed hundreds of millions of dollars of computer equipment. Max wondered if maybe that was the point, to hide it in plain sight.

Max worked his way around to the side of the complex.

There were no guards, so he inched closer to the fence. When the camera swept away, he stepped out of the forest and shot it. He took a gamble that it was the only one covering this part of the fence line, but he did not want to wait around to find out.

He jogged over to the fence and pulled the multitool out of his bag. He found the plyers and started snipping the wire fence.

The plyers were fairly cheap, so it was hard work getting through each wire. It took longer than he wanted to cut enough to climb through, but eventually he made it onto the compound.

As he put the multitool back in the bag, one of the security guards from the front door walked over to the corner of the fencing and looked up at the security camera which he had shot.

Max hid behind a small section cut out of the complex wall. He grabbed a rock and tossed it at the fence near the guard.

The guard heard the rock hit and turned to face it.

He started cautiously walking towards Max. He waited until the guard got to within three metres then ran out. He startled the guard who scrambled for his rifle.

Max jumped up from his left leg and drew back his right fist, slamming it into the guard's face, then crouched as he landed and swung a savage left hook into the guard's abdomen. As he hunched over, Max kneed him in the face, knocking him out.

Max heard the other guard call out and start walking in their direction.

Max crept to the corner of the building and waited. He heard the footsteps approaching and readied himself.

The guard called out again, just as he rounded the corner.

Max threw a savage uppercut, his fist colliding with the guard's jaw and knocking him out cold.

Max ducked his head around the corner to check for any other guards who may have come out of the complex. It was clear, so Max grabbed both the unconscious guards by the vests and dragged them back against the building and searched them. He found a couple of magazines which fit the pistol he had, so he stuffed them in his pocket. He took two spare magazines for the assault rifles the guards were carrying and put them in his bag, then took one of the rifles and slung it on his back, next to the bag.

The guards were carrying flexicuffs, so he used them to tie the two guards to each other.

Max headed around to the front door. It was locked and had a high tech looking electronic keypad. There was no way of guessing the code and he was not sure he had time to try to rewire it, so he knocked on the door.

"What?" came the reply through the door.

"I've got to pee," Max said. "Open the door."

"Jesus, that's twice already," the man said, opening the door. "You have got the smallest bladder in the world."

"Maybe I should see someone about it," Max said to the confused doorman as the door swung open.

"Who are you?" he said as Max smashed the butt of his gun down on his head.

"I'm the anti-IT guy," Max said as he stepped over the semi-conscious guard and checked the hallways.

He grabbed the guard by the shirt and dragged him in behind a wall, out of the doorway. The guard groaned and Max realised he was not quite knocked out. He found a small unoccupied office across the short hallway and dragged him inside, closing the door behind them.

Max opened a storage cupboard and shoved the semi-conscious guard inside, as he struggled in vain against Max's strength. Max pushed him in against the back wall and as he started to try to fight his way forward weakly, Max punched him in the face. He collapsed into the dark space and Max closed the door on him.

He was not sure if these men were good guys in the wrong place or bad guys, so he didn't want to shoot them. Not yet anyway. He would have to keep going the hard way.

He opened the door, snuck a look around the frame, then headed out. He went left down a long stark corridor. It was a bleak and boring building, and from what he could tell, it seemed pretty empty. Something wasn't adding up.

He circled through the building and cleared the rooms as he moved.

Nothing. Just empty offices.

He stood in the hallway thinking, until he heard a conversation coming from one of the rooms he had already cleared. He spun back around and ducked into the nearest room.

He snuck a look around the doorframe as two men came out and headed for the main entry way. He watched as they moved, they were both tall men – one a thin, pale fellow and the other a massive hulking unit.

Max waited until they were clear of the hallway then found the room they had come out of and walked in cautiously. It was the same boring grey walled office he had cleared already. A desk and chair with small filing cabinet, and a two-seater stiff grey fabric couch on the left wall.

Max turned to his right and looked at the flat grey wall. It looked perfectly normal. He ran his hands over the smooth surface.

Nothing.

He stood thinking with one hand resting on the wall, when he felt a small draft tickling his fingers. He turned to the wall and got his face in closer. He felt the cool air run down over his face and looked up to where the wall joined the roof. He had not noticed it before, but the wall was not actually touching the roof. There was a small gap between them and there was air gently pumping out into the room.

It was a false wall.

Max looked around the room, studying every single detail. He walked over to the desk and noticed the keyboard was covered in dust – expect for the up and down arrows.

Max hit the up arrow and the wall rose up into the roof.

There was a small space behind it which was filled with a cold mist. As it flooded into his room, he saw the gleaming glass elevator doors.

Max walked over to the elevator and an alert flashed across the surface. *Please wait,* it said with a graphic of a hand with its fingers pointed skyward in the stop gesture. He stopped and waited as the wall sunk back into position behind him. The small cavity glowed a bright red from the elevator's warning message.

Sanitisation in progress, appeared on the doors with a series of graphics as the mist returned, filling the space from his feet up.

Once it was all around him, he noticed the second graphic light up. It was a face of a god blowing air from his mouth creating a cloud. Max was suddenly blasted with cold compressed air. He felt it penetrating his clothes and pockets, and felt it running over his now shaved head and face.

Seconds later, the graphic changed to the third image, which looked like a snowflake. The high-pressure air stopped and the space was again filled with the cold mist. When it made it to his eye level, a green *Proceed* replaced the graphics on the elevator door as it opened.

Max walked into the lift and found two rectangular buttons displayed on the glass. He hit the bottom one and the elevator sank into the ground beneath the building. Three storeys down, the elevator filled with a blue light from the rear. Max turned around and took in the scene.

A giant hangar space, larger than Max could have imagined, stretched away beneath him with rows and rows of black servers with their blue and green flashing lights. There were a handful of people milling about and working on the servers. Max had no idea what they were doing. Andrew was right, IT was not his strong suit.

The elevator continued down until he reached the floor. He walked out and strolled through the huge space. He wandered around to the side of the server room in the cold air and followed the wall in the shadowy darkness, out of sight.

There were thousands of servers all emitting their low rumbling and soft beeping, with their constant flashing lights. Each row was behind a tall walled metal mesh fence, compartmentalising them. The workers had plastic cards which they pressed against a sensor to gain access to each cage.

About halfway down the room, along the wall, Max found a set of double doors. They had two porthole type round windows in them and he looked through the closest one. A long white hallway, like a white tile lined hospital corridor, stretched on beyond the door.

He took a final look at the server room and entered the hallway.

"Hello, Agent Shaw," a woman's voice said, echoing through the hallway, startling Max as the door closed behind him.

He looked around for the source of the voice, confused, until he found the small camera in the corner above the door he had just entered.

"That's right," the voice said. "We have been expecting you."

"Really?" Max asked the camera. "What gave me away, shooting the camera on the fence?"

"No, Mr Rixon revealed your identity and, well, as you can see, we have a lot of tech. It was not hard to find out all about you, your tragic past and selfless sacrifices for the world. And, that you are Witness S, a recently escaped war criminal on trial at the International Criminal Court."

"It was you who took out the convoy, after I left the court?"

"Yes, of course. We were not sure what Mr Rixon told you and could not risk you getting away."

"But I did, that must have pissed you off."

"It did. You killed several of my men."

"They started it."

"But I will finish it and thankfully, you have just walked right in and handed yourself to us."

"Max!" Andrew shouted from one of the nearby rooms. "Max, I'm in here!"

"I'll be with you in a minute," Max said, smiling to the camera then running in Andrew's direction. "Where are you, Andrew?"

"I'm here! Here, Max! Please help me!"

Max ran until he found what he thought was the right door. He drew his pistol and kicked open the door.

Andrew was sitting in a metal chair and looked like he had been beaten to within an inch of death. His eyes were swollen and his arm was sitting in a broken cast which looked like it had been shattered against the chair. The room smelt of blood, sweat and piss.

Max had tortured people in the past, but never to this extent. Andrew looked like he had been tortured for days. He cried when he saw Max.

"I'm so sorry, Max," Andrew said, unable to control his emotions, seeming relieved or maybe even excited to see Max. "Look what they did to me."

"It's okay, Andrew," Max said, pulling his knife and cutting away the duct tape on Andrew's arms and legs. "Can you walk?"

"I think so," Andrew said, gingerly getting to his feet as Max found some clothes on a nearby table and threw them at his feet.

"Put these on," Max said, guarding the door. "It's time to go."

Max had his knife in his left hand and was resting his pistol wielding right hand on top of his left wrist, ready to take anyone who came through the door.

"Are you ready?" Max asked over his shoulder.

"Yes, but I can't see much," Andrew said, feeling his swollen face for the first time.

"Do you trust me?"

"Yes," Andrew said, nervously.

"Okay, hold still," Max said, walking over and holstering his pistol.

He took his knife in his righthand and Andrew's neck with his left.

"Ready?" Max asked.

"For what?" Andrew asked.

"It's going to hurt a little. Don't flinch."

"Okay," Andrew said, breathing deeply.

Max used his razor-sharp hunting knife to cut Andrew's swollen eyelids.

"Jesus Christ," Andrew said as blood and other fluids started pouring out of the cuts. "What the fuck did you do?"

"I helped you see," Max said, grabbing a rag from the table and tossing it to Andrew. "Clean it up a bit and I'll get you fixed up when we get out of here. Let's move."

Max resumed his stance by the door, knife in his left and pistol in his right, then he walked out into the corridor. There were two men down to his right, running towards him in full security gear with their weapons drawn, and three to his left in similar positions.

Max fired one bullet, hitting one of the three on his left. It threaded between the other two colleagues and hit the guy at the back in the face. He fell to the ground as his two comrades turned back to watch. It gave Max enough time to spin and drop to one knee, and fire four shots into the guards from his right. Both men fell, but Max did not wait to watch them fall.

He spun back and started running towards the other two guards who were starting to raise their pistols. Max whipped his right hand to the side, pushing the guard's gun away from himself. As the guard tried to pull the gun back up towards him, Max caught his wrist under his arm and clamped down, then turned his own pistol towards his prey's temple. He pulled the trigger and the bullet exploded through his head showering his comrade with blood and brain matter.

The second man was too distracted to worry about the blood because as Max had trapped his friend's arm, he was also using his knife to devastating effect. Max had stabbed it through the second guy's forearm, between the bones severing the nerves, forcing him to drop his gun in pain as Max ripped it free and stabbed him violently in the neck twice. The shock and terror in his eyes quickly faded as he died, just as his comrade's blood and brain exploded over him from Max's pistol shot.

The pair fell to the ground in a bloody mess.

"Fuck me," Andrew said, walking out of the room and seeing the bodies and the blood on Max's white camouflage gear.

"Welcome to field work, Analyst Rixon," Max said, wiping the knife on his coveralls. "It's a bit different to riding a desk. Keep your shit together, stay behind me and you'll be fine. Let's move."

"Got it," Andrew said, following Max down the corridor. "Should I have a gun or something?"

"Do you know how to use it?"

"No."

"Then there's your answer."

Max looked up at the camera he had spoken to earlier and stuck his finger up and smiled.

He kicked the door to the server room open and saw all the tech guys running away. He saw a couple of security guards coming from both sides, so he ran straight across the gap and ducked between two of the server rows. Andrew closely followed as the guards opened fire, narrowly missing the big analyst as he clumsily fell in behind Max.

Max checked the main walkway running up the centre of the hangar sized space. There were guards at both ends, but it was otherwise clear. He quickly paced out into the corridor, still leading with his pistol.

As he walked past each open aisle, between the servers, he quickly checked it was clear. Left and right, before quickening his pace towards the exit.

Four aisles down, he found one of the guards who had obviously spotted him moving out of the double doors. Max shot him twice and started searching for the second guard.

He heard the rustle of wire too late and looked up to see the missing patrolman flying through the air towards him. He had climbed on top of the security cage and used his partner as a distraction.

The guard tackled Max to the floor, and he dropped his pistol and knife. They scattered across the concrete as the pair wrestled. Max's new opponent was not without skill, but he was no match for Max.

Max headbutted him, then punched him. The blow was aiming for the man's nose, but he instinctively pulled his head back and away, trying to protect it after the headbutt, which meant Max ended up punching him in the neck. His throat collapsed and for a moment he looked like a fish out of water trying to get air, until the life drained from his eyes and he fell to the ground still clutching his throat.

"Jesus, Max," Andrew said. "That was brutal. Was it necessary? The throat I mean."

"If you want to start fighting to get us out of here, go right ahead," Max snapped, turning back to face Andrew. "Until then I'll do it my way, but for what it's worth, he moved."

"It was just..." Andrew said, trailing off seeing the unimpressed look on Max's face.

Max got to his feet and reached down to grab his knife as Andrew picked up his pistol.

"Max! Look out!" Andrew screamed as another guard came running at them.

Max was still standing up after retrieving the knife and quickly looked up. He sighted the guard and flung the knife towards him. It tumbled through the air until it pierced itself into the guard's shoulder. The guard stumbled backwards and squeezed the trigger on his rifle, loosening off a volley of bullets towards the pair.

Andrew jumped to his left, back toward the aisle between the servers, tossing Max the gun as he launched. Max caught the pistol and in one fluid motion spun back towards the injured guard and put two bullets in him.

A second stream of bullets hit the servers beside Max and he turned back to see more of A&A's goons coming up quickly from the rear. He ran over and grabbed Andrew dragging him up to his feet.

"Run!" Max ordered, pushing Andrew's head down. "Keep low. Get to the elevator."

Andrew took off as Max opened fire on the chasing guards. He gave Andrew a few seconds to get moving before following. He kept firing, holding the guards back as he ran.

When he got to the fallen guard, he pulled his knife out of the guy's shoulder and sheathed it.

When the gap between Andrew and the chasing guards was wide enough, Max turned and sprinted after Andrew.

The men gave chase, still firing, but their shots were erratic given the growing distance between the groups and that both they and their targets were moving.

Max dodged left and right, giving them an even harder target.

Max looked ahead and saw Andrew stopped in his path.

"What are you doing?" Max yelled. "Get to the lift."

Then he saw the Andrew's hands raise in surrender. He looked past Andrew and saw two men dressed in matching grey security outfits at the elevator.

Max shot the first guy. The bullet flew past Andrew's head and sensibly he dropped to the ground, giving Max a clear shot, which he took.

The second guard fell.

"Get in!" Max ordered again, dragging Andrew up to his feet, part leading, part dragging him to the elevator.

Andrew fell in the lift and scrambled to the far corner. Max hit the other rectangular button to return them to the surface as the doors closed.

The lift started to rise, but when they got to about two storeys above the ground it stopped. They were stranded in a glass box overlooking the hangar as the remaining guards gathered and raised their guns towards them.

"Fuck me," Max said, dropping to the ground beside Andrew as the glass above them shattered, raining shards down inside the small box.

Max holstered his pistol and inched forward to the edge of the steel floor he was laying on. He pulled the rifle he had stolen from one of the outside sentries and opened fire on the growing number of men below as the pings of the incoming bullets hit the steel beneath him.

"Can you get this moving?" Max asked.

"I'm not sure," Andrew said as more bullets smashed into the elevator.

"Well, try!"

Andrew slowly crawled across the floor towards the control panel. He started dragging his fingers across the touch screen opening dialogue boxes as Max fired at one of the guards in the open, hitting him in the leg and stomach. His screams temporarily distracted his colleagues.

An electronic keyboard appeared on the touch screen and Andrew started typing away as fast as he could with only one hand, given his other arm was throbbing in pain and he could not use his other hand properly.

Max drew a line in the concrete in front of the guards with bullets, forcing them back. He wanted to keep them at some distance to limit the chances of getting a good line on him or Andrew.

One of the men got brave and started running towards the elevator shaft, unleashing a wild spray from his rifle. Max put four bullets in his chest. He fell squeezing his trigger and scattering bullets all over the hangar, including into one of the nearby servers.

The server exploded into flames which quickly spread to the next server, then the next as their internal batteries caught fire.

Max watched the flames spreading quickly. There was a group of guards across the main walkway, hiding behind a row of servers. He knew they were there, because they had not long ago been firing at him. He sighted the closest server and emptied his clip into it.

It burst into flames as its battery exploded, throwing burning plastic and metal into the wire fencing. Like dominoes, the other servers in the same row exploded sending smoke billowing up to the roof.

The fire sprinklers burst open, showering the whole sunken bunker, as the lift started to rise. Max pulled the rifle inside the elevator just before they lost sight of the hangar below and climbed towards the building in the woods.

"Well done," Max said, helping Andrew to his feet and clicking his spare magazine into the rifle.

"You too," Andrew replied. "How many guys did you just kill?"

"Doesn't matter. We wanted to leave and they didn't want us to. I cleared a path."

"Thank you, Max."

"Don't thank me too early," Max said as the elevator reached the top, "we aren't out yet."

The elevator opened and the mist surrounded them.

"It's a cleaning protocol to keep dust out," Andrew said, scooping the mist into his hands.

"We don't have time for this," Max said, stepping forward and kicking the wall.

The plaster cracked. Max stepped back then sprang forward, shouldering the wall and shattering it. He crashed through into the boring office then checked the hallway.

It was clear, so he headed out, closely followed by Andrew. They made their way back to the front door.

"Wait here," Max said as he ducked into the small nearby office.

He opened the cupboard and found the guard who was starting to come to. He searched his pockets and found his access card, then punched him, knocking him out again.

"Here take this," Max said, passing Andrew the card. "Get through the gate and head into the bush for cover. I have a car. It's about two hundred metres north and three hundred east. I will meet you there. There are a couple of guards out here. I left them unconscious and they may have come to by now. I need to be ready."

"Okay, but why did you just knock them out?" Andrew asked. "It's not your style."

"I didn't know if they were genuine bad guys or just the hired help. I didn't want to shoot them, not knowing."

"Well, look at me, what do you think?"

"Yeah, yeah, I get it now. Actual bad guys. I will handle them. You just get to the car."

"Okay, Max."

Max opened the door and went to look to his right to see if the guards where anywhere to be seen, but before he got the chance two massive hands grabbed him and dragged him through the door by the shoulders.

Max was a big guy, but the man that had hold of him was a monster. He had a good couple of inches on Max, plus about twenty kilos or more. He tossed Max like a ragdoll onto the stone covered driveway. Max dropped the rifle and it skidded as he hit the ground.

Max rolled to face Leonid, drawing his pistol as he moved, but before he could get the shot off, the big man kicked his wrist and the pistol flew out of his hand. Max scrambled back, crab walking away as Leonid stomped down where his chest would have been.

Max kept moving back until he reached the fence.

Leonid smiled, having easily cornered his prey.

Max used the fence to stand up, without taking his eyes off the big Russian who was getting closer and closer.

Leonid threw a haymaker and Max dodged the blow. His big fist smashed into the stiff wire fence, as Max drove a punch up in under Leonid's ribs. The big man just laughed and smiled.

Max threw another punch, but the bigger man caught his fist and twisted his arm around to the side.

"Go!" Max yelled to a frozen Andrew. "Get out of here!"

Andrew came out of his trance and ran for the gate. He used the access card to open it and started running down the road.

The big Russian looked over to see Andrew fleeing through the gate and smirked.

"He will not get far," Leonid said, turning back to Max. "Nor will you."

Max threw a left jab into Leonid's jaw. It shook him, but not enough. His head turned away, but quickly turned back.

He was still smiling, almost taunting Max.

Max threw a second jab, but this time, Leonid caught his fist and turned it, twisting Max's other arm so both forearms were facing the sky. The angle was awkward and Max was struggling against Leonid's strength.

Max was trying to think, questioning how he was going to be able to break the hold, when the two security guards he had knocked out earlier came around the corner. Max saw them and smiled. He looked at Leonid and nodded to his left. The big man took the bait and looked.

While he was distracted, Max kneed him in the balls and he hunched over. Max took the chance as he felt the grip loosen on his hands and launched a second knee into the big man, this time into his stomach. He doubled over and let go of Max's hands, stepping back trying to get his breath back. Max launched off his left foot into the air, drew back his right fist and slammed it down onto the Russian's head. He landed and threw the left jab, this time generating power up through his legs and body, and out through his shoulder.

Leonid stumbled back and fell on his arse.

Max ran, grabbing his pistol as he moved and the two security guards gave chase, raising their weapons.

Max shot at them as he ran. Two bullets each.

They fell to the ground clutching their chests.

Max turned the pistol on the big Russian and went to pull the trigger, but saw the slide had clicked open.

Empty.

Leonid breathed a sigh of relief. "I will find you both and kill you!" he yelled as Max fled into the scrub.

Max ran fast and hard, high stepping over branches and small bushes. Twigs broke as his boots crunched down on them. There was a small gully which he slid down.

At the bottom, he ran through the shallow water trickling along the tiny creek, towards his car.

After a couple of hundred metres, he climbed the small bank and jogged the remaining distance to the car.

He found Andrew out of breath, hunched over behind the BMW, having only just arrived himself.

"Get in," Max barked. "Quickly."

"How did you get away from him?" Andrew asked.

"I got lucky. Now, get in."

The two men climbed into the car and Max reversed hard through the scrub on his makeshift track. The branches scratched at the paint and squealed as they dragged along the metal.

When he got to the main road, he found a gap in the traffic and hit the accelerator. The powerful SUV sprang forward, kicking up rocks and muddy dirt before gripping the tarmac and charging forward.

"Where are we going?" Andrew asked.

"As far away from here as we can get," Max said. "We need to find a place to patch you up and regroup. We need some time to come up with a plan. How long have we got?"

"The system will start attacking the intel agencies in a matter of hours."

"How do we stop it?"

"We need the tablet."

"What tablet?"

"Apollo's control tablet. The one Isabella had at the launch. It is the only way to control him."

"Him?"

"Apollo. The program."

"Right. Where is it?"

"With Isabella. She won't let it out of her sight."

"And where is Isabella?"

"Paris."

"You're sure about that?"

"Yes, she has a series of events to mark certain milestones. Tonight's event is almost like a farewell to the world as we know it party. She's got a bunch of rich arseholes and world leaders who will be there. Almost rubbing their faces in it without them knowing that's what she is doing."

"And it's tonight?"

"Yes."

"Please tell me you know where."

"It's at the…" Andrew started to say when Alexei sprung up from the backseat and looped a strand of piano wire over his head, choking him.

Max swerved, trying to hold the car on the road, while fighting Alexei with one hand. Andrew was struggling, clawing at the wire trying to get some relief. Max turned the cruise control and lane keeping on, and undid his seatbelt. He grabbed one of Andrew's arms and placed it on the steering wheel. Andrew had a look of sheer horror on his face.

"Drive!" Max said to Andrew as he dragged himself into the backseat of the BMW next to Alexei.

He punched Alexei in the face, but he didn't let go of the wire. He was thinner and a bit sick looking, but clearly he was just as tough as his friend Leonid.

Max pressed his feet against the door and grabbed Alexei by the head as the car swerved wildly in the traffic as Andrew pulled on the wheel, struggling as he fought to breath, let alone drive.

Max slammed Alexei's head into the window, pushing hard with his legs to give it extra force. He repeated the move three times, before Alexei finally let go of the piano wire.

Andrew dragged in a deep breath as he reached over and took the wheel with his good hand to avoid colliding with the rear of a hatchback. The BMW swerved just in time, but rocked wildly, fishtailing and beeping insistently as the car changed lanes without indicating.

Alexei used the momentum to turn and come at Max.

The pair traded blows in the tight space. Max landed a punch, but it was quickly followed by Alexei getting the upper hand. Max fell back against the door behind the empty driver's seat. Alexei grabbed him around the neck and started to choke him with his bare hands. Max couldn't get free. He punched the Russian in the stomach. Five short hard jabs, but it did nothing to loosen his grip.

"Oh shit!" Andrew said, looking out the front window at three lanes of banked up traffic at a dead stop in front of them.

Andrew steered the car into the emergency space at the side of the freeway, unable to reach the cruise control.

The car slammed into a bunch of wooden guideposts, ripping them from the ground or snapping them, bang after bang as they slapped into the front grill. Cars in the closest lane beeped their horns as they raced past.

"Max!" Andrew yelled, trying in vain to reach the cruise control button, seeing a solid barricade ahead.

They were out of road.

Andrew's fingers danced across the steering wheel towards the cruise button. Inch, half an inch, then finally he hit it and the car stopped accelerating, but didn't slow much. Momentum was carrying them forward.

Max gave up trying to fight Alexei and instead looped his legs through the far seatbelt and his arms through the belt behind his back.

The BMW's autonomous braking system activated, throwing Alexei through the gap between the front seats and knocking Andrew's hand off the wheel. The car skidded hard, tearing tread from the tyres, but without Andrew controlling it, the car pulled left and slammed into a nearby vehicle in a cacophony of breaking glass, metal on metal and plastic breaking.

The airbags all deployed and seatbelts tightened, as the car stopped dead in its tracks.

Max felt a pinching pain in his shoulder as it popped out of joint.

The car came to rest with steam and smoke billowing out from under the hood.

Max opened the door down by his feet; the one near his head was wedged against a parked car. He climbed out as other drivers and passengers were getting out of their cars to see what was going on.

Max walked over to a street sign and slammed his shoulder into it, and he groaned through gritted teeth as it went back into joint.

He opened Andrew's door and checked his former colleague over. He looked across the small space and saw Alexei was trapped under the steering wheel. He was moving, but he was stuck as the steering wheel was pinned to the seat.

"Wake up!" Max said as he slapped Andrew across the face. "Andrew, can you hear me? We have to move."

"Yeah," Andrew replied, waking groggily from the impact of the airbag against his face. "What happened?"

"You crashed."

"Again?"

"Yep. Remind me not to let you drive again. Can you walk?"

"I think so. Weren't you driving?"

"Just get out and start moving."

Andrew climbed down and stumbled. He hunched over and threw up as Max saw Alexei draw a pistol.

Max grabbed Andrew and ducked behind the wheel arch as the bullets flew out the open door.

"Go!" Max yelled, grabbing his bag and fleeing after Andrew down the freeway.

Fifty metres down the road, Max realised it was hopeless running this way. The traffic was too banked up.

"Andrew," Max yelled and pointed, "this way!"

Max headed across to the far side and leapt the concrete barricade into oncoming traffic. He raised his rifle and sighted the nearest car. It slammed on its brakes and stopped only metres from him.

"Get out of the car!" Max ordered to the terrified driver who put up his hands and nodded.

He climbed out, and Max and Andrew got it.

Max hit the accelerator, burning his tires, spinning the wheel and dragging the car around one hundred and eighty degrees in a storm of smoke and squeals, then he dropped the clutch and raced off down the slipway beside the road.

Chapter Thirteen

"With all due respect, Mister Justice," Blake said from the witness stand at the International Criminal Court, "Witness S is one of the finest agents the Australian Intelligence Service has ever produced."

"If he is your finest, it leaves a lot to be desired," the new prosecutor stated. "The man breaks out of custody, kills a number of people and brings disrespect to this august institution."

"Given the circumstances leading up to the attack, I would argue that this institution is the architect of its own undoing. There was a deal reached between the previous prosecutor and the defence, and the justices had been informed, and so far, we have been given no answer and no reasons for the court's decision to press ahead with this trial. As for the deaths, we have no evidence that it was Witness S, nor do we know if he was in fact the intended target, but it is highly likely he was. Following the events at the prison, where he was attacked, I think it is a pretty safe assumption he was in fact the target and victim in all of this, not the perpetrator."

"You have a lot of faith in your agent. Could it be because of your personal relationship?"

"The witness and I have been colleagues for many years."

"But it is more than that, is it not? You are in fact lovers?"

"The witness and I are close friends, and that is all I will say on the matter."

"Do you think it is appropriate for someone in your position to be conducting such a relationship? Both as a witness here today, but also given he is your subordinate."

"I have given you the answer to your question."

"No comment?"

"I suggest we move on."

"I want to place it on the record that Mister Smyth has refused to answer my question."

"Vice Admiral Smyth."

"What?"

"My title is Vice Admiral, not Mister, not Agent. Vice Admiral."

"Moving on, your Prime Minister's letter has caused a stir in the global media."

"I didn't hear a question," Blake said, after an awkward silence.

"Do you agree and do you have any comments?"

"I have seen the media and no I do not have any comments."

"Surely you take an interest in these matters?"

"I take an interest in a great deal of matters, that is my job."

"So you have no comments? You would not like to provide some context to the letter?"

"The Prime Minister has formally noted, through his public statement and the statement I delivered in this very room only moments ago, his thoughts on this trial and the context in which it is taking place. His words are his own and I would not seek to provide commentary on them."

"So, given his hostile view of the court, why are you here today?"

"Because I was invited and I believed it was important to place on the record my very strong opinion that the witness is not only innocent of the crimes for which he has been charged, but also to state unequivocally that I believe he was the target of an assassination plot in the attack on his convoy after leaving here. He is not the perpetrator as he has been presented. My agency is looking into it and I am sure I will have evidence to clear him very soon."

"How can you of all people be trusted to present such evidence? How can we believe you?"

"That's a question only you can answer. The witness, like all of my agents, is one of the good guys. You may not believe it, but there are people out there who wish to bring about death and destruction. Who seek to kill the innocent in the name of faith or for their own greed. We exist to stop them. It is that simple. Nothing more and nothing less, and we do so within the laws and powers given to us by our governments and under international law. My agency seeks to protect democracy and freedom, protect the very organisations that give the power to the people, not the ruling elite. I will always stand opposed to tyranny and terrorism. As do all of my agents, including Witness S. Tell me this, counsellor, what do you stand for?"

"I stand for life, Vice Admiral. Every life is precious. No one deserves to be treated in the way you and your agents have treated people, and no one is above the rule of law."

"You are so naïve. The people we target do not believe in our rule of law. They believe only in the rules that they create. If we don't meet them on their level, we will never win, and millions will die, while millions more will be subjected to a fate worse than death as their liberties and freedoms are eroded and taken from them. You should be thanking him, not putting him on trial. You should be putting a medal on him, not handcuffs. He has saved your life more than once and lost more than anyone in the process. This trial should be immediately abandoned until we can determine what other factors are at play here, including why the deal was overturned without notice or cause and why this court has allowed itself to become the political plaything of certain states. Questions need to be answered, but rest assured, I will be looking into it, even if the court won't."

Blake left the trial slightly frustrated in himself that his usual stony persona, that he always presented in these types of hearings, including testifying before the parliament, had cracked. He knew it was because the trial was a fraud and that clearly someone was pulling the strings behind the scenes, but he was still kicking himself for showing emotion. He also knew it was because the questioning of his relationship with Max had hit a nerve.

And he was kicking himself for showing it.

He was riding in the backseat of his bulletproof BMW which was flanked on both sides by two other black SUVs with agents of the AIS on board which formed his elevated security detail.

He was en route to the embassy after the hearing when his phone pinged with a unique chime. Its distinct double beep was from a secure AIS app for deep undercover agents.

He pulled out his phone, scanned his thumb and enter his passcode. There was a new message.

Hermes, en route to Brussels. Small window. Need an assist. Château Vaux-le-Vicomte. Invite tonight. Please advise. Prince.

Blake immediately opened his secure line and called AIS to ask his top French analyst to pull together a brief on the château and whatever event was taking place tonight for Max. He also organised a drop for Max in Brussels with the local freelance team AIS used on the ground.

Within twenty minutes he had the briefing.

He opened the app and started typing.

Prince, package will be delivered to the Musée Belge de la Bande Dessinée. 1600 hours. Find Alix. Good luck and Godspeed. Hermes.

Chapter Fourteen

Max had arrived in Brussels and dumped the stolen car. He changed into his suit, collected his bag and was walking briskly with Andrew down a back street in the bustling city. He had sent a text to Blake en route and was pleased to find the reply letting him know AIS was preparing a package for him.

He had a short window to get Andrew some medical help before he needed to get to the comic book museum where the drop was to be made.

The pair ducked into a dirty alley running behind some light industrial style buildings.

At the third building, Max knocked on the door and, very quickly, a short man with pencil moustache opened it.

"Bonjour, Mr Shaw," the man said, opening the screen door. "It is a pleasure to see you again. What trouble have you gotten yourself into today?"

"For once it's not me who needs your help, Gabriel," Max said, nodding at Andrew. "This is a friend of mine, Andrew. Any chance we can get some help?"

"But of course, please come in," Gabriel said, holding the door open.

"What is this place?" Andrew asked, looking around.

"It is a backup option for when we are trying to keep a low profile," Max said. "Gabriel was a contact of mine within the DGSE, the French General Directorate for External Security."

"And what sort of help can he provide?"

"I am a former member of the Légion Etrangère," Gabriel said proudly. "Commandant, Medical Corps."

"Legionnaire?"

"Oui!" Gabriel said. "I moved to Brussels years ago. I had enough of the cloak and dagger world, but that did not stop young Maxwell here from dragging me back in occasionally."

"I am sorry, Gabriel, but I need to duck out," Max said. "Can I leave him in your capable hands? He's got a fractured or maybe broken arm, and he's been in two car crashes."

"Two?" Gabriel said, dramatically gesturing with his arms and farrowing his brow. "And look at his eyes. Did you do that?"

"Man can't drive, what can I say?" Max said, smiling at Andrew. "Yeah, I cut him, so he could see."

"That's not the whole story," Andrew interjected. "The last crash in particular was mostly your fault."

"You had the wheel," Max joked, heading for the door. "I'll be back in an hour."

"Parfait," Gabriel said, patting Andrew on the back. "Let me get to work."

Max headed back out into the alley and took a circuitous route through the city to the Musée Belge de la Bande Dessinée in downtown Brussels. The art nouveau building designed in 1904 by Victor Horta was formerly a textile building, but had been repurposed in the eighties to house the national comic book museum.

Among its many permanent displays was an exhibit dedicated to Tintin, one of the most popular local comic magazines, which included among its titles *Alix*, which Blake had mentioned in his text.

Max wandered through the fun space admiring the childlike innocence of the comic books and exhibits on display. Large colourful plastic sculptures and props were scattered amongst the beautiful concrete, tile and intricately crafted iron railings and balustrades.

He meandered aimlessly like any of the other tourists in the centre, seemingly showing interest in the exhibits, all the while checking his back and making his way to the Tintin gallery.

When he arrived, he found the space was divided into three. The most popular by far was the *Adventures of Tintin* exhibit, but he wanted the one on the far end, *Adventures of Alix*.

Alix was a series based on a young Gaul adopted by a Roman noble in the years of Julius Caesar and the start of the Roman Empire. The gallery space portrayed some of the visually stunning artworks from the comics as well as busts and sculptures in Roman style of the main characters.

Max studied each bust and artwork, until he found Alix himself. It was an intricate sculpture of the hero. Max checked he was not being watched, then got closer to the bust. He searched either side of it, then found what he was looking for behind it on the stand. A small paper token stamped with the museum's logo. He grabbed it.

"Please do not touch!" a security guard snapped from his right.

"Désolé, sorry," Max said, nodding and walking on.

He took the ticket to the cloak room and handed it to the young girl behind the counter who was more interested in her phone than in her job. She checked the ticket and opened a locker.

She wandered over and dropped the leather satchel on the desk with a fake smile and nod, then went back to her phone.

Max smiled and said thank you, then dragged the bag over his shoulder.

As he turned around to leave, he saw a familiar face in the doorway.

Alexei.

Max walked back into the museum under protest from the guards who noted he should not take his bag in, but Max ignored them and walked briskly through the doors. He did not need to look to know Alexei was following him.

He quickly turned down an aisle on his left, then sprinted.

Guests, tour guides and museum guards alike all turned to see what the commotion was as the guards shouted for him to stop.

Max ran on, quickly checking over his shoulder as he heard Alexei collide with a guard. Alexei punched the young man and screams rang out around him from nervous patrons.

Max faced forwards again, but not in enough time to see the trolley pushed into the aisle in front of him. He crashed into it, toppling it over and dragging its books off onto himself and the floor.

An apologetic worker pulled the cart off him as he scrambled to his feet, the old volunteer chastising him for running, while at the same time apologising. Max said sorry as he started running again.

Alexei leapt the cart as the old man screamed at him to have some respect. Alexei just ignored him and ploughed on, gaining on Max.

Max was shocked at the man's speed. The last time he had seen him, he was crumbled under a steering wheel after a violent crash. How he was walking, let alone running, was incredible, especially at this speed.

Max hit the rear exit door, sounding the alarm. He was only a metre out the door when Alexei dove through and tackled him to the ground.

Max fell forward, rolling over, feeling Alexei's grip drop as the pair hit the concrete driveway. Max used his own momentum to scramble to his feet and keep running.

He reached the end of the driveway and jumped up on a large commercial skip bin, using it to get over the fence.

Alexei caught his ankle as he was going over.

Max pulled his knife out and slashed the top of Alexei's hand. He fell over the solid sheet metal fence as Alexei let go.

He hit hard, but was not going to wait for his pursuer to join him. He got up and ran hard, as he heard Alexei land on the gravel behind him. He heard the stones crunching under the Russian's feet as he gave chase.

Max ran out between two buildings onto a busy street. He dodged the traffic to the sound of beeping horns and expletives yelled from windows, then he ran into a dress shop.

He looked back through the large window to see Alexei dancing between cars on the street. Max kept running as woman in the shop screamed. Max pulled over three clothes racks as he ran, apologising each time to the owner, who was irate. He crashed out the back door as Alexei jumped through the glass window of the store, showering the carpet with glass to more screams from the shoppers and shopkeeper.

Max drew his pistol as he ran and aimed back at the door, while still jogging backwards, breathing hard. Alexei flung it open and Max put two bullets into the bricks either side of him. Alexei did not flinch. Instead, he pulled his own gun and gave chase. Max spun, dodged left and right, trying to make himself a harder target as bullets ripped into the ground either side of him.

Occasionally, when he got the chance, knowing the path was clear, Max returned fire. He did not want to hit any onlookers.

As Max turned back to fire, he ran out onto the road and was collected by a car.

Luckily, it was not going too fast.

Max landed up on the bonnet with a thud, before the driver hit the brakes, sending him rolling off onto the bitumen. He crawled and clambered to his feet as Alexei fired four shots into the car, one hitting the driver who slumped forward, falling on the horn and releasing the brake.

Max rolled to the side as the car moved past him.

Max scurried along on all fours trying to get back to his feet, shaken after the impact of the vehicle, as bullets hit all around him.

He saw a small truck coming in the opposite direction towards him. He spun on his heel and started running in the same direction.

Max used the truck as a shield as the bullets kept coming, then jumped into the back. The driver braked slightly, but when a bullet sailed into the back window shattering it, he stomped on the gas to get out of there.

Max used the momentum to climb into the rear tray and used the raised gate for cover. He tried to line Alexei up for a shot, but there were too many civilians in the way. He could not risk it, so he held fire.

Alexei smiled smugly as the small truck carried Max out of sight around a corner.

Max waited until the driver pulled over. He was clearly in shock, but Max did not have time to comfort him. If Alexei had found him, Andrew and Gabriel could be at risk. He jumped down from the back of the truck and ran as fast as his legs would carry him towards Gabriel's.

Gabriel opened the door and let him in, and Max explained what had happened.

"How could he have found me?" Max asked. "The only person I told where we were was Blake."

"And you trust Blake?" Gabriel asked.

"With my life," Max said, turning to Andrew. "I used the old deep cover app. It should be the most secure channel, right?"

Andrew did not reply, he just grimaced and frowned.

"What?" Max asked. "What did you do now?"

"It's too early," Andrew said. "He shouldn't be accessing those channels yet."

"He?"

"Apollo. How many times are we going to have to go over this?"

"You gave it access to the secure apps?"

"Yes. Well, not intentionally. He is smart. He learns where to look."

"Jesus, Andrew. How could you be so stupid?"

"I thought I was building a system for them to use as a company, to help people and grow, not as a tool to destroy others. But we don't even know if it was the app. Did Blake call anyone?"

"I imagine he called AIS to get their help, but it would have been on his secure sat phone."

"It wasn't the app. It was the phone. Those systems were first, remember? That's why I came to see you. You can't trust the phones."

"Even sat phones?"

"Yes."

"Do you have any idea what you have done?"

"Yes, Max, and I said I'm sorry. I want to help you stop them."

"Well, you'd better or I will make this very difficult for you."

"You don't need to threaten me, Max. I'm here to help."

"You're going to need to explain this all to me in detail en route," Max said, turning to Gabriel. "Is he ready?"

"Oui," Gabriel said. "As good as he can be given the circumstances."

"The man who is pursuing me a tall lanky Russian. He's fast and strong, and pretty ruthless. Can I convince you to come with us?"

"No, Max. I am not running from anyone. If I see him, I will take care of him."

"Well, just keep your head down, will you?"

"Of course, I will be fine."

"Thank you, Gabriel," Max said, handing the old man a wad of euros. "I owe you one."

"You have paid for a service. You do not owe me anything. What is it your friend Hulk says? Good luck and Godspeed."

"And to you, old friend. Stay safe."

Max shook hands with Gabriel as Andrew said thanks for the cast and stitches. Max opened the back door.

"Max," Gabriel said as Max turned around and caught the object Gabriel had thrown him. "It is parked two blocks down. White Honda."

"Are you sure?" Max asked, studying the keys.

"Now, you owe me," Gabriel said smiling.

"I won't forget it."

"I know. Now, get out of here. Go kick some arse."

Chapter Fifteen

Lyadova paced back and forth in front of the grand fireplace. It was a white painted brick opening in the wall which was easily six foot high and almost the same wide. It had a roaring fire behind a small antique iron fence. Above the fireplace hung a massive portrait of one of the French aristocrats who had owned the Château de Vaux-le-Vicomte decades before A&A had purchased it.

The baroque French château was built in Maincy, just over fifty kilometres to the south east of Paris. Until very recently when Lyadova bought it, the château had been a major tourist destination with caves, rolling immaculate grounds and gardens, period costume hire, water shows and one of the largest collections of art and antiquities in France, including hundreds of chariots and carriages.

A colossal gold statue of Hercules was one of the main attractions at the site. It was visible from up to a mile away and stood over ten feet tall on an over six-foot-high concrete pillar.

The room Lyadova was in had originally been used as a guest bedroom, but she had converted it into an office. It still held its old worldly charm with antique period furniture and ornate gold framed oil paintings, but it had been upgraded subtly to include all the modern electronics she was used to in her offices. Speaker and computer systems were hidden in the old walls and ceilings.

Lyadova stopped in front of the fire, letting its warmth run over her as she pulled a folded picture from her pocket. It was frayed around the edges and the fold had worn a solid stripe down the centre of the photograph from years of opening and closing the photo.

It was a black and white picture of a women in her late teens, maybe seventeen or eighteen. She had a loose summer dress on and Lyadova had always imagined it in a bright yellow, warm and friendly to match her beaming smile. She was holding a newborn baby, only a week or two old at most. She looked proudly and lovingly at the camera, like the child was the only thing that mattered to her in the whole wide world.

It was the only photo Lyadova had of her mother. It had been left in the basket along with Lyadova at the front door of a small cathedral in Moscow only days after the photo had been taken.

Lyadova had been sent to an orphanage and raised by strict nuns who taught only the love of Christ, while showing absolutely no love or affection for any of the children in their care.

Lyadova lived there with them until she turned fifteen. She was a rebellious teen, not very academic and not interested at all in the teachings of Jesus Christ, and she had become too hard for the nuns to control, so they asked her to leave.

Lyadova felt she had been abandoned yet again and fell into depression. Her world turned into a living hell as she was forced to find shelter on the streets. She had to fight, beg and scrape for food. She stole clothes and blankets to survive the long winter nights. It was not long before she fell in with the wrong crowd and started running drugs to make cash. She even sold her body on more than one occasion and she was raped within her first month on the streets.

Within a year, she moved on to selling drugs and controlling a dozen runners. She was determined to drag herself up and off the streets.

Soon enough Lyadova was making enough money to find a place to live. She rented out the spare rooms to make extra income and frequently had friends she had made staying on the couch. She was happy to be able to provide people with a warm place to sleep in from the cold, but sadly, they were not all thankful. She was robbed almost monthly and beaten by men who tried to take advantage of her. She learnt the hard way how to fight and defend herself.

One evening, Lyadova let a young man she had met stay over in the guest bedroom. He was freezing and hungry, and was turning tricks in back alleys for cash from older men.

During the night, he came into her room and pinned her to the bed. He ripped her underwear off and tried to force himself upon her.

Lyadova bit his lip, gnawing and ripping her head back, until his bottom lip came completely off. He let go of her bruised wrists to hold his face and while he was distracted in pain, she sliced his balls off.

With every setback and heartbreak, with every attack and loss, Lyadova hardened her resolve. She was going to get out of that life and make something of herself. She was determined and nothing was going to stand in her way.

There was a knock, then the oversized door opened and Nina, her head of security, walked in with her long white trench coat.

"Sorry, boss," Nina said, walking over. "Your guests have started to arrive."

Lyadova was still lost in her own thoughts.

"Ma'am?" Nina asked. "Is everything all right?"

"Nina, apologies," Lyadova said, folding the picture and putting it back in her pocket. "I was lost in my own little world there for a moment."

"It is completely fine. Was that your mother?"

"Yes."

"She was beautiful."

"She was a prostitute. Did you know that?"

"No, ma'am, I did not know that, but it does not change the fact that she is beautiful."

"Thank you. She is part of the reason we are doing all of this."

"How so?"

"I found her, years ago, and she told me why I had been left at that orphanage with those bloody nuns. I was seeing a guy. He was handsome and treated me well. We were in love and we had crawled out of the gutters and were finally starting to make some real money. I finally felt we were getting close to leaving our awful lives behind. But we were into some things with the wrong people. He got in too deep and owed a lot of money to some very nasty individuals. One night he came home and asked me for all the cash I had saved, and when I refused to give it to him, he beat me. He beat me until I lost consciousness."

"Jesus, I am so sorry to hear that. What happened?"

"When I woke up, I had no idea how long I had been out, but our house was turned upside down. He had been through every draw and slashed open every cushion and pillow looking for the cash. I scrambled over and slid the lounge back to find the loose floorboard I hid the cash under. As soon as I saw the tin was still there, I realised my mistake. He was there with three other men. One of the men shot him in the face and he fell dead on the floor, then the shooter walked over to me. He pointed the gun at my head and took the tin. I thought I was going to die, but instead they just left with a warning. Leave town or I would be next."

"Well at least he got what was coming to him, for what he did to you."

"He did."

"So, you left?"

"I gathered whatever I could carry and fled, back to the only place I could think of, that fucking orphanage. The sister let me in and they provided shelter for the night. While I was there, Mother Superior presented me with this photograph and told me it was left in the basket with me. She told me they had tracked her down, years ago, but she was terrified when they approached her. They decided to keep it from me, but they figured I was old enough now to hear about it. They had her name, Katrina, and they knew where to find her."

"And now you did too."

"Yes. The following day I left the orphanage and went straight to her house. She was home and we both broke down into tears when she opened the door. She invited me in and told me how she had become pregnant at seventeen to a wealthy aristocrat. A man who had a wife and family, and wanted nothing to do with her or with me. She gave me up, because she did not know how to raise a child. She did not have a house and thought she could not provide the care I would need. She thought the nuns would do a better job."

"That must have been a terrible decision to have to make."

"It was and it broke her heart."

"So, did you ever find out who he was?"

"Yes. I went to his office in downtown Moscow and met with him, but as you would imagine, I was not welcome. He spoke for only a minute, then went to his safe, handed me a bundle of roubles and told me he never wanted to see me again. I was upset, but then he threatened me. He told me if he ever saw my mother or me again, he would kill us, so I took the money and left. I just wish…"

"Wish what?"

"I just wish my mother had taken the threat seriously," Lyadova said, turning to face Nina. "Maybe then she would still be alive."

Lyadova stared for a few moments at the fire, then turned to Nina.

"Are we ready to go?" Lyadova asked, breaking the silence.

"Yes, ma'am," Nina said. "Everything is ready and your guests have started to mingle in the courtyard. We need to get you to the rendezvous point. The helicopter will be waiting."

Chapter Sixteen

Max had found a small electronics retailer in Maincy. He and Andrew gathered a few supplies, including a new laptop and printer. None of the items they bought were up to their usual standard, but they would have to do.

Max found a tailor and purchased a new suit and overcoat with a crisp white shirt with shiny white buttons. He also bought a vest, bow tie and flat cap, and pair of boots and set of clear framed reading glasses. The pair then made their way to an old rundown motel on the edge of town.

Andrew hooked up the laptop to the television to give himself another screen to work with as Max showered and got ready. When he walked out of the bathroom Andrew saw the various scars from bullet and knife wounds, from years of fighting, covering Max's toned and athletic body.

"Jesus," Andrew said, unable to look away. "How are you still able to function? How are you not dead?"

"Plenty of people have tried," Max said, pulling on his shirt. "It's just a matter of time until one of them hits the right spot."

"Why do you keep doing it? Why keep putting yourself through all this?"

"Because someone has to."

"You're a better person than me. I would have walked away from all this years ago."

"I made a choice when AIS offered me the job. I agreed to do whatever it takes to protect the innocent. Unfortunately, I haven't always succeeded, but I have to keep trying. It was a choice that led to a lot of pain and suffering, and loss, but I made a promise to never stop. I'm going to keep that promise until one of these arseholes finally puts the bullet in the right place."

Max pulled the bowtie around his neck and started to tie it.

"Where are we at?" Max asked as he pulled his boots on. "Are you ready to go?"

"Yes," Andrew said, turning back to the laptop and television. "The drive that Blake left for you at the comic museum had an invitation to the party on it. I've printed it out and it's sitting next to your bag."

"Thank you. What about the venue? What can you tell me?"

"The drive had some specs and a blueprint. The villa used to be a tourist site, open to the public, which means there was more detail available then we would usually have, which is nice. A&A bought the place and delisted it. Lyadova uses it as her own European home and office. I've put the files on your phone so you can refer to them if needed."

"So what's the party and who's going to be there?"

"It is a celebration of the launch of Alexandria 2.0. The hype has been building since her dramatic announcement about the project in Greece. The guest list is a veritable who's who of politicians, dignitaries and celebrities from around the world. Look at the list."

Andrew pulled the guest list AIS had put on the drive for him up onto the television screen.

Max scanned the list. Andrew was right, it was a list of the world's elite. He recognised the names of over a dozen world leaders as well as sports stars, academics, singers and Hollywood heart throbs.

"Wow, did you see her in *After the Sun Sets*?" Andrew said, pointing to an American starlet's name on the list. "Amazing tits, perfect body."

Max didn't reply, he just starred at Andrew unimpressed.

"Oh right, yeah," Andrew laughed. "Not really your thing."

"Not really the time either," Max snapped. "So, who am I?"

"You're Professor Maximilian Stanthorpe, an Australian academic from the University of Sydney."

"And what am I a professor of?"

"International relations."

"Are you taking the piss?"

"What? You studied that right?"

"Given where I have been for the last few months you could have come up with something else."

"Well, at least you know the system and the basics. Enough to get you through the small talk."

"Yeah, okay, fine," Max said, giving Andrew another unimpressed look. "So, why am I invited to the party?"

"You are representing the university and the thousands of students who, at the end of the week, will have all their projects funded and will be given access to the combined knowledge of the world thanks to Apollo and Alexandria 2.0."

"What else do I need to know?"

"The project is getting mixed reactions from people around the world. Some are claiming their copyright is being stolen. They aren't able to negotiate with Apollo and they are complaining that they are being given take it or leave it offers, but even if they choose not to sell, Apollo is still taking it anyway."

"Is it?"

"Probably."

"So, what is it taking?

"Everything. He is vacuuming up the internet. He is basically programmed to copy everything."

"Including the deepest secrets of national governments?"

"Yes."

"I should have let them torture you some more for helping build this thing."

"I have already apologised, Max. What more can I do to make it up to you? I'm here helping, aren't I?"

"We need to fix this."

"We will."

"So, what am I looking for?"

"You need to find her tablet computer. She never goes anywhere without it. If she hasn't got hold of it, her personal assistant, Elias Laskaris, he will have it and he is always within reach."

"So how do you suggest I get it?"

"There will be hundreds of security guards there and heavy surveillance."

"That's not an answer."

"I don't know is my answer. That's your part."

"Great. Guess I will have to see what I can do. What do I do with it once I have it?"

"Bring it to me."

"You don't seriously think I'll be able to get it out of there do you? With all that security. You are going to have to walk me through what I need to do."

"Okay, shit, well, that's going to be more of a challenge."

"We got the camera and earpiece for this, didn't we?"

"We got them so I could see and hear what was happening, not to try to walk you through hacking into one of the most secure devices on the planet."

"Well, you need to figure out how you are going to do that. I have to get going."

"Okay," Andrew said, turning back to his laptop and frantically scrolling through lines of code.

Max pushed the earbud into his right ear. It was larger than the comms units AIS used, but it was going to have to do. Andrew had connected it to Max's mobile. He also pinned a small silver lapel pin onto his suit jacket and turned back to the television.

"Have you got it?" Max asked, holding up the jacket.

"Just a sec," Andrew said, tapping on the keyboard.

The television changed and Max's face filled the screen. The vision was broadcasting from the pin. The quality was not very high given it was a store-bought surveillance hidden camera. It was not designed for this, but Andrew had repurposed it.

"The quality is a bit shit, but it should do the job," Andrew said. "It's normally for spying on nannies to make sure they are looking after your kids properly."

"Can you tell what it is from there?" Max asked.

"Nah, it just looks like a normal lapel pin."

"Good," Max said, putting on a pair of clear framed glasses and the flat cap which matched his vest.

Max walked over to the mirror. His new suit was a good fit for a young academic. It was grey with a hint of blue herringbone with brown checks. His bow tie was the reverse of his suit, brown with light grey blue checks, and it matched his flat cap. He adjusted the glasses and gathered his things.

"Okay, I'm going." Max said. "Be ready."

"Okay," Andrew said, not looking up from the computer. "Good luck."

"Thanks."

Max walked into the city centre and found a brand new black hire car waiting for him. The driver opened the door and called him sir as he sat in the back of the big town car. Lyadova wanted all her guests to arrive in style.

The driver climbed in and drove the relatively short distance to the Château de Vaux-le-Vicomte.

The car joined the long line of matching vehicles inching forward towards the grand gates of the old manor. The fence itself was impressive enough with concrete pillars carved to look like large statues of some type of guardians. Max could see the immaculate grounds stretching out beyond the gates.

They drove through into the first quadrangle which was divided into four large open expanses of lawned areas until they reached the far side. The driver stopped briefly as another man in a crisp tuxedo opened Max's door.

"Good evening, sir," the valet said. "Welcome to the Château de Vaux-le-Vicomte. Invitation please."

"Thank you," Max said, climbing out. "I appreciate it."

Max handed over the invitation Andrew had printed for him. The man scanned the barcode and the small screen revealed a green tick with a little blurb.

"Professor Stanthorpe," the man said. "Ms Lyadova is very pleased to have you joining us tonight. She has asked me to make you feel welcome and to let you know she hopes to be able to find time to discuss your upcoming paper on the role of technology in international diplomacy and cross border relations."

"I would very much welcome such an opportunity," Max exclaimed, getting into the overly excitable academic character. "It is a fascinating topic and it would be a privilege to talk to her about it. How exciting!"

"Excellent," the man said, feigning interest. "If you would please make your way over the bridge into the courtyard the proceedings will begin momentarily."

"Yes, quite right. Tremendous. Thank you."

"I hope you have a wonderful night, sir."

"And you, too."

Max did up his jacket button as he walked across the small bridge slung over a square sided moat which ringed the château. He took out his earbud and threw it and his mobile into a tray before walking through a metal detector. When he was cleared, he pocketed both items and wandered into the event.

There was a massive rectangular courtyard lined with white marquees serving champagne, wine and beer, as well as an array of hors d'oeuvres. Max wandered through the courtyard taking a glass of champagne excitedly from a waiter, playing it up with an over the top thank you, like an academic enjoying his moment in the sun.

There were various big groupings of people, circling around someone important who was holding court. There was a roped off section for the media who were snapping off photos of guests as they arrived and broadcasting live to every country on earth. He watched as the cameras all turned and the flashes started rapidly firing as a young couple climbed out of their town car. Max had never seen them before, but pretended to know who they were and smiled broadly, as a woman behind him revealed it was a Canadian singer and her television star boyfriend, the latest 'it couple' on the world stage. She was wearing an impossibly short dress which barely covered her, and he was wearing a linen suit with an open white dress shirt unbuttoned to below his chest. The media went wild, snapping away with their cameras and yelling questions for the good-looking couple.

Max continued to wander through the crowd, until he found himself joining a circle near the front of the courtyard. A small grouping of guests was gathered to listen to someone waxing lyrical about the state of world affairs. As a professor of international relations, he guessed this was a good group to be in.

He edged further in until he saw the man holding court. It was the British Prime Minister, Timothy Birmingham, the very man who had subjected him to months of torture, who had handed him over to the International Criminal Court and the man who had spent months campaigning on the abolition of the Five Eyes intelligence system, using Max as an example of everything that was supposedly wrong with the system.

"...And it is time for the British to admit we have been a part of some of the most heinous crimes in history," Birmingham continued, "and it is time that we change."

"What do you think about Witness S escaping?" one of those gathered asked.

"Well, it is indeed a sorry state of affairs. How the court could let this happen and let this man walk free is outrageous. He is no better than a terrorist."

"Wouldn't you say he did more than your own government to save your country from terror?" the same women asked. "I heard he was the one who stopped a nuclear bomb from detonating in London."

"He did some terrible things."

"Stopping a nuclear bomb is a terrible thing?"

"That is not what I meant and I am sure you know that."

"Can you confirm the rumour about the nuclear bomb?"

"It is classified."

"Are you seriously going to argue about classified material with all the nonsense you have been spouting about tearing down the national security apparatus? Now you want to hide behind it."

"No, I am not. It does not matter what else this man did. One good deed does not counter all the bad ones he committed."

"I think we should pin a medal on him," the woman said to the delight of several onlookers, "especially now you have confirmed he saved London. What other bullshit have you been spreading?"

Max smiled to himself as Birmingham excused himself abruptly from the group. He shouldered past a couple of people before walking straight into Max. Birmingham looked at him like he was a piece of shit for not moving.

"Prime Minister Birmingham," Max said, excitedly putting out his hand to shake it. "Professor Maximillian Stanthorpe, University of Sydney, if you have a moment, I would love to speak to you about a paper I am writing…"

"Not just at the moment, Professor," Birmingham said, shaking his hand. "Wow, that is an impressive grip. Why don't you find me later and we can discuss it then? If you will excuse me."

"Of course, how wonderful," Max said, stepping aside, allowing Birmingham to pass.

Max watched him walk away, completely unaware he had just shaken hands with Witness S.

"I don't know how you could shake that man's hand," the woman who had been debating Birmingham said. "He's the one who should be on trial."

Max turned around to find the elegantly dressed woman standing behind him in a stunning yellow evening gown. Her dark skin and black hair glistened under the rows of string lights which were strung between the marquees. She wore a matching yellow shawl and gloves which ran up to her elbows.

"Occupational hazard, I am afraid," Max said, pushing his glasses back on his nose. "I need to speak to politicians to help my research. Well, mostly to try to get funding for my research."

"And what do you research, Mister..." she asked, pausing not knowing his name.

"Maximillian Stanthorpe," Max said, shaking her hand. "How rude of me. I am a professor of international relations at Sydney University."

"Maximillian, nice to meet you. I am Verity Hughes. He's right about one thing."

"And what's that, Ms Hughes?"

"That's a hell of a grip for an academic."

"I work out."

"I'm sure you do."

"So, what do you do Ms Hughes?"

"I am a software engineer."

"Really?"

"Yes, Oxford graduate. I have been working with A&A for a couple of months."

"Well, how wonderful. A couple of months you say?"

"Yes, why is that?"

"Great timing, to be here for this, I mean."

"Yes, I have been very lucky," Verity said, smiling with some small hint of sarcasm.

"Hell of a handshake you've got too," Max said, raising an eyebrow. "Can I buy you a drink?"

"Please," Verity said, taking Max under the arm and walking with him for the closest marquee.

"Does A&A know you confront world leaders with such challenging questions?"

"I think we both know that he needed to be confronted."

"Indeed, different times we are in, Ms Hughes."

The pair got fresh glasses of champagne as an announcement was made for the crowd to make their way through the villa into the rear courtyard where dinner would be served.

They joined the crowd wandering and chatting as they made their way through the château taking in its magnificent art and architecture. At the rear of the building a large, tiled foyer with huge glass windows framed their dinner venue. They walked out the rear door and down the steps into the rear gardens.

If the front of the opulent building and gardens was impressive, the rear was another level up. It was exquisite.

Two long rectangular gardens overflowing with blooming flowers ran away on the left and right of the building. A wide concrete path running between them held the longest table Max had ever seen. It must have been two football fields long.

Water features and foundations dotted the landscape behind the gardens on the left and right, and a long pond framed in the far end. The path continued through a round intersection of concrete to a bridge over the pond and ran for the same distance further away from the château.

The rear section was marked with pines on each corner and two huge fountains were lit up on both sides of the path, perfectly symmetrical. There was a series of pools and concrete sculptures drawing your eye until it hit a huge clearing in the thick pine forest. The lawn in the clearing was a vibrant green, although it was dusted with snow, and a series of lights like a runway guided the view up to the towering gold statue of Heracles or Hercules, depending on a preference for the Greek or Roman version of the hero's name. It was simply amazing and awe-inspiring.

The crowd murmured and spoke excitedly, pointing out the garden's features as they moved to their seats. Heaters and fire pits lined the edges of the pathway, surprisingly providing enough heat on the cold night.

Max found a seat towards the château end of the table and Verity took the seat opposite.

"Ladies and gentleman," a man said over the speakers, "please join me in welcoming the official party. British Prime Minister Timothy Birmingham, Canadian Vice President Nora Pelletier, vice President of the United States, Carl Moore, along with the ambassadors of India, China, Australia, New Zealand, the United Arab Emirates, Germany and Italy."

The crowd applauded as the world leaders moved to their seats. Max watched Carl Moore take his seat. The pair had met in Washington only months earlier. He had been FBI director and his leadership in helping take down a major terrorist organisation had flung him into the spotlight. He was the obvious choice to take over as vice President when the former Veep retired early due to illness.

The announcer then introduced a long list of Hollywood A-listers and global acts from stage, screen and music. Max recognised only a few of the names, but staying in character clapped loudly and smiled broadly with each addition. Verity smiled at him and clapped along too. The A-listers took their seats as a thumping sound beat in the distance, growing louder as it drew ever closer.

"And the moment we have all been waiting for," the announcer continued, "the woman of the hour, Chairwoman and Chief Executive Officer of A&A Enterprises, Isabella Lyadova, accompanied by the President of the Russian Federation, Nicholai Sukhanov, and the President of the Republic of France, Cosette Moreau."

Just then a massive Russian made Mi-8 VIP helicopter came in low over the château and flew over the long table to the gasps and awe of the crowd seated below.

It flew up into the clearing and landed in front of the Heracles statue.

The white aircraft with its distinctive red and blue stripes was the Russian equivalent of the United States' Marine One. It was the Presidential helicopter.

The side door opened and a solider opened the door and saluted as the three VIPs climbed down the stairs and began their long walk towards the table.

The crowd all stood and applauded for the full four minutes it took for them to walk to their positions in the centre of the colossal table.

Lyadova gestured with her hands to ask everyone to take their seats. Max felt like he was in some alternate reality. Only hours ago, he had been in prison and now he was sitting at a table with the world's elite. He was still trying to figure out what the hell was going on, but he was clapping in an overexcited way like he imagined his character might if he had been thrown into this world. It was a far-flung reality from that of an academic's stuffy office jam-packed with textbooks and unmarked papers.

The appearance of the Russian President was an interesting development. He was clearly involved. Max needed to find out how and why, and what his and his government's goals were. Max knew Lyadova was born in Russia and spent most of her early years there, though she had never ever really provided any information on her upbringing to the public, from what he could tell.

At the age of thirty, she had sprung onto the world stage buying up stocks in global IT powerhouses until she had controlling interests in several of the biggest global players. She used her influence to merge the parties into a single entity which she called A&A Enterprises when she became chair and CEO.

Max had read a short brief on her from the files AIS had compiled for him. The combined intel from the Five Eyes community was that they had no idea where the money came from. They all agreed there was a significant investment in some early start-ups which helped catapult her into the billionaires' club, but they could not trace the original investment money. In fact, there were no records of an Isabella Lyadova before those earliest share records.

He let his mind drift to the possibility that the Russians might be involved in all this and how deeply the President and others were in the conspiracy. The very thought sent a cold shiver through his body. The Cold War restarting or turning hot would likely only lead to one inevitable outcome – World War III.

Max had seen the entourage of security and advisers following the three VIPs down from the helicopter. Lyadova was closely followed the whole way to her seat by a massive woman in a long white coat. Andrew had described her on the road down to Maincy. Nina, Lyadova's head of security and the boss of the two arseholes who had tortured Andrew and chased Max through Brussels.

There was a younger guy in a suit with them. He was probably in his late twenties. Tall, but not as tall as Nina, and thin. He had a carry bag slung over one shoulder and he was clutching a tablet computer like his life depended on it. It was the same guy who handed her the tablet in Epidaurus, Greece, when she announced Alexandria 2.0, her personal assistant Elias Laskaris.

Laskaris stepped forward and handed the tablet to Lyadova as the crowd took their seats, then he stepped back beside Nina. Max wondered if Nina would be constantly within reach of the tablet too. His odds of success were shortening, not that they were good before.

"Ladies and gentleman, welcome to the Château de Vaux-le-Vicomte," Lyadova said. "I want to thank you all for coming and I want to acknowledge the official party, world leaders and influencers from around the globe. I am honoured you could all be here on this special occasion. I want to especially thank the President of France for agreeing to be host to our event in this beautiful country and the Russian President, not only for providing our incredible transport to tonight's event, but for his years of support."

The crowd all rose to clap the officials and celebrities as Lyadova took a sip of her champagne.

"As you all are aware," Lyadova continued, "Alexandria 2.0 is in its final stages and a world of free access to knowledge is but days away. The next pandemic will be stopped by sharing research, thanks to the twenty-first century's most incredible project, Alexandria 2.0. The next war will be stopped by opening up our borders to allow the free flow of information, thanks to this generation's greatest gift to the world,

Alexandria 2.0. The next financial crisis will be averted by dragging our brothers and sisters out of poverty, thanks to research and knowledge shared by the largest philanthropic donation in global history, Alexandria 2.0."

The crowd all burst into applause and sprang to their feet. A few of the rowdier celebrities whistled and cheered.

"Someone should get her a cape," Verity quipped across the table making Max smile.

Lyadova continued her speech, which was interrupted by applause every few minutes. She name dropped countless people at the tables who each stood to receive their acknowledgements from the crowd.

"I have received thousands of emails from around the world," Lyadova stated. "Academics the world over have written to me to let me know what A&A's funding for their research was buying. Professor Wilfred Holt from the University of Notre Dame says he is studying the impact of global warming on our food supplies. His research is contributing to a field of knowledge which impacts our very survival. Professor Jenny McMillan from the University of London is exploring the likelihood of water on planets in our solar system. A project which will one day tell us if we are indeed alone in the universe. And Professor Maximillian Stanthorpe from the University of Sydney is researching a subject very close to my own heart, the impact of technology on international relations, diplomacy and cross border affairs. The professor's work is focused on the disconnect between governments investing in cyber security as the highest priority for defence spending, outstripping traditional guns and tanks, and the rate our citizens are growing closer to our neighbours, sharing information and engaging via technology to learn and grow. All three projects are just examples from countless projects which aim to improve our world and further humanity."

Max was surprised to hear his alias named and his heart skipped a beat briefly when Lyadova asked all three researchers to stand for a round of applause. Andrew had done too good a job on his CV. Verity smiled and clapped exaggeratedly in his direction.

Lyadova went on to introduce other academics, celebrities and world leaders. It was a variable list of beneficiaries, donors, and contributors to the Alexandria 2.0 project.

"As we speak, Apollo is scouring the internet for knowledge," Lyadova said. "He has been busy. Apollo, are you there?"

"Good evening, Isabella," the AI program said over the speakers. *"How can I be of service?"*

"Apollo, the crowd is wondering how you are progressing in building Alexandria 2.0. Can you tell us where you are up to?"

"I am pleased to report that I have reviewed sixty-seven percent of the internet, cataloguing content and building the database. I have executed one hundred and eighty-seven million, two hundred and ten thousand, five hundred and nineteen contracts for academic research."

"That is simply amazing progress. How long before Alexandria 2.0 is up and running?"

"I estimate the time to competition as three days, fourteen hours and twenty-one minutes."

"Thank you, Apollo, I know you are busy, I will leave you to get on with the job."

"Thank you, Isabella. Please enjoy your evening."

"Just over three days!" Lyadova said, raising her arms as if summoning praise.

The crowd responded by again getting to their feet with rapturous applause.

"Now, I know that not everything has gone perfectly," Lyadova conceded. "But, like every large-scale project there will be some teething issues. My commitment here to you tonight and to everyone watching is that we will remedy any of these issues and address your concerns, but for now, I would like everyone to remember the goal of Alexandria 2.0, to bring us closer together through sharing knowledge and breaking down barriers. The god Apollo is said to have helped build the impenetrable walls of Troy and now his name's sake is helping remove the obstacles which stand in the way of human evolution and greatness. Thank you all for coming. I look forward to speaking to you all throughout the evening. Please enjoy your meals and your time here."

An army of waiters marched in behind the guests, each holding a long, elegant shot glass and a plate of appetisers. They moved in and placed them down for their guest.

"Na Zdorovie!" Lyadova said, taking her shot glass, raising it in cheers and drinking the shot of vodka.

The diners all drank their shots then clapped wildly as Lyadova made her way to the table and took her seat. Max watched as Laskaris took the tablet back from Lyadova. He clenched it tightly to his chest with both arms crossed over it.

"Well congratulations, Professor Stanthorpe," Verity said as they took their seats. "It seems you are now an international celebrity."

"So it would seem," Max said as a few of the guests either side of the pair shook his hand.

"What are you thinking about?"

"The comment on the walls of Troy. They were impenetrable, but for human error and rat cunning."

"Everything is fallible, Professor."

"That's what worries me."

The guests all made small talk over dinner, but Max spent most of the time with one eye on Laskaris and the tablet. His thoughts were interrupted as someone bumped into him. Max turned to see Birmingham hurrying off towards the château with one of his aides in tow. The staffer apologised for the Prime Minister running into him, but Birmingham just kept walking. Max nodded and said it was fine. He watched the pair enter the massive complex and disappear down a corridor.

"He's such a prick," Verity said, nodding in Birmingham's direction. "How could they have been so stupid to elect him?"

"He was saying all the right things for a certain crowd, at the right time, given everything your country had been through," Max said, "plus he had money, a lot of it, to get their attention. That is basically all you need these days to win – name recognition and money. Although, public sentiment versus the PM's language and policy announcements does call into question how many silent voices there are. People who vote, but don't respond to the pollsters maybe?"

"Are you suggesting foul play?"

"I teach international relations and dabble in politics. I like to inject a question, albeit often at the extremes, into conversations to gauge the room. Foul play would not surprise me."

"Do go on," Verity said.

"The public have never seemed to be on the side of tearing down the very institutions that have protected our countries for decades, centuries even, but out of nowhere, Birmingham's popularity and eventually his vote skyrocketed. Such a quick turnaround is relatively unheard of."

"But not completely unheard of," Verity said. "Isn't democracy grand?"

"It's the best we've got I'm afraid, but I have faith in the people. When a person's true colours are shown, the people for the most part do the right thing and use their votes to cast judgment."

"That's a romantic way of looking at it."

"Well, it doesn't mean there won't be shit bits in between, but ultimately I do believe in the people," Max said honestly.

"I hope you are right, because they have made some mistakes along the way, including electing Birmingham."

"We all do, but when given the chance we can make it right. Vox Populi, Vox Dei."

"The voice of the people is the voice of God."

"Exactly."

Max saw movement out the corner of his eye and turned to see Lyadova and Laskaris briskly walking off towards the château.

"Will you all excuse me?" Max asked getting to his feet.

He walked along the table shaking hands with various people who wanted to congratulate him on the mention in Lyadova's address. He played his part while always keeping one eye on the tablet. Laskaris followed his boss down the same corridor to the right that Birmingham had taken.

Max spoke briefly to one of the guests before excusing himself for the bathroom. He climbed the broad concrete staircase into the château and headed right after Lyadova. He put his ear bud in as he walked.

"A, are you there?" Max asked.

"Yes, I'm here," Andrew replied. *"Do I call you by your name?"*

"No, use my callsign for now. I don't know who else is listening."

"Got it, Prince it is. What can I do for you? I saw you on the television by the way, how good's that, getting a mention?"

"I would have preferred to be a little more subtle."

"I fed the letter in at the last minute and got it to her attention. I didn't know she would use it in the speech, I just thought it might be a good way to get some time with her."

"Yeah maybe, but I think given the global hunt for Witness S, I could have done without the press thanks."

"I didn't think about that."

"Clearly. It doesn't matter now, what's done is done. I'm following the tablet. What do I need to do if I can get to it?"

"I've been thinking about it and I have a new app to try. I've sent a link to your phone. If you open it and hit the scan button when you are within range it should start the hack."

"Within range?"

"Yes, you need to be within a few metres."

"A few metres, Jesus. Okay, well, how long will it take?"

"That's the thing, Ma— sorry, Prince. It's going to take about ten to fifteen minutes."

"You must be joking?"

"This isn't easy, especially with this budget equipment you bought. This isn't AIS."

"Fine. I will see what I can do. Stay on the line."

Max walked around the corner of the long corridor and watched Lyadova disappear into a room. Laskaris waited until she was inside, then ducked into the room next door.

Max waited a couple of minutes to make sure he wasn't being followed and to avoid some stray guards.

When he was sure it was clear, he silently opened the door and snuck into the room Laskaris had gone in. He pushed the door closed without a sound.

He was not sure what he had expected, but he certainly didn't imagine the scene he found.

Laskaris was sitting with his back to the door. The room was in darkness, except for the glow coming from the tablet which Laskaris had propped up on his chest. Max saw Laskaris was completely naked and masturbating.

Max initially thought he was just watching porn, but then he saw the artwork and features of the very building he was standing in, in the background on the screen. It was CCTV footage coming from somewhere in the château of two people having sex on an office desk. The man's pants were around his ankles and the woman was laying on her back on the desk. She reached up and hugged him, showing her face to the camera.

It was Lyadova and the man with her was the British Prime Minister, Timothy Birmingham.

Max snapped a couple of photos of the pair on his phone, then took two incriminating photos of Laskaris with the tablet in the shot.

Laskaris noticed Max in the reflection of the tablet as he changed positions and let out a short scream as he tried to get to his feet. Max grabbed his shoulder and pulled him back down into the chair, then walked around in front him.

"Don't move," Max ordered as he showed Laskaris the photos he had just taken. "Sit there and listen to what I have to say. Do you understand?"

Laskaris nodded.

"Do you understand?" Max asked in a harder tone.

"Yes," Laskaris managed to cough out.

"Good. Now, we both know you are in some trouble. I can't imagine your boss would be impressed with your use of her tablet?"

"No," Laskaris said, sheepishly looking down.

"Look at me," Max said, waiting until Laskaris looked up before continuing. "I presume you like your job?"

"Yes," Laskaris nodded with tears welling in his eyes. "I really do."

"Well, there is no need for anyone to find out about this."

"Oh, thank you," Laskaris said, smiling in relief. "You don't know how much this means to me. What can I do to thank you? Do you want to join me? I could…"

"No," Max said, shaking his head. "I need to borrow that tablet for a few minutes."

"I can't do that," Laskaris said, the panic rising in his voice.

"No one needs to know. I'm just going to borrow it then you can have it back and do whatever you like with it."

"I really can't. I would get fired."

Max showed Laskaris the photos again.

"And what happens when I send her these photos?" Max asked. "Promotion? I doubt it very much. She will throw your arse out of the company and make sure you never get another job for the rest of your life. She will wreck your life."

Laskaris sat thinking about it for a moment, then without saying a word handed over the tablet.

"Good choice," Max said. "Stay there and don't move."

Max walked over to a nearby bench and sat the tablet down next to his phone.

"A, I've got it," Max said. "What do I do?"

"You got the actual tablet," Andrew laughed. *"That's great! Although I didn't need to see what you did. Even the grainy footage was a bit much. He was having a good time wasn't he?"*

"Shut up and focus."

"Okay, right, the tablet, that will speed up the process. Open the link I send you and hit the go button. I made it simple so even you should be able to work it. I know you aren't good with technology."

"Okay," Max replied, clicking the link then hitting the go button on his phone.

The phone started scanning and within a few seconds found the tablet.

"Okay, good, it's found it," Andrew said. *"Starting the hack."*

"How long?" Max asked.

"Still going to be about eight minutes."

"Try to make it sooner."

Laskaris sat forward and started reaching for his clothes.

"I said don't move," Max reminded him.

"I was just getting my clothes," Laskaris said.

"Did I tell you that you could get them?"

"No," Laskaris said, sitting back.

Max watched Birmingham and Lyadova. Birmingham had finished and was pulling his pants back up.

"Now we've handled your business," Lyadova said, *"it's time to handle mine."*

"Jesus Christ," Birmingham said, *"can't a man catch his breath first?"*

"Why haven't you shutdown MI5 and MI6 yet?"

"It is not that simple, Isabella."

"Bullshit. I did not finance your campaign and rig all those polls, so you could just fly around and make speeches. I put you in there to get this done."

"And I will. I just need some more time."

"I want it done within the next few days."

"That's probably not possible. Why do you need it done so soon? I thought I would have a few months."

"Will you do it or not?"

"I don't think I can get it done in such a short timeframe."

"Well, that is disappointing. I am sorry she is going to find out."

"Who is going to find out?"

"Your wife."

"What? You are going to tell her about us? You have just as much to lose if that secret gets out."

"No, I am going to tell her about the affair you are having with your chief of staff. She's here with you tonight. Very pretty girl. Then I am going to turn the machine which helped get you elected around and completely destroy your career and your life. Your wife will leave you and getting a job will be impossible. If there is anything the public is sick of it is politicians who are not able to keep their cocks in their pants. I will turn every employee I have into a social media commentator and they will all call for your resignation. You see, Tim, I giveth, I can taketh away. Oh and before you try to get out of it, you should know I have photos and videos. It is amazing what Apollo can find."

"Your program hacked my phone?"

"Yes, among other things, including your Chief of Staff's phone, her messages and photos were particularly interesting. You have twenty-four hours to shut them down and turn off their connections to Echelon or I will release the photos and start the social media campaign to remove you from office. Your choice. Enjoy the party."

Max couldn't believe what he was hearing. Isabella had bought the Prime Ministership for Birmingham and had rigged the election; now she was forcing him to turn off his country's national security systems. And making matters worse, he was going to do it just as her program hacked every intel and defence system in the world. The British would instantly become vulnerable to collapse as every system connected to the internet was exposed. From telecommunications to electricity and gas, everything was connected and Max knew they were all currently shielded by British cyber security. Without it, the kingdom could fall and start a domino effect across the west.

Max was staring at the screen when the hairs on the back of his neck stood up. He spun around as Verity shut the door. She looked at Max then saw Laskaris sitting in the chair completely naked.

"Well, well, well, what's happening in here boys?" Verity asked with an amused look on her face.

"We were just having some fun," Max said, trying to cover his tracks.

"Is that why there are security guards all over the place sweeping the corridors?"

"I wouldn't know."

"Agent Shaw, glasses, a shave and a new hat might fool some, but I have been around for a while," Verity said, walking over and shaking his hand. "I work for MI6."

"MI6, well it's about time you guys started paying attention."

"I will admit we dropped the ball a couple of times and can thank you for picking it up and running with it, but as you know our hands were tied."

"That, I'm afraid, was nothing compared to the situation you are in now," Max said, turning the tablet around for Verity to see. "She funded his campaign, rigged the election and has just given him two days to shut you guys down."

"We knew the money was coming from her, but we were not sure why. That is why I am here. I took the position with A&A to try to find out. Do you know why she is so adamant about getting it shut down?"

"Alexandria 2.0 is a cover. It is about to start a global hack on intelligence systems. With yours out of the way, Echelon could fall, let alone British industry and defence."

"Jesus, what is she going to do with all that information?"

"My guess would be to sell it to the highest bidder."

"That information in the wrong hands would start wars."

"Yes, but I have also been wondering for a while now, how much we would pay."

"We would pay?"

"Yeah, how much would we pay to get our own information back?"

"Our countries held to ransom? At gunpoint? It's going to have a lot of zeros."

"Exactly, but it might stop something far worse."

"What's worse than the total collapse of our intelligence systems?"

"War with Russia at the same time as our systems are down."

"Russia?"

"I think they're involved. I just need to work our how deep the rabbit hole goes."

"So, what is the game plan?"

"My phone has started a hack on the tablet and Apollo's systems, trying to pinpoint all the locations of the data storage facilities and to get control of the program. It needs a bit more time. What is the story with the security guards?"

"They are down the far end of the mansion checking rooms. A few too many people have gone walkabout."

"Okay, well we need to get back out there then."

"What are we going to do with your naked friend here?"

"He has to play along," Max said, turning to Laskaris. "Elias, you've heard what your boss is up to, what do you think?"

"Please don't kill me," Laskaris said, shaking in pure fear. "I didn't know she was doing any of that. Please!"

"I'm not going to kill you, not yet anyway."

"Oh, please, I don't know anything. I'm not involved. I just wanted to work for A&A, good for my career. I swear I didn't know what they were doing."

"I believe you, but the question is now that you do know, what are you going to do about it?"

"Anything you want, please just don't hurt me."

"You are going to get dressed and go back to work. You are not going to say a word about what you have heard, but you are going to keep the tablet unlocked and within a few metres of me at all times, so the hack can continue."

"What happens when the hack has finished?"

"You go back to work like nothing happened and start looking for a new job."

"How am I supposed to just go back and pretend I don't know what they are doing?"

"It is more dangerous if you leave without warning or just disappear; they will find you and if they figure out you know their secrets, then they will kill you. When this is all over, I will come back for you and get you out."

"Do you promise?"

"Yes," Max said, tossing Laskaris his pants. "Get dressed, it looks like your boss is done next door."

"Are you sure about this, Max?" Verity asked. "It is a lot of faith to trust some kid you have just met."

"Elias, have you heard about Witness S?"

"Yes," Laskaris said.

"You know what he is accused of doing to people? The torture and assassinations?"

"Yes."

"I am Witness S. If I think for one minute you have given us up, I will hunt you across the Earth until you are simply dead. You won't even see me coming. You will just be here one minute and not the next. I was in gaol only days ago and now I am here in a party with the world's elite. There is nowhere I cannot go and that I won't find you. Am I understood?"

Laskaris nodded his head in pure fear.

"I am going to need you to look me in the eye and tell me you understand," Max said.

"I understand," Laskaris said with a trembling voice.

"It may not seem like it, Elias, but I'm the good guy. I do what I do to protect people. I don't want to hurt you. I want to stop your boss from putting millions of peoples' lives at risk. I will come back to get you out and look after you. I just need you to do what I have asked or you could join their team and terrorise the world, which puts you and I on opposite sides of all this."

"No, I understand," Laskaris said with a steadier voice.

"Good lad," Max said, passing Laskaris his shirt.

Laskaris got dressed and headed into the corridor just as Birmingham and Lyadova emerged. He followed the pair down the corridor and out into the courtyard.

When they cleared the corridor, Max and Verity headed out of the room and ran into a security guard. She showed her A&A security tag and they got waved through.

"Prince," Andrew said in his ear, *"I've lost the signal. You need to get back within range of the tablet."*

"I know," Max said. "We are moving into position."

"Who are you talking to?" Verity asked.

"We've got our own inside man. I'll fill you in later."

The crowd was all mingling on the lawn, drinking and laughing, chatting amongst themselves, and warming their hands over the fire. Max saw Lyadova and a still nervous looking Laskaris making the rounds.

"The kid is shitting himself," Verity said.

"So he should be," Max stated, smiling and nodding to a man who said hello as they walked past. "I have already had a couple of run ins with their security team, they aren't mucking around."

"You mean the Russians?"

"A massive guy and thin guy, both hard as nails."

"That's them. Former KGB. MI6 has a file. From what we can tell they were in organised crime before joining the KGB. They joined just before it was shut down, but continued operating for a couple of disgruntled generals, including their current boss, Nina."

"The woman in the white coat?"

"Yes, she was one of the first women to ever make it in the world of Soviet intelligence. She is just as tough as her underlings and twice as big a bitch."

"Great. The Russian President and Russian security guards have their fingerprints all over this. Do you think they are involved?"

"I hope not, but that was a hell of an entrance earlier."

Max and Verity joined a circle not far from Lyadova. Laskaris moved around a little to be closer to Max.

"Signal's back, Prince," Andrew said. *"Try not to move."*

Max just ignored him and went back to his fake conversation with the circle he had joined.

Lyadova moved on to a new group. Laskaris held his position until he got an evil eye from her, a look he knew all too well, she wanted him closer. Andrew told Max the signal was lost, but he was stuck in a conversation, so Verity walked past him and he handed over the phone. She followed Laskaris and joined a new conversation, while Max changed angle to keep them in view.

Andrew told him the signal was back and Max nodded at Verity, so she knew she was in range.

The game of cat and mouse continued with Max and Verity leap frogging each other to stay close enough without giving themselves away. Andrew chimed in occasionally to tell Max he had lost the signal. Max was getting frustrated at how long it was taking. He wished he had AIS's support for the operation, but given he was technically a fugitive on the run, Max could not risk getting them involved.

"Why is this taking so long?" Verity asked as Max joined her to walk along a path to a new conversation.

"We are on our own," Max said. "We are doing what we can with off the shelf kit. I can't involve my usual team given everything that has been happening."

"Even so, this is ridiculous."

"I agree. A, how much longer?"

"You are currently out of range," Andrew said through the earbud, *"but I'd say about five more minutes."*

"Five minutes," Max said, looking at Verity who just rolled her eyes. "Make it sooner."

"I'm trying..." Andrew complained but Max muted the call.

"Something is happening," Verity said as a hush fell over the crowd and the tension built in the large space, like everyone there was holding their breath.

Max looked around and noticed the world leaders. One by one they were looking at their phones and excusing themselves. Birmingham and his security detail headed for the château and the exit, as the French President put the phone to her ear. Within seconds, she too was being whisked away by her security guards.

The crowd looked back and forth between themselves and the leaders, not sure what was happening.

"It's started," Max said. "They're getting warning calls."

"Look," Verity said, grabbing Max's arm and pointing him towards the big Heracles statue in the distance.

Lyadova and the Russian President were both running towards the big helicopter escorted by the President's personal security team. Nina and Laskaris were also in tow. The rotors started before they even got to the grass.

The assembled guests didn't need any further warning. Panic set in and people started running for the exits.

Max and Verity followed the crowd towards the exits as Max unmuted the call.

"You are out of range, Prince," Andrew stated. *"Prince, can you hear me?"*

"I can hear you," Max said. "The world leaders all got messages and calls and headed for the exits. Turn on the news. Has it started?"

"Hang on, looking now. Shit. It's all over the news that the party is being evacuated."

"Apollo is attacking?"

"They won't put that on the news, but it would seem so. He's started to breach their firewalls."

"Did you finish the hack?"

"No, we still had a minute or two to go."

"Fuck."

"What's the plan now?"

"We need to get out of here. We will meet you at the motel in a couple of hours. Start thinking about how we can get in with what we have."

"I'm not sure…" Andrew started but Max hung up on him and removed the earbud which he put in his pocket.

Max and Verity reached the château to find the entrance blocked by the US Secret Service who were holding the vice President inside waiting for his bulletproof limousine to arrive. Max saw the vice President walk past the door; he was pacing back and forth.

"Mister Vice President," Max yelled past the guards, removing his glasses and hat.

Moore stopped in his tracks on seeing Max and hung up on his call.

"Let him through," Moore ordered his protection detail.

"I don't think that is a good idea, sir," the head of his guard said, recognising Max.

"I'm giving you a direct order, let him through."

The Secret Service agent reluctantly moved aside to let Max and Verity through.

"What are you doing here, Max?" Moore asked. "You are an international fugitive."

"You and I both know that is total bullshit," Max stated. "You wouldn't have let me through if you believed it."

"I couldn't believe the Brits handed you over."

"Torres let them take me. They snatched me off the street in Washington and shot my partner in the process."

That was clearly news to Moore, he looked genuinely shocked.

"Is Blake okay?" Moore asked.

"He was shot in the leg," Max clarified. "But either way, it happened on your soil and we couldn't risk accusing you of being involved."

"So why are you telling me now?"

"Because last year I put my life on the line to stop a terrorist leveling your country and I'm hoping that's bought me two minutes with you to try to put a stop to what is happening here."

"What is happening here?"

"It's Lyadova and her Apollo project. It is hacking global intelligence systems, including Echelon."

"How do you know this?"

"I know someone who helped them build it."

"How?"

"He came to see me at the prison. A&A security tried to kill me after the hearing at The Hague and they captured and tortured him. They didn't want their secret getting out. I escaped and came straight here to try to stop her."

"It looks like you failed."

"I'm doing this one off the books. I need you to get the court to drop the case, so I can get AIS and the CIA and NSA involved."

"I don't know how I can do that, Max, but I can let our government and the Aussies know, and the other Five Eyes or four, I guess. What about Birmingham?"

"Verity here is with MI6. She will talk to the Brits, but don't trust him."

"He's the Prime Minister."

"And he's sleeping with the enemy."

"Lyadova?"

"Yes. She rigged the election for him."

"Jesus."

"We need them to hold the line and stop him from turning off their security systems."

"Why would he? After what's happened tonight?"

"She's threatened to turn the world against him, including his wife, with details of his affairs and election funding."

"Okay, so how do we stop this thing?"

"We are trying to work it out, but we think we have a couple of leads."

"And they are?"

"I would rather not say at this stage, sir. If I am wrong, it could have grave consequences."

"You are asking for a lot of faith on my behalf, Max. I'm going to need something."

"We think the Russians may be involved," Max said, after a few tense seconds. "But we don't know how involved. That's what I plan to find out."

"If they are, you know what will happen?"

"Yes, sir. At best, the return of the Cold War."

"And worst, a very hot one."

"Yes, sir, I'm afraid so."

"Do you know how the attack is being coordinated?"

"My inside man has more details which I will get to you when I can. How can I reach you?"

"Here is my number," Moore said, quickly scribbling down his mobile number on his business card. "Let me know as soon as you have any more details."

"Yes, sir. Thank you, sir."

"I'm putting a lot of trust in you, Max. Don't let me down."

"I'll do my best, sir."

"Thank you," Moore said as his detail hustled him out of the room and into his waiting limousine.

Max and Verity started making their way through the château to exit through the front courtyard, when Max stopped in his tracks.

"What is it?" Verity asked as Max pulled her back into the château.

"Not what," Max said. "Who."

"Who is it?"

"Alexei, one of the Russians."

Verity snuck a peak around the doorframe and saw the thin Russian pointing at the front door of the château and yelling. A handful of guards were running towards them.

"Time to move," Verity said. "Come on, this way."

Max didn't need to be told twice. He followed Verity back through the château and out into the rear courtyard where they had had dinner. They ran along beside the long table and Max grabbed a knife as the first volley of bullets flew by and slammed into the table, smashing glasses and plates.

They ran around the fountain along the path and past a huge rectangular reflecting pool, then they came to a long moat like pond, known as le Grand Canal.

A grand bridge had been built over it for the occasion to allow Lyadova and the Russian President to access the gardens while staying in the line of sight. Max and Verity ran over it and up to the concrete sculpture wall two thirds of the way up the rolling gardens.

La Cascade, as the sculptured wall was known, was a series of massive columns and arches between which several embedded scenes of gods in their flowing robes were carved out in amazing detail. Beyond it were the rolling grasses and clearing in the trees and the massive gold statue of Heracles.

"This way," Verity said, grabbing Max's hand and pulling him through a clearing in the tree line.

"What is this?" Max asked as they arrived at what looked like a stairway into the earth itself.

"The River Styx."

"What pray tell is the River Styx, other than the mythological gateway to the underworld?"

"That's where the name came from. It's a diverted river. A series of tunnels built when the château was constructed to channel all the water around the grounds for the water features. It's all built on real river systems."

"Great," Max said. "Why are we going down there?"

"I would have thought that was obvious. There are men with guns shooting at us up here."

"Is there another exit?"

"I hope so."

"You hope! You haven't been down there?"

"MI6 sent me some reading before the dinner. I remember seeing it on the sitemap."

Max could hear footsteps fast approaching.

"I don't think we have a choice," Max said. "Let's go."

Max and Verity bounded down the stairs and into the freezing cold, knee high flowing water.

"This way," Verity said. "Any luck and it will link back up to the other tunnels they built."

"I hope you're right."

They ran through the water as best as they could over the slippery stones and potholes. Max could hear someone in the tunnel behind them. There was minimal lighting which gave the place an eery vibe. Max could see the sweeping flashlight just around the corner behind them.

There was a small drop in their path and the water was teeming over it like a waterfall. They jumped down hoping it was loud enough to cover their movement. Verity started down the row, but Max had another thought. He grabbed Verity and put a finger to his lips. Then he led her back to the waterfall. He sat down in the icy water and Verity gave him an unimpressed look, but followed suit. She sat beside him and the pair pushed themselves back against the drop letting the waterfall flow over their heads.

The clearing behind the water was just wide enough to cover their faces and they tangled their legs in sideways, to get them out of the path of their pursuers.

Then they waited.

A single man jumped down into the water in front of them. Max gave Verity the signal to just hold and be quiet. Then Max pushed his face through the waterfall before slowly and silently getting to his feet behind the guard.

He grabbed the guard's head, slapping his hand over his mouth and yanked it back so he was looking at the roof, then with ferocious force Max drove the blunt knife he had taken from the table outside, down into the guard's neck. It wasn't sharp enough to slice his throat, but it had punched a hole right through his windpipe. Max pulled the knife out and pulled it down again, this time just above the spot where the guard's collar bones met.

The guard fell to his knees as Max took his gun and spare magazine from him. He splashed down into the water still clutching his throat as Verity emerged from under the waterfall.

"That was brutal," Verity said as Max raised the guard's pistol and aimed it in her direction. "What the fuck are you doing?"

Max fired two shots beside her head. The first bullet hit another guard as he rounded the corner and dropped him into the water. The second hit the wall chipping the old brick, next to Alexei's face. Alexei pulled back behind the wall for cover.

"Move! I'll cover you," Max ordered and Verity ran past him, as best she could in her long wet dress, to look for the exit.

Alexei took a glance around the corner at waist height and Max put a bullet into the wall next to him again, forcing him back, then he ran hard after Verity.

He slipped on a stone as two bullets hit the wall and the roof near him. He turned back and fired at Alexei who dived for cover. Max got to his feet and ran while firing back at Alexei trying to hold him back.

Max rounded a corner and found Verity climbing a set of spiral stairs. The old metal creaked and groaned when Max hit them at speed, taking three at a time. He fired two warning shots into the water near the corner knowing Alexei could not be far behind, then he ran into the back of Verity who had stopped in his path.

He looked around her at the old iron gate and the modern padlock. He fired two shots into the lock, then spun back to cover them as Verity pulled the chain through to open slats in the gate.

"Got it, Max," Verity said, just as Alexei turned the corner and fired a broadside of bullets into the metal stairs.

The bullets pinged off the stairs as the pair ran through the gate.

They took off down a long sloping tunnel with its arched roof. It was dimly lit by a string of old lights. Max was not sure, but he thought they were running back towards the château.

Verity rounded a corner up ahead as Alexei made it into the long corridor and exchanged fire with Max.

Max ducked around the corner and found a huge row of wine barrels. He fired a shot at the lock holding them in place, then kicked the small metal bracket and the wine barrels started to roll. One after the other they rolled out into the tunnel he and Verity had just been in, each barrel going faster as they went, gathering momentum. The sound of a hundred wooden barrels with their metal straps roared as they rolled in the echoing tunnel.

Verity had found another doorway. It led into the more formal cellar. There were rows and rows of wine, some of it caked in dust from decades ago. As they got closer to the kitchen, the wine bottles got newer and there was also shelf after shelf of rum, whiskey and vodka.

Max grabbed a bottle of what looked like very expensive vodka and threw it, smashing it on the metal shelving unit, then he fired two shots into the vodka-soaked shelves. The metal bullet and metal shelves sparked and the vodka caught alight.

"What a waste," Verity said, grabbing another bottle and bursting through the kitchen door.

Alexei ran into the cellar as the other vodka and rum bottles exploded into a huge fireball. Max jumped through the kitchen door and kicked it shut as the fireball hit it.

Verity helped him to his feet.

"Pretty quick thinking," Verity said. "I hope you didn't burn the whole building down."

"I hope so too," Max replied. "But I'm not waiting around to find out."

"This is the service hallway," Verity said as the pair made their way through the kitchen and into a small corridor. "It runs under the building to various locations, so the servants don't walk through the house."

"We need to find an exit."

"From memory, this should lead us to the Carriage Museum."

"Please tell me you have a better idea to get us out of here than by horse and carriage?"

"When Lyadova bought the place, she gifted most of the carriages to the French government for display in various museums around the country. She uses it to house a bunch of her own much more modern chariots."

They followed a corridor along until they found a staircase. It spiralled up to a door which Verity pushed open and she smiled sighting the room before her. Max walked in behind her and saw the rows of gleaming and spotless sports and luxury cars.

"Normally I would suggest something that blends in," Max said. "But I don't think that description fits anything in here."

Verity laughed, then walked over to a metal lock box on the wall. She pried it open with a screwdriver and revealed the key fobs for the cars. Mercedes, BMW, Lamborghini, Ferrari, Alfa Romeo, they were all there, but Verity found a black fob with silver writing and a sharp trident on it and pressed the unlock button.

A brand new Maserati MC20 beeped and the blinkers flashed. It was the top of the line sports car. Zero to one hundred kilometres an hour in less than three seconds. Top speed three hundred and twenty-five kilometres an hour.

"I take it you're driving?" Max asked.

"Hell yes," Verity said as fire brigade units arrived on site.

Max found the button for the old Chariot Museum doors as Verity climbed in behind the wheel and started the car. Max got in as the doors to the old museum opened.

Verity wound her way through the emergency vehicles, down the bridge and through the gates out onto the road.

"Where to?" Verity asked as she hit the accelerator and the powerful sportscar leapt into action.

Chapter Seventeen

Max and Verity had wound their way through the traffic then headed into Paris. They switched cars twice and number plates once on their final car, which was a small European sedan, picked as Max had mentioned earlier, to blend in.

They had driven back out of the city and had taken a long circuitous drive through the country until they had found their way back to Maincy and the motel where Andrew was still busily typing on his computer.

"Jesus Christ," Andrew exclaimed as the pair entered the motel room. "I thought you must have been captured or killed. Where the hell have you been?"

"We didn't want anyone following us," Max explained. "So, we took the long way. Andrew Rixon, this is Verity Hughes of MI6."

"Actually, it's Verity Humphries," Verity corrected. "Hughes was my cover name."

"Nice to meet you," Andrew said as Max smiled and nodded at Verity.

"I introduced you to the vice President with your cover name," Max said, shaking his head as Verity smiled and nodded.

"I was going to say something, but he seemed to be in a hurry," Verity laughed.

"MI6 is involved?" Andrew asked, as Verity opened the vodka she had stolen from the château.

"We have been watching A&A for a while now. They have their fingers in so many pies, we thought it deserved another harder look."

"Yeah, like the British Prime Minister's election campaign," Max added.

"Well, the UK has been in a constant state of turmoil for years following the death of Prime Minister Morgan," Verity explained. "Not that I need to remind you of that."

"He got what was coming to him."

"Yes, he did and so did the princess."

Several years ago, Max had found out that the then British Prime Minister Stephen Morgan and the third in line to the throne, Princess Victoria, the Duchess of Cambridge, were both involved in a terrorist organisation secretly pulling the strings of global disorder. He had killed both of them, and while the AIS and MI6 spin teams had gone to work explaining the deaths and covering up certain facts to ensure the deaths didn't inflame tensions, the British public had remained sceptical. The two major political parties used Morgan's death to drive political unrest, while republican proponents used the death of the princess and rumours of her involvement in nefarious activities to push for the removal of the monarchy. It was a second scandal within the decade for the royal family and the public was growing tired of the outdated system.

"Didn't stop your boys coming and capturing me?" Max said. "They knew what had happened, so why was the order given?"

"Orders are orders," Verity said. "Our guys had to follow them. Many of us argued against your arrest, but the government was getting a lot of pressure to act from the parliament's intelligence committee and the election was only months away."

"It didn't matter, that arsehole Birmingham still got elected."

"Yes and now we know he had help. Clearly, he got cash from Lyadova, but you said she might have rigged the election. I want to know how. Andrew, can I borrow your laptop?"

"Sure," Andrew said, getting to his feet, vacating the seat.

Verity worked away on the laptop, while Max checked over their weapons and supplies.

"Here," Verity said after a frenzied period typing away on the keyboard. "ManuBrit. It's the organisation which the government got to run the electronic voting and tallying for the election. Let's see where this goes."

For several more minutes, Verity and Andrew exchanged tips and thoughts on tracing the corporate entity. It was a maze of organisations and dummy corporations which channelled revenue into tax havens, but eventually they started to find the major players behind ManuBrit and right at the top of the chain was A&A.

"Holy shit," Andrew said, "they could have been manipulating the results."

"We don't have anything convictable," Verity said, "but considering what Max heard in the exchange between Lyadova and Birmingham, anything is possible."

"Surely MI6 and others would have looked into ManuBrit?" Max asked.

"Yes, but even if all roads led back to A&A it would not have raised many flags. Half our IT capability comes from them. It was probably seen a good thing to have the backing of a safe global platform to ensure security of the vote."

"I've seen plenty of those intel reports. So, Birmingham and Lyadova fuelled the political fires in the UK to help him get elected. One of his campaign platforms was to dismantle the intelligence system, falling on the side of the former PM and princess as the victims of a system without bounds. He inherited me in custody, the man responsible for these events, and turned me over to The Hague using my capture as fodder against his opponents and blaming them for illegal rendition, which technically it was. And he has been campaigning every day for them to throw the book at me, but what does he do now? MI6 and the other agencies would know Apollo is hacking their systems, so does he go ahead with the plans to shut it all down?"

"I'm not sure he can. The intel committee and others would be briefed by now and surely they will call it out for what it is, pure madness."

"Yeah, but maybe it plays right into his hands."

"How do you figure?"

"I've been thinking about what I would do in his position. The spin machine could say they are only hacking us because we have stuff to hide, we don't want to hide any more secrets. He could pre-empt the hack and release it all early. Promise kept."

"I forgot you used to work in politics. You could be right, but I think we have a bigger problem."

"What?"

"The Americans and the other Five Eyes countries are not going to want the British to release their secrets, because they could harm them too."

"So they will want to stop him?"

"Exactly. The US could launch its own attack on the UK."

"Moore can hopefully hold them off."

"I hope so."

"We need to figure out what Lyadova's plans are, and Sukhanov's, and we need to do it fast. Andrew, did you have any luck with the tablet?"

"No," Andrew said bluntly. "You moved too much and the signal kept dropping out. We still needed a few minutes."

"What outdated systems were you using that it took so long?" Verity asked. "It was taking way longer than I would have thought."

"Look what I'm working with," Andrew said, gesturing to the old television and small laptop. "It's not like any of this is AIS standard equipment."

"Still," Verity said, running her hand through her hair. "Did you find anything? Surely a few snippets of information came through?"

"Yes, I found a series of data point pings."

"That's it?"

"Can someone explain this to me?" Max asked. "What are the pings?"

"Apollo isn't real, right," Andrew asked rhetorically. "It's a program. Not a person or even a satellite. It is hosted like any other program on a server or servers across the globe. The pings I got were from the servers."

"Tell me you know the locations?"

"I know some, but they are the strongest pings."

"Where?"

"Outside Moscow," Andrew said, reaching over and pressing the on button on the television which showed a map of Russia.

Verity and Max exchanged worried looks.

"What does the strength of the pings mean?" Max asked.

"It means the main three servers where Apollo is working from are based there," Andrew replied.

"I need you two to figure out exactly where they are and how we access them."

"What are you going to do?"

"I'm going to make a phone call," Max said, walking out of the room and into the street as Verity took a swig from the vodka bottle.

Chapter Eighteen

Max hung up the phone.

He had driven to a small village not far from Maincy to make the call.

He stood in the small, glass walled, public phone box gathering his thoughts.

He wasn't sure what his next move was, but he was starting to run out of time. He stared at the phone until the tiny cubical began ringing with a shrill tone bouncing all around him.

It wasn't the phone.

Max turned to see blue lights reflecting in the windows of the nearby shops and homes. Max stepped out of the box as the first police car came into view.

He paused briefly hoping they were looking for someone else, but his hope faded when one of the officers in the lead car pointed in his direction.

Max spun on his heal and ran.

He darted down a side street leaping some crates and rubbish which was piled in the lane as the lead police car rounded the corner and followed him.

He jumped up onto a skip bin as the chase car ploughed into it. The sudden impact unbalanced Max and he fell backwards, landing flat on his back on the bonnet of the cop car. His head hit the windscreen and for a moment his head spun, but he didn't have a choice, he needed to get up.

Max got to his feet and leapt back onto the skip, as the officers were climbing out. He jumped the fence beside the bin and ran as van den Berg yelled after him.

As Max ran, he heard van den Berg shouting orders to the line of cars which had followed him into the lane, calling for them to move back and circle around.

Max reached the end of the lane and made the split decision to turn right. He ran as fast as his legs would carry him.

He made it halfway down the block when the first of the police cars arrived. It spun its wheels rounding the bend and then drove straight for him, turning at the last second, trying to pin him in.

Max dove across the bonnet and then kept running as the second and third car arrived.

Max ran between them, jumping into one of the police car's doors as the officer tried to block him. The door slammed shut to the curses of the French officer.

Max sprinted into traffic, pivoting suddenly to tackle a man off his motorbike. The pair fell to the bitumen as the bike revved and skidded along the ground.

The bike owner was lying on the ground moaning in pain, but Max was already on his feet. He jogged over to the bike as the police vehicles started reversing towards him.

He stood the bike and revved it, spinning the wheels as he dragged himself into the saddle.

One of the flashing cop cars reversed into him. He wrestled with the handlebars getting it back under control, before tearing off down a side street.

The old dirt bike whined as he rode it hard, closely followed by van den Berg in the lead chase car.

Max rode up onto the footpath so they couldn't ram him. He dodged pedestrians and A-frame signs outside the small boutiques, and weaved between the rows of seating outside a small bakery.

Ahead Max saw the shops were ending. Soon enough the police would be able to stop him with force.

Van den Berg smiled as he looked over and saw the realisation on Max's face. He was going to be known the world over as the man who caught Witness S, one of the most highly trained spies in the world.

When Max passed the last shop, he hit the brakes and pulled the bike left, zooming across the open, green park, tearing up the soggy lawn which was covered in a thin layer of snow and ice.

Mud flung up from the back wheel as he skidded and turned, cutting a track across the park. He stole a quick look behind himself and saw the three police cars racing across the park. They too were ripping the lawn to shreds and throwing mud into the air behind them as they slid, giving chase.

Max took a right at the fence line, following it along a flowing river. One of the police vehicles was now only inches from his rear tyre. Mud flicked up and splattered on its windscreen. The driver hit the windscreen wipers, but it just smeared the brown liquid and dirt across the glass. There was no way to see, so they slowed down.

Max saw a small road and bridge ahead, which he took in a tight turn. The mud covered vehicle missed the turn and ploughed on, as the remaining two hit the brakes and skidded hard, still giving chase.

The bike and two chase vehicles drove hard down a muddy road hitting potholes and splashing water and mud everywhere. The third car had eventually made it to the road and was now closing in on them.

Max saw an old tractor and a farmer walking over to open the gate to his property. He flung open the gate as he heard the bike and police cars coming towards him. He stopped to watch, just as Max crossed the road and hit the small causeway running along outside the farmer's property.

Max accelerated hard up the side of the causeway, throwing more mud as his back wheel ran through the bottom of the channel. The farmer danced back towards his tractor with a concerned look on his face as Max shot past him and onto the wide-open paddock.

Max looked back to see two of the cars make the turn as the farmer screamed at them and gestured wildly.

The muddy windowed cop car had tried to follow Max. It was a stupid decision. It smashed into the side of the channel and stopped dead in its tracks. The accelerator must have got stuck, because the front wheels of the hatchback were spinning madly in the mud, sending torrents of brown drops flying back across the road. Steam and smoke poured out from under the bonnet. The two officers climbed out to assess the damage as the farmer approached yelling at them.

Max rode across the muddy field, as the two remaining vehicles skidded, losing traction trying to follow him. He was thankfully pulling away, but one of the cars made a turn and was heading back towards the farmer's driveway which would be a slightly better surface.

Max twisted the throttle and rode fast across the paddock. He looked back and saw the second police car spewing mud from its wheels. It was bogged and digging itself deeper into the icy ground.

Max reached the end of the paddock as the last police car turned onto the side road from the driveway and headed straight for him. Max turned the bike to face it, then hit the throttle.

The car and bike both stopped on the road as if daring each other to drive.

"You have nowhere to go," van den Berg said through the vehicle's megaphone. "Just turn yourself in. An innocent man does not run. We will find you."

Max stared at him from a distance, then shook his head and hit the throttle.

The bike tore off the spot, racing towards van den Berg. Van den Berg turned to the driver and nodded. The driver hit the accelerator and the police car spun its front wheels, putting itself on a collision course with Max.

The two vastly different vehicles raced towards each other on the farm's dirt road. Max had no intention of moving and nor, it seemed, did van den Berg's driver. Metre by metre they sped towards one another, until with only seconds to spare the police vehicle pulled right giving Max the chance to dart past.

He saw van den Berg and the driver yelling at each other as he went past.

Max took a quick left and made his way towards the farmhouse, as van den Berg's car took an off road track through another field to give chase.

Max shot past the farmhouse as an angry and confused woman came outside to see what all the noise was. He waved and kept moving. She watched as moments later the police vehicle roared its little engine and hammered past her family home.

Max has made it to the back of the property and was stopped, assessing his options as the police vehicle pulled closer and closer at incredible speed.

Max spun the bike around to face the police car, accelerating towards them, and for a moment van den Berg wondered if they were in for another game of chicken. The driver sensed it too and gripped the wheel tighter, knowing this time he wasn't going to budge. But then, Max spun the bike back around, flinging mud towards them.

Van den Berg watched as Max rode hard up to the end of the paddock and disappeared. His driver accelerated hard up the little hill and crested the top at speed.

"Fuck!" van den Berg yelled as the car left the ground.

"Merde!" the driver said, clinging to the wheel as the car began to fall back towards the earth.

Ahead in the distance, Max was racing hard across the frozen dam, moving fast and feeling the back wheel sliding as it tore up the thin layer of ice. It was barely thick enough to hold his weight, so he was riding flat out to try to stay ahead of the cracks and to stay out of the water.

Van den Berg's car on the other hand was way too heavy. It splashed down in a tsunami of mud, ice and water. The airbags deployed and only seconds later steam and smoke started pouring out from under the hood.

Van den Berg climbed out into the knee deep water. He was shaken and the water was freezing, but he still managed to look across the dam to see Max stopped on the other side.

"You okay?" Max yelled out, his voice echoing through the cold air.

"I would be better if you just cooperated," van den Berg yelled back.

"I can't do that. Not yet anyway. I didn't kill those agents."

"Hand yourself in and we can talk about it."

"Open your eyes, Commander. Not everything is what it seems."

Max kicked the bike over and revved the throttle, before tearing off into the distance, leaving van den Berg in the mud.

Chapter Nineteen

Lyadova sat in the comfortable high back leather chair and sipped on champagne. So far, everything was going to plan, and she felt like a reward.

Even though she was in a calm mood, her mind kept slipping back to the conversation with Nina about her mother. She was on edge and the champagne was helping dull the nerves.

"Are you okay?" Nina asked, walking into the lavish hotel suite. "You look stressed."

"We have just started the biggest computer hack the world has ever known," Lyadova said. "Global intelligence systems are already starting to fall, and the Five Eyes and others are trying to track us, so yes, I am a bit on edge."

"I guess that is understandable."

"In truth, it's not that though," Lyadova conceded, gesturing for the seat opposite her. "I have been thinking about our conversation from earlier."

"About your mother?" Nina asked as Lyadova poured her a glass of the sparkling wine.

"Yes. Mostly about the night she was killed."

"Do you want to talk about it?"

"We had been meeting each other regularly for coffee or sometimes dinner. Every time we met, I could feel her changing, growing somehow more confident, but somewhat more embarrassed by what she had done. She felt shame and guilt for giving me up and for what I had been through. She kept blaming herself and flashing to anger whenever my father was mentioned."

"She could not move on?"

"No, she was stuck on repeat. She started to talk about confronting him and attacking him, but I told her of the threat he had made. I made her promise to stay away from him."

"But she did not listen?"

"I was walking through a quiet street in Moscow when I heard the sirens. I was late for dinner with her, so I just marched on quickly. It was freezing and had started to snow. The pavement was getting slippery with ice, I remember I had to be careful not to slip. When I got to the restaurant, even though I was late, she was still not there. So I waited. I waited for an hour, with every passing minute my worry began to grow. I could not wait any longer, so I left the restaurant and started walking towards her house. Halfway there, I started to jog and eventually started to run. Something was wrong, I was convinced of it. I used the spare key to let myself in. She was not home, but then there was a knock at the door."

Lyadova took a sip of wine.

"I ran to the door to find two police officers," Lyadova said. "They had found my mother. She had been in an accident only a few blocks away. The sirens I had heard were going to her aid, emergency vehicles going to the accident. But it was no use, she was dead. Her car had left the road and slammed into a tree. It was likely an accident they told me, but I did not believe them. I spent a full year investigating and trying to track her movements for the day and to unpick all the details of the accident. The more I read of the case reports and spoke to witnesses the more I was convinced it was not an accident. There was an indent with black paint from a collision on the back panel of her white car. Someone rammed her off the road."

"They rammed her into a tree?"

"Yes. She lost control and with the ice on the road could not stop the car in time."

"Who do you think did it?"

"My father."

"How do you know?"

"She went to see him. She made a note in her diary. It said she was overcome by guilt and needed to confront him. She was going to his office to force him to acknowledge what he had done."

"What was she hoping for?"

"I think she wanted an apology and maybe closure of some sort, but I cannot help but feel she was doing it for me."

"You cannot blame yourself for the actions of either your mother or father. Their actions are their own."

"That is true. And my actions are my own too."

Lyadova took another sip of her champagne and smiled to herself.

"Anyway, did you come in for something?" Lyadova asked, breaking her faraway stare at the wall.

"Yes, ma'am," Nina said. "I think we have found them."

"Where are they?"

"We intercepted a call. They are coming here."

"Got to hand it to them, they are good at their jobs, especially considering their agencies are not helping them. Go to phase two with him. Release the photos."

"With pleasure," Nina said, standing and walking towards the door.

"Oh and Nina," Lyadova said, stopping Nina in her tracks. "Send Alexei and Leonid, but this time, don't miss."

"Yes ma'am," Nina replied, before leaving the room.

Chapter Twenty

Max had come back to the motel over two hours ago. He was covered from head to toe in mud after following the river back to Maincy. Several kilometres from the motel he ditched the motorbike in an old farm shed and wandered back, careful to monitor who was around.

He had spent most of the time since returning, talking through everything and making plans with Andrew and Verity.

Verity and Max racked their brains trying to figure out how van den Berg found him, but they figured it didn't matter, they weren't staying for long.

All roads were leading to Russia.

Andrew had been able to steal a few files while he was hacking into Lyadova's tablet. Not only were the server pings near Moscow, one of the uncovered files revealed the Russian Government had provided land and some funding for Alexandria 2.0. They had even gone as far as to pay for the server bunkers and some of the equipment A&A were using to store the world's knowledge and now its intelligence.

Max had showered and changed into some comfortable brown chinos and a white T-shirt, which he had purchased earlier, and he was pacing, thinking through their plans.

Verity was getting dressed in the bathroom as Andrew typed away at his laptop. He stopped typing and it took Max a moment to notice the missing sound of the tapping plastic keys, but he could feel a tension in the air.

He turned to Andrew.

"What is it?" Max asked.

"You need to see this," Andrew said, moving to the side so Max could see the television screen.

There was a bright red breaking news banner on the bottom of the screen.

"Ladies and gentleman, please forgive the interruption," the news anchor said. "We have just heard that there is a major cyber-attack unfolding across the world. While we are still waiting for official comment from the government, we have had numerous sources confirm the threat is real and that we are in fact under attack.

"Major corporations, government agencies and the military are said to be encountering a highly sophisticated and coordinated hack," she continued. "It is unclear at this stage what the hacker or hackers may be after. We are reaching out to the government to try to get more information."

Verity walked out of the bathroom in a burst of steam. She was drying her hair as she wandered over.

"What's happening?" Verity asked.

"BBC has just broken the story," Max replied.

"What? What do they think will come of that? All they will do is start a panic."

"I am just being told," the newswoman said, pressing her ear, listening as she spoke. "I am being told the Prime Minister, Prime Minister Birmingham, is back from France and he is expected to speak shortly. We will bring you the press conference live from Number Ten when he steps out."

"This will be interesting," Max commented as his phone pinged.

Max read the message: *P, get out now! Cover blown. H.*

"Get your things!" Max snapped, running to the bed to pull on his shoes and jacket.

"What?" Andrew asked.

"We've got to move. Now!"

Verity did not wait another second, she tossed her towel on the ground and started pulling on her coat, socks and shoes. Andrew was a bit slower to react.

"What are you doing, Max?" Andrew asked.

"Get your shit together," Max snapped. "I just got a message from Blake. They know we are here."

"Oh shit," Andrew said, dragging himself out of the chair and pulling on his coat.

Verity and Andrew grabbed their gear and ran for the door.

Max took the firelighters he had purchased earlier out of his bag and tossed them onto the bed. He lit them and instantly the cheap bedspread caught fire. He threw their old clothes and files into the fire.

Max ripped the cords from the laptop and ran out of the room.

He had checked out a few of the cars in the parking lot when he had gone out earlier. He had spotted a late model Ford sedan and opened his app. He had already set it up in case they needed a quick getaway. He tapped a couple of buttons and the car came to life as sirens rang out in the distance.

The three climbed into the car and Max threw it into reverse before Andrew had even closed his door. It slammed shut as he pushed it into drive and hit the accelerator.

"Jesus!" Andrew protested.

Max looked into the rear-vision mirror, but did not make a comment. Andrew was in the car and safe, he was alright.

"Where are we going, Max?" Verity asked from the passenger seat ignoring Andrew.

"Slight change of plans," Max said, pulling his phone out. "We are going to have to go to Plan B."

Max dialled the number and held the phone to his ear as he drove the car through the small town.

"It's Prince," Max said. "We need to reroute to Option Bravo. Yeah, Nangis. We will be there in fifteen minutes. Potentially coming in hot."

Verity could not hear what was being said, but the person on the other end of the line was protesting about the 'coming in hot' phrase which she knew meant they could be under gunfire.

"Yes, I know I already owe you one," Max said. "Now I'll owe you two."

He listened for another minute before saying thank you and ending the call.

"He'll be there," Max said.

"Birmingham's walking up to the podium," Andrew said from the back seat, staring at his laptop. "I'll turn it up."

"Are we right to go?" Birmingham asked the gathered journalists through the tinny speakers on the laptop. *"Alright. Good evening or I guess good morning, I apologise for the earliness of the hour. As you are aware, last night I was at an event near Paris. The event was interrupted when a number of world leaders left abruptly. I know there has been speculation as to the circumstances for the sudden end to the event. I have spent the last few hours on the phone with other world leaders and I stand here this morning without their blessings to speak. They in fact begged me to refrain from telling you what I am about to tell you, but I made a promise to run an open and transparent government, and trust you the people with the knowledge I share."*

"Our government and various other governments around the world are being targeted by a highly sophisticated cyber-attack," Birmingham explained. *"I have received intelligence to say that the man behind this attack is none other than Witness S, the former Australian Intelligence Service Agent who violently escaped custody in The Hague in recent days."*

Verity and Max exchanged worried looks at Birmingham's blatant lie.

"Enough is enough," Birmingham continued. *"Witness S is a traitor and a terrorist. It is time you all knew the truth. Witness S killed former Prime Minister Stephen Morgan. The public was told he had been in a car accident which was true, but we were not told it was Witness S who forced his car off the road. He murdered the Prime Minister. He was also responsible for assassinating Princess Victoria. We all remember the footage. He shot the Duchess of Cambridge in cold blood, choosing to believe there was some global conspiracy against him. The man is a psychopath. He is a murderer and now he has unleashed a global cyber virus to try to cripple the world's information technology systems in an attempt to get away with his crimes."*

"As I said, enough is enough," Birmingham proclaimed, producing an A4 sized photograph and showing it to the camera. *"This is former Australian Intelligence Service Agent Maxwell Kenneth Shaw, otherwise known a Witness S."*

Max's heart pounded in his chest. He had just been outed by Birmingham. His identity was no longer a secret. He thought about the thousands of terrorists and criminals he had spent a lifetime trying to defeat who now knew who he was and had his photo, let alone the global police force who would now be after him, hanging on Birmingham's version of reality. He clenched the wheel in anger, but kept the car moving through the countryside towards their destination.

"Former Agent Shaw," Birmingham explained, *"is one of the most highly skilled and deadly agents the Five Eyes intelligence system has ever created. As the earlier press conference from The Hague mentioned, he has escaped from custody after killing his prison guards. If you see this man, report him to police, but do not approach him. He is to be considered armed and extremely dangerous. This photograph was taken last night at the event near Paris. He was able to sneak into one of the most secure places on earth, undetected. We have determined that he was at the event to try to hack into A&A's Apollo program. We believe that A&A's system is the only one strong enough to counter his attack and he was there to try to shut it down. I promised to end the Five Eyes agreement and this morning I am here to announce I have terminated our participation in the program. We can no longer be party to an institution which creates people like Mister Shaw. In twenty-four hours' time, our secrets will be published for the world to see. Our history and our wrongs will be righted. For extra security against Mister Shaw's attack, I have ordered a transfer of all our data to A&A's servers, including our medical and health data, citizenship data and military and intelligence data. Mister Shaw wants to bring down the intelligence system which wronged him and I cannot let your data become corrupted or compromised by this man. Isabella Lyadova has provided me with personal assurances of the*

British people's privacy and security. Your personal data is safe. I have also this morning spoken to the head of MI6 and have given him the order to shut down the organisation. I want to thank all the people involved in the organisation for their service, but acknowledge their services are no longer required. The same goes for MI5 and I thank those people for their work. Today, we turn over a new leaf. One which puts us on a path to world peace. And I want to reassure everyone that Mister Shaw will be found. His program will be stopped and his reign of terror will come to an end. Mister Shaw is now considered Britain's enemy number one and I have issued a warrant for his arrest. There is no stone he can hide under and no place we cannot find him."

Birmingham turned and walked back into Number Ten as journalists shouted questions which went unanswered.

The three sat in the car without saying a word. The news anchor came back on and it was clear from her tone and speech she was in shock. She was listing off the various analysts and thought leaders they were lining up to interview on this breaking news.

"Turn it off," Max finally said after a couple of minutes. "I don't need to hear anymore."

"Are you okay, Max?" Verity asked, putting her hand on his arm as Andrew shut the laptop lid.

"It doesn't change anything," Max said defiantly. "We have a job to do. We have to stop the attack."

"Well, I just got fired on national television, so I have nothing else to do anyway," Verity joked, smiling at Max.

"Without MI6 and the British in the Five Eyes agreement, the whole system will crumble. It's like pulling a foundation block out, the tower will fall."

"And that is exactly what the Russians would want. They have wanted the west to fall for decades and now they have their chance with the support of the British Government who are willingly handing over their files for safe keeping to one of the biggest corporations on the face of the planet. All while trying to pin the blame on you."

"Thanks for the reminder."

"I am sorry, Max, but this is getting out of control."

"I know, which is why we have to stay the course. By now my photo is all over the world, so we are lucky we moved to Plan B. There shouldn't be anyone waiting for us here."

Max drove on through the early morning darkness until he found the access road he was looking for. A man in the security hut walked over as Max wound down his window.

After a brief exchange in French, Max handed over a wad of Euros and the man opened the gate for them. Max drove through and gave the guard a quick wave of thanks.

They dumped the car near a little shed as sirens sounded from across the field.

"No one waiting, hey?" Verity said, taking cover in the long grass.

"They must have intercepted the call," Max said, taking the sim card out of his phone and snapping it in half.

"I told you they are everywhere," Andrew said. "A&A must have got into your phone. Did you give it to anyone at the dinner?"

"No," Max said, thinking back to the night before, "but it did go through an x-ray at the security check point."

"That's all the time they needed," Andrew explained. "They would have bugged everyone's phones at the event."

There was a faint whirring of engines above them then out of nowhere a small jet landed on the short country runway of the Nangis Aerodrome. The original plan had been to meet the plane at Orly in Paris, but thankfully Blake's message had been enough warning to avoid major airports. Max would have easily been arrested after Birmingham's press conference.

The plane quickly turned and taxied, outrunning the police cars which had now made it onto the aerodrome at the far end of the facility. The door lowered as it taxied closer and Max, Verity and Andrew all ran for it. Verity crossed the field without effort and jumped up the still moving stairs. Max was almost pushing Andrew trying to speed him up.

"Come on," Max demanded. "Move it. He can't risk stopping."

"I'm trying," Andrew protested. "I don't spend all my time at the gym or running from bullets!"

The jet started to turn on the taxiway around the bend ready to get back on the runway. Andrew grabbed the closet handrail and tried twice to jump on board. Max grabbed him by the back of his pants and on the third time lifted him, helping him get a foothold. He tripped on the step, but thankfully didn't fall. He climbed the steps as Max gave chase to the sleek jet. He could hear the engine revving up as the sirens drew closer.

Max grabbed the rail and pulled himself onto the steps as the first police car arrived at his side. Van den Berg was sitting in the backseat.

One of the officers in the front fired a shot at Max. It went wide, but Max still gave the officer a disapproving shake of his head as van den Berg started yelling at the officer.

Max hit the button by the door, and the stairs retracted up and the door locked shut.

Verity and Andrew were in the main cabin strapping themselves in as Max stepped into the cockpit.

"Let's go," Max said, taking the co-pilot's seat next to Gabriel.

"When you said you were coming in hot," Gabriel yelled, "I did not anticipate you meant from the police!"

"I'll explain en route. Just get us off the ground."

Gabriel turned the jet onto the runway and revved the engines. Two of the police cars had come onto the runway in their path. Gabriel paused on seeing them, but Max grabbed the throttle and pushed it forward to take off speed.

The police officers were not playing chicken, but instead they abandoned their cars, leaving them on the runway. It was going to be tight. Max pulled back hard on the controls willing the plane to lift off. They were roaring down the runaway at full speed, closer and closer to the two deserted vehicles.

Within metres of the flashing blue and yellow lights the jet lifted from the runway.

Gabriel sighed in relief.

"This is why I retired you know," Gabriel said. "To stop having to do this shit."

"If you thought that was bad, wait until you find out where we are going," Max said, turning the dials on the autopilot when they reached their cruising altitude and walking back to talk to Verity.

"What? Where are we going? You didn't say on the phone."

Chapter Twenty-One

Gabriel had arranged a private hangar in a small airport a couple of hours drive from Moscow. He hated Moscow and Russia, and he had not let Max hear the end of it since he found out their destination.

The group had driven into the city and found a quaint motel which was happy to take cash.

The freezing cold air of Moscow and the fresh powdery snow fall gave Max the excuse to wear a snood around his neck and up over his mouth and nose. He also donned a pair of reflective Oakleys and a large dark blue overcoat with an upturned collar. He stole a black woollen cap as they walked down the high street to cover his freezing shaven head.

The Russian press was running his photo on every channel and in the morning papers. They were having a field day at the west's embarrassment, but it also meant he would be easily recognisable to anyone paying attention.

The main newspaper in town had written up a story accusing Max and the AIS of crimes against Russia. In fairness, its sources were pretty good. Max and his team had carried out several operations in Russia both with and without the support of the local government.

He and Verity moved quickly through the streets looking for the pickup location. They turned the corner into a side street and followed it along to an unmarked door.

Verity stepped forward and knocked twice.

A small slide window opened and a piercing set of eyes stared out at the pair.

"What?" the man said in Russian.

"When the snow is white and the sky is blue," Verity stated.

"Darkness cannot be seen for light."

"But it is still right in front of you."

The window shut and the door opened as Verity's MI6 colleague recognised their code.

Verity walked in closely followed by Max as the MI6 agent closed the door behind them.

The MI6 safehouse was an old rundown apartment with faded green curtains and matching benchtops and carpet. The walls were a yellow shade of off white and the furniture looked like it was purchased in the mid-seventies. It had the familiar smell of close quarters living.

There were several computers and a bunch of surveillance gear in the former lounge, and Max guessed there would be some normal apartment rooms, like bedrooms and bathrooms, but there would also be an arsenal which was the second reason for their visit.

"What are you doing in Moscow, Verity?" the agent asked.

"It is good to see you too, Michael," Verity said, pulling down her scarf and peeling off her overcoat. "It has been a while."

"It has," Michael said, looking Max up and down. "And who is this?"

Max pulled down his snood and put his glasses into the front of his shirt.

"Jesus Christ," Michael said. "You are the most wanted man in the world today, Agent Shaw. What are you two doing together?"

"Max was at the A&A event," Verity explained. "They are up to their tits in this. Max is being made the scape goat. You and I both know the charges at The Hague were bullshit. We would both be with him in there if they ever looked at our records."

"That's probably true."

"I'm sorry for barging in," Max said, shaking Michael's hand. "But we're running out of friends fast and time is running out."

"What's going on?"

"A&A are orchestrating the massive cyber-attack on global governments and institutions. We're not sure what their endgame is, but we think the Russians are involved."

"Jesus."

"Exactly," Verity said. "We know the Russian President has been providing funds to the Alexandria 2.0 project under the cover of philanthropic donations to help a supposedly worthy cause and he has even built and is hosting a number of servers here in Moscow. But we're starting to think there is more to it. Birmingham has shut us down. I have been ordered back to London. MI6 is out of the picture. He is fucking Isabella Lyadova. She funded his campaign and rigged the election to get him into office. That's why I was at A&A to uncover the links. Max here found it for us."

"So Birmingham is a Russian spy?"

"We're not sure yet," Max jumped in. "He definitely isn't clean in all this, that is for sure."

"He issued an arrest warrant through Interpol for you and outed you to the world."

"He needed a distraction."

"Well he got it. I'm supposed to arrest you."

"You said it yourself, Michael," Verity said. "MI6 has been shut down."

"True. Looks like I won't be doing that then. So how can I help?"

"This thumb drive has everything we have so far on it," Verity explained, passing Michael the USB device. "We need you to get it to headquarters. They need to ignore Birmingham's order and stay online."

"You need to get it to Blake Smyth too, at AIS," Max said.

"Okay, I can do that," Michael said, reaching for his computer. "I'm not sure how the brass will take this when it arrives."

"Hopefully they do their jobs," Verity said.

"And if they don't or they can't?"

"I need you to get it to Carl Moore," Max said.

"Carl Moore? As in, vice President of the fucking United States, Carl Moore."

"The one and only. Tell him it is from me. He will know what to do."

"Are you sure, Max?" Verity asked. "With everything that is happening, the Americans may not trust you."

"Moore might. We've got to take the chance. We can't do this on our own."

"I will send the files," Michael said. "Can't promise they will read them, but they will get them."

"Thank you," Max said.

"We've got to take some kit," Verity said, walking towards the hallway.

"Go for it," Michael said. "I haven't done the stocktake yet. Take what you need."

Max and Verity went into one of the spare rooms. She entered a six digit code into the panel, unlocking the armoury. Max took a standard Glock pistol from the shelf and checked it over, then loaded a magazine, chambered a round and stuck it in the back of his pants, under his coat.

Verity gathered some electronics and a new laptop in a leather backpack, while Max took off his coat and hung an MP5 over his shoulder. The gun was slung on a long rope attached to the base so it sat beside his hip. The tip of the barrel would be just covered by his long coat when he put it back on, but it was low enough not to be seen under it. He put the coat back on to check the length. He was right, it was just long enough to hide the gun.

Max grabbed a few magazines and stuffed them in his pockets. Left pocket for the MP5 and right for the Glock. Finally, he spotted a long row of hunting and throwing knives. He moved along the line and one by one tested their weight, until he found a matt black carbon knife like the one had used for years with AIS. Perfectly balanced. He clipped the holster to his belt and sheathed the knife.

"I think we may need a couple of these," Max said, tossing Verity three smoke grenades and three flashbangs.

"Can't hurt," Verity said, placing them in the bag. "Got what you need?"

"Yeah, I think so," Max said as he heard a rap on the front door.

He exchanged a quick look with Verity who jumped up and moved to the shelves to gather her weapons.

Max pulled the MP5 up to his shoulder and walked with purpose into the front room. Michael had drawn his pistol and was walking towards the front door.

"You expecting company?" Max asked.

"No, only you," Michael said.

"I'll cover."

"Got it," Michael said, sliding the window open in the door as Max took up position a few metres from his right arm aiming the MP5 at the door. "What?"

"When the snow is red and the sky turns grey," the man in the street said in Russian.

"Darkness grows and calls the dead."

"To march with him today," the man said as a small package dropped through the window and landed at Michael's feet.

Max leapt forward and grabbed Michael, dragging him away from the door and back into the main room.

Just as they rounded the corner, the package in the foyer exploded, blasting the door out into the street and tearing chunks out of the plaster walls.

Michael groaned in pain as some shrapnel ripped into his leg just below the knee as the pair fell onto the carpet. It was bleeding badly – it must have cut an artery – but Max couldn't help him, he needed to get up and cover the door.

Max dragged himself up and fired two warning shots into what was left of the doorframe, hoping to keep any attackers at bay.

"Can you move?" Max asked.

"No, I'm fucked, Max," Michael said through gritted teeth. "Get Verity out of here. There is a back way out. She knows where it is."

"I can carry you," Max said, reaching down to lift him.

"No, Max," Michael groaned, pushing Max's hands away. "I will only slow you down. The files are still uploading anyway. I can hold them off for a couple of minutes. You both need to get out of here and finish this thing."

"Thank you," Max said, firing another couple of rounds towards the front door.

"You don't have to do that, Max. It's my job. You go do yours."

"You got my word," Max nodded, patting Michael on the shoulder before jogging down the hallway.

Michael fired a round into the first man through the door, hitting him in the neck. His knees buckled and he dropped to the floor as blood pumped out between his fingers.

Michael looked over to the computer and saw the copying documents progress bar still filling as the files moved off the USB drive.

He grabbed the laptop and dragged it off the table to the floor beside him.

He flipped the old brown coffee table over and took cover behind it as a flashbang grenade bounced into the room. He curled himself up in a ball with his arms over his head, pressing his ears into his biceps as he closed his eyes.

As soon as the grenade went off, he fired wildly over the top of the table hoping to hold back the incoming attackers.

A torrent of gunfire pierced the tabletop and he felt the sharp stinging pain as the hot metal sliced through him and hit the wall behind him. He looked down and saw his hands covered in blood as he fell to his side, bleeding out on the floor.

Three men walked into the room. Two of them ran down the hallway to check the rest of the MI6 safehouse. The remaining man was Leonid. He walked over and looked down at the dying figure before him and smiled.

"You will never win," Michael said, spitting blood onto the carpet as he reached over and hit the enter button on the keyboard.

Leonid fired his magazine dry.

Michael's body was filled with holes and the life left his eyes.

Leonid picked up the laptop. *Message sent,* was sitting in the window. He tossed the computer onto the sofa and walked after his men.

Max had found Verity waiting for him near the back door, but when he arrived, they didn't use it. Instead, she pulled him into a side room and bolted the door shut, then she reached up and pulled a small string hanging from the roof. An American attic style ladder slid down into the room.

Max followed Verity up into a narrow crawl space, then pulled the ladder and cord back up behind them. They army crawled over the beams until they reached a small open space where it was high enough to stand.

Verity pulled down another ladder and the pair climbed. It was much longer in length then the previous ladder and this time stopped at a dead end. She removed a small panel, entered a code and a section of the roof lifted up.

The pair climbed the final steps out onto the roof.

On the adjacent building's roof, Alexei was standing there smiling broadly on sighting his prey. He gave Max a short wave, then pulled his assault rifle up to his shoulder.

"Move!" Max yelled as he grabbed Verity by the back of the shoulders and pushed her forward.

Bullets slammed into the concrete roof and the hatch they had just used.

As the pair ran forward, a line of bullets impacted the concrete behind them as if Alexei was tormenting them.

"Please tell me there is a way off this roof," Max said as they took cover behind a concrete shelter protecting a staircase into the building.

"Yes, down the far end," Verity said. "It leads over to the next building. There are four in a row, before a ladder down to the street."

"Are any of the others connected?"

"Yes. He is on one of them."

"Fuck."

Max ducked his head around the structure to see Alexei coming across a small walkway. He fired when he saw Max.

Verity grabbed out two of the smoke grenades and tossed them around the concrete roof for cover.

Instantly, smoke started to hang in the air between them and Alexei.

Alexei fired wildly into the smoke, hoping to deter them from running.

As soon as the smoke was thick enough, Max and Verity ran. They both fired in Alexei's direction, forcing him to take cover. They fled across to the next building as Alexei emerged from the smoke and opened fire.

Max stopped and returned fire as Verity ran across the small bridge to the next building, before she turned and unleashed a stream of bullets towards Alexei.

He dived to the ground as Max ran across the bridge.

Alexei was slowly making up ground as they reached the last building and started to climb down the ladder.

As Max went over the edge, he saw Alexei in a full sprint.

"Find us a car," Max shouted down to Verity who was nearly at the ground.

"What are you doing?" Verity asked, watching as Max climbed in through an open window behind the escape ladder.

When he didn't reply, she just ran for the nearby lane where she hoped to find Michael's car.

Max waited patiently in the hallway near the window, until he heard gunfire ring out. Alexei was firing after Verity from the roof.

Max saw her duck down an alley as bullets tore into the wall behind her.

Max waited, listening to the sound of Alexei's feet on the ladder getting closer and closer, then he saw it. Foot number one. It landed on the ladder as his other foot swung out behind him to go down to the next rung, but it would never get there. Max fired a bullet through Alexei's load bearing ankle. He screamed in pain as he slipped off the rung and fell. He smashed his chin on one of the rungs as he frantically tried to catch himself.

Max watched him fall, then clutch the rung just above the window.

Alexei hung with his arms outstretched and his face right in the window in front of Max. His face was contorted in pain, until he saw Max and his eyes widened.

Max punched him as hard as he could, right on the bridge of his nose. Alexei's face was instantaneously covered in blood as his nose broke and the skin split under the force. The pain was too much to bear and he lost his grip, falling the last three storeys and smashing through some boxes and rubbish stacked against the building.

Max climbed through the window and made his way down the ladder as Verity pulled up in a black SUV. She jumped out and got some cable ties out of the back, as Max pulled the bleeding and groggy Alexei from the pile of rubbish. He couldn't stand on his wounded ankle, so Max carried him to the SUV.

Verity tightened the makeshift handcuffs around his wrists, then they tossed him in the back, before driving off.

Chapter Twenty-Two

Gabriel patched Alexei up in the bathroom of the motel. It wasn't enough to repair the wound, just enough to stop him from bleeding to death.

They had rented adjoining rooms. Verity and Andrew were next door continuing to work up leads.

Max had cable tied Alexei to a chair in just his underwear and opened the bathroom window. It was freezing inside thanks to the cold winter air rushing in through the window. Max was giving Alexei a few minutes to get very cold, in an attempt to speed up what would follow.

"Do you want me in there?" Gabriel asked, nodding to the bathroom door.

"No, old friend," Max said, "you have already done more than I could have asked. Thank you again."

"It is no problem, Max. You helped me out of more than one jam and if this is as serious as you say it is, well, I cannot sit on the sidelines."

"I'm starting to think it is the worst case scenario."

"That, my friend, is a feeling we share."

"Why don't you go in and see if Verity could use your help. Maybe there is another angle they haven't seen."

"Of course, let me know if you need me."

"Will do."

Max stepped up to the bathroom door as Gabriel went through into the next room. He took a deep breath, opened the door, then walked in.

Alexei was awake, thanks to the cold air, and he was shivering. His lips were blue and he was ghostly white, which was most likely from blood loss. His skin was splotchy with purple veins and marks from the cold.

"You know who I am, right?" Max asked.

Alexei just stared at him.

Max stepped forward and backhanded him. It would have hurt on a normal day, but in the freezing conditions it would have been twice as painful.

"I'm going to ask you again, do you know who I am?" Max asked.

"Of course, I do," Alexei said. "Witness S. Agent Max 'Prince' Shaw, formerly of the Australian Intelligence Service."

"Good. And you are Alexei Kuznetsov, formerly of the KGB, now hired goon of Isabella Lyadova at A&A Enterprises. Alexei, I'm going to ask you a few questions. You know how this works, if I get an answer I like we will move to the next question. If I get an answer I do not like, I will hurt you until you tell me the truth. I understand you tortured a colleague of mine recently, so I will just take that to mean you get what I am saying."

Alexei just sat there breathing in and out deeply trying to psych himself up for the pain.

"Where is Isabella Lyadova?" Max asked.

"I don't know," Alexei said, smiling broadly.

"Okay, what about your boss, Nina Yahontov, know where she is?"

"Probably with Lyadova."

"What about Leonid Goncharov? Where is he?"

"Looking for you. Could be anywhere. Maybe even right outside."

"I hope he is. That will save me some time. But let's say he's not at the door. Where would he be?"

Alexei just sat staring at Max, almost tempting him to act.

"I will ask you this," Max said, walking around behind Alexei. "What is worse than death? Especially for someone like you, so fit and strong. So tough and capable. I think it would be permanent injury. Now, I know what you are thinking, that ankle is going to give you a permanent limp if you don't get to hospital soon, so it can be operated on. But humour me, say you were to get the surgery you need, you would mostly be yourself. Am I right?"

Alexei didn't move.

"I want you to think about it for a minute," Max said, putting the plug into the bath and turning on the cold tap. "I'll be back to hear your answer."

Max walked out of the bathroom and picked up the rubbish bin as the cold water started to fill the tub. He pulled the small bag out of the bin, then walked out of the hotel room. He used the bin as a scoop to gather snow, then walked back inside. He dumped the snow into the filling bath then walked back out. He repeated the process over and over. On the seventh trip, he turned off the cold water and did a couple more trips out into the cold to gather snow.

Max grabbed a handful of the slushy, icy water and dumped it into Alexei's lap. He squirmed and thrusted, trying to get the freezing ice water off his crotch.

Max walked back around to face Alexei. Without saying a word, the pair locked eyes and Max grabbed him around the throat pushing him and the chair back to the edge of the bath. He pushed hard and the chair tilted, lifting its front legs off the ground, then with his other hand, Max lifted the nearest leg and used the edge of the bath to lever Alexei and the chair into the freezing water.

The chair fell back first to the bottom of the bath, dragging a thrashing and wide-eyed Alexei under. His feet were cable tied to the chair legs and they were up out of the water. So were his legs, until just above the knees where the water started. But his head, upper body and legs above his knees were under the freezing water.

Max left him under for around thirty seconds. He figured a former KGB operative could hold his breath for some time, but given the coldness of the water, that time would be reduced.

Given he had zero percent body fat, the cold would also affect him faster than most.

Max reached in, grabbed the back of the chair, behind Alexei's closest shoulder and pulled him up out of the water. He coughed and spluttered and shivered, as Max sat him upright.

"You see, Alexei," Max said. "Now you are wet in this cold air, not only are you rushing towards hypothermia, but your limbs are starting to shut down as the blood rushes back into your core to try to keep your vital organs pumping. Your feet are both now in the freezing cold water and I would guess they are already starting to numb. In a few minutes, the numbness will be replaced by excruciating, burning pain and within no time at all, you will start to suffer permanent damage. Frostbite is a bitch. If I leave you in there too long, no surgery will be able to fix the damage. The most likely scenario will be that you lose both your feet, maybe even a good portion of your legs. See, I'm not going to kill you, Alexei. You are ready for death and welcome it. No, death is too good for you. I am going to force you to live in pain, permanently crippled for life. Now, I am going to go grab a coffee, because it is freezing in here and I need to warm up, but while I'm gone, do me a favour and think about the answer to this question – is Lyadova worth it?"

Max walked out and closed the door, leaving Alexei to freeze and think about his answer.

"How's it going?" Andrew asked, walking over to the kitchen where Max was making coffee.

"The KGB operate on a different wavelength," Max said as the kettle started to boil. "He will be tough to crack, but I have given him some things to think about."

"What was all the snow for?"

"Ice bath."

"Jesus. He will die of hypothermia."

"Hopefully not," Max said, pouring the hot water into a plunger and letting the coffee circulate in the glass container. "Why do you care anyway? He tortured you or have you already forgotten that?"

"No, of course not. Fuck him. He deserves what he gets."

"What have you found out?"

"Blake left some new intel in your app. Satellite images of the three server locations."

"Great. What do they show?"

"Almost exactly the same as the one in The Netherlands. Brick office above ground, surrounded by a huge fence. A few guards on the grounds."

"Did Blake leave anything else?"

"Just a message."

"What did it say?"

"We don't know, it is encrypted. We need your fingerprint to access it."

"Okay," Max said, pushing the plunger down and grabbing four mugs, before following Andrew into the other room.

"How's it going?" Verity asked.

"Work in progress," Max said, handing over the mugs and pouring the coffee. "Have you got the phone?"

"Yeah, here it is," Andrew said, passing Max the phone.

He pressed his finger to the scanner and once it recognised him, the message began to play.

"Prince, I got your message," Blake said through the tinny speaker. *"This is worse than we thought. The Americans, Canadians, Kiwis and every spare agent and analyst we have in Australia are working on trying to block the hack, but it is learning and adapting. We won't be able to fight it off for much longer. MI6 has left us exposed, but some of them have seen through Birmingham's bullshit and they are fighting back, but I'm not sure how long they will be able to work before the Army are sent in to take over. I spoke to our friend in the US. He got your message and while it is safe to say they are sceptical, for now, he believes you, but he wants proof of the Russian involvement before he can act. If they are involved, we may be about to start World War III. Find out what you can and get back to us. We might be able to de-escalate this thing before it is too late. Hulk, Alpha and Bravo are stuck in Australia, and I'm stuck in the embassy awaiting my flight home. I'm sorry we*

can't get there to help you, but we will keep working up leads. You are on your own, but we will do what we can to assist. Good luck and Godspeed. Hermes."

The recording crackled and Max looked down at the phone. There was a long pause.

"Be careful, Max," Blake said. *"I love you."*

The recording ended and everyone sat there thinking about what they had just heard.

Max could hear the fear and uncertainty in Blake's normally unwavering voice. But he heard the words that gave him all the inspiration and strength he needed to keep fighting. *I love you too,* he thought to himself.

"You and Blake, hey?" Andrew said. "Always thought there was something between you."

Max just ignored him.

"He got one thing wrong," Max said. "I'm not on my own. I'm glad you are all with me. Keep at it. I'd better go talk to our friend."

"You got it, Max," Verity said, turning back to her laptop with Gabriel.

Max walked into the bathroom and instantly felt the cold air hit him.

Alexei was shaking and his white skin was turning blue. There was anger in his eyes, but it was fading. The fight was leaving him as his body was screaming in pain. Max could tell he wanted the pain to end and end quickly.

"So, is she worth it?" Max asked, before taking a sip of his coffee.

"No," Alexei conceded with the final bit of fight leaving his body.

"I didn't think so," Max said, walking over and pulling the plug on the bath, letting the freezing water flow down the drain. "Where is Lyadova?"

"I don't know. All I know is that she was with the President."

"Is the President involved in all this?"

"That's above my paygrade."

"You say Nina will be by her side, so what about Leonid, where will he be?"

"At one of the server bunkers."

"I know of three, which one?"

"The biggest one, the one to the south of Moscow."

Max walked over and closed the bathroom window, then walked over and turned the cold water tap on. The shower water hit Alexei's skin and he groaned and squirmed. Compared to the freezing conditions he had been in the water would have felt like acid or fire pouring over his skin. Within a couple of moments, he stopped moving about as he started to warm up. Max added some hot water to the mix then left the room.

"Verity," Max said, grabbing his guns. "It's time to move."

Chapter Twenty-Three

Max fired a single shot into the camera on the corner of the compound. The bullet went straight through the glass lens shattering it, before ripping through the back of the camera.

Glass and plastic exploded from the small unit.

He turned and nodded to Verity, and she quickly ducked out of the snow covered tree line and started to cut a hole in the metal wire fence.

Max jogged along the fence line until he reached Verity as she snipped the last wire. He pressed the linked flexible metal back allowing Verity to enter then followed her through.

As his foot touched down on the concrete, an alarm sounded and four guards who had been at the front and rear entrances of the small office like building on the compound came running around their respective corners, firing their weapons wildly.

Max threw back his jacket, grabbed the handle of his MP5 which was hanging at perfect height and dragged it up, spraying a line of bullets towards the guards from the front.

Verity pulled two Glocks from her holsters and fired both at the guards from the rear as she ran sideways, following Max towards the building.

Verity took down one of her attackers with a bullet to the face. He fell into the path of the second guard, tripping him, and giving her the seconds she needed to line him up and take the shot which took him down. His body fell just in front of his comrade.

One of Max's guards fired a bullet which grazed his left arm, tearing a hole in his overcoat, but thankfully it didn't do much damage to his arm. More like a long burn than a hole or cut.

Max dropped to a knee to lower his profile, giving himself fractions of a second to line up his shots. Two blasts rang out then the gunfire stopped.

Max stood and checked out his arm, as the two guards he had shot in quick succession fell to the ground.

"Are you okay?" Verity asked as she fired a bullet through the alarm unit hanging on the side of the structure, silencing it.

"Yeah, I'll be fine," Max said, using his fingers to open the hole in his coat. "Just a graze."

"You getting slow, old man?" Verity laughed.

"Aren't we all? I think it is safe to say we lost the element of surprise."

"Agree. The camera or the fence must have triggered the alarm. What's the game plan?"

"Unchanged. Let's get in there and take it offline."

"After you."

Max turned on his heel and walked towards the front of the building with his MP5 pressed against his shoulder, ready for anything that might come around the corner.

When he got to the guards, he pointed down at them, then continued on to the corner. He snuck a peak around the brick edge and was happy to see there were no more guards.

He turned back to Verity who was checking the guards. She was intently studying one of the guard's wallets.

"We've got a problem," Verity said, tossing it to Max.

Max looked down at the leather folding wallet. He opened it and was shocked to see the badge and laminated official identification of an officer of the Russian Federal Security Service. The FSS was the main successor to the KGB and leading security agency of the Russian Federation.

"Fuck," Max said as he put the ID in his pocket. "Their fingerprints are all over this."

"It looks like it," Verity said, taking out the other guard's ID and checking it.

She flashed it to Max and he nodded, acknowledging the same FSS logo, then she pocketed it.

"Let's move," Max said, grabbing the closet guard's coat and dragging him to the front door.

When they arrived, Max pressed his hand to the biometric sensor, but the door didn't open. He tried again, but the panel flashed red. Max dropped the guard, then studied the door. There was a small round hole burned out of the metal, like an explosive charge had been used to open it. He pointed to it and Verity gave him a puzzled look.

He pushed the door and it swung open. Max went right and Verity took the left corridor. The pair swept the offices until they met at the rear of the complex.

All clear.

Max walked into one of the offices and pressed the up arrow on an old keyboard, and like the facility in The Netherlands, the wall retracted. The pair went through the decontamination and dust procedures, before taking the elevator down into the basement.

"Wow, this is a much bigger complex than I was expecting," Verity said as the enormous complex came into view beneath them. "I don't know what I was expecting, but this isn't it."

"This is four times the size of the one in The Netherlands," Max noted, taking it all in.

"What is that?" Verity asked, pointing into the distance where flashes of light were just visible.

"It looks like muzzle flashes," Max said. "What is going on here?"

"No idea, but it can't be good. So, are we still sticking to the plan?"

"Yes," Max said as the elevator reached the bunker floor. "Follow me."

Max led the way, hugging the right-hand wall. They could hear the gunfire ringing out, but Max hoped they would not have to get involved. He found a doorway and peeked through the glass viewport. It was clear, so he opened the door and entered the hallway with his gun pressed against his shoulder. Verity was in close step, guarding their flank.

He found the control room and burst through the door, firing four shots into the men at the controls. Max pushed one of the fallen men from his chair and started pressing various buttons as Verity checked the men. They both had FSS IDs.

"We don't know how many of these guys are here, Max," Verity said, tossing the ID wallets up onto the computer system beside Max. "We might need to take more drastic measures then trying to shut it down here."

"What did you have in mind?" Max asked.

"Well, even if the virus Andrew gave us to upload works, they could eventually overcome it and get the system working again," Verity said as Max pushed the USB drive Andrew had given him into the computer and started the virus upload.

"I have never really believed in all this technology shit anyway, so it can't hurt."

"Do you know where the cooling rooms are?"

"Yes, but you're not going to like it."

"Why? If we can take down the cooling system the servers will overheat and burn themselves out."

"Okay, let's hope they are too busy to see us," Max said, walking back out of the room closely followed by Verity.

The pair followed the right-hand wall of the main server room, sticking close to it, in the shadows. The gunfire had stopped and Max was wondering what he was going to find when they drew closer to where the action was.

"Clean up this mess and get these arseholes out of here!" Leonid yelled to their left. "Think they can just take over, what a joke."

Max and Verity crept quietly along the wall until they found another hallway. They silently entered and quickly moved towards the cooling room.

Inside the cooling room were hundreds of air-conditioning units. The modern machines were covered by sleek black metal housings which made them look remarkably similar to the high-tech servers in the other room. Some of the units had a thin layer of ice forming on them.

They walked to the far end of the room and split up.

Max took his hunting knife out of its leather sheath and slid it in under the back panel on the colling system. He pried the panel off and discarded it. He looked at all the wires and tubes running around the system. He wasn't exactly sure which one he was looking for, so he grabbed the bottom tube leading into the system and cut it.

It didn't take long for him to realise he had cut the right one. Gas started pouring out into the air around him.

He moved quickly along the line of cooling units, cutting the tubes on every second or third one. Verity was doing the same on the other side of the room, weaving between the machines.

When they got to the halfway point, a small alarm sounded and a voiceover rang out in the space. *Cooling system alert,* it said. Verity and Max exchanged looks before moving quicker through the room, this time only stopping to cut every fourth or fifth unit.

"Agent Shaw, you are back, I see," a woman's voice said over the facility's speakers. *"I would have thought, being a global terrorist, you would have just given up and gone back into hiding, but the faithful servant of the people returns to his duties. You don't give up do you?"*

"Nina, I presume?" Max said, running to his next unit and prying off the panel. "I must admit I was a bit annoyed Birmingham started blaming me for you and your boss's crimes, but it's just given me a renewed purpose to find and kill you both."

"And how exactly do you plan to do that, when you and the recently unemployed Agent Verity Humphries of the MI6 are trapped in that room?"

Verity looked over to Max acknowledging she was now in their sights too.

The door they had used to enter the room burst open and Leonid and his men ran in. Leonid came running towards Max, knife and pistol in hand, as two men ran towards Verity.

Max knew he couldn't risk firing a bullet with the gas levels rising, so he kept hold of his knife. Leonid smelt the gas and tossed his pistol on the ground, but held tight to his knife.

"You think you can just come in here and takeover, like those other dogs?" Leonid asked.

"I have no plans to take over," Max said. "My plans revolve more around the break part of break and enter."

"You will be what is broken. You slipped away before, but history will not repeat itself."

"We will see about that, but why don't you tell me what the Russians were doing in here? Trying to take over, you said. I thought they were working with you."

"They built this facility. The President himself has visited and provided a lot of the money to make this all happen. He wanted it all for himself."

"So they tried to remove A&A from the process and I take it Lyadova wasn't keen on that arrangement?"

"All I care about is that the west finally gets what is coming to it. I spent years in the KGB fighting to help Mother Russia dominate. The Cold War may have ended for you, but it was just the beginning for us. The west will finally fall."

Leonid ran forward slashing his knife towards Max. Max jumped back as the knife sliced his overcoat across the left breast and shoulder. He lunged forward again and Max dodged to the side, slicing Leonid's arm with his own knife. It was a good cut, long and deep. Blood began running down his arm into his hand and over the handle of the knife.

On the other side of the room, Verity picked up one of the metal panels she had removed from the cooling unit and was using it partly as a shield and partly as a blunt weapon. One of the men ran at her and threw a haymaker. She clutched the panel and moved it into the path of the incoming fist. She heard the familiar snap of bone breaking after the thud on the metal.

As the attacker cradled his broken hand, Verity launched, raising the panel over her shoulder and swung it through the air. It slapped down hard on the guy's face, knocking him to the floor.

Leonid slashed at Max, but Max was faster than the big man and moved away from the blade. He caught Leonid's wrist and pushed it to the side, opening up his chest and stomach for attack. He stabbed his own knife in under Leonid's left ribs and twisted it. Leonid flashed to pain and anger. He grabbed Max with his left hand then slammed his forehead down on Max's.

The force of the blow dazed Max and he stumbled back. He shook his head trying to focus.

Leonid took the opportunity to capitalise and ran forward with his blood covered knife in both hands high above his head. Max caught his forearms as he tried to stab the knife down into him.

The pair fell and Max's back pressed against one of the air-conditioning units. He was struggling, trying to hold back the knife in Leonid's outstretched arms which was inching closer, fighting its way through the space aiming for Max's skull. The angle was making it difficult for Max and Leonid's sheer size and strength was starting to overwhelm him. His head was still ringing from the headbutt as the knife inched closer and closer to his head.

Max moved his head to the side and dragged Leonid's arms in the opposite direction. If he was going to get stabbed, he thought, the shoulder was better than the head.

As he moved his head, he caught a glimpse of his own knife still lodged deep in Leonid's ribs. He exploded right and pushed Leonid to the left, getting himself out from underneath the knife, then grabbed his own knife and dragged it towards Leonid's back before ripping it free.

Leonid sliced his own knife through Max's overcoat, jumper and shirt, and traced a line down his back, but Max was still moving. He spun around behind Leonid and stabbed him violently in the back three times.

The third impact found its mark. Leonid stopped in his tracks as the knife severed his spine. He instantly fell to the ground, as his legs gave out. He dragged himself painfully forward and propped against the air-conditioning unit.

"Where is Lyadova?" Max asked.

"Fuck you!" Leonid spat as blood ran from his mouth.

He tried to lunge at Max with his knife, but Max kicked it from his blood-soaked hand then stabbed him through the shoulder, pinning him to the cooling system.

Leonid screamed in pain and cursed, but quickly started to fade as the blood was draining from his body and the pain was starting to take hold.

Max looked over and saw Verity. She had climbed onto the second attacker's back and had him in a headlock or more specifically, a sleeper hold. He fell to his knees as his body started to shut down without oxygen, and Verity got her footing, then with incredible force she twisted his head and snapped his neck. He fell to the ground at her feet as she tried to get her breath, but the gas was making it hard to breath.

Max looked down at Leonid. The fight was gone and he knew it, so he just sat there in excruciating pain as Max searched his pockets.

"We need to get out of here," Verity said, arriving at his side.

"Agree," Max said, standing up and ripping the knife out of Leonid's shoulder. "Let's move."

Leonid screamed in pain and hopelessness.

Max and Verity ran for the door. As they moved, Max picked up Leonid's gun from the floor. He clicked out the magazine, but left one round in the chamber. He turned and tossed it back towards Leonid. It hit the floor and spun on the polished concrete until it stopped and spun on the spot right beside him.

Leonid picked up the gun and pointed it at Max who was now standing in the doorway. It would have been a good shot on any day, but with an unsteady hand, the distance with a pistol was unlikely. Leonid knew it too.

He nodded to Max in a sign of respect for his opponent, then put the gun to his head and pulled the trigger. The muzzle flash was enough to spark the gas in the cooling system room. One by one the air-conditioners exploded in both directions and Leonid disappeared in a ball of flames and smoke.

Max ran after Verity across the large hangar and the pair took the elevator up to the surface, as the fire spread to the servers.

"Why do you still have that?" Max asked as they climbed into their car.

"Because of this," Verity said, turning the panel from the air-conditioning unit over in her hands.

Max looked down at the panel Verity had used as a weapon in the bunker. On the inside there was a white sticker with the embossed logo of the Russian Government.

"It says 'Property of the Russian Federation'," Verity read aloud. "This is a military base."

Chapter Twenty-Four

Max had dropped Verity back at the hotel and asked her to relay the evidence to their respective agencies and to Moore in the US. The logo and sticker from the bunker as well as the ID she had taken from one of the FSS agents were enough evidence for the Americans and their allies to declare war against the Russians, but Max was determined to try to find a way to stop the cyber-attack before the world rallied its armies. If he could disable the program, maybe the Russians would back down.

Before he left, he gave Verity a swipe card for the Four Seasons in downtown Moscow. He had taken it from Leonid. It was his best guess at where Lyadova and Nina were going to be.

"He has been getting agitated," Gabriel said, nodding towards the bathroom door. "The painkillers we have are not strong enough."

"I will take him with me," Verity said, opening the bathroom door to see Alexei. "I will get you some morphine, Alexei, if you promise to tell me all I need to know about Lyadova and Nina."

Alexei was still tied to the chair, but was no longer in the ice-filled bath. He was dry and warm now, however his injured foot was clearly causing him a lot of grief. His normally stoic and gruff demeanour was being overcome by pain.

"I need to get to a hospital," Alexei said. "The damage is going to be permanent if I do not get to see a doctor soon."

"You know the deal," Verity said. "Information for pain relief."

"Okay," Alexei said after a full minute, "but I want to know what you are planning to do with me. If you are going to hand me over to the authorities, do it now so I can get some help."

"I have a problem with that because the authorities we need to get you to are many hundreds of miles from here. And they don't speak Russian."

"I might be able to help," Gabriel interjected, walking into the small bathroom. "I have a friend who may be able to help you. Between the two of us, he and I will be able to fix your ankle and get you some pain relief."

"You said may be able to help," Alexei said. "Not very reassuring."

"He hates Russians even more than I do."

"Yet he is in Moscow."

"The joys of the line of work we all find ourselves in. You of all people should appreciate that."

"Are you sure?" Verity asked as Alexei just shook his head and looked away. "I know you only agreed to help us get out of France, not to take on the Russians."

"Yes, I am sure. An old friend of mine has a place I used to use on missions here in Moscow. You can drop us off on your way to the hotel."

"Information first," Verity said, turning back to Alexei.

Alexei told Verity everything he knew about Lyadova and Nina, which it turned out was not much more than they already knew. He did confirm the hotel where they were staying. He and Leonid had rooms one floor down from Lyadova, who was in the Presidential penthouse suite, and across the hall from Nina.

Verity stole an old sedan with greying white paint. It was reliable enough to get them to the drop off, but she doubted it could do much more than that. She changed the licence plates, swapping them with a nearby car, then bundled Alexei into the boot.

Gabriel rode beside her in the passenger seat giving directions to his friend's place.

The Russian street was lined with old industrial concrete and brick buildings. Some were rendered and painted in white, while others were exposed red or white bricks. The architecture could only be described as brutalist. Standard designs, limited or no outdoor space, and no doubt very similar floorplans. The old Soviet machine built them and modern Russia had not bothered to bring them into the twenty-first century.

Street after street looked the same and the roads, parks and outdoor spaces, as well as the rooftops, were covered in snow which was helping to blend everything into one big landscape of sameness.

They turned into a busy suburb and drove along the long road until Gabriel found the apartment block he was looking for. Verity was not sure how he could have recognised the building among its similar rectangular designed neighbours, but she drove down into the building's basement and parked.

"Are you sure you will be okay with him?" Verity asked. "I can stay if you need."

"He cannot get far on that leg," Gabriel said. "I am not that old and incapable just yet, mademoiselle, plus he will be unconscious for most of his surgery. But, more importantly, you have a job to do. I will be fine. Go get that bitch."

"Okay, well just be careful. Here are the keys. I will meet you back at the motel."

"Good luck," Gabriel said, taking the keys and placing them in his pocket.

"You too," Verity said, before walking up the concrete ramp and into the cold snow covered street.

Verity turned up the collar on her overcoat and wrapped the scarf around her face and ears for warmth for her walk to Lyadova's hotel.

The Moscow Four Seasons was an impressive five-star hotel with views of the Kremlin. It was a large white rectangular building with unique façades on each end. The big hotel dwarfed most of the other, more spectacular buildings in Manezhnaya Square.

Verity walked through the sculpted courtyard admiring the domed water features even though it was too cold for them to be running, taking her time to see if she was being followed.

When she was comfortable, she stole a glance up to the Presidential suite on the off chance she could see Lyadova, but she was nowhere to be seen.

Verity crossed the courtyard and a doorman in a heavy black overcoat opened the big glass door into the lobby for her. She said thanks and headed into the cream marble tiled two storey lobby. She heard the conversations and music coming from the restaurants and cafés inside the grand hotel as she crossed the foyer.

Verity took the elevator up to Alexei's floor, the second from the top, and used his key to access his room. It was immaculate. Subtle light coffee coloured walls and carpet, with slightly darker shaded curtains, with large white, black and caramel artworks and expensive looking white and grey furniture.

She looked through his belongings and his suitcase which was laid out on a baggage holder in the bedroom. She opened each and every drawer and cupboard, but did not find anything useful.

Verity walked back out into the lounge room and was about to leave when she spotted a small black wire running up the wall behind the television. Normally she would not have given it another thought, but the other cords for the pricey stereo, DVD player and cable television boxes were all concealed in the walls it got her attention.

The cord was connected to a small black box which had a short thick cylindrical pole, like a satellite phone, angled out away from the wall, and it had a glowing green light blinking on the front.

Verity walked over and turned on the television set. The large flat screen came to life. The adult movie channel was playing. Verity shook her head and scrambled for the remote to turn down the loud moans coming from the stereo. She wiped the remote control on the quilt before lowering the volume and flicking the source over to HDMI where she found the signal being received by the small black box on the wall. It was broadcasting footage from the hallway outside Lyadova's suite. She used the remote to scroll through the options and was surprised to see not only various angles of the hallway, but rolling footage from numerous cameras inside Lyadova's suite.

Lyadova was there pacing in front of Laskaris. Verity was happy to see him alive. He had obviously played his part and kept his word, otherwise he surely would be dead. Verity noticed he still looked nervous, but thought she might have been reading too much into it.

Laskaris was frantically typing on the tablet computer, taking dictated instructions from his boss.

Verity hit the volume button and Lyadova's voice echoed in the room.

"Dear Mr President," Lyadova dictated as Laskaris typed. "I thank you for your offer, however given the quantum of intelligence we have so far been able to obtain from your nearest neighbour, I am afraid it is rejected. I think you need to add another zero or two to the end of that figure if you would like to buy that intelligence package. Now, as for your security information, I am willing to consider a slight reduction in the monthly costs for securely storing it for you. You will however need to reconsider your bid for your enemy's intel, then we can talk. The clock is ticking, Mr President, I came to you first, but I am giving you two hours, before I start negotiating with the other side. Think fast. Signed blah, blah. Send it to the President's private email. I am going to have a shower, I have not stopped since the party."

"Yes, ma'am," Laskaris said, his voice cracking slightly, without looking up from the tablet.

Verity watched Lyadova walk out of the room and as soon as she was gone, Laskaris wiped tears away from his eyes. She was right, he was clearly petrified. He looked around, then stared at the door as if willing himself to get up and make a run for it, but soon enough his shoulders slumped forward in defeat. Verity knew he was too scared to run, given everything he knew.

Verity tossed the remote onto the bed and left the room. She took the stairs up to the top floor and walked into the empty hallway.

She took a punt on Alexei's key opening the door to Lyadova's suite, pressing it softly on the black card reader.

A soft mechanical click let her know the door was unlocked and she gently turned the handle and opened the door.

Verity snuck through the huge apartment, having memorised its layout from the camera footage, and into the room where Laskaris was sitting.

"Elias," Verity whispered, causing him to jump. "Do you remember me?"

"How could I forget?" Laskaris asked, wiping more tears from his face and looking around the room. "You should not be here. They know you were coming. It's a trap."

"We promised to get you out. Get the tablet, let's move."

"It won't matter, she will find us."

"We will sort Lyadova out soon enough."

"It's not her I am worried about," Laskaris said, shaking in fear and looking to the door.

The door flew open and Nina stormed into the room.

Verity moved fast, covering the ground to Laskaris in no time at all. She grabbed the young man and pushed him in behind the nearby marble bar as bullets tore into the windows and walls behind them.

"When I say," Verity whispered to Laskaris, "you are going to run for the door. Got it?"

Laskaris was shaking, panic was taking over. His breaths were heavy and fast. Verity slapped him across the face to get his focus. They locked eyes.

"Get your breathing under control," Verity said. "You will be fine. You are going to get out of here. The door. Ready?"

"Yes," Laskaris managed to get out, slowing his breathing.

"Good."

Verity leapt up and started firing towards Nina. The first shot went wide and the second narrowly missed her chest as she jumped behind a wall.

"Move now!" Verity said, dragging Laskaris up and pushing him for the door.

The pair ran across the room with Verity exchanging shots with Nina. Her bullets were slamming into the wall, keeping Nina behind cover.

Laskaris opened the door and ran out into the hallway as Verity's pistol ran dry.

Nina heard the click and sprang out, loosening off bullets in groupings of two. Two into the carpet, two into the wall. Verity ducked out of the room as two bullets followed her.

One hit the hallway wall. The other drove itself deep into Verity's thigh.

"Fuck!" Verity said as she fumbled for a new magazine and stumbled forward holding her leg.

Laskaris caught her and helped her walk towards the elevator, but then they both heard Nina laugh from behind them as she walked into the hallway.

"Stop where you are," Nina ordered, aiming the gun in their direction. "Elias, I am so disappointed in you. Bring the tablet to me and I might not kill you."

"No," Laskaris said shyly not looking up. "I will not help terrorists."

"We are not the terrorists. We are simply trying to right some wrongs."

"You are trying to start a war," Verity interjected, pulling Laskaris in behind her.

"Not a war. It will probably be a number of wars, but who knows, I guess it may turn into one big war over time. It does not matter. All that matters is that we succeed."

"You are insane."

"No, insanity is continuing to get in our way. We will win and you will die. So why try, when even your own country does not want you, former Agent Humphries."

"That is because your boss has bought Birmingham off, but he won't get away with this and neither will you."

"We will see about that," Nina said, pulling the trigger.

Laskaris flinched, but Verity sprung forward as fast as she could on her injured leg and tackled Nina.

Verity had been counting and she knew Nina's gun was out of bullets.

They hit the floor hard, and grappled and wrestled over the top of each other. Verity elbowed Nina in the mouth as she rolled on top, only for Nina to dig her thumb into Verity's bullet wound and use the pain and momentum to roll her over.

Nina started pummelling Verity, punch after punch aimed squarely at her face. Verity blocked most of the blows, but a few snuck through and landed. Verity waited for the moment, then punched Nina in the stomach, taking the wind out of her.

The elevator arrived and chimed behind them, and they both looked over to Laskaris.

"Go!" Verity yelled as Nina punched her again.

Verity struggled under Nina's constant assault. She was looking for an opening, anything, then she found her window. Nina's attack slowed slightly, giving her enough time to throw a hard jab up into her jaw. Her head flew back and as Verity started to pull herself out from under the bigger woman, Laskaris appeared at her side and slammed the tablet into Nina's face, sending her sprawling backwards. Nina hit the floor and moved only very slightly, very gingerly. She was dazed, semi-conscious, but she was fighting it, trying not to pass out.

"Come on," Laskaris said, helping Verity to her feet.

He looped her arm over his shoulder and they climbed into the lift and took it downstairs.

They made their way to the valet parking area and Verity stole a set of keys from the open storage box behind the concierge desk. She pressed the fob until a set of indicator lights flashed then passed Laskaris the keys.

"You're driving," Verity said, holding her leg and limping to the passenger side of the sleek Mercedes.

"I don't really drive," Laskaris said nervously.

"But you know how, right?"

"Yes."

"Good enough. Get in."

Laskaris was fumbling nervously looking for the ignition button when three bullets hit the windscreen. He screamed as Verity reached over hit the ignition button and yanked the shift into drive.

The car lurched forward and Verity grabbed Laskaris's closest hand and put it on the steering wheel.

"Drive or we both die!"

Laskaris spun the wheel and hit the accelerator.

He drove for the exit ramp as another two bullets thumped into the back of the expensive luxury sedan.

Laskaris pulled the car out on the Moscow street and hit the gas.

He was right, he was not a good driver, but they were free and clear. Now he needed to get Verity to the hotel before she bled out.

Chapter Twenty-Five

Before Max had left Verity, the two spies had spent quite a bit of time discussing their plans. They sat in the car and planned their attack.

Verity was going to make a play for the tablet. It was risky, but necessary. Andrew needed the tablet to stop the cyber-attack. Max wanted to go with her, given the seriousness of mission failure, but he had his own mission. Verity had tried to talk him out of it, but his mind was made up. All roads were leading to one place and he was not going to stop. He could not stop. The world was about to go to war and not only that, the West's entire intelligence and defence system was under attack. If the cyber-attack succeeded, they would be going to war blind.

Max knew he had to do whatever it took to try to stop that from happening and to try to stop the war, regardless of the personal cost.

They eventually agreed they needed to divide and conquer. So while Verity was going after Lyadova and the tablet, Max was going after the Russian President.

The Kremlin was one of the most recognisable and secure places in the world, easily rivalling the White House. Security was tight on a normal day, but Max knew it would be even more difficult given everything that was going on.

"You are suicidal," Andrew said over the phone. "Do you have a death wish?"

"Can you do it or not?" Max asked, cutting out the photo he had just taken of himself with a sharp pair of scissors, while holding the phone to his ear with his shoulder.

"Yes, but it will take a little while and you will need to send me the photo too."

"Done. You have thirty minutes."

"Thirty minutes isn't enough…" Andrew said as Max hung up the phone cutting him off.

Max gently glued the photo down on top of the FSS agent's ID he had taken from the bunker earlier. When he was satisfied, he ran the plastic card through the laminator and made sure the air pockets were pushed out. He then glued the embossed plastic protector back on over the top of the photo and ID. He memorised the card's details and practiced saying his assumed name over a couple of times.

Russian was not one of his favourite languages or his best, but he knew enough to hold a conversation and get by.

Max walked out of the office building and back into the street. He turned the collar up on his new coat and pulled the snood up over his nose. He took a long circuitous route through the Moscow streets, doubling back on himself to see if he was being followed. Occasionally, he stopped to look in a shopfront window to use the reflection to check if he was being watched, while feigning interest in whatever product was on display.

He was doing it for security reasons, but also to give Andrew time. Max had asked Andrew to hack into the FSS personnel database and alter the details of the agent whose ID he had taken at the server bunker. Andrew needed to upload Max's photo to replace the agent's and give the agent a promotion to help his movement throughout the building. He also asked Andrew to get him a meeting with a senior adviser to the President.

Max knew his photo was running in the media, but he had no other option, he needed to get in. He just hoped the security guards were not glued to the media. Given everything that was happening, he was hopeful they were too busy to have seen the papers or broadcasts. But, he had to admit, he wasn't feeling positive.

Max joined a long line at the staff entrance to the Kremlin and waited dutifully as if he had all the time in the world. When a man joined the queue behind him, Max knelt down to do up the laces on one of his boots. As he got back to his feet, he stumbled backwards into the man behind him.

Max apologised in Russian and gave the man a friendly pat on the shoulder to say thanks for catching him. The staffer was a bit confused, but just smiled and told Max not to worry about it.

Max turned back around and stepped forward with the line.

When it was his turn, he scanned his fake ID and walked through the metal detector.

Nothing. He had left most of his weapons in the car.

The security guard was checking the photo and looking back at Max's face, then he looked over to his comrade at the computer. It was still searching, but then the screen changed and Max was relieved to see his photo starring back from the screen. Andrew had come through for him.

The guard with his stolen ID was still cautiously eyeing him, as if he recognised him. He started to walk back over, still holding the ID and a questioning look on his face, when the metal detector alarms rang out behind Max, distracting him.

The guard tossed Max the ID and briskly walked towards the metal detector, completely forgetting Max.

Max turned to see the man in the queue behind him pull a Glock from his pocket. He was puzzled and shocked as he pulled the weapon out.

Instantly guards swarmed around him, drawing their own weapons and forcing him to drop the gun and hit the floor. The man was protesting that the gun wasn't his and that he understood the directions he was being given. He was shaking and incredibly nervous as the agents surrounded him and moved in.

Max smiled and walked away as the screen changed and his photo disappeared.

When he had dropped the gun in the man's pocket, after stumbling into him, he had hoped to buy some time and cause a distraction. It had worked better than he had hoped.

Max walked out of the security building and across the expansive grounds of the Kremlin. The buildings were simply stunning. The incredible architecture stretched up into the sky with their colourful peaks and spirals, and the bright red bricks. A number of the spires had large gold stars at their peaks. Other buildings were painted in a crisp white, with green roofs or golden domes and spires.

The footpaths between buildings had been cleared of snow, but the huge quadrangles were covered in a thick layer of white powder as were the more gently sloped rooftops.

Max walked with purpose towards the main administration building and flashed his badge at the door. Two guards opened the doors for him and saluted.

Inside the foyer a young nervous looking junior officer in a Russian Army uniform asked who he was there to meet and Max told him the name of one of the President's senior advisers. The young officer was clearly excited on hearing the name which meant Max had picked the right person. Senior enough for people to know him and get their attention, distracting them from him.

"I will call his office and get someone to come down," the young officer said in Russian.

"That's okay," Max replied. "What level is he on?"

"Level four, but I should really get someone to escort you."

"It is fine, son. I have been here many times and do not wish to waste their time. Thank you for your help."

"I will ring and let them know you are on your way."

"Thank you," Max said, not waiting around.

He found a set of stairs and bounced up them two and three at a time. He got to level four and instead of heading in, kept going up the stairs until he made it to the top floor. He opened the door into the short but opulent hallway leading to the President's office.

Dark wood panelling lined the lower half of the wall, with an off-white, almost grey paint at the top. Several paintings of former Russian leaders were framed in gaudy thick gold frames. The carpet was bright red with gold edges and every few metres a sculpture or potted plant sat lining the march down to the President's somewhat modest dark oak door.

There were two guards by the door on sentry duty. Max waved and greeted them like they were old friends.

"It is good to see you again," Max said, covering the distance between the stairs and the door quickly. "How is your wife?"

Both guards looked at each other, wondering who he was talking to, but before either replied Max had arrived and stood between the pair. They turned to face him and he smiled broadly.

The guard on the left went to speak, but before he uttered a word, Max threw a hard right jab into his jaw, knocking him out. The other guard was speechless for a second, until his training kicked in and he reached for his pistol. Max spun on his heel and caught his wrist. He pulled him forward and threw a violent headbutt, shattering his nose. As he fell back, Max pulled the gun from his hand and punched him in the broken nose, knocking him out.

Max opened the door to the outer office where he found the President's personal assistants. He pointed his gun at the three of them and held his finger to his lips. They all nodded their understanding, then he told them to get up and walk into the President's office.

The first assistant opened the door and they filed in after her with Max hidden at the rear.

The Russian's big office was lined with the same dark oak wood panels and greying paint. It also had the same bright red and gold trimmed carpet, and matching red and gold curtains with gold rope holding them in place. Behind his desk, the President had a huge painting of himself in full military attire in a thick gold frame.

"Ah, Annika," President Nicholai Sukhanov said, holding up a document, "this brief is not the one I wanted. Wait, what are you all doing?"

"I am sorry, sir," Annika said as she led the other two assistants to the side.

"What are you doing?" Sukhanov said, before sighting Max who had turned to barricade the door. "Who are you?"

Max pushed the door closed and stuck a chair under the doorhandle, wedging it shut, and flicked the latch to lock it. He pulled his snood down, letting Sukhanov see his face.

"You," Sukhanov said, standing and letting his large leather chair roll back against the sideboard. "You are in a lot of trouble, Agent Shaw. Breaking into the Kremlin is not a smart idea. I do hope you did not kill anyone on your way in here."

"Call it off!" Max demanded as he aimed his gun at the Russian leader.

"Call what off?"

"You know exactly what I am asking, Mister President. Call off the cyber-attack."

"You do not know what you are talking about, Max," Sukhanov said, taking his seat again at his large wooden desk and opening the draw.

Max fired a shot into the ornate desk only inches from the President's other hand.

"Put both hands where I can see them," Max ordered.

Sukhanov just sat there completely unfazed. His right hand was still in the draw. The pair stared each other down, waiting for the other to blink.

There was a knock at the door and Max stole a quick look behind himself to make sure the door was still closed.

Sukhanov pulled his hand back out of the draw and Max turned back to see him wielding an MP-443 Grach or Pistolet Yarygina – a Russian service pistol the troops called PYa. He fired a shot as Max was turning back to face the world leader.

Max turned just enough for the bullet to only graze his arm. The Russian President fired a second shot as Max started to bring his own gun back up. The bullet hit the weapon and it dropped from Max's hand onto the red carpet.

"If I wanted to kill you, Agent Shaw, I would not have missed with either bullet," Sukhanov said, aiming the pistol at Max's face. "As I am sure you are aware, I was in the KGB for many years and the military before that. I keep my weapons training up to date. Do you understand me?"

"Yes," Max said, looking at the graze on his arm and pressing it gently with this other hand.

"Things are not always as they seem, but I am afraid certain actions may force my hands."

"What do you mean?"

"I am not responsible for the cyber-attack."

"Then someone in your government is helping Lyadova. Everything I have heard and seen and experienced over the last few days has led me to you and the Russian Government."

"It is true I helped A&A Enterprises to build their supercomputer and to store their systems in Russia, but I can assure you, I had no knowledge of this attack. We suffered for years in the cold, during a war which devastated my country and left a lasting scar. I do not want history to repeat itself. I have no intention of going to war with the west, because all that would be assured is our mutual destruction."

"How do I know you aren't lying to me now?"

"You are unarmed standing in the Kremlin with a gun pointed at your head. Your death would take but a split second. Why would I lie to you? I have nothing to gain from such deception."

"We encountered some FSS guards at one of the server rooms. What were they doing there?"

"One of my generals tried to take a couple of the server sites, to give himself command of the system, but A&A was too prepared. They took control of one of our new drones and threatened to level several suburbs in downtown Moscow, unless I got the general to back down. In all honesty, he did not send enough men anyway, he would never have taken the centres."

"Can you get control of the drone back and reorder your military into the A&A servers and destroy them, and takedown Lyadova?"

"It is not that simple, Agent Shaw," Sukhanov explained, turning his computer monitor around.

Max saw the red flashing box on the President's computer monitor. It had a countdown timer with only hours remaining on the clock. He looked from the screen to Sukhanov's now sullen face.

"In only a few hours the entire Russian military and intelligence systems will be exposed," Sukhanov said. "The West is not the only place A&A is attacking. Every spare agent and soldier are preparing for war. We don't think we can regain control of A&A, so we need to prepare for the bigger battle, while our systems are still up and allow it."

"So why are you telling me all this?" Max asked.

"I need to understand what you have told your country and your allies."

Max just looked at the President without saying a word.

"I know the Americans and their allies, including your own country, are rallying their troops," Sukhanov said. "Within hours, the first strikes of a very hot war will be taken and when they are there will be no stopping retaliation. Even I have limits on how much I can control my generals and military. Blood will mean blood. An eye for an eye. If they believe, as I suspect, that we are behind the attack, they will come for us with everything they have."

"They will," Max agreed.

"Mister President?" a male voice asked over the intercom. "Is everything okay? We cannot open the door."

Sukhanov pressed the intercom as Max's heart skipped a beat. Spending the rest of his life in a Russian prison would be hell on earth. That is, of course, until the war started and left nothing but complete and utter devastation in its wake.

"I am fine," Sukhanov said. "Tell your men to stand down."

"We heard gunshots," the agent said.

"Everything is under control, Captain," Sukhanov said, walking over and opening the door. "Stand down."

"Yes, Mister President," the agent said after looking Max up and down, but when he saw the President had a gun in his hand he saluted and turned from the door.

Sukhanov shut the door.

"We have only minutes before they do a full breach on this office," Sukhanov explained. "If they get hold of you, word will spread and your forced entrance will be seen as the first shot of the war. I can hold them back for a while, but as I said I cannot stop the train once it leaves the station. You need to escape unseen."

"You're letting me go?" Max asked, surprised and honestly disappointed in himself, given what the President had said about his actions potentially starting the war.

"I believe that you had good intentions in coming here, to try to stop a war. It does not escape me the courage it took to do what you did. You had to know you would be coming to your death, but I can only assume you thought the cause worthwhile. I trust that your skills and that same desire to stop any needless bloodshed will help do what needs to be done."

"What would you have me do, sir?"

"You were right to suggest that there may be forces within my government seeking to bring about war with the west. They think I am trying to change the country and reform it, and they are right, but they do not wish for change. They have spent their lives looking at ways to get retribution and vengeance on the West for the Cold War. I cannot afford to look weak in the face of western aggression in the eyes of these men, but they also cannot be allowed to start an unprovoked war. I need you to find them and stop them."

"You want me to kill senior Russian officials and military officers?"

"Yes."

"Why don't you just have these men arrested?"

"As I said, Max, Russia is not Australia. I cannot be seen to be undermining my generals or seen to be weak. Having a foreign agent take the men out gives me plausible deniability. I want to reform Russia and open it to the world, but there are many people who lived through the Cold War who have long memories and still believe the West is our enemy. I am not one of them.”

“But you could put an end to Lyadova’s program and these generals with a phone call.”

“Again, it does not work like that. My military know your countries are moving into position, they will think I am backing down and will just take matters into their own hands. If I look like I am hesitating or putting the Russian military in harm’s way, there will be a coup.”

“So, you expect me to find these people, kill them, then find Lyadova and stop her.”

“Yes, and I need you to call off the Americans and their allies. Once they back down, I can deescalate and get my troops to turn around.”

“What assurances can you give me that you will also stand down your troops when the allies do?”

“There is nothing but my word.”

Max starred at the President. He had no choice, but to take him at his word. After years of hunting people and using any means necessary to get the truth from them, he wasn’t sure what to make of what he’d just heard.

“I will do what I can,” Max said finally.

“As will I, you have my word,” Sukhanov said, handing Max his pistol as a sign of trust. “I do not want war, Max, but if it comes to us, I will fight it like no war has been fought before.”

“I understand. You have my word I will do whatever I can.”

“The man you are looking for is General Sacha Kuznetsov.”

“The head of the Strategic Missile Force?”

“Yes. You know him?”

“I’ve heard of him. Where is he?”

“Tagansky Protected Command Point.”

“I thought that was a tourist attraction? A relic of the Cold War.”

“Not exactly.”

"What does that mean?"

"The old bunker was sixty-five metres underground and used to host a communications and anti-missile defence centre. The new bunker is much bigger and much deeper; we built it under the old site and kept it secret, a bit like your supposedly hidden AIS facility at the military college in Canberra."

"Fair enough," Max said, raising an eyebrow at the mention of AIS's apparently not so secret headquarters. "How do I get in?"

"Take this," the Russian President said, passing Max an access card. "This will open the door. You are going to need to do the rest, but I am sure you will manage."

"I will see what I can do," Max said, wondering for a moment if he should try again to convince the Russian to just arrest Kuznetsov, but thought better of it knowing he had made up his mind.

"Good. Thank you, Max," Sukhanov said, shaking Max's hand, before opening a secret panel in the wall exposing a hidden elevator. "You have three hours."

"Three? The timer says four."

"At three, I am going to hit the kill switch, but if it gets to that stage war will be inevitable."

"The kill switch?"

"Yes."

"I thought it was just a myth?"

"It is not."

Max stood for a moment considering what he had just been told. The kill switch was real.

"You need to go now," Sukhanov said. "Take this down to the basement. When you get there, I will have a man waiting for you. He will take you wherever you need to go."

"Thank you, Mister President," Max said nodding.

"Remember if you are caught, I will deny this conversation ever happened. You will be treated as a foreign operative and tried, no doubt tortured and thrown in a hole somewhere for the world to forget. Russia has not forgotten your previous missions here, let alone what you might do here today. I am sorry I cannot be more helpful, but my hands are tied. If you can get to Lyadova and Kuznetsov, I will be able to turn our ships around and stop our defence build up, but if you fail or the Americans shoot first, I will have no choice but to respond in kind."

"I understand, sir. I will get a message to AIS."

"Thank you," Sukhanov said, stopping himself on seeing Max's expression. "What is it?"

"I know this isn't really the time, but can I ask why you had the men jump me in the prison in The Hague?"

"I didn't, Max. They may be Russian, but it did not have anything to do with me. Kuznetsov sent them."

"Okay," Max said, nodding and thinking about that as the elevator arrived.

Max stepped into the elevator and the doors shut behind him, before he felt it sink into the earth. He wasn't sure who would be waiting for him in the basement. It could be a man to take him wherever he wanted, as promised, or it could be a dozen men with a black bag ready to move him to a prison where no one would ever find him.

He couldn't help but believe the Russian President. He knew Sukhanov was a reformer and knew that any change would take years, especially after the last President finally left office, but to sign off on the torture and assassination of one of his own top generals by a foreign agent meant the Russian was in more trouble than he let on. Let alone to confirm the kill switch was real. Max knew that was the Russian President's way of showing Max he was on his side. The West had spent decades trying to find out if the kill switch was real. The President was a former KGB agent though, anything was possible. He guessed he see whose side the President was really on when the elevator doors opened.

Max knew that his message would have gotten to AIS and the Americans by now which meant they too thought Russia had some involvement in the cyber-attack and the western allies would be preparing for war. He needed to get a message to Blake to let him know what Sukhanov had told him, including that the Russians were getting attacked too.

Max felt guilty. How could he have made such a massive error of judgment? He blamed the Russians, now the world was heading to war. He felt the failure and fear wash over him.

At the bottom of the elevator shaft the doors opened and Max stepped out to find a seriously tough looking older man. Without doubt, Max knew he was a former solider and most likely a spy, seasoned and well versed in the dark arts of covert operations. He reminded Max of his mentor Hulk, not so much in looks but in the overall gruff mood and demeanour.

He just nodded towards his car and walked off in that direction. Max followed and climbed into the passenger seat next to the Russian.

"I have been told to take you to Tangansky," he said. "You will be able to buy a ticket like a normal tourist, but getting any further will be challenging."

"Any suggestions?" Max asked.

"Depends."

"On what?"

"On whether you mind getting a bit wet," the Russian said with a sly smile.

Chapter Twenty-Six

As directed, Laskaris drove in circles around the old city until Verity was sure they were no longer being followed. She then gave him the directions to the hotel where Andrew and Gabriel were bunkered in.

He helped her out of the car and they walked the remaining few blocks to the motel.

"Sacrebleu," Gabriel exclaimed when he saw the wound in Verity's thigh. "What happened?"

"That bitch, Nina," Verity said. "Got a shot off when my mag ran empty."

"Andrew, go to the bathroom and get some towels and the med-kit."

Andrew got to his feet begrudgingly and went to fetch the supplies.

"And who is this young man?" Gabriel asked, looking Laskaris up and down.

"This is Elias Laskaris," Verity explained. "Lyadova's personal assistant."

"And how did he come to be chaperoning you?"

"He's not a bad kid, just in the wrong place at the wrong time. Max and I met him in France and Max promised to get him out. I saw the opportunity to make good on it."

"And Nina?"

"Still breathing, for now. So is her boss. But we got the computer."

Verity looked to Laskaris who nervously held up the tablet. Andrew re-entered the room and quickly passed the med-kit and towels to Gabriel, and reached for the tablet, almost fixated on it.

"I will be in the other room" Andrew said, without taking his eyes off the tablet.

"I am fine by the way," Verity said.

"Oh good, I'm glad to hear that," Andrew said only half listening and occasionally looking up from the tablet.

"Partir!" Gabriel snapped with a wave of his hand, telling Andrew to go away, which he did. "Unbelievable!"

"It's okay, Gabriel," Verity said. "I won't take it personally."

"He is a pig," Gabriel said, pulling a face in disgust. "Anyway, let us get you patched up."

"Thank you," Verity said, climbing onto the table. "Where is Alexei?

"Back in the bathroom. Tied to the chair again."

"Is he patched up?"

"Yes. Luckily for you, I got extra supplies while I was out."

"Yeah, thank you."

"Let's see what we have here," Gabriel said, going to work on Verity's leg.

"Did you guys do something to the modem?" Andrew yelled from the other room.

Gabriel swore under his breath and rolled his eyes as walked to the bathroom to clean up.

"No," Verity yelled back. "Why?"

"The wi-fi has gone out and the mobile service has too," Andrew said, wandering in. "I got cut off and can't get any internet."

"What happens if it doesn't come back on soon?"

"It means we will need to get to a dedicated communications tower or satellite relay station to try to get to the servers."

"What about the tablet?"

"It needs to connect to the system. Can't do that without the net. Unless you get it to a few metres from the A&A servers.

"Lyadova?"

"Could be. Part of the plan was always to hack into the telecommunications companies and take control of them.

Could also be our countries making a pre-emptive strike on Russia."

"And we are cut off from them and can't find out either way?"

"That's correct. So, what do we do now?"

"We need to mend Verity's leg before we do anything," Gabriel said, walking back into the room. "I need to give you a sedative to numb the pain."

"Okay, but not too much," Verity said. "I need to stay lucid."

Gabriel went to work, directing Laskaris as his new medical assistant. He injected some pain relief at the site of the wound and Verity gritted her teeth. He used a small set of medical plyers to hunt for, then remove, the bullet.

Whether it was pain or relief, Gabriel wasn't sure, but either way Verity passed out on the table.

Gabriel stitched up her wounds and bandaged her thigh, letting her sleep while he tidied up. The bullet had missed all the vital arteries and he suspected she would make a full recovery in time.

Gabriel was washing the towels in the bathtub when he heard a thud in the main room.

"Everything okay out there?" Gabriel asked over his shoulder.

There was no reply, so he washed his hands and turned off the water. He stood and picked up a clean towel to dry his hands.

"What is going on?" Gabriel asked as he walked out of the bathroom.

He saw Laskaris unconscious on the floor, then quickly turned his attention to Verity who had been sleeping on the table. Andrew had a pillow pressed tightly over her face, smothering her.

Gabriel ran forward and while he was not as fast as he used to be when he had worked missions with Max, he covered the few metres in no time and shoulder charged Andrew.

Andrew let go of the pillow and took the full impact in the sternum and bounced into the wall.

"What the fuck are you doing?" Gabriel asked. "You are still working for Lyadova."

"I never stopped working for her," Andrew said. "When I found out Max was in The Hague I knew I could finally get my retribution for what he did to me and I knew I had found someone we could pin all of this on."

"You are an idiot. Max has some very powerful friends and there is no way they will believe anything you and that bitch try to spin."

"You may not have noticed, but the world we currently know is about to go to war, forever changing it. A&A will own all the secrets and have all the codes. Lyadova is basically privatising global government."

"Others have tried to take over the world and they had whole armies working for them and could not do it. She will fail too."

"This isn't the story of Alexander the Great or even Hitler, old man, wars aren't fought on the beaches anymore. Although we'll have the Russians to do that if we need them. Information is key and soon we will have it all. And when we do, we will tell everyone Max was behind it and rewrite history as we see fit."

"Max will find a way to stop you and when he stands over your dying fat arse, know you have lost and I will be smiling."

"No, you will be dead," Andrew said, lunging forward.

Gabriel stepped to the side and punched the bigger man in the face as he went by. Andrew turned around unfazed and lunged again. Gabriel repeated his sidestep, but this time to the other side, and punched Andrew again.

On the third attempt, Andrew read the step and tackled Gabriel to the floor. The pair grappled and traded blows as Verity started to stir. Gabriel was clearly the more skilled fighter, but Andrew was twice his weight and size, and he was starting to dominate. Gabriel's training kicked in and he looked around for a weapon. He reached up and pulled the drawer out of the bedside table with all his remaining strength and slammed it into the side of Andrew's face. It was enough to loosen Andrew's grip and Gabriel capitalised with a hard knee to the balls.

Andrew rolled to the side as Gabriel tried to recover. He scrambled on all fours towards the side table where Verity's pistol was sitting. Andrew saw the gun and pushed through the pain to get to his feet.

The pair arrived at the pistol at the same time. Gabriel grabbed the handle and spun the gun towards Andrew, but Andrew held the old man's wrist and dragged it away as Gabriel fired a shot.

It missed Andrew and lodged in the wall between the motel rooms.

They wrestled against the wall and the table, where Verity was coming to, trying to take control of the gun. Gabriel elbowed Andrew in the face, knocking him back and then pulled the trigger. The bullet sliced through Andrew's side, just below his ribs. He was a big guy and the bullet had easily missed the vital organs, but it got his attention. He grabbed the pistol with both hands and started to overpower Gabriel.

Verity rocked to the side as the pair ran into the table and she woke.

Within a few seconds, Verity had an idea of what was happening and wrapped her hands around Andrew's throat trying to strangle him, but she couldn't get a good hold. She rolled off the bed, wrapping her arm around his neck and locking it into her other arm. One of her feet bounced on the ground as she dangled from his neck, not wanting to put too much weight on her injured leg. Andrew was starting to choke and she knew she had a good lock on him, but he was fighting for his life and had not let go of the pistol.

Gabriel tripped and fell back into one of the bedside tables, and Andrew took his chance. He raised his leg and stomped down on the old man's leg. Gabriel had been half sitting on the bedside table still holding the pistol, his legs awkwardly out in front of him.

Andrew's blow was devastating. Gabriel's knee cracked and his leg bent at an unnatural angle. He screamed out in pain, but before he even hit the ground, Andrew fired two shots into the old man's chest.

Gabriel sank to the floor with blood dripping from the corners of his mouth and pumping out of the holes in his chest.

His eyes were wide and the life was gone from them.

Andrew turned the gun around and pressed it up under Verity's ribs.

"Let go," Andrew ordered, "or I will put a bullet in you too."

"You son of a bitch, you won't get away with this," Verity said, letting go of him and stepping back. "Whatever you think is going to happen, won't. Max will find you and kill you, especially when he finds out you killed Gabriel."

"I think the aging Prince will have bigger problems. There is no way he will be able to pull off his next mission. They will black bag him on sight and then they will torture him to death."

"Then someone else will stop you. You cannot win."

"Unlikely. Before the internet and phones stopped working Max sent me a message. The Russians aren't to blame, we just made it look like they were. Max spoke to Sukhanov and the President gave him safe passage out of the Kremlin. He has got to take down a couple of rogue generals and officers to try to stop the Russian military launching a pre-emptive strike on the West. But I didn't send the message on. Blake doesn't know. AIS and the Americans, and what's left of your own MI6 still think the Russians are responsible and by now they are preparing for war. You see, the world will be too busy fighting each other to come for us. And, my old friend, Max Shaw, will be buried in a hole somewhere and forgotten, or maybe they will just shoot him on sight."

"You arsehole, you have been feeding Lyadova information and withholding it from the allies. That's how Nina knew I was coming wasn't it? You told her! And now you are starting World War III!"

"Yeah, but I will be fine. I must say though I was surprised Nina didn't kill you, but she will."

"First chance I get, I am going to kill both of you. You should put a bullet in me too, because it will be the only way you get to live. You betrayed us. You betrayed your country. You are a selfish son of a bitch and I hope I am there when Max finds you. If there is anything that he hates, it is traitors! And he is going to make you suffer."

"Shut up!" Andrew yelled, whipping the pistol across her face.

Verity stumbled back against the makeshift operating table.

Andrew kept the gun aimed at her while he found the cable ties Max always had in his supply bag. He threw them to Verity and made her flexicuff herself, while she starred at him with nothing but hate and contempt. When she was cuffed, Andrew kicked Laskaris in the ribs, then pushed him over with a hard kick to the shoulder.

"Wake up," Andrew said as Laskaris started to cough and come to.

"What, what happened?" Laskaris asked, rubbing his head.

"I knocked you out. Now get up, I need you to drive."

Chapter Twenty-Seven

"Well, Mister President, I just do not think I can make the deal at that number," Lyadova said down the camera of her videocall. "I am going to need at least another five billion."

"But, Miss Lyadova, we are only a small nation," the male voice replied with a heavy African accent. "We do not have that sort of money laying around."

"Mister President, with all due respect, you and I both know your country has been holding onto stockpiles of conflict and other rare diamonds. If you want access to your enemy's files you need to get me the money."

"I will try to get the money."

"You have one hour, Mister President, before I make the same offer to your opponents and I think they will happily pay for your secrets."

"You would not dare."

"Make it thirty minutes," Lyadova said, ending the call.

"The North Korean chairman is on the line," Nina said, handing Lyadova the phone.

"Mister Chairman," Lyadova said before listening intently.

Nina tapped her stylus on her tablet, impatiently waiting for details. She saw her boss's eyes widen and she grinned.

"That is a generous offer," Lyadova said. "How can I be sure you can make the payment?"

She listened again for a minute before pointing to the tablet in Nina's hand. Nina unlocked it and opened the appropriate app, then spun it to face her boss.

"I see the money is in the account," Lyadova said. "In return, as promised, I will send you the details of all American assets in South Korea, including their secret operations base in Seoul, plus the placements of their missile storages. When you transfer the second half of the payment, I will fire three missiles from the South Korean military at the designated buildings you put forward. The missiles will be your call to action and you will be able to strike back, first taking out the US stores."

Lyadova listened again as the North Korean dictator spoke and she nodded along.

"I can assure you," Lyadova said, "I have not made the offer to sell your secrets to the South. They have a do not negotiate policy, like the Americans, so they will get what is coming to them when you attack.

"For a modest monthly fee, Mister Chairman, yes I can happily house your sensitive information and ensure nothing like this ever happens again," Lyadova said before pausing again to listen. "Yes, sir, I imagine if you win the coming war with the South, you could pretty much afford anything I put forward.

"Yes, you are correct, you will win with the information I provide," Lyadova said. "I can assure you it is worth the investment. I would also be happy to put together a package on Japan for you, if you are interested?"

The pause this time was longer as the dictator considered his options.

"Yes, of course," Lyadova finally said, breaking the silence. "It isn't if, but when, the information turns out to be correct and helps you secure victory, I will happily walk you through the second package. Thank you, Mister Chairman."

Lyadova ended the call and sat her phone of the table.

"Give me a status report," Lyadova commanded. "When will we have full control?"

"Apollo has worked his way into every system on the planet," Nina said, "and in about four hours we will have control of the Russian defence system and you can launch the attack."

"What about the Americans?"

"The program is being blocked and countered, but it will eventually overcome them. It is learning their every move and it is just a matter of time."

"And they think it is the Russians?"

"Yes, I heard from Andrew. He has blocked the messages from the AIS team on the ground and passed on only what we wanted them to hear. They are preparing for all out war. As are the Russians."

"Good. Andrew played his part. I wasn't sure he had it in him."

"Me either. Have you given any thought to the fact we might be about to start World War III?"

"I have, but all that matters is that the Americans and their allies take out the Russians or at the very least the Russians are blamed for everything."

The phone on the table rang and Nina answered. She listened for a moment then passed the phone to Lyadova.

"General Sacha Kuznetsov," Nina said, handing over the mobile.

"Hello, General," Lyadova said, "how are your plans coming?"

"We are about to take out the first two targets," Kuznetsov said. *"Both CIA in downtown Moscow."*

"It will be public?"

"Very."

"And then?"

"We have four targets in St. Petersburg. They will be very public too."

"Good. And the President?"

"He is soft. Sitting in his office, hoping the cyber teams can stop the hack and that the Americans walk away."

"So you do not think he will launch a pre-emptive attack?"

"I do not think so, which is why I am going to give the order myself. Following the CIA agent takedown."

"Thank you, Sacha."

"The West will finally meet its match and we will return Mother Russia to her rightful place as the world superpower."

"God willing. Good luck, my friend. Keep me informed of your progress."

"I will," Kuznetsov said, ending the call.

Lyadova smiled broadly. Her plans where finally coming together and the world was about to change forever.

Chapter Twenty-Eight

Three CIA agents and one AIS agent had been held up in a safehouse for weeks in St. Petersburg. They had been watching a Russian intelligence operative they suspected was buying and selling secrets. They had suspicions that a New Zealand based intelligence agent was selling him Five Eyes secrets and were hoping to catch him in the act before putting them both out of action.

Their room was full of recording equipment and paperwork, as well as empty bottles and food containers, and the general stink of four men in close quarters for an extended period of time.

The four spies were frantically dismantling equipment and trying to send off intelligence reports, but the internet was not working and their satellite phones and modems were having intermittent failures. The Australian was shredding paper and had started a fire in the bathtub to burn photos, USBs and CDs they had gathered over recent weeks.

The door of their apartment exploded into hundreds of pieces. Two of the CIA agents opened fire on the open doorway as the remaining CIA and AIS agents kept trying to send the files and burn intelligence in the bath, respectively.

A flashbang grenade lobbed into the room and exploded in a bright white light with a deafening sound. The two shooters emptied their clips into the open doorway, blind, disorientated and in pain from the blast.

When their weapons clicked dry, a Russian special forces team swarmed into the room. The first three soldiers riddled the two American agents with bullets.

One of the soldiers fired a single bullet into the face of the CIA man at the computer trying to upload their files to Langley. His head flew back as his blood and brain matter splattered on the wall behind him.

The Russians moved quickly through the apartment and found the locked bathroom door. The lead solider kicked the door in and was met with two bullets from the AIS agent's pistol.

He fell back into the hallway.

The next two soldiers didn't stop to check their fallen comrade, they knew he was dead. They flicked their rifles to fully automatic then both men aimed around the doorframe and emptied their guns randomly into the bathroom.

A cameraman who had been filming the whole event walked into the bathroom to find the AIS agent bleeding heavily from various holes in his chest and from the mouth. He smiled as the cameraman and soldiers entered the small, tiled room, then dropped his lit match into a small jerrycan of fuel he had been using to burn the documents and IT equipment.

The can exploded showering the whole room with burning petrol and fragments of the metal jerrycan. The cameraman and the team behind him dropped to the floor, rolling to try to put out the flames.

While this was occurring in St. Petersburg, a black sedan raced through downtown Moscow. It was being pursued by three Moscow police cars with their sirens blaring and lights flashing, and two black SUVs with dark tinted windows.

The snow and ice on the roads meant the powerful cars were skidding and losing traction on tight turns, giving the cars time to catch up with each other. When they got close enough, the passengers in the black SUVs would open fire on the sedan and the passengers in the sedan retaliated.

People in the streets ran and ducked into alleys and shops for cover. They screamed and tripped over each other trying to evade the incoming bullets.

The odd bullet went astray and hit other cars or pedestrians and the carnage they were leaving in their wake was catastrophic.

It was not long before local news helicopters were on the scene following the chase and reporters were in the streets interviewing witnesses.

One of the black SUVs rear-ended the black sedan and it spun out on the icy road. It did two full revolutions before both SUVs slammed into its passenger side and drove it up over the walkway. Its wheels hit the gutter and flipped it onto its side.

The big SUVs mounted the curb and slammed into the bottom of the car flipping it onto its roof, then they smashed into the driver's side of the car which was now facing them.

They pushed the sedan through a chain link fence to the crest of a small slope. The SUVs stopped as the sedan slid away from them on its roof down an icy slope towards the frozen Moskva River.

The sedan slid out onto the ice and spun on its roof. The two men inside climbed out on the far side as it came to a stop and drew their weapons.

At the same time, eight men in full military fatigues climbed out of the SUVs and drew their own assault rifles.

The two men behind the sedan opened fire as the eight men on the hill started firing. The bullets hit the sedan's now exposed bottom and riddled it with holes. Fuel started pouring out onto the snow-covered ice.

The two men smelt the petrol and oil, and started to run.

The first man was hit in the back with bullets from the military attackers, mowing him down in the path of his colleague. The second man looked up at the news helicopter just before the sedan exploded in a huge fireball. The force knocked him off his feet and shattered the ice. The concussive wave knocked him off his feet and shrapnel tore into his body.

Moments later the twisted frame of the burning sedan and the bodies of both men fell into the river and sank out of view.

Chapter Twenty-Nine

Tagansky Protected Command Point was a Soviet-era missile bunker which had been converted into a restaurant and family entertainment centre. It housed a laser tag arena, conference centre and Cold War Museum, all open to the public as a popular tourist destination.

The original bunker was sixty-five metres deep and covered around seven thousand square metres. From the outside, the entrance was disgusted as a plain old building in a non-descript Moscow street.

According to the Russian spy who dropped Max off, Tagansky was still an operational facility. A double bluff. A secret facility which was supposedly closed after it became known to the public and now open to the public as a tourist attraction, but it was in fact still a highly secret military facility hiding in plain sight like the days of old. The difference being that the new facility was a hundred metres deep and covered approximately fourteen thousand square metres.

The base was under the command of General Sacha Kuznetsov, the head of the Russian Strategic Missile Force, and former KGB operative who was the rising leader of the anti-President Sukhanov brigade. Kuznetsov thought Sukhanov was too soft and too willing to make peace and be friends with their former enemies. He was a zealot with wildly anti-west rhetoric, but he was too powerful for Sukhanov to remove from office. For now anyway. And, he had control of the Russian military's missile arsenal.

Max swam under the frozen ice sheet on the Moskva River. His thermal wetsuit was working hard to keep out the cold as he approached the intake from the river for Tagansky.

A relatively new metal grate was fixed to a concrete frame in the riverbed.

Max pulled out a small mobile underwater oxy acetylene torch and began cutting the metal beams on the grate.

Eventually he was able to pry the grate from concrete and he let it fall to the bottom of the river. He discarded his oxy torch too, letting it float down gently to the thick sentiment on the river floor.

Max swam into the intake which declined at around thirty degrees. His rebreather scuba gear only just fit through the tunnel with his big frame. He held a small flashlight out in front of himself to see where he was going, not that there was much to see.

After around one hundred and twenty metres, Max reached a section of the tunnel which plateaued and ran horizontally. He had been told by his Russian escort that about twenty metres along the tunnel there was an access port he could use to enter Tagansky.

At the far end, the tunnel divided into two separate sections, one for the IT cooling systems and one for the drinking water filtration systems of the base.

Max was moving slowly through the last twenty metres of his swim, not wanting to miss the port, given he couldn't turn around in the tight tunnel and because he knew he would not fit in either tunnel further along.

All of which meant death and he could not think of a worse death than drowning, other than drowning and failing his mission at the same time.

Max saw the opening for the port approaching. He was expecting a round gate-like door in the side of the tunnel, but instead found a small tunnel cut out of the roof and leading up about four metres to a door with a large round handle, like a steering wheel.

Max reached up into the tunnel to hold himself in place. He felt the push and pull of the water in the tunnel, which was stronger here then he had felt on the descent, presumably from the pull of the pumps ahead of him. He tried to enter the vertical tunnel, but his scuba gear was holding him back. He realised he couldn't get to the door with it on.

Max looked up and assessed the situation. It would only take a few seconds to reach the door, but opening it could be tricky. If he needed to use a lot of force, it would deplete his oxygen levels fast.

He had no choice, this was a one way ride. He took the oxygen tank off, keeping hold of the mouthpiece as he moved into the vertical section. He was in a sitting position with his legs facing back in the direction he he had come from and his head towards the port hole above him. The scuba tank was resting on his legs, the cord was taut.

He took a moment to calm himself and slow his breathing, then dropped the mouthpiece and struggled into the vertical shaft. It was just wide enough from him to get in.

As he pushed up from the tunnel floor, he felt the oxygen tank wash away towards the tunnel divide at the far end.

No turning back now.

Max kicked with his big flippers up to the port hole, hoping he would be able to turn it, especially now he didn't have his tank.

When he reached the big wheel locking the tunnel, his worst fears were realised, as he tried to turn the wheel.

It didn't budge.

He felt the panic rising slightly as he pulled on the wheel willing it to turn, but it stubbornly held its position.

Max got his torch and wedged it into the crossbar of the wheel and used it to lever against the door itself. He could feel his lungs starting to burn as he pushed with all his might, against the torch. His brain was screaming for him to take a breath and he knew if the door didn't open soon, his body would make the decision for him and involuntarily take a breath.

Max pushed hard on the torch. It bent then shattered, casting him into complete darkness. He felt the broken pieces of torch fall through his fingers and the batteries fell out and dropped away into the darkness beneath him.

Now he was starting to panic.

After everything he had been through, the gunfights, the knife fights, the car chases and the countless bombs and the hand to hand combat battles he had been in, he was going to take a full breath of the Moskva River and drown.

Mission failed.

His mind turned to Blake and the pain he felt in knowing he wouldn't hold him again.

It was the motivation he needed. He didn't want to die like this and he wanted nothing more than to be with Blake.

He pushed his back hard against the wall and used both his hands to push against the wheel. He put his knees into the opposite wall for leverage and pushed as his body was starting to convulse, screaming for air.

Then it turned.

An inch.

Max dug in and used the last of his strength to push the wheel and it spun. He quickly unwound it and thrust the metal hatch open.

He used the wheel to drag himself up into the maintenance room of the new Tagansky Protected Command Point bunker.

He pulled himself up over the lip of the shaft, out of the water and rolled onto the floor, sucking in deep breaths to recover.

As he lay on the floor, a maintenance worker approached with a worried expression on his face.

Max waited until he was close enough, then kicked his legs out from under him. As he fell, Max grabbed his head and slammed it into the wall, knocking him out.

Max got to his feet, kicked off his flippers and slid out of his wetsuit, before undressing the maintenance man and donning his clothes.

As he stood over the unconscious man, a Russian solider walked into the room.

"What is going on here?" he asked in Russian.

"Come quickly," Max replied in Russian.

"The alarm said the port was open. Who is he?"

Max spun around when the solider was within arm's reach and grabbed him by the shoulders, then kneed him in the nuts. The solider buckled over and Max slammed his head into the porthole lid he had used only minutes ago. The solider was still, just conscious, so Max repeated the move, slamming his face into the hard metal. The door closed as the soldier fell to the floor.

Max dragged both men into a nearby storage room and tied them up using an old extension cord, then left the room.

He grabbed his silenced pistol and holstered it under the maintenance man's jacket, then got a clipboard and left the maintenance area.

He walked purposefully through the modern facility, following the directions he had been given, towards Kuznetsov's office.

The facility was an underground labyrinth of tunnels and rooms, all painted in a very military grey.

On each corner street signs were painted on the walls pointing towards the various meeting rooms and storage units.

On one corner, Max was alarmed to find a sign for missile storage. It seemed the Russians were in fact not only using it as a command centre, but also as a missile silo. Kuznetsov had an arsenal and was willing to use it.

He kept walking towards Kuznetsov's office, until he found the door to the outer office. Max knocked and entered, and a young solider greeted him.

Max drew his silenced pistol and pointed it at the young man, who was probably all of eighteen years old.

"Is he in there?" Max asked.

"No," the young solider said, raising his hands in fear.

"Where is he?"

Before he could answer, the door opened behind Max. Max stepped to the side, using the door to cover himself. An older man walked into the room, reading a note.

"Oleg, I need to you to get this message to the general," the man said, looking up for the first time to the younger man. "What are you doing?"

"I," the younger man, Oleg, stammered as he held his hands in the air.

Max stepped out from behind the door and shot the newcomer in the back of the neck, causing Oleg to flinch. The older man turned to face Max as he pulled the small dart from his neck and looked at it, before he passed out.

"Where is Kuznetsov?" Max asked, aiming the pistol back at Oleg. "Oleg, isn't it? I don't want to hurt you, but I will if I have to."

"Control room, Alpha," Oleg said.

"Where is that?"

"Right, then second left," he said using his hands to point.

"Thanks," Max said. "Now, come drag him into the office."

Oleg did as he was asked and dragged the unconscious officer into Kuznetsov's office. Max told him to tie him up, which he dutifully did.

"What happens now?" Oleg asked.

"I'm going to find Kuznetsov while you have a nap," Max said, raising the pistol and firing the sleeping dart into the young man's neck.

Oleg grabbed at the dart as his eyes rolled into the back of his head and he fell to the floor. Max tied him up next to his comrade, sitting his pistol on the desk, then searched the nearby cupboard.

As expected, Max found a clean spare uniform of Kuznetsov's in his cupboard. He got into the uniform, holstered the pistol, then left the room.

He marched quickly through the corridors, like he owned the place. Younger officers and junior soldiers stopped and saluted him as he walked. He returned the salutes, not stopping to give them a chance to look at him twice. They were all well trained; they saw and respected the rank of general on his uniform, not looking at the name badge.

Max walked into the command room to find five soldiers, including Kuznetsov. They were all facing a large screen on the wall and Kuznetsov was barking orders to a group of soldiers on the other end of the videoconference.

Max locked the door behind him and picked up a hardback operations manual which was sitting on a nearby desk.

He walked up behind the man closest to him and hit him hard in the base of the skull with the manual. The officer fell to the ground, as Max lunged for the second man, who was turning to see what happened, when the hard spined book slammed into his temple knocking him out.

Max threw the book. It spun lengthways through the air and collided with the webcam, knocking it off its stand.

Max fired the pistol twice as the three men all watched the book hit the camera.

The two officers in the room, dropped to the floor, unconscious from the darts, then Max levelled the pistol at Kuznetsov.

"Call them off," Max demanded, having heard the general's orders to fire on the American fleet in the Pacific.

"You might be wearing my uniform, but you are not giving the orders here."

"Call them off, now!" Max yelled, stepping closer to the general.

"Never," Kuznetsov said, smiling and looking to a nearby computer monitor. "I am impressed you got in here, but you are too late. The first shots have been fired. The war is here and finally the West will be brought to its knees."

"Do you see me kneeling before you?"

"In time, I will see you all kneeling before Mother Russia."

"Not if I have anything to do with it," Max said, moving forward to engage, but the general lunged for him instead.

The older man had not lost much of his KGB training over the years. He was fit and strong and covered the ground between them fast. He got in a couple of good punches as he reached Max.

Max stumbled back and the pair wrestled over the gun. Max headbutted the general, breaking his nose, but he did not flinch, just took it in his stride and keep wrestling. He held Max's wrists outstretched above his head, then used his other arm to punch Max in the stomach and ribs. Max's mid-section was aching in pain, as the blows kept coming. He felt his arms giving up the fight, they wanted to protect his organs. Kuznetsov felt it too and let his arms lower.

Max's pistol was now pointing straight up, but the two men were trying to get the edge to aim it at the other.

The pair struggled for a full minute before the gun went off. They looked at each other for a moment, before Max fell to his knees.

"I see you kneeling now," Kuznetsov said.

"Fuck y…" Max managed to get out, seeing the sleeping dart lodged in his stomach, before his world went black.

Chapter Thirty

Max's head ached as he tried to open his eyes. The light burned and his nostrils flared, smelling the sharp chemical compound from the ammonia stick which had been snapped under his nose to wake him. He tossed his head back trying to avoid the smell.

"You know, I thought you were using bullets," Kuznetsov said, "not sleeping darts. Luckily for you, my friend. We found the men you knocked out, including my personal assistant. I can tell you, you are going to die, but had you been using bullets, you would be dead already, because I have zero tolerance for western agents killing my men."

"So why am I still alive?" Max asked.

"I wanted you to see your failure."

Max blinked and felt the room spinning as he tried to shake the sleeping chemical still pulsing through his system. His vision was blurred, but he could make out the general and the new officers in the room.

He could also see the computer systems and blinking control terminals, as well as the monitors at the far end of the room. One monitor in particular got his attention. It showed a dotted line tracking for the middle of the Pacific Ocean.

"In twenty-two minutes, the Pacific Fleet will be nothing but a radioactive smear on the ocean," Kuznetsov said proudly.

"You know they will retaliate," Max said. "Lyadova is using you to start World War III. You won't win, everyone will lose."

"So be it, if it means the West loses."

"So you would sacrifice the lives of millions, possibly billions, in a game of mutually assured destruction just to see us lose?"

"I am old, I have played this game for too long, and now is the time to make the move."

"You are doing this because you are sick of waiting?"

"I want to leave a legacy for my family and write my name into the history books as a proud Russian who took action after having endured the pain of watching as his country suffered through a long cold winter."

"What you are doing will bring about nothing but death and destruction. There will be no history books left to write in. You are sentencing your country and our whole world to death."

"It is too late for you to try to talk me out of it."

Max was about to respond when the phone rang. One of the junior officers picked it up and listened for a moment, before pressing the command buttons on a nearby keyboard.

The main screen in the room changed to vision of President Sukhanov.

"Sacha, what the hell are you playing at?" Sukhanov asked.

"I am doing what you are too weak to do," Kuznetsov replied. "I am taking the first steps towards war with the west. A long overdue battle to return our nation to superpower status and to cripple our enemies."

"You may very well cripple us in the process. I gave no such order because it is too soon. You must abort the missile."

Too soon, Max thought to himself, unsure of his thoughts as the haze from the sleeping dart was still coursing through his veins, and blurring his thoughts and vision.

"I cannot do that, sir."

"You can and you will."

"No, Mister President. I will not."

Sukhanov turned to one of the military men in his office and asked a question. The general in the room nodded and picked up the phone. He spoke for a few seconds, before the President spoke again.

"This is President Sukhanov." The President's voice boomed through the speakers throughout the facility, having asked the officer in his room to connect the call to the base's sound system. *"General Sacha Kuznetsov is hereby relieved of his command and on my authority is to be placed under arrest.*

The missile headed for the pacific must be aborted, that is an order."

"Nice try, Mister President," Kuznetsov said, "but my men are loyal to me. They follow my orders, not yours."

"We will see. Any solider in that base found to be complying with former General Kuznetsov's orders will be branded a traitor and put to death. I am the President and I am taking command of the base. Carry out my orders or you will suffer the consequences."

"It is good to see you are finally trying to show you have some balls, Nicholai, but it is too late. Your plan will fail, that's why I needed to step in."

"Well one of the things we have in common, Sacha, is that I do not always just have one plan. I have contingencies in place."

"Oh, I guess you are referring to the western spy you let into my base," Kuznetsov said, stepping to the side so Sukhanov could see Max tied to the chair. "If he is here on your orders, then you, sir, are the traitor."

Max had been watching and listening to the conversation intently, but he was still hazy. With Kuznetsov's back turned and the whole base distracted by the President, he had taken the opportunity to pull his belt around his waist until the buckle was at the back, near his handcuffed wrists. He had pulled out one of the pins that held the buckle and used it to pick the handcuffs.

Max stood as the President watched his monitor.

"Agent Shaw and members of the Russian military who are loyal to me and to Mother Russia," Sukhanov said, *"on my authority you may arrest or kill any person on that base who tries to stop you carrying out my orders to abort that missile."*

Max smiled and nodded as he stepped forward quietly and drew a pistol from the holster on one of the officer's hips.

The officer spun around to protest, but Max pulled the trigger and shot him between the eyes. He then levelled the gun at Kuznetsov.

"You are but a pawn, Agent Shaw," Kuznetsov said. "See you in hell, Nicholai."

Max didn't hesitate. This man had just fired a missile at an allied fleet and had to be stopped. He fired two bullets into Kuznetsov's head and chest.

Two of the other officers in the room stared each other down, before they drew their own pistols and fired, killing each other.

Max heard gunfire ringing out through the corridors as he moved towards the control panel.

"Thank you, Max," Sukhanov said.

"Don't thank me yet, sir," Max said. "I need to know how to abort the missile."

"General Preobrazhensky here will walk you through it."

"General, talk to me," Max said, scanning the panel as the door opened behind him.

Max ducked behind a chair as the soldier's head exploded in the opened the doorway.

Oleg entered and aimed his gun at Max. He held his gaze for a minute, before lowering the gun.

"I can help," Oleg said, walking into the room.

"You want to help me?" Max asked.

"Yes. I hate Kuznetsov and I am loyal to Mother Russia."

"I wish I had known that earlier."

"Me too. My head is still spinning from that shit you shot into me."

"Mine too. Sorry."

"It doesn't matter, let's get on with it," Oleg said, walking over to the control panel and handing Max his gun. "You watch the door."

"With pleasure."

As Preobrazhensky walked the young officer through the abort procedure, Max aimed both pistols at the door, vigilant, waiting for any incoming attacks.

He did not have to wait long. Two junior soldiers marched into the room, firing wildly.

Max grabbed Oleg and dragged him behind cover, then sprang up and shot both the attackers. One of the men fell, firing his gun dry as he went down. The second was hit with several of the bullets his comrade fired and he fell in a bloody mess.

"Agent Shaw," a man yelled from the doorway, "hold your fire. I am here to help you secure the room."

Max let the officer into the room and they fired at a pair of soldiers running towards them firing their own weapons. The duo fell, as the hairs on Max's neck stood up.

The officer he had let in the room was aiming his pistol at Max's head.

"Sukhanov is a traitor, Kuznetsov was the real leader," the officer said as he squeezed the trigger and the bullet flew from the barrel.

Max fell to the floor and felt the blood running over his hands, but it wasn't his.

Oleg had dived over the console and tackled Max to the floor, just before the officer fired. The bullet hit Oleg in the back and went through into the wall behind Max.

Oleg fell on top of Max. His blood pumped out and ran over Max's stolen shirt.

The officer in the room levelled his gun at Max's face and was squeezing the trigger as his neck was ripped open by a bullet from a young female sergeant standing in the doorway.

"I am Sergeant Lelyah Yahontov," she said, running over to help Max up.

"Max Shaw," Max said as he rolled Oleg onto his back to check on him. "He has a faint pulse. Keep pressure on it and watch the door, will you?"

"Yes, okay," Yahontov said, turning back to Oleg. "Oleg, stay with me."

"General, where are we up to with the abort?" Max asked, back at the control panel.

"Enter the following code," Preobrazhensky said from the screen, before reading a short list of Russian numbers and letters, which Max typed into the command panel.

"Done."

"Now, press the blue button to your right."

Max hit the button and watched the monitor. The dotted line was still moving towards the Pacific Fleet. It was only minutes away from its target, billions of dollars of military equipment and thousands of innocent crew sailing across the vast ocean.

"How long until the abort code reaches the missile?" Max asked.

"It should be there any second," Preobrazhensky said nervously.

Max watched the blip on the screen as another man tried to enter the room, but was taken down by Yahontov. Max turned around in time to see the solider fall in the doorway.

"There it goes," Preobrazhensky said. *"Congratulations, Mister President. Missile aborted."*

"Thank you, General, and thank you, Max," Sukhanov said. *"We have bought ourselves some time, but the Americans will have seen that. Their systems are still operational. They will be preparing for war and retaliation."*

"I need to get out of here so I can speak to AIS," Max said.

"I can help you," Yahontov said.

"Sergeant Yahontov," Sukhanov said, *"it is a matter of national importance that Agent Shaw gets that message to the allies, they need to pull back or the world will be plunged into war."*

"I understand, sir. I will do what I can."

"Thank you both. Good luck."

"Thank you, sir," Max said as the screen went black. "Oleg?"

"He's gone," Yahontov said sadly. "He was a good kid."

"He saved my life."

Max paid his respects to the young man, before heading for the door.

He was met there by a large group of soldiers. They raised their weapons as a huge explosion rang out through the complex. The whole facility shook, giving Max and Yahontov the chance they needed. They fired into the group of soldiers, taking them down.

As they ran into the hallway, they picked up two new guns and tossed their empty ones on the ground.

"What the hell is that noise?" Yahontov asked. "It sounds like water."

"It is," Max said. "We need to move!"

The pair ran into the corridor as a huge crack in the concrete wall opened further and started gushing thousands of litres of water into the facility.

Unknown to anyone in the facility, Max's scuba equipment had lodged in the cooling system's intake blocking the flow of the cold water needed to regulate the heat generated by the computer systems.

The system had been heating up since Max had arrived. The engine powering the blade of the intake didn't have a failsafe on it and continued running until it exploded, causing the oxygen tank to explode with it. The oxygen helping spread the flames.

The combined explosion, coupled with the sudden rush of cold water back into the overheated system, caused the server units to explode. The water now rushing into the hallway was running out of the IT server room. Without the pumps and regulators in place, and thanks to the cracked walls, the Moskva River was now free to run down into the bunker. The facility needed to be evacuated or everyone inside would drown.

"This way!" Yahontov yelled, leading Max towards the water.

Max ran after Yahontov covering their rear. Yahontov took down a man who ran into the hallway in front of her. He fell as the water reached him and he was completely underwater before Yahontov got to him.

Max fired at two men who had come into the corridor behind them, forcing them back into cover as the water rose to his knees. It was freezing and he suddenly realised how good his wetsuit had been earlier.

The water was at waist height as they got to the staircase and started their climb.

Three bullets slammed into the wall in front of them at the first landing, pinning them in position. Yahontov checked around the corner to see a solitary officer holding position on the stairs. He fired as she ducked back behind cover.

They were stuck. The rising water was making its way up the stairs and the gunman was keeping them from making the climb out of the bunker.

"The President says it is vital to national security for you to get out of here," Yahontov said, "but we are cornered."

"I need to speak to my government and let them know your President is not behind this attack," Max said. "Without confirmation, they will likely take it as a further provocation and retaliate."

"A further provocation?"

"The cyber-attack."

"They think that was Russia?"

"We found evidence to suggest your government was behind it or at least condoning it. I sent word and now the missile has been fired they will have little to no doubt of Russian involvement."

"Plus the death of the agents."

"What agents?"

"Kuznetsov ordered the assassination of a number of CIA and AIS agents in Moscow and St. Petersburg in the last couple of hours. It was broadcast on national television. They broke into a CIA safehouse and shot everyone, and they drowned two other agents not far from here in the Moskva River."

"Jesus, the Americans and my own country will see that as an act of war."

"I am afraid you are right. So, he was wrong."

"Who?"

"Sukhanov. It is not about national security, so much as it is about global security."

"Yes," Max said as the water started lapping at his feet.

"Take the stairs to the top, exit through the back. There is a blue Peugeot in the lot, the keys are in the glovebox."

"What are you going to do?" Max asked, but before he could protest, Yahontov ran up the stairs.

She took three bullets and kept running, then opened fire on the officer on the stairs. The solider and Yahontov traded shots until they both fell.

Max ran up the stairs, pausing briefly to check Yahontov, but she was gone.

He took the stairs up to the surface, found the Peugeot and fled the scene.

Chapter Thirty-One

Max circled around for a while, before he found a payphone. He dialled a memorised number then heard the clicks on the line as it found its path through the international switchboards. There was a sound like the old dial up internet modem connecting to the internet, before a woman's voice came on the line.

"Access code?" the woman asked.

"India, Delta, Juliet, one, eight, seven," Max responded.

"This is an old code."

"This is an old agent. I've been away. Put me through to Hermes."

"Please hold."

There were another series of clicks as the call connected.

"Prince?" Blake asked.

"Hermes, it wasn't the Russians," Max said. "It's a long story, but you need to call off the troops."

"That is easier said than done, Prince. They killed six agents, including one of our own, live on television. It is being broadcast across the world as we speak. They are accusing our guys of espionage."

"We were spying on them."

"And they spy on us all the time too, we don't take out their agents on live TV!"

"No, but we do take them out."

"It's not only that, they fired an intercontinental missile at the Pacific Fleet."

"And ditched it in the ocean."

"How could you know that?"

"I was in the room."

"What?"

"I told you it was a long story, but let's just say I spoke to Sukhanov and I know for a fact it was a disgruntled general named Sacha Kuznetsov who launched the missile, without Sukhanov's authorisation."

"You spoke to Sukhanov?"

"Yes and I shot Kuznetsov in the head."

"You assassinated a high level Russian general?"

"Yes, Sukhanov authorised it, he was watching on videoconference."

"What the hell is happening?"

"They are under attack too and they thought it was us at first, then they found out it was Lyadova and A&A."

"How do you know it was Lyadova? A few hours ago, you told me it was the Russians."

"Yes, but I also sent a message through MI6, Agent Verity Humphries. You should have received it hours ago."

"I didn't get the message, Prince."

"Shit. How could that happen? I left them with a message to send to you and I was hoping she had the tablet by now too."

"What tablet?"

"Lyadova's tablet. It controls that program, Apollo."

"How did she get it?"

"Verity was going to steal it, because we couldn't keep it in range long enough."

"In range?"

"Yeah, Andrew explained how I had to keep the tablet within a certain range to let him hack it."

"That's not how it works, Prince. You only need to connect once and the program can hack in. Andrew told you that you needed to stay in close proximity?"

"Yes."

"I'm sorry, Prince, but that's bullshit and he knows it."

"He knows?"

"He built the program."

"Son of a bitch."

"Where is he now?"

"With the others at the safehouse."

"I think he is playing you."

"God, how could I be so stupid? He still works for her."

"Lyadova?"

"Yes. Shit. I've got to get to the safehouse. He didn't send the message and he lied to me. The others are at risk."

"Good luck, Prince. Be careful."

"I will."

"I will do what I can on my end, but the wheels are already in motion."

"Talk to Moore, tell him everything. Tell him to pick up the phone to Sukhanov. He told me he was going to hit the kill switch if I didn't stop Lyadova in the next few hours. I've only got another ninety minutes."

"Did you say the kill switch?"

"Yes."

"I read the briefs, but I thought it was bullshit. He actually threatened to use it?"

"No, Hermes. He told he will use it. If I fail, he will shut down the internet and everything connected to it, instantly casting the world back into the dark ages."

"Not to mention, crippling our defence and intelligence networks."

"If Lyadova doesn't get there first."

"The program is only a couple of hours from breaching our systems, so whatever you are going to do, you'd better do it quickly."

"No pressure. I'd better go."

"Wait."

"Yeah, what is it?"

"I love you. Be careful."

"I love you too," Max said, ending the call.

Max jumped back into the blue Peugeot and hit the accelerator. He didn't bother with the circuitous route, he just drove straight to the motel.

He drew his pistol and kicked open the door. The room Andrew had been using was empty. He checked the bathroom and it was empty too.

He walked through the shared door and into the second room, leading with his gun. He saw the makeshift operating bench and the obvious signs of a struggle in the room.

Max quickly checked the bathroom, finding it too empty. As he wandered back out, he saw Gabriel.

The old man's body had fallen to the side and was laying on the floor. His eyes were wide, but the life once in them was gone. Max gently closed Gabriel's eyes and stopped to pay his respects to an old friend who he worked with over many years. He felt sick to the stomach knowing he had got him involved.

His thoughts then turned to Verity and Alexei. Neither of them were there.

He quickly scouted about in the room looking for the tablet, but didn't find that either.

As he was about to leave, he heard sirens blaring and saw the flashing lights approaching. They must have left them off until they got to the motel entrance because he hadn't seen or heard them approach.

Five police cars pulled up outside his room.

Max grabbed his old watch from the table nearby and put it on his wrist, then he got down on his knees and put his hands in the air as the officers all climbed out and ran for the room with their guns drawn.

The first officer kicked Max in the chest and forced him to the ground.

"Interpol and Russian police have been looking for you, Mr Shaw," van den Berg said, walking into the room. "And here we find you with yet another dead body. You are in a lot of trouble."

"I didn't kill him," Max said. "He was a friend of mine. Please, you need to call President Sukhanov. He will explain everything."

"The President's office told us you were here," ven den Berg said, handcuffing Max and getting him to his feet. "The President himself authorised me to operate on Russian soil. Do you think I am stupid?"

"I'm starting to," Max said as the officer who kicked him earlier backhanded him. "Call the Kremlin. I have a mission to complete. You don't know what you are doing."

"I am arresting the world's most wanted man. A man who escaped The Hague and got away from my officers in France. A man who needs to go back to gaol."

"I want to change my answer."

"To what?"

"Whether I think you are stupid. Yes is the answer. I do."

The officer with van den Berg bundled Max out of the room and into the back of a police car as forensic teams arrived to investigate Gabriel's death.

Max sat in the back of the police car. Andrew must have Verity and Alexei, and maybe even the tablet. And he had killed Gabriel. He felt his anger rising. He shouldn't have trusted him. He should have trusted his gut. Andrew had gone bad early and he hadn't changed. This time Max was certain he was going to kill him.

Max was sitting calmly in the rear of the police car as it drove down the busy Moscow road. The driver kept looking at him in the mirror and Max just smiled smugly at him.

"How did you know I was at the motel?" Max asked. "You said Sukhanov's office called."

"Good police work," van den Berg said. "We tracked your plane to Moscow and I followed."

"No, really? How did you find out about the motel?"

"You don't think we are good at our jobs, Mister Shaw? I tracked you across multiple countries, didn't I?"

"Not that good. I was only there, at the motel, a couple of minutes. You got a tip off. You were waiting for me to get back? Who in Sukhanov's office called? I have to warn him, he has a traitor in the ranks."

"You can think that if you like, but I think it was more like good police work."

"An anonymous call led you there and you are taking the credit," Max said.

"Sukhanov himself called the Chief of Police."

Max sat in silence thinking about what he had just heard. It didn't make sense. Sukhanov called. Why would he give Max up?

"I am going to make my career on you," the driver said interrupting Max's thoughts as the car pulled up at a set of traffic lights. "Your photo was on every newspaper and television channel. You are going to get me a promotion. I will be a national hero for arresting you."

"I wouldn't count on it," Max said. "You will be lucky to have a career once I am done with you."

"Are you threatening me?" he asked, turning around to face Max.

"No, I am making you a promise."

Without warning, Max threw a violent punch into the driver's face.

He had pulled a hidden pin from his old watch and used it to pick the cuffs. The Russian police car didn't have a screen between the front and rear, so when he saw the chance, he took it.

As the officer fell backwards, van den Berg turned to face him.

"You don't have to do this, Mister Shaw," van den Berg said. "Just come with us and we can talk through your side of the story. If you are in trouble, we can protect you."

"No, you can't," Max said. "Come find me when all this is over and we can talk. Until then, I have a job to do."

"How will I know when this is all over?"

"Make some calls. You'll figure it out."

"Who do I…" van den Berg managed to get out, before Max punched him in the face, knocking him out.

"Sorry. You don't seem like a bad guy, but you are getting in my way."

Both officers were unconscious and the car rolled gently into the car in front of it and stopped.

Max tried the back door, but it was locked, so he climbed over into the front and crawled over the driver and out his window.

The driver came to as Max put his first foot on the ground. The Russian officer grabbed his other foot trying to stop him.

Max steadied himself, then kicked the officer in the face, knocking him out again.

He reached in and stole both officers' pistols and a taser, then fled through the traffic to sound of horns and the shocked expressions of the nearby drivers.

Chapter Thirty-Two

Sukhanov was sitting watching the news while he had a bite to eat. He was not hungry given everything that was happening, but knew he needed to keep his energy and blood sugar up. The next few hours were going to be critical.

"Companies across the country and around the world are protesting the launch of A&A Enterprises software program, Apollo," the reporter said. *"The Alexandria 2.0 project was launched by Isabella Lyadova and heralded as a world changing platform to store and distribute global knowledge, but instead it has been accused of stealing intellectual property. Suddenly the program has lost its shine, as businesses around the globe protest the inadequate and often nil payments they have received for their property. Some businesses claim the program forged signatures and blatantly stole from them.*

"Pharmaceutical companies say years of research and development costs have been sunk into projects creating drugs to treat and cure the world's ills, but these formulas have now been published for free. While television and film industry executives, as well as on-demand streaming and pay television networks are up in arms at A&A's promise to make their content free for all users. Likewise, writers, composers, singers and bands the world over, are upset at the token payments they have received as a one-off payment for their songs and albums. They say the moves will send artists broke."

Sukhanov shook his head at the scale of program's capability. Not only was it hacking these companies and the sophisticated systems they had in place, but it was also singlehandedly taking down the global defence and intelligence services. Lyadova had made a massive promise, but this was even bigger than he could have imagined.

The door to his office opened and members of his security team walked in.

"Sorry for the interruption, sir," the head of his security detail said, "but it is time to move you to the bunker."

"Do you really think that is necessary?"

"Yes, sir. The military has indicated that the Americans and the allies have not changed course. It is their, and our, assessment that war is now inevitable. We need to get you to safety."

"Where are my wife and children?"

"They are already en route, as are the key members of the security council and cabinet."

"Okay then, let's go."

Sukhanov was led out of the office and down into his waiting limousine.

There was a bunker on site, but the Americans knew that and so it was determined they would move the President to their doomsday bunker in the mountains just outside Moscow.

The Presidential limousine was flanked by a full motorcade with police and military escorts. It left the Kremlin and sped through the streets.

As the motorcade was reaching the city limits, there was a commotion at the front of his limousine. Sukhanov lowered the window between the compartments.

"What is going on?" Sukhanov asked.

"Hold on, Mister President," the head of his detail said as a rocket propelled grenade hit the lead vehicle blowing it apart in a violent ball of flames and twisted metal.

"Jesus Christ! Get me out of here!"

An explosion rang out behind them as a second rocket hit the trailing police vehicle and it too exploded into flames.

The roofs of the cars second in at each end of the motorcade both blew off in a controlled explosion and two mounted machine guns popped up, manned by two highly-trained military officers. The two officers opened fire on the locations of the rocket launchers.

Over the noise of the gunfire, came the thump of rotating blades on military helicopters.

Sukhanov saw the big choppers coming in, one at the front and one at the rear of the motorcade, and was thankful for the billions he had spent on the military since taking office.

The chopper at the front launched two missiles and Sukhanov's thanks turned to fear as the missiles headed for the motorcade, instead of his attackers. The missiles hit the turreted car in front. It was a solid car, but took catastrophic damage and the missile had left a huge crater in the roadway. The decoy limo ahead of Sukhanov's hit the debris and crater, and stopped dead in its tracks, blocking the freeway.

As his driver threw the President's limousine into reverse, the second helicopter at the rear launched its missiles and tore apart the rear turret-mounted vehicle, with the same effect.

The motorcade was stuck with nowhere to go.

Sukhanov's security team dutifully filed out of their remaining cars and returned fire at the helicopters and at the rooftops, but it was futile. The rocket launcher teams were joined by an army of troops with high powered rifles who started raining down bullets on the guards. They were cut down in the street where they stood.

"I am sorry, Mister President," the lead agent said, turning back to face him. "I am sorry I let you down."

Sukhanov just stared blankly at the agent unsure what to say and in shock.

The helicopter in front hovered menacingly in line with the President's limousine's front window, as the one from the rear landed on the bitumen not far from the luxury vehicle.

Five heavily armed men jumped down from the chopper and ran for the President's car.

The driver and lead agent both climbed out and started firing at the incoming force, but were easily overcome, but not before taking down two of the men.

The remaining soldiers got to Sukhanov's door and waved him out. He did not have any options, his detail was all dead and he was unarmed, so he complied.

One of the soldiers riffled through the President's pockets until he found his locator chip. He dropped it on the ground and crushed it with his boot.

"Where is your mobile phone?" the solider asked.

Sukhanov handed it over and the solider dropped it on the ground then put a bullet through it.

"Time to move," the solider said, waving his hand in the air to tell the chopper to power up.

He led Sukhanov to the chopper and they all got on board, before the big bird revved hard and climbed into the sky.

The two helicopters sped off into the distance and towards the setting sun.

Chapter Thirty-Three

Tsaritsyno Palace is a magnificent architectural marvel south of Moscow city. It was built in the sixteenth century and bought in 1775 by Empress Catherine the Great.

The main palace was constructed of red bricks with exquisite white features, including the towering window frames and pillars. There were four towers along the front of the palace which were in diamond formation and the roof and accents were in a muted green copper.

The grounds also held a church, four cavalier houses, an Opera House, four massive greenhouses, an architect's monument, three impressive stone bridges and the Bread House kitchens which joined to the main palace.

There are monuments and gardens spread across the massive estate and a visitors' centre and museum, which were no longer open to the public.

The grounds and roofs were all covered in snow, but the scale of the buildings and surrounding gardens was still impressive as the sleek silver town car pulled up at the front of the palace.

Three men climbed out and dragged a fourth man with a hood over his head out of the rear of the car. They walked up to the front door and let themselves in.

The four men walked through the grand ballroom with its highly polished wooden floors and multimillion dollar art collection, then into a connected hallway before taking an elevator down into the basement.

The man in the hood was forced down to his knees on the cold concrete floor.

"Well, thank you gentleman," Lyadova said, walking into the room. "I hope it was not too much trouble for you to collect him?"

"No, ma'am," one of the three soldiers said. "Quick helicopter ride and a couple of vehicle changes and here we are."

"Good to hear. You can take off his hood now. Hello, Mister President, welcome to my home away from home."

"Isabella," Sukhanov said, blinking in the harsh neon light. "What is going on here? This is not part of our plan."

"Oh please, I just killed your security detail, took out your motorcade and kidnapped you, one of the most powerful people in the world, and within the hour I will have control of your military. This was always part of my plan. The allies will not know what hit them. Well, actually yes they will. That is also a big part of my plan."

"Why are you doing this?"

"I want you to suffer. I want you to be blamed for the collapse of the world as we know it, then I want you to die."

"Why? I was supposed to return our Mother Russia to her former glory, now you have spat on that chance."

Lyadova walked over and sat the photograph of her mother on the ground in front of him. She saw the instant recognition in his eyes.

"Katrina Lebedev," Lyadova said, pacing in front of the Russian leader. "You remember her, right?"

The Russian leader knelt in stunned silence, before finally agreeing.

"I do," Sukhanov said, resigned to the fact Lyadova clearly knew that he knew Katrina. "Why?"

"She was my mother."

Sukhanov's eyes darted from the photo to Lyadova.

"That's right," Lyadova said. "It is good to finally meet you, Dad."

Sukhanov was shocked. He had met with Lyadova countless times over the last few years, scheming with her to build Alexandria 2.0 and to finally cripple the West's intelligence systems. Never once had he even suspected Lyadova was not who she claimed to be, let alone his own child.

"It was a different time," Sukhanov said, apologetically. "I was engaged to be married and had just started my political career, I could not be seen with a prostitute, let alone impregnating her with a bastard child out of wedlock."

"Fuck you," Lyadova said, backhanding him.

"I made a lot of mistakes, Isabella, including what I did to your mother and to you, but I tried to make it right. I gave you and your mother money to ensure you could get a good education and live comfortably."

"You selfish arsehole, you have no idea, do you? You were so worried about yourself. Did you even stop to think about what it would do to her? Single and pregnant back then?"

"No," Sukhanov said, ashamed. "No, I didn't."

"She gave me up. Dumped me on steps of the cathedral with nothing but that photo. It was lucky I didn't freeze to death, although given what those heartless old bitch nuns did to me over the years, there were times I wished I had."

"I am sorry, Isabella, but this is between the two of us. What you are doing will kill millions of Russians and, as you said, destroy the world as we know it. You cannot want that."

"I have wanted nothing but that since the day I found out you were my father. You had the perfect life and rose through the ranks, and now well, here you are, President and one of the most powerful men in history. I am going to destroy your legacy and ensure your name will be forever written into whatever history books survive the war as the biggest criminal and murderer in history. A history written thanks to Apollo and Alexandria 2.0 by me. You will be responsible for starting World War III and you won't have the western intelligence and defence systems I promised to defence Russia. I will orchestrate the whole war to ensure you are blamed for everything."

"You are insane. You will not get away with this."

"Maybe so, but I am willing to be labelled a criminal and admit what I have done, at least in this room to you. Where you are unwilling to admit what you have done."

"I apologised."

"For abandoning me, but what about for killing my mother? You are a murderer! All to protect your perfect life!"

"I did not kill your mother."

"Bullshit! You paid her off and threatened her, but she couldn't help herself, she wanted you to acknowledge me and wanted you to accept your past, but you could not let her just go. What if she told others and your world came crashing down? No, you certainly could not have that, so you had her killed!"

"You may hate me for abandoning your mother and for not playing a role in your life, and that is understandable, and I am sorry. But Isabella, I did not kill your mother. I swear on the lives of my children."

"The ones you love!"

"All of them, you included. I swear I did not kill her."

"It was only a few blocks from where you had met with her."

"It was, but it was a tragic coincidence. I am sorry for your loss."

"And what about the hitman you hired to kill me?"

"That was not me."

"But you admit there was an assassin who targeted me, because I am your daughter?"

"A senior member of my party found out about you. He was trying to protect me."

"By killing me?"

"No," Sukhanov lied.

"I can see it in your eyes," Lyadova said grabbing Sukhanov by the throat. "You've almost convinced yourself you did nothing wrong, but I can see it. I grew up on the streets, thanks to you. I dealt with liars and rapists and drug dealers and thieves every day. You're no different. Admit what you did, and I will spare your wife and children."

"They are your brothers and sisters. You can't hurt them."

"You are my father, and I am willing to kill you. Why should I care about them? Admit what you did or they will suffer."

"Okay. Okay. Just don't hurt them."

"Admit it!" Lyadova said, punching the president in the face.

"I did it!" Sukhanov screamed. "I killed your mother and I tried to kill you too. She was a whore, and you were a mistake. Your very existence threatened my career and everything I had built. You needed to disappear. Forever."

"Did you grieve when they told you I was dead?"

"I did."

"You are a good liar, old man, I will give you that. I guess you can't get far in politics without being good at it, but not good enough."

"Believe whatever you want to believe, Isabella. I'm done talking to you."

"You're done talking to me? After only minutes. I have spent a lifetime waiting for this moment you son of a bitch. You will hear me out and answer my questions. She died because of you! And, you have no idea the pain I endured. I was alone. I was afraid. I knew my own father was trying to kill me. I fled the country. I changed my name and underwent countless plastic surgeries to change my appearance. All in countries with very sketchy records on health and hygiene, but it was worth the risk if I was to live. But for all the years of looking over my shoulder, I plotted my retribution. Your career was more important to you than anything, certainly more important than my mother and me. So I set about finding a way to bring you down. I could not just go public, because I had no proof. Some nobody daughter of a prostitute against the future leader of the party. No, I had to find another way and I had to be patient. I knew one day you would become President, so that is where I started. How better to destroy a world leader than by making him look insane and inviting others to destroy him for me? Over the coming hours I will use your military to provoke the Americans into all out war and you will take the blame. I have already fired a warning shot at them and killed several of their spies. They are going to be upset already, but that was just the warmup."

"You are a psychopath! The world will know what you have done."

"Shut up!" Isabella snapped, slapping him hard across the face. "You did this! Not me! Tie him up and get the terminals ready."

Two of the men who had brought Sukhanov into the basement tied him to a chair which had been sitting in the corner, while another two workers set up the computer monitors and televisions in the basement.

"Get comfortable, Dad," Lyadova said. "It is going to be a long night."

The monitors all came to life, each showing a countdown clock with a final thirty seconds ticking down. When it hit zero, the screens all showed the Russian Government's seal before flashing to the launch controls from the Russian version of the nuclear football.

"Russian missile and nuclear arsenal operations system online, Isabella," Apollo said over the audio system. *"Please select your targets."*

Chapter Thirty-Four

"The President and Prime Ministers have decided to stay on the war footing," Blake said over Max's comms unit. *"They say the Russians are still moving troops, ships and weapons, and they fear both systems will be compromised by the Apollo program within the hour, if they haven't been already. They won't back down until the Russians do."*

"And the Russians won't back down until the allies do," Max said. "We are going to war because no one will blink."

"I'm still trying, Max."

"Did you speak to Moore?"

"He is locked in the war room, but I have left several messages for him. I will keep you posted."

"If I can shut down the system, will they pull back?"

"Not unless the Russians do, but we also have some other problems. Intelligence has come in that the North Koreans are moving troops and so the South is responding, and we have massive weapons and equipment movements in parts of Africa."

"She's been busy."

"Yes, but we can't influence these other nations and get them to stand down, while we are preparing for our own war with Russia. We need them to deescalate."

"Okay, well, one thing at a time. I will try to stop Lyadova and the program first to protect our systems."

"Okay. Are you sure you can manage this on your own?"

"I don't have a choice."

"I'm mobilising as much support as I can."

"Thanks, Hermes. I know you will do your best."

"Likewise."

"Okay, I'm in position," Max said, laying in the undergrowth just back from the tree line outside Tsaritsyno Palace. "Is the signal still coming from inside?"

"Which building is it coming from?"

"It is under the palace. I presume from the basement, but given the number of heat signatures I am seeing around the site, it might be better to enter via the Bread House, which is the square building at your two o'clock. Our report on the building says it is connected to the main palace via two walkways, one above and one below ground."

"What about security? Any idea where they are set up?"

"Check your phone."

Max pulled out his phone and clicked the link Blake had sent him. It was a map of the complex and satellite imagery dotted the heat signatures over the grounds. The facility was massive, but even still the number of heat signatures dotting the landscape and the buildings was overwhelming. The main palace showed at least twenty, while the Bread House had around ten.

The greenhouses and cavalier buildings all had a handful each, but the one which was drawing Max's eye was the Opera House. There was a tight cluster of dots in the Opera House. There were also various guards milling about in the meadows and scattered along the perimeter and on the bridges.

"What are the three long streaks of red?" Max asked, trying to zoom in for a better look.

"Looks to me like a heat exhausts," Blake said. *"It must be freezing there. The heat could be from underground heating units."*

"Or server rooms?"

"That's certainly possible, given who we are dealing with."

"Three streaks: Opera House, Bread House and palace."

"The largest heat signature is from the Opera House."

"And it is the easiest for me to get to."

"Take a screenshot of the map, Prince. I don't know how long I can keep access to this satellite before it is repurposed for the war effort."

"Done. Stay with me as long as you can. I'm going to need some support."

"You've got it. Be…"

"I will," Max said, cutting him off as he started his trek across to the Opera House.

The sun had almost set and the temperature was dropping rapidly as the darkness spread. Max had stolen an overcoat, gloves and a beanie from a car in the city before Blake rang and told him he had tracked Andrew through the tablet.

Andrew had used a backdoor into the AIS servers to use the intelligence systems. Blake had found the breach and back traced it to the tablet.

Max had the two pistols and the taser he had stolen from the police officers. It wasn't the ideal kit and attire for what he was about to attempt, but it would have to do.

Max snuck over the fence and headed toward the southernmost greenhouse at the rear of the property. It was easily the length of two football fields and around thirty metres wide. It was framed by the same ornate architectural designs as other buildings on the property, but was roofed and walled by thick glass.

Max crept in for a closer look.

Through the glass walls he could see the huge indoor field of red flowers. Poppies to be exact. Millions of them arched up towards the UV lights which were coming on as the sun was setting.

The four massive greenhouses would be worth millions in drug money when the poppies were processed. Max could not help but wonder why a woman, worth billions, would be risking everything with drugs.

As he moved along the building, a door opened and a man walked out and lit a cigarette. He turned to his left and saw Max.

Max smiled and fired.

The two prongs shot out of the taser, trailing their cords. The first stabbed into his neck and the second into his chest, then Max squeezed the trigger. The guard started to convulse and stiffened, before falling backwards through the open doorway as the electricity coursed through his body.

Max checked the surroundings then ducked his head in through the door of the greenhouse. He could not see anyone, so he dragged the unconscious guard inside and tossed him three rows deep into the poppies.

He pulled the man's belt off and tied his hands, and used some of the sprinkler hose to tie his feet.

"What do you think you are doing?" a guard asked from behind him.

Max looked around for anything he could use. He didn't want to fire his gun without a silencer. Not yet anyway.

"He fell over in the poppies," Max said. "Come help me."

"What was he doing in there?" the guard asked, lowering his weapon and walking into the garden.

"You know what he's like," Max said, waiting patiently.

When he heard the guard was within a few feet, he stood and swung around, clutching a shovel. The metal head flew through the air and connected with the guard's face, making a satisfying, if not frightening thunk.

The handle broke leaving Max wielding a long spear-like wooden handle which was split down to a sharp tip.

He tied the second guy into the garden hoses, not that he needed to, he was close to death from the hideous blow from the shovel. Max took a couple of spare magazines, then wandered back out into the open air.

Max ducked across a short open field until he reached a long narrow pond. There were guards on either end, but it was covered in ice and snow. Max walked over and poked the ice with his broken shovel handle. It felt solid, so he gingerly stepped out onto the ice. He was a big guy and halfway across he heard the ice cracking under his weight, so he started moving quicker.

When he got to the other side, Max saw a small restroom facility for guests who had been allowed to wander the gardens, before Lyadova bought the palace. He sprinted across the snow-covered grass, as another one of the A&A goons emerged from the bathroom.

He saw Max coming and drew his pistol, but Max was already on him. The broken shovel handle sliced through his windpipe, then lodged in his spine. The mortally wounded solider stood for a few seconds, blood pumping from the corners of his mouth, then Max pulled the bloodied spear out and he fell in a heap.

Max dragged the body into the toilet and tossed him into a cubicle.

There was a wide open meadow between the toilet block and the baroque grape gate which stood proudly beside the Opera House. The shortest distance was straight across the field, as the crow flies, but Max didn't want to get caught in the open, so he hugged the tree line to his left.

He moved as quickly as he could through the snow.

Max made it through the trees and the growing darkness to the path which led through the Grape Gate up to the Opera House.

There were two guards smoking and bouncing from one foot to the other, trying to keep warm.

Max moved silently in the darkness, inching closer to the edge of the tree line. He found a tight pinecone resting in the snow at the base of one of the towering trees. He picked it up and tossed it in the air, then swung the broken shovel handle like a baseball bat and whacked the pinecone at the trooper on the right.

The pinecone sailed through the air like a Babe Ruth special at Yankee Stadium.

The guard on the left had heard the impact of the makeshift bat and ball, but didn't see the pinecone. It smashed into his comrade's face with a thunk and he stumbled back holding his eye. As he moved back, the guard from the left turned to see what had happened and check if his mate was okay.

Max certainly hadn't planned on hitting the guard with the pinecone, he thought it would just land somewhere nearby, but smiled when it did.

Max ran hard out of the shadows, while the pair were distracted. When he was a couple of metres from the left-hand guard, he dropped into a baseball slide on the icy ground. The closest guard had started to turn back to try to find the source of the original sound, but saw Max sliding towards his feet.

He was too slow to react. Max's feet collided with his, taking his legs out from under him.

The guard fell face first towards Max as Max angled the broken shovel up towards him. He fell hard onto the spike and it pierced through his thick jacket and into his chest. As his weight hit it, Max let go and the guard fell onto it. His momentum and mass forced the other end of the handle into the ground and it dug in. The guard's big frame was heavy enough to force the handle in deep, puncturing his lung.

As the guard had been falling, Max had raised his taser and fired the remaining charge into the sentry the pinecone had hit. Both prongs stabbed into his hand, which had been covering his swollen eye. He tensed up as the electricity flowed through him, until he hit the ground, convulsing.

Max slid to a stop beside him. He was semi-conscious, so Max kicked him in the face, finishing the job, putting him out cold.

Through the gate, Max saw the long rectangular Opera House. It was built of the same red bricks, with the tall but narrow, ornate white gothic windows which rose up to sharp points, while the windows on the second floor were white gentle arches. The roof was bordered with spires and arches in a mix of the red bricks and white concrete.

Max pulled out his phone and checked the satellite image.

"Hermes, are you there?" Max asked.

"Yes, Prince," Blake said. *"I have you by the Opera House."*

"Yep, just confirming there are still six in there?"

"Looks like just four. They are still all down the opposite end of the building."

"Think the two I just took out were our missing men?"

"I'm not sure, but I don't think so."

"So I'm missing two?"

"Looks like it. Wait, one is on the move."

Max looked back down at the phone and saw one of the dots moving towards the middle of the long wall running down the left of the building. It stopped then stepped closer to the wall, before it started to fade, then completely disappeared.

"It dropped off," Blake said. *"There must be an elevator in there."*

"I guess that's where the others went," Max said. "I'm moving in."

"Ack."

Max walked quickly to the main entrance of the Opera House. He drew one of his pistols, flicked off the safety and marched inside.

The interior was nothing like he was expecting. It was basically a large ballroom, adorned with expensive artwork and huge velvet curtains. At the front of the room, the three men were huddled around a banks of computer monitors, which were the obvious out of place items. Max could just make out the white text coding on the screens with their black backgrounds. Thick electric cables ran from the panel across the old polished floor until they disappeared through a gap where some of the wooden panels had been ripped up.

Max was halfway to the men as the door closed behind him and one of the men turned around to see who had entered. No sooner had he locked eyes with Max, then he was hit between the eyes, the bullet driving in before bursting in a red mist through the back of his skull and into the computer monitor, shattering the screen and showering the table with blood, glass and circuits.

The man on the right drew his own pistol and started spinning around to face Max, but it was too little, too late. Max fired and the bullet ruptured his skull, just above his left temple. He fell on top of his comrade and his pistol dropped at the third guy's feet. He nervously looked down at it.

"Don't even think about it," Max commanded.

The man was sweating and his eyes were darting between the gun and the floor in front of Max. He never actually made eye contact with Max. He was starting to shake and twitch, and Max knew what was coming. The sweaty IT nerd quickly dropped to the floor, reaching for the gun.

Max pulled the trigger of his own gun and the bullet tore through the man's hand.

He dropped to his knees, crying in pain and clutching his wounded hand.

Max walked over and pressed the pistol against the younger man's forehead and he sobbed in fear.

"How many people are downstairs?" Max asked.

"Just one," he replied.

"Bullshit. I know there are at least three."

"I forgot, shit, I forgot. I'm sorry. There are three."

"Are there only three?"

"Yes."

"What is down there?"

"It's a server room. One of the main servers for the Apollo program."

"What was your role in all this?"

"I was just running the servers and keeping them operating optimally."

"Do you know what they have been doing with that program?"

"Yes," he said, letting his head sink and he sobbed softly.

"You're a terrorist."

"I did not mean to be and I don't want to be a terrorist. I just applied for a job and then all this happened. They threatened to kill me if I didn't do the job."

"What is the program doing now?" Max asked, looking to the scrolling code.

"It is in the final stages of taking control of the Russian military intelligence and weapons system."

"How long until it takes over?"

"It is only a matter of minutes."

"Can you stop it from here?"

"No. Apollo has control now, but—"

"But what?"

"But I could slow him down."

"How?"

"I could use the system to overheat the servers here on site, forcing a reboot."

"Do it."

"If I do, will you let me go?"

"If you do it, I won't kill you."

"Okay, please I am sorry, I want to help you. I do not want to die."

"Get up," Max said, dragging the man to his feet. "Do what you need to, but if I find out you are playing me, I will shoot you and dump you here in the pile with your friends."

"Okay, I will do it. Please just don't shoot me."

Max dragged the chair out for the man and bounced it impatiently to force him to sit.

He quickly got into the chair and started to type with one hand. He typed just as quick with one hand as most people did with two good hands.

"What do you plan do to?" Max asked.

"I am going to shut down the servers," he said. "It will force the program to look for the problem and relocate."

"Relocate?"

"Apollo is primarily based here. If I shut down these servers it won't kill him, but it will force him to move to another server. That will give you some time."

"Can you shut down any of the others from here?"

"No, only Lyadova can do that."

"Where is she?"

"The palace."

"What about this guy?" Max asked, showing him a photo of Andrew. "Seen him?"

"Yeah, he was here earlier checking on the system. He built it, you know? The whole system. He programmed Apollo and oversaw construction of the servers."

"Did he have anyone with him?"

"No, not that I saw."

"Where is he now?"

"Probably in the Bread House. He hangs around there. I think because that's where the kitchens are."

"Hermes, did you get all that?"

"Yes, Max. I'm checking the heat signatures in the Bread House, but this is the last time I will be able to help. They need the satellite back. The Prime Minister and President just gave the orders to move the fleets into the Baltic and the Black Seas. They are expecting heavy resistance."

"Have you spoken to either of them or Moore?"

"Still waiting. I will try again."

"Thanks," Max said, turning back to the man at the computer. "How long?"

"It would be faster if I had both hands," he snapped.

"Hurry up," Max said, pressing the gun to his knee, "or you will never walk without a limp."

He didn't respond, just typed quicker.

"Prince, the elevator is moving," Blake said. *"One heat signature on board."*

"Ack," Max said, spinning back to face the elevator.

"The satellite feed is gone. I'm sorry, Prince, you are on your own now."

"Great. Let me know if you get it back anytime soon and tell me when you hear from Moore."

"Ack," Blake acknowledged.

Max raised his pistol and ran across the room, ducking in behind the wall as elevator doors opened with a short ding.

"What is going on up here?" the woman asked, wandering out of the lift. "The servers are going offline."

She paused in her tracks when she saw the bodies and her injured colleague at the keyboard.

"What the fuck?" she asked as Max pressed the gun against her temple. "Who are you?"

"I'm the man about to fuck up Lyadova's plans," Max said.

"Not likely," she said, grabbing Max by the wrist and pulling it forward as he fired a shot.

The bullet sailed passed her face, within an inch, and she turned around to look at Max with eyes full of hate and anger.

Max tried to free his wrist, but she was twisting his arm awkwardly, then before he knew it, she threw a savage headbutt, busting the skin under his eye. She used the distraction to knock the gun from his hand and it scattered across the floor.

The man at the computer stopped to see what was happening.

"Get back to work!" Max yelled.

"Don't do anything he has told you!" she countered.

The IT guy just sat watching as the pair traded blows.

She was fast and strong, and Max was taking a pummelling. He stumbled back into the wall, next to one of the velvet curtains as she came in with another round of punches.

Max blocked several, but missed just as many.

As she came in with another punch, Max ducked and she punched the wall. She groaned and swore, and danced backwards holding her hand as if trying to take the pain away.

When she stepped back, Max grabbed the rope which had been holding the curtain in place. He unhooked it, just as she recovered and came in for another go.

Max looped the rope around his attacker's wrist, pulled it tightly, then spun and dragged her arm over his shoulder using the rope. He pulled down hard and heard the snap of both her ulna and radius forearm bones.

With the rope still around her wrist, Max looped it behind her head so it was around her neck and her broken arm was pulled up close under her chin.

He tied the rope in a strong knot. If it wasn't for her trapped wrist blocking it, the knot would have been tight enough to cut off her air supply. Max then punched her in the back of the head, knocking her out, and let her fall face forward to the floor.

Max limped over to the man at the computer who was smiling.

"She's not going to be happy with you," he said.

"She's unconscious," Max said. "So who cares what she thinks?"

"Not her. Nina."

"What's she got to do with it?"

"That's her girlfriend Lydia."

"She nearly got the better of me."

"I know. Nina trained her well."

"Not well enough."

"Okay, it's done. The servers are all shutting down. It should buy you some time. Can I go now?"

"Is there anything else that needs to be done?"

"No."

"Okay, thanks," Max said, punching him in the face.

He fell on top of the other two IT guys, unconscious.

Max walked over to the elevator. He pressed the call button and the doors opened, then he dragged a heavy old wooden bench over and left it half in, half out of the elevator, ensuring it would not move. Trapping anyone left downstairs in the server room.

As he turned to leave, he heard the click of the safety on a pistol behind him. Lydia, with her broken arm still choking her, aimed Max's pistol and fired.

Max dropped down behind a row of tables and chairs as the bullet sailed through the air where his head had been only fractions of a second before.

Bullet after bullet slammed into the chairs and tables as he ran, crouched over to keep a low profile. Splinters of wood and plastic, and strips of leather and puffs of cotton stuffing exploded up into the air all around him.

As he ran, he drew his other pistol and when he got to the end of the line of tables and chairs, he dived into the open and fired two shots.

Lydia fired her last bullet and it hit Max just under the ribs, grazing his side. His first shot missed, but the second perforated Lydia's cheek. She sat for a minute staring blankly, before falling to the side, her eyes wide.

As Max turned to leave, the butt of a rifle hit him between the eyes and he passed out.

Chapter Thirty-Five

"Targets confirmed, Isabella," Apollo said over the basement's speaker system. *"Initiating launch sequence."*

"You are insane!" Sukhanov yelled. "Call it off! This is about you and I. Punish me, not the millions of innocent people you are about to sentence to death."

"Oh, but you see, Mister President," Lyadova said, pacing in front of Sukhanov, "you are about to go down in history as the man who started World War III. I am punishing you in the only way which seems to matter to you, by trashing your reputation and legacy. Besides, you were happy enough to play along when you thought you would be the one in control and the Americans would be the ones to suffer."

"I don't care if the Americans or any of the allies die, but you will kill millions of Russians. You need to stop this."

"There is a problem," Apollo said, chiming back in. *"Emergency protocol enacted."*

"Emergency protocol? What is that? Get Andrew in here now."

"Send the technician over," Nina ordered into her radio.

Two minutes later Andrew walked into the room in a fluster, breathing heavily.

"What is happening?" Lyadova asked. "Why is Apollo offline?"

"Something has happened at the server room," Andrew said. "His emergency protocol is to move himself to another server to protect himself. Once he is in position, he will come back online."

"The launch was initiating. What does this mean for that sequence?"

"It means it will be delayed for a few minutes until Apollo is back to fully operational. He has to run some tests when he boots up."

"How long?"

"Shouldn't be any more than twenty minutes."

"Jesus. This is my hour of glory. Fix it, will you!"

"The problem is with the Opera House server."

"I have spent millions on this complex. You told me it was secure and unhackable."

"It can't be hacked. That's not what happened."

"Well, what happened?"

"I think someone took it offline. The server."

"If they cannot hack it, that means they are here, on site."

"Yes."

"Put out an alert to all guards on site," Lyadova said, turning to Nina, "and then take Andrew and find out what happened at the Opera House."

"Let's go," Nina snapped at Andrew, before the pair left the room.

"There is something I have been wondering," Sukhanov said, "and since it seems we have time, I thought I would ask."

"What is it?" Lyadova asked with a bemused look on her face.

"Where did the money come from? How did you become the richest person on the planet and how did you create the biggest brand known to mankind?"

"You mean how did the illegitimate daughter of a prostitute make something of herself?"

"Well, yes," Sukhanov said bluntly.

"When I was younger, I sold everything, including my body, to feed myself and keep a roof over my head. I begged, borrowed and stole until I climbed out of the gutter and could finally afford a comfortable place. I started to turn away from a life of crime and heartache when I was assaulted by the man I loved. He beat me and stole everything I had. That's when I returned to the orphanage and those awful nuns who pointed me in the right direction to find my mother. I found her and you killed her, but you already know that bit."

"The money."

"You gave my mother a suitcase full of cash as hush money when she came to see you, but it was taken as evidence after the crash. When I tried to claim my mother's possessions, including the suitcase, they didn't believe me. I had no proof and only a faint resemblance, which was not enough. They buried her in a field with a small plastic sign for a headstone. No ceremony, no celebration of her life, not even a prayer. They treated her as a criminal and wouldn't listen to me. They figured a dead hooker and her illegitimate daughter, who happened to be a known criminal, could not make any real fuss and didn't deserve to be treated as human beings."

Sukhanov sat in silence.

"I cried, uncontrollable sobs, for days. I had nowhere to go and nothing left in the world. I thought about killing myself. I dreamed of ways I could do it. But then one day, the crying stopped and I stopped thinking about killing myself and started thinking about killing you instead. You were the answer to every question about why my life was so awful. I met Nina in the weeks that followed and we planned an attack on the police station. We raided the station and recovered the suitcase you had given my mother. We also helped ourselves to some other things too, including guns, money, jewellery and drugs. As much as we could get into our van from their evidence hold. Then we ran."

"Drugs?"

"Bingo!" Lyadova said, pointing into the air. "You see, my abusive ex-boyfriend had made some enemies in the depths of the drug cartels and I knew where to find some of them. I bought my way out. I paid them every cent he owed them, knowing they would think I was in it with him, then I sold them all the drugs we stole from the police station."

"And that was enough?"

"No," Lyadova laughed. "The cash in the suitcase you gave my mother and the drug money, plus the proceeds from selling the jewellery and some of the other things we stole, was seed funding."

"You started a trillion-dollar company with that money?"

"Yes, but not in the way you think. I gave Nina the option to walk away with her share, but she decided to stay. When I say seed funding, I mean it quite literally. We started with cannabis, but quickly moved into heroine. The money bought us the seeds and enough to bribe a local farmer and a few others to look the other way. Your assassin tried and nearly succeeded in killing me, which was when I knew I had to leave. While Nina got the business up and running, I fled the country to change my appearance. I couldn't risk you finding out who I was or where I was again. So I did the plastic surgery and months of pain and fear and loathing. Months of pain, all the while looking over my shoulder waiting for my father to finally kill me. I later returned, ready to take over the business. After my first year back, we had enough money to buy the land and, after the second, we expanded and grew our operations. After five years, we had more money than we knew what to do with and I started investing it, but as the dot com boom was starting, I saw an opening. I pumped millions into creating a new company and hiring talented staff, and A&A grew. We aggressively bought out competitors. Those who refused were met by an army of my loyal soldiers who persuaded the directors to sell using whatever threats and non-disclosure waivers were necessary. Others I just had killed and their colleagues got the message. And while the company was growing, so was the drugs business. Both legitimate and illegitimate businesses were making millions."

"How did you get away with this for so long?"

"I silenced everyone who stood in my way, one way or another. Everyone has a price. Some took money, some took jobs, some took bullets. And, you forget, A&A controls what people see on the internet and social media. If I wanted someone or something to disappear, it would simply be gone. That's why I know you will be blamed for this and I will be free to help write history and our new future. I will control everything."

"You will fail."

"How exactly do you think that will happen?"

"There are people out there who fight even harder for what they believe in, than you can imagine. They will see you brought to justice."

Chapter Thirty-Six

Max woke.

His head was spinning and aching from the rifle blow.

He ran through his mental checklist to assess his various aches and pains. His face and ribs were sore, but he couldn't feel anything more serious, just the crushing cold.

His feet were freezing and he blinked a few times, willing his eyes to open.

As he started to fully regain consciousness, he felt the cold pressing on every inch of his body.

He opened his eyes and looked down to see his feet in two buckets of freezing cold water. The water line was a couple of inches above his ankles.

But that wasn't the worst of it, he was also completely naked outside in the sub-zero temperatures.

Max was shackled at the wrists with both arms up and out to the sides above his head, like a human Y. He struggled against the chains, but it was no use; they were fastened to two nearby trees.

"It seems we have had a little role reversal," Alexei said, smiling as Max looked up. "You have caused us a lot of trouble and I have a few debts to settle."

"I knew I should have just killed you," Max replied.

"Well, thanks to your friend, Gabriel, I am surprisingly feeling all right. He told me I would likely get back to my old self in a few months, but I feel better already."

"And you let him die."

"Yes, he was still a friend of yours after all, so he had to be punished."

"You should kill me, because if I get out of these chains, I will not hesitate to kill you for what you did."

Alexei limped over and punched Max in the face. Max's head flung back and to the side.

He slowly turned back to face Alexei and before he could say anything, Alexei punched him again and again, left, right, left.

The chains on his wrists cut into the skin as he pulled against them trying to protect and free himself.

When Alexei finished, Max spat blood at his feet, reddening the white snow.

"What was it you told me about staying in the icy cold water at the motel?" Alexei asked, walking back to a small bag on the ground. "That's right, the water will permanently cripple my feet after only a short time in the extreme cold. Now you have that same problem."

"Are you going to push me off a building too?" Max asked. "Just to make it even."

"I should shoot you in the foot too."

"Then we would be even. So, what are you waiting for?"

"I have to find out some information first, then we will get to that."

"You might as well get to it, because I'm not telling you shit."

"We will see," Alexei said, smiling as he turned around holding a hunting knife. "Everyone talks eventually."

"We'll both freeze to death out here, before you get me there."

Alexei held the knife up in front of Max's eyes, then slowly lowered it and dragged the blade across his chest.

A six inch cut was sliced into the skin over Max's left pec and he just gritted his teeth and looked at Alexei with eyes burning with hate.

Alexei saw the defiant look in his eyes and sliced another gash into Max's exposed torso, this time below his right rib line.

Max held his gaze and locked his jaw to get through the pain.

Alexei saw the bullet wound Lydia had inflected and drove his thumb into the hole.

Max groaned and gnawed his teeth, but never once blinked, focusing his anger and hate into his stare.

"You are tough, I will give you that," Alexei said, "but do you really want to die out here?"

Max didn't say anything, just stared at his torturer.

"Maybe I need something a bit stronger to get your attention," Alexei said, walking back to the bag and removing a box like item. "This should do it."

Max watched as Alexei sat the car battery in front of him and connected the leads. He touched the opposite ends of the cables in front of Max's face. It was a move Max himself had used to intimidate several terrorists over the years. He knew exactly what was coming.

Alexei just smiled and locked eyes with Max as the sparks lit up the shadows between them.

Two of A&A's private soldiers were walking past and stopped to see what was happening. One was wheeling a barrow full of wood and the other was carrying two axes. They had been chopping firewood for the old palace's fireplaces.

They both smiled and moved in to watch what happened next.

Alexei sat the leads on Max's chest. The electricity coursed through his body and into the buckets of water. Max spasmed and squirmed as all of his muscles tightened and his head flew back. His whole body arched and shook, as water splashed out of the buckets.

Alexei pulled the cables off his skin and Max instantly dropped. His head fell forward and his knees went weak. His whole body weight was hanging on the shackles around his wrists.

"Who did you tell you were here and what did you tell them?" Alexei asked. "Tell me and I will just kill you and put you out of your misery."

"Kill yourself and I'll be out of my misery," Max said.

"Wrong answer," Alexei said, placing the ends of the leads on Max's chest.

Max convulsed again as the two guards smiled and laughed behind Alexei.

Max fell forward as the jumper cables were taken off his skin. His head slumped and he didn't budge. He didn't even look like he was breathing.

Alexei slapped him across the face as the axe men continued to smile and laugh. Max didn't flinch, so Alexei slapped him again.

When he didn't flinch the second time, Alexei got worried and moved in to check his pulse.

He couldn't feel it. He moved in closer again to see if he could hear or feel his breathing.

"He's dead," Alexei snapped at the two guards who instantly stopped smiling. "Come help me get him down."

The two guys ran over and took Max's weight as Alexei unlocked the cuffs on Max's wrists.

When his hands were free, Max kicked one of the buckets forward and drove it into Alexei's stomach.

Both of the guards had moved in under his arms to hold him up and Max took them both in headlocks. The guy on the right was the first to fall as Max snapped his neck.

As the dead guard was falling, Max flung the second bucket forward and hit Alexei in the face as he hunched over from the previous blow.

Alexei fell back and started crab walking backwards away from Max.

The second guard was clawing at Max's arm trying to get free and Max punched him three times in the kidneys, immediately weakening him. He dropped to the ground in front of Max and started crawling through the snow to the axes he had dropped only moments before.

Max jumped on his back and the two men grappled and wrestled in the snow, inching closer to the axes with every roll. The guard got to one first and tried to get Max to fall on it.

Max held himself up as Alexei ran in wielding a hunk of firewood high over his head. He swung it down towards the back of Max's head, but Max had seen the attack coming and rolled to the side.

The block of wood smashed into the guard's face and instantly killed him.

Alexei stumbled back, as Max swung the big axe towards him.

Alexei rolled to the side as the blade drove into the snow beside him. He rolled and scrambled away, getting to his feet as Max did too.

Alexei ran, dodging left and right, heading back towards the palace as Max hurled the axe through the air in his direction.

The axe narrowly missed Alexei, slamming into the trunk of a tree and lodging itself in deep as the handle vibrated, expelling its remaining energy.

Alexei radioed in for back up as he ran as fast as he could on his bad leg.

Max had watched Alexei run. There was no way he should be running on that injured foot. He was clearly on some heavy drugs.

Max pulled on his pants, shoes and jacket. He tucked a pistol into his pants, then gathered the other axe and knife, and ran deeper into the thick trees before Alexei's back up could arrive.

Max made his way around the tree line, dodging patrols, until one unit got too close. He used the shadows to hide, but they kept coming.

He scaled a nearby tree, climbing as fast and as silently as possible.

Two guards arrived at the base of the tree and scanned around the area.

Eventually one of the men saw Max's footprints in the snow. They followed them to the tree he was in, then looked up.

As the duo raised their heads, they saw Max falling fast through the air towards them. He had jumped when they were close enough.

Max was wielding the second axe high over his head and brought it down brutally into the head of one of the guards. Blood sprayed everywhere, including onto the face of his comrade who was falling away in shock.

The horrified blood-soaked fighter fell into the snow scrambling away from Max. He had dropped his gun as he fell and was desperately and frantically trying to find it in the white powder. Just as he clenched the handle, the axe blade sliced through his wrist, taking off his whole hand.

The guard sat up in shock and blinked as he saw his now handless arm. Blood pumped out onto the snow as his eyes rolled into the back of his head and he passed out.

Max left the axe and the fatally wounded man, and trod quickly away through the snow. He found the Opera House again and snuck past it en route to the main palace.

When he arrived, he realised it was being renovated and each end of the old palace had metal scaffolding up to the roof. He used the closest scaffold to climb up on top of the grand old structure.

At the top, Max saw a guard smoking and watching the driveway.

The palace was divided into three buildings. The centre building was around three storeys tall with a high pitched roof, which had rounded weathered copper curved surfaces running around the edges and a long flat rectangular section running down the centre.

The two buildings on each end were only two storeys, but on each corner they had three storey towers offset in diamond formation. Each tower rose like a guard tower on an ornate gothic castle. In the centre of the two lower buildings' roofs were raised white concrete platforms, surrounded by gently sloping green copper which went back down to the edge of the building.

The smoking terrorist was on the raised part in the centre of the first roof, leaning over the railing casually.

Max crept up the slippery copper and climbed over the opposite railing onto the platform. He walked up behind the smoking guard and cracked him over the head with the butt of his pistol.

The terrorist toppled over the railing and slid on the ice and snow towards the edge, but thankfully stopped just short of falling over. Max didn't need another body giving away his location as the patrols ramped up.

Max headed for the main building's roof and started to climb up. When he got near the top, he heard the familiar sound of the safety clicking off on a rifle. He looked up and found a sentry aiming an assault rifle at his face.

The guard reached for his radio to call it in, as Max reached up and grabbed his ankle, pulling it out from under him.

The private solider fell backwards, as Max swung to the left, and fired a short burst of bullets which slammed into the roof, narrowly missing Max.

The guard slipped off the roof, down a full storey to the roof Max had just been on. He hit hard and lay still.

Max climbed down, hearing the man's radio.

"Unit One, respond," the radio commanded. "Was that weapon fire?"

"Ahh, sorry," Max said in Russian. "The roof is slippery, I fell and accidently let off a couple of rounds. I am fine though. Apologies. All clear here."

"Watch what you are doing, Unit One, and keep your eyes open. We cannot afford mistakes tonight. Be on the look out for the prisoner."

"Roger that," Max said, pocketing the radio.

Chapter Thirty-Seven

Max army crawled along the centre roof, getting low in the snow to hide from the A&A guards along each ledge. They were watching the yards and gardens, looking for signs of intruders, but the cold was slowing them down and the boredom was kicking in, meaning their bodies were starting to semi-hibernate.

Suddenly, all their radios erupted waking them from their stupor.

"Red alert!" Nina said. "Alexei tells me Agent Max Shaw is on the grounds. He got away from this idiot. The Opera House has been breached. All guards check your areas and report in."

Max watched the four men on the roof with him. They all turned to each other, then turned to look at the centre of the building. They began walking up the sloped snow covered copper towards him.

He had no choice, eventually they would see him.

Max pulled out his pistol and, while laying prone, fired two shots into the man coming up the slope on his right, then quickly changed position and discharged two shots into the man on his left.

Both men fell and slipped down the icy surface before disappearing over the edge of the roof.

"Who is shooting?" Nina asked as the remaining two guys on the roof watched their comrades fall over the edge of the building.

Max rolled onto his back then sat up. He fired at the man on his left, hitting him in the arm and the leg. He fell to his knees as Max fired again, but the bullet sailed over his head as he dropped onto roof and rolled left.

Max turned to fire at the last man, but he was moving fast and started firing. Max laid back down and rolled hard to his left, tumbling down the roof towards the edge to escape the rapid incoming fire.

As he slid, the two guards unleashed a wave of bullets towards him. The bullets hit the snow all around him, puffing the white ice up into the air.

Then Max went over.

The two guards approached cautiously, but they were optimistic. There were no ledges or decorative spires on that side of the building.

The soldier Max had shot limped along holding his arm behind his comrade as he arrived and looked over the edge, then suddenly his face exploded as the bullet hit its mark.

Max had caught the concrete lip above the gothic window on the top floor as he went over the edge and he was hanging precariously. He dropped his now empty pistol after shooting the guard and it fell harmlessly into the soft snow below, and disappeared in a puff of powdery ice.

Max heard the second sentry, slowly inching closer to the edge. He could tell it was the guard he shot earlier, he could hear the hop steps he was taking, quick step then hard landing on his good leg. Max heard the hard landing, then the quick step and pulled himself up, reached over and he grabbed the guard's ankle on his good leg pulling it out from under him.

He fell onto his back, then came over the edge, dropping his gun into the snow next to Max's three storeys beneath them.

As he fell, he caught Max's shoulders and scrambled to get a hold.

Max grabbed the ledge with his other hand to hold their combined weight.

"You are coming with me," the guard said through his pain into Max's ear.

"I don't think so," Max said, throwing his head back and breaking his nose.

The guard's grip failed and he slipped. He fell, but grabbed Max's jacket at the last second. Max was losing his grip, but could feel the guard's hands starting to twitch on the fabric. Max just needed to hold on a little longer.

The guard slid again and Max kicked back with his heal hitting him in the balls. His attacker's reflexes kicked in and he instinctively let go with his good hand to protect himself, but the other arm was the one Max had shot earlier and it was not strong enough to hold him any longer.

The guard fell and hit the ground beside the guns, in a puff of powdery snow, but it wasn't a soft fall. He hit hard and there was no doubt he was dead.

Max pulled himself up as several of Lyadova's soldiers ran across the garden towards the palace and opened fire at him.

Max ran hard as the snow kicked up in white icy puffs behind him as the bullets from the guards' guns hit the roof.

He turned and ran to the other side of the roof. When he got there, he found one of the safety ropes which was tied to the scaffold. He used it to slide down to the arched gate and façade that bridged the gap between the palace and the Bread House.

Bullets slammed into the massive concrete and brick gate, and tore through the air all around him as he ran.

As he got closer to the massive Bread House, he threw the knife he had picked up earlier into the nearest window, shattering it, then he dived through it.

The glass was scattered across the floor as Max flew into the room, rolling into a somersault and stopping down on one knee scanning the room. He quickly gathered his knife as one of the mercenaries came through the door. He reached for his gun, but didn't get the chance. Max put the knife into his neck.

"Max!" Verity yelled from a room nearby.

Max took the knife and the guard's gun, then scurried out of the room, leading with his gun. A lookout entered the hallway and Max, fired taking him down. Then he saw Verity in the room on his left.

Verity nodded quickly to her right. Max nodded his understanding and dived into the room, landing on his right side.

He took aim at Verity's right, where the gaoler she had pointed out was hiding, and he opened fire.

The guard had been waiting for him, but her first shot went wide having not expected Max to dive into the room. The second hit Max in the left arm. Max's first two shots missed, but the third lodged in her chest. She fell back against the wall and then slid down, trailing a heavy blood smear on the ancient looking wallpaper behind her.

"Nice shot," Verity said. "I was getting sick of that bitch. How are we faring?"

"I've taken out one of the server rooms and a few guards," Max said as he walked over and started untying her wrists. "I could use a hand though. Here, hold this."

"Thanks," Verity said, taking the gun from Max to watch the door, as he undid the other ropes. "Here we go!"

Verity fired over Max's head, taking down a portly older man in the hallway. Max undid the last of the ropes holding her arms, then loosened the rope holding her legs. She stood up and fired again, forcing another guard behind cover. She fired three times into the wall he was using for cover. The bullets punched through the plaster and they heard him fall in the hallway.

"Back up?" Verity asked.

"Not coming," Max said. "They are busy preparing for war. Andrew didn't send my messages, but it didn't matter anyway, Lyadova launched an attack on the American fleet."

"Jesus."

"I aborted it, but it was enough to get their attention. Now that psycho bitch has hacked the Russian military systems and is preparing to launch World War III."

"Where's your shirt?"

"I didn't have time to put it on after Alexei tortured me. Just the jacket."

"He did? Are you okay?"

"Nothing like a few cuts and some high voltage to get you in the mood to kill some fuckers."

"I'm sorry about Gabriel, and Andrew, I didn't see it coming. He busted Alexei out."

"Neither did I. Gabriel was a great man. Andrew, on the other hand, has always been a piece of shit and he is soon to be a dead man. And so is Alexei."

"Let me look at that arm," Verity said, tearing the wide fabric belt which had been holding the curtain in place off the wall. "Where is Lyadova?"

"I think she's in the palace," Max said, wincing as Verity tightened the fabric around his arm to stop the bleeding from the bullet wound. "Or under it, in the basement."

"So, what's the plan?"

"We need the tablet to stop the cyber-attack and any other attacks she is trying to launch, then we need to get word to all the governments to get them to stand down."

"And Lyadova and her crew?"

Max walked to the door, picked up one of the dropped guns and clicked the safety off.

"Your choice in the moment," Max said. "I don't care either way. Arrest if you want. Shoot if you need."

"Done, let's move," Verity said as she followed Max out into the corridor.

They cleared the rooms, then headed down into a large room which took up the centre of the Bread House.

As they walked in, Nina and Alexei marched in at the opposite end. Well, Nina marched in tall and proud, ready for a fight, while Alexei limped in, having reopened the wounds in his foot as he fled from Max. His cast was breaking and falling away, but his eyes were wide in anger. Max could only assume he was on a heavy cocktail of drugs to keep him moving through the pain, but it was also giving him some big intense angry eyes. The drugs were one thing, but the arse kicking he would have gotten from Nina for letting Max escape was probably also playing a role. That and his wounded ego.

"I've got her," Verity said, locking eyes with Nina. "We have unfinished business."

"Looks like the crackhead is mine," Max said.

"You killed Lydia," Nina said, pointing at Max. "Once I take down your friend here, I am coming for you."

The four of them stood facing each other for a few seconds, before Nina and Alexei both raised their weapons. Max and Verity followed suit, and the room erupted in gunfire.

All four moved and returned fire as they ran. Bullets flew through the air and slammed into windows and walls.

Max shot Alexei twice, but the crazed Russian started running at him with wide, wild, screaming eyes.

Max fired again, but the Russian tackled him and the pair rolled around on the floor. Max fired a shot into the wooden floorboards beside Alexei's head as he pinned him down.

Max pushed all his weight down onto the pistol and tried to angle it towards Alexei, but the tough Russian threw a vicious headbutt breaking Max's nose.

Max dropped his gun and involuntarily recoiled. Alexei capitalised, punching Max in the chest and the face, then rolled him over and unleashed a violent blast of punches into the Max's sternum and ribs.

"You killed my father!" Alexei screamed.

"I don't know your father," Max said, ducking a punch.

"General Sacha Kuznetsov!"

"Oh yes, I remember him now, I did kill him, but he got what was coming to him," Max said as Alexei unleashed a flurry of punches. "No wonder you were so keen to torture me alone in the woods without back up. Pity your dad's not here to see how incompetent you really are. Must run in the family."

"Fuck you!" Alexei spat as he threw another series of punches and elbows.

Out of the shadows, Laskaris, Lyadova's young personal assistant, crept up behind Alexei and slammed a closed laptop over his head, shattering it and showering the ground with plastic, glass and electronics.

Alexei was dazed by the blow, but it seemed to just anger him more. He turned to see his new attacker and grabbed Laskaris by the throat. The young man's eyes filled with panic.

Max reached up and grabbed Alexei by the throat, then punched him twice in the face. Alexei let go of Laskaris and he stumbled backwards.

Max jumped on top of Alexei and unleashed his own flurry of blows, until Alexei fell backwards, dazed and semi-conscious.

"Thanks, kid," Max said, standing and searching for his gun. "Where did you come from?"

"They had me tied up across the hall," Laskaris said. "But one of the guards asked me for a hand with his computer."

"Sounds like he underestimated you."

Laskaris just nodded shyly, reflecting on killing the guard.

"It was the right thing to do," Max said, walking over and picking up his gun. "You did what you had to. I owe you one."

"Look out!" Laskaris shouted as Alexei got to his feet.

Max spun, lowering his body and dragging his leg along the ground. It collided with Alexei's injured foot and Alexei moaned in pain as he fell back to the ground. Max stomped on the cast, once, twice, three times. On the fourth, the cast finally broke away and he stomped down again, undoing the last of Gabriel's surgical work.

Alexei gritted his teeth as he clawed backwards, trying to reach one of the pistols on the ground. Max darted around and kicked him in the ribs, then stomped on his hand, shattering it.

Alexei pulled his hand in close to his chest, clutching it in pain. Max levelled the gun at Alexei's face. Alexei went to speak, but Max had had enough. He pulled the trigger and the bullet carved through Alexei's face and exploded out the back of his head. He fell in a heap as Max's gun clicked empty.

While Max was distracted and had his back to the door, Andrew snuck into the room. He fired six shots in Max's direction, but he was a hopeless shot. The first bullets sailed past harmlessly.

Max turned around, grabbed Laskaris and dragged him down to the floor. Laskaris hit the floor beside him with a heavy thud, and Max crawled over him to use his own body to protect the young man.

A bullet tore into Max's thigh and he clenched his teeth.

Andrew disappeared back through the door and Max rolled to the side to check Laskaris. The young man's face was blank. His eyes were wide. Max checked his body and found three bullet holes in Laskaris's back. The thanks Max had felt for Andrew's shots missing him quickly faded on realising they weren't meant for him.

Max closed the young man's eyes, then screamed in anger.

"Rixon, I'm going to kill you, you son of a bitch!" Max yelled, getting to his feet, chambering a new magazine in his pistol and running into the corridor as best as he could with his wounded leg.

Across the room, Verity and Nina's initial shots both went wide, but the pair kept running towards each other until they met by the large French doors near the middle of the wall.

The two women danced around each other, like Olympic boxers getting ready to spar.

Nina was almost two metres from Verity and without warning she launched herself through the air and tackled Verity. Her shoulder drove up under Verity's ribs and buckled her over. The force of the tackle was enough for both women to drop their weapons.

Verity fell backwards with Nina holding on around her waist. The pair crashed through the glass French doors and tumbled down a small concrete staircase onto a narrow path which lined the building. It was covered in snow and now fragments of glass too.

Verity felt the cold ice pressing through her thin shirt as she lay on the snow trying to get her breath.

As she got to her feet, she saw the blood stains on the snow. The glass in the door was thick to keep out the cold and it had cut her in several places, but she was so cold she couldn't feel it.

Nina stood up, wielding a large shard of the glass which she held in a stabbing grip like a dagger.

The strong and fearless women danced around each other again leaving a rough circle in the snow, then Nina lunged. She was fast, but Verity was ready for her and blocked the incoming blow. She grabbed Nina's wrist and twisted it back, then punched her in the face. As she threw a second punch, Nina countered and freed her wrist, swiping the glass at Verity, slicing her forearm.

Blood dripped down over her hand and fingers then dripped off, splattering on the snow by her feet.

Verity dodged the next two wild swipes with the makeshift knife, but the third sliced a long cut in her shirt and a thin red line in her chest. She swatted at Nina's hand hoping to dislodge the glass, but she held fast, so Verity grabbed Nina's glass wielding hand and squeezed hard.

The glass cut open Nina's fingers and palm, and she groaned and cursed in pain.

Verity saw a brief opening and threw a savage headbutt. Nina moved her head back, but not fast enough. Verity's forehead still slammed down onto Nina's mouth.

Nina lost two teeth and two others were close to coming free from the blow. Verity's forehead was sliced open by a couple of Nina's teeth and the blood was streaming down over her right eye.

Nina tried to punch Verity with her glass welding hand, but Verity saw it coming and grabbed the hand and squeezed. Again, the glass drove itself deeper into Nina's palm and cut her index finger down to the bone.

Blood poured out of the pair, who were again dancing their dance in the pink, red and white snow.

Nina ran in, swapping the glass to her other hand and slashed Verity down the right side of the face causing her to scream in pain.

Verity tried to tackle Nina, but the bigger woman was too strong and held her ground, then stabbed the glass into Verity's already wounded back.

Verity rolled to the side and Nina lost her grip on the glass. As she tried to reach for it, Verity threw a brutal left-right combo, jab and hook, into her face, knocking the other two loose teeth out.

Nina stumbled backwards, then spat blood onto the snow and wiped her swelling lips.

Verity pulled the glass shard from her back and ran for Nina. She slashed the air as Nina dodged and ducked the incoming attacks. Verity faked another slash and as Nina dodged, Verity kicked her in the knee. There was a sickening snap as one of the ligaments broke.

Nina screamed in agony and fell to her good knee.

Verity came in to finish the job, but Nina was not going to make it easy. She grabbed Verity's legs and swept them out from under her, then dragged herself on top and started punching, letting her pain fuel her.

Verity used her free arm to block some of the blows, as she searched the snow with her other hand.

Then she found it.

Her fingers slid over the smooth, bloodied surface of the glass shard. She picked it up as the blows kept coming, then stabbed it hard into Nina's side, snapping the end off between her ribs, as Nina kept punching. It took her a few blows before Nina could feel the glass and when she did, she stopped swinging.

Nina felt her ribs and saw the blood on her hands. Anger flashed in her eyes and she drew her arm back to start punching again, but Verity lunged.

The remaining piece of the glass shard lodged in Nina's neck and she went still. She blinked and raised her hand to her neck, but then fell to the side as blood poured from her wounds and mouth.

Verity kicked Nina off onto the snow and laid in the freezing icy powder, thankful she was numb so she could not feel all her wounds, aches and pains.

As she started to get to her feet, Nina reached out and grabbed her leg.

Verity planted her foot, the one Nina had hold of, and spun on her ankle, swinging her opposite leg through the bitter winter air. Her boot slammed into the end of the glass which was still embedded in Nina's neck and it drove in. The life drained from Nina's eyes and she fell backwards and laid dead in the snow.

Inside, Max rounded the corner as two bullets shattered the picture frame beside him. Max returned fire as Andrew fled into a nearby room. One of the bullets slammed into the door, narrowly missing Andrew, as he flung it closed.

Max walked as fast as he could on his wounded leg.

As he got closer to the door, his pace quickened until he was almost running.

He kicked open the door and burst into the room.

Max found himself staring down the barrel of Andrew's pistol. Three A&A security guards were standing behind him with their batons drawn.

Andrew squeezed the trigger.

Max with lightning speed reached out and slid the slide back on the gun, jamming it open, before Andrew could fire. He furrowed his brow and locked eyes with Andrew over the pistol sights. Max was beyond angry, he felt as if he could almost crush the pistol with his bare hands and Andrew knew it.

Max tore the pistol free and holding it by the top, he swung it handle first like a hammer into the side of Andrew's face, knocking him down to one knee.

The three guards circled around Max and Andrew, who was still on his knees.

"All right, boys," Max said, looking each one up and down, sizing them up. "The Americans and their allies know what

Lyadova has done. They will be here any minute. Is she really worth it?"

The men stopped moving forward and looked at each other. While they were distracted, Max dashed forward, slamming the butt of Andrew's stolen pistol into the side of the first guard's head. As he was falling, Max shot the man on his right with his own pistol and his dead body fell backwards and sprawled out on the floor.

The third foe slammed his baton into Max's shoulder. Max dropped his gun and groaned.

He spun to face the third guard, as Andrew tried to get to his feet. Max kicked him in the back and he fell to the floor. The guard took the distraction as a gift and swung his baton like a baseball bat. It hit Max under the ribs and he felt one crack.

As his attacker moved in for another shot, Max caught his wrist and swung Andrew's pistol through the air towards his face.

The guard caught his wrist and the pair stood facing off, trying to free themselves from each other's hold. The guard threw his head forward and smashed it down on Max's already swollen eye. The skin split and blood ran down his cheek.

Max's eyes blazed with anger and he returned the blow with his own vicious headbutt. The wannabe soldier staggered back, dropping his baton and letting go of Max's wrist to clutch his face. Max unloaded strike after strike on the terrorist with the butt of Andrew's gun as the guard cowered and roiled trying to block the attack. Max hit him in the side of the head and he dropped to his knees. In one fluid motion, Max tossed Andrew's gun up and caught it by the handle, pressed it to the guard's head and pulled the trigger.

The body fell to the floor beside Andrew.

Max stepped forward, leaned down next to Andrew's ear and pressed the gun in under his chin.

"Get up," Max said, his tone as cold as the icy snow outside.

"Don't kill me, Max," Andrew said. "I was just doing what I had to, to survive. You, of all people, should understand that. We are the same."

"We are nothing alike. You are a traitor and a terrorist. You killed Laskaris. He was young and had a full life ahead of him. He didn't need to die."

"He tried to kill Alexei."

"He hit Alexei with a laptop. It hardly dazed him, let alone come close to killing him. If anyone was going to kill Alexei it was me. Not the kid. He was a good guy and you are a piece of shit."

"So, what happens now?"

"I killed Alexei. Now I am going to stop Lyadova and you are going to help me."

"Why would I do that?"

"Because you built the program for her. Apollo is your handiwork."

"Apollo is my masterpiece!" Andrew said with a mix of pride and anger.

"But it wasn't just building Apollo and killing Laskaris, you also murdered Gabriel. What did he do to you?"

"I didn't like him and we couldn't take him with us. I needed to get the tablet back to Lyadova and I only needed a couple of hostages."

"So you killed him!" Max yelled, pressing the gun harder in underneath Andrew's jaw.

"Like you can judge. How many people have you killed just today alone? All guns and death. Aren't you tired of it?"

"I am actually, but you had to turn up at The Hague and drag me into all this. Why? Why me?"

"We needed someone to get the western allies fired up. Feed them information about the Russians and get them on a war footing. You were an easy target. I knew you wouldn't be able to let it slide. You will always be the hero, even when they toss you out with the trash, you can't help yourself. Like when you arrested me, you just see things in black and white. There is no grey with you. Always the boy scout, always the saviour. I knew you would get involved. I could then manipulate you and you didn't disappoint. You gave the information to Blake and Moore, and helped start World War III. Then I outed you in the media, so you would be the fall guy. The world would look to you and to Sukhanov as the ones responsible for all this, and Lyadova would get away with it. But I didn't anticipate after all these years and everything we threw at you, that you would make it this far. I was waiting, so patiently, to watch you die. After all those years in prison I served because of you. Your death when it comes will be elating."

"How did you know I was Witness S?"

"Birmingham."

"Timothy Birmingham, the British Prime Minister?"

"Yes, he's fucking Lyadova. They are in on this together. He was supposed to tear down the Five Eyes treaty and weaken their intelligence systems making it easier for Apollo to strike. He had to keep his end of the deal after Lyadova rigged the election so he could win. The plan was for the western intelligence system to fall and while it did for Russia to strike."

"I know."

"Then why did you ask?"

"Because I remembered what you said about me not being so good with technology. You're right, I'm not, but my friend Hermes, well, he is very good with technology. He has been listening and recording everything you have said."

"Well congratulations, Agent Shaw. You got me. I confessed on tape, but I will still get to watch you die."

"How do you figure that?"

"I know where Lyadova is."

"I'm sure I can find her without you."

"Yes, I'm sure you can. But, can you get into the room without killing Sukhanov?"

"Sukhanov?"

"Yes."

"That was who the men led in from the town car? I saw it arrive. She kidnapped the Russian President?"

"Bingo. And he's right in the crossfire path. You wouldn't want him to take a bullet. You would be responsible for starting the war after all. Even if Lyadova fails, a stray bullet into the Russian President would be the next shot heard around the world. The starting pistol of war, but this time the allies won't win."

"Why did she kidnap Sukhanov? Apollo is attacking the Russians too. I saw it with my own eyes when I met him."

"You're as big a fool as he is. He has been involved in this from the start. Lyadova made him believe she would only attack the West and he would have free rein to take out the allies and return Russia to its former glory."

"So, they are intending to go to war?"

"They were, but Lyadova is taking control of their military and she is going to be the one calling the shots."

"Why? What does she hope to achieve?"

"She wants Sukhanov to be written into the history books, stored in Alexandria 2.0, as the greatest war criminal in history and the man responsible for starting the war to end all wars. And she wants A&A at the centre of information and government for all time. It will be her legacy."

"Why does she hate Sukhanov?"

"He is her father, and she wants revenge for all the terrible shit that happened to her in her life."

"And what do you want? Why are you telling me all this?"

"I want to live."

"I should just put a bullet into you and be done with it," Max said as he clicked back the hammer on his pistol. "And rest assured, I will if you do anything I don't want you to. Now, tell me how to get to Lyadova without harming Sukhanov or the stray bullet will have your name on it."

Chapter Thirty-Eight

"Apollo, are you back online?" Lyadova asked, pacing in front of Sukhanov.

"Apologies, Isabella," Apollo said. *"The main server room was taken offline and I needed to relocate my main programming to one of the backups. I am back online and fully operational."*

"Recommence with target acquisition."

"Yes, Isabella. Acquiring targets."

"How long until you can strike?"

"Approximately two minutes until launch. The first missile will then hit its targets within seven minutes."

"Stop this, Isabella," Sukhanov said. "You can kill me. You will have your revenge."

"That would not be enough," Lyadova said. "I cannot just kill you. I have to destroy your name and legacy too."

Sukhanov had two sentries standing behind him. Both men had their weapons trained on his head. After the attack on the server room, Lyadova told them if anyone tried to enter the room, they were to kill him.

Sukhanov looked across the room and saw a small window in the door. He squinted at first, then pretended to stare off into space, but kept his eyes trained on the door, not wanting to give his captors any warning.

Max's face reappeared in the window, then he held up three fingers. Two, one.

Sukhanov fell forward onto his stomach, anticipating the room entry, and trying to avoid the shots from his kidnappers.

Lyadova turned to see what he was doing. The room was still and otherwise silent.

"What are you doing?" Lyadova asked, walking over to Sukhanov.

"Umm, I fell," Sukhanov said, confused, but then the door opened, just not in the way he had been expecting. He had expected Max to come in guns blazing.

Sukhanov saw Max walking into the room and felt relief, until Max put his hands on his head. One of the terrorists was leading him into the room with that other guy, Andrew, smiling broadly and trailing closely behind.

"Ah, Agent Shaw," Lyadova said, turning to face him. "You were the one who took my servers offline."

"Guilty as charged," Max said. "Why don't you let the President go and turn the others off?"

"I am sorry, but that doesn't work for me. As a matter of fact, you being alive doesn't work for me either."

Lyadova pulled out her pistol and shot Max in the leg. The same leg Alexei shot him in.

He dropped to the floor, clutching the wound and gritting his teeth.

"You have caused me quite a bit of trouble!" Lyadova said, slapping Max across the face. "I thought Birmingham and his new Attorney-General, that piss weak pretender Maher, had sorted you out. We paid that judge, Stafford, in The Hague to keep you locked up, which ultimately forced you to escape and go on the run again, as planned. You should be dead or at least back under arrest. I don't know how you have avoided van den Berg and the police, and intelligence agencies, we have been tipping them off the whole time. Let alone all my men. I should have hired you instead of them."

"I'm sorry to disappoint," Max said, moving in beside the President. "But I'm not for turning or for sale."

"How did you find him?" Lyadova asked her agent.

"I led him into a trap," Andrew said proudly walking out from behind the agent, smiling at Max.

"Good work. Now, why don't you help get Apollo's main servers back online?"

"Yes, ma'am," Andrew said, walking towards the door.

Max watched in anger as Andrew walked away, but then he stopped in his tracks and turned back to the room.

Andrew started moving back towards Lyadova slowly.

"What are you doing?" Lyadova asked.

"What he's told," Verity said, ducking out from behind Andrew and shooting one of the kidnappers behind the President.

Lyadova dropped to the ground and crawled fast behind cover, as Max grabbed the other sentry and dragged him to the ground before he could shoot the President.

He wrestled with the would-be shooter, until finally he got in behind him.

"Missiles ready, Isabella," Apollo said.

"Fire!" Lyadova yelled from behind the cabinet.

"All missiles launching," Apollo said as the computer screens all changed to show footage and radars of missiles launching from Russian ships and silos around the world.

Max snapped the guard's neck as four new A&A security men ran into the room.

Verity and Max both covered Sukhanov, returning fire at the guards. Verity shot one gunman and he fell, exposing Andrew. She fired, but couldn't be sure if she hit him.

Max pushed over a table and the three of them took cover behind it, as Andrew and the guards bundled Lyadova out of the room. Max took down one of them as he fled.

"We need to stop the warheads," Sukhanov said, looking up at the monitors. "War with the West won't end well for any of us."

"Especially while our systems are still online," Max said.

Sukhanov's eyes revealed his surprise. Max knew his secret.

"That's right," Max said. "I know you lied to me. You have been involved in this from the very beginning. You sent those arseholes to get me in the prison and got me to take out your general to silence him. You will answer for what you've done."

Their conversation was interrupted by gunfire as more men ran into the room.

"She took the tablet," Verity yelled over the incoming barrage. "What's the plan, Max?"

"We need to get the table," Max said. "Then we need to track them down and stop the warheads."

"What do we do about him?" Verity asked nodding to Sukhanov as she took down the last guard in the room.

"I am not going to run or hide," Sukhanov said, grabbing Verity's gun and pulling her in front of him as a human shield. "I need these missiles taken down and I need to speak to the Americans to get them to backdown. I must convince them it was all Lyadova's fault."

Sukhanov stood up, dragging Verity with him for the door making sure to keep her between him and a very pissed off Max. Max held his gun's sights on the President.

"Shoot him, Max!" Verity said defiantly.

"Shut up!" Sukhanov said, pulling her tighter.

"You won't get away with this," Max said. "Just let her go. Do the right thing and call the Americans. Back down and stop a war. You can reverse the damage Lyadova's done."

"You may be right, but what about you. You will tell the world what I have done."

"If we stop a World War, I'm sure that will play well for you. You saw the light and had a change of heart."

Sukhanov paused thinking about what Max had said.

"I can't take that chance," Sukhanov said levelling his gun at Max and firing.

The bullet hit Max in the side as he tried to dodge it. He hit the ground and scrambled behind cover as a second bullet slammed into the table. He heard Sukhanov swear, then Verity groaned before the unmistakeable sound of a body hitting the floor, before a door slammed.

Max sprung out from cover to see Sukhanov shoot the control panel on the other side of door and take off running.

Then he saw Verity on the floor and quickly bolted to her side to checked her for wounds.

"I'm okay," Verity said slowly opening her eyes and clutching her head. "That arsehole pistol whipped me. That fucking hurt."

"Are you okay?"

"I'll be better when I can return the favour," Verity said as Max helped her get to her feet.

He tried the door, but it was dead.

"Any ideas," Max asked.

"Let me look at it," Verity said, stepping over and slamming her gun down on the top of the electronic control panel.

It fell open exposing a bunch of wires and Verity set about cutting and splicing wires, until a few minutes later the door clicked open.

"Great work," Max said. "Let's head out."

Max moved relatively fast, limping in front of Verity as he led them up to ground floor of the palace.

He shot a guard at the top of the steps, then another in the foyer. They searched the ground floor looking for Lyadova and Sukhanov, but there was no sign of either.

"Max," Verity said, pointing to the front door of the palace.

There were blood droplets in the doorway. The two agents pushed open the door and saw more blood drops on the snow.

They followed the growing trail, which led them around the building, where they found Andrew on his knees, shallow breathing like a fish out of water and swaying in the breeze.

"Where is she Andrew?" Max asked as Andrew's eyes rolled around in his head.

Max slapped him hard across the face getting him to focus.

"Where is she?" Max asked again.

Andrew whispered something Max could not hear, so he moved closer, then he saw Andrew smile. Max looked down and saw the grenade in Andrew's hands. There was a small metal click as the lug and spring flicked the lever up, firing the pin, setting off the short timer.

"Get back!" Max yelled to Verity back around the corner of the building.

Max grabbed Andrew and pulled the big man forward. Andrew fell face first into the ground, covering the grenade, as Max fled back towards cover. He dived to the ground just as the grenade exploded.

Andrew's body absorbed a huge amount of the grenade's energy, but it tore him to pieces.

Four massive windows shattered and the snow around the explosion was covered in blood and dirt, and a huge divot was carved out where Andrew had been laying.

Max got back to his feet as Verity turned the corner and saw the hole, before they looked at each other having heard something in the distance. They scanned the sky looking for the source of the familiar sound.

A helicopter was coming in fast and the pair spotted Lyadova and her security detail running across the open gardens towards the greenhouses.

They gave chase but, given their injuries, neither Max and Verity were not as fast as they needed to be.

The Russian President and former KGB agent was running across the palatial garden after Lyadova. He was faster than Max in his current condition, but Max still doubted he would make it to Lyadova in time.

Sukhanov ran like his life and his country depended on it. He leapt small garden beds and hedges, as Verity and Max took down the guards running towards them.

Lyadova's goons were chasing Sukhanov, but Max and Verity opened fire, taking them down. They couldn't let Sukhanov die, not before he called off his troops anyway.

Suddenly, Sukhanov stopped and Max and Verity were closing in. Max was not sure what he was doing.

Sukhanov raised his pistol and started firing.

Max looked ahead and saw a flame shoot out of the gas tanks at the back of the middle greenhouse. Seconds later, the tank exploded setting off a chain of explosions throughout the other greenhouses as the fertilisers and gas caught the flames.

The explosion threw Lyadova and her bodyguards off their feet, as the fireballs burst up into the air. Billowing black smoke, licked with intense orange flames.

The helicopter was engulfed, but powered through. It came in circling over Lyadova as she moaned, laying in the snow.

Sukhanov and the two agents were closing in as she got to her feet.

Sukhanov fired, taking down one of her guards, before discarding his now empty pistol. Max and Verity fired past the President, taking down a sentinel each before they too ran out of ammunition.

The three remaining guards got to their feet and were searching the snow as Sukhanov arrived. He squared off with the first guard, trading blows. The older man had not lost much of his skill. The KGB training was kicking in and he was beating the guard to death.

Max and Verity arrived and took a guard each. Max ducked as his opponent swung. Verity dodged as hers lunged. Max countered and threw his own punch as Verity kneed her attacker in the stomach.

Lyadova climbed into the helicopter and started yelling at the pilots.

Sukhanov climbed in behind her and started fighting with the crew member who was in the chopper. The crew member tackled Sukhanov out of the helicopter and the two men fell out into the snow. They wrestled each other until they got back to their feet and started trading blows.

The crew member pushed Sukhanov back into the helicopter and slammed his head against metal door. Sukhanov caught himself and stopped his attacker from repeating the move, then dragged the airman around and traded places with him. He slammed his head into the chopper's frame, before the crew member pushed him back towards the tail rotor.

Max jumped into the air and drew back his right hand, slamming it down into his foe's face. As he landed, he sprang up, forcing himself to endure the pain, and sent a left hook into the guard's stomach. The winded assailant buckled over and Max drove his good knee into his face, knocking him out.

Verity kicked her attacker in the knee and his leg collapsed with a sickening crack. As he fell to his knees, she grabbed his chin and the back of his head and twisted with all her remaining strength, snapping his neck.

Max and Verity saw the President get pushed towards the rotor blades, but were thankful when he stopped only inches from it. They ran for the chopper.

Sukhanov could feel the blades only inches behind him and he was trying to move away, when he saw Max and Verity coming over his assailant's shoulder.

He waited, watching the guard, but keeping one eye on the two approaching western agents.

When they were within two metres, Sukhanov dropped to the ground.

Verity had launched herself into the air and kicked the airman in the back. The guard stumbled forward and Sukhanov tripped him. His momentum launched him face first into the rotating blades at the back of the chopper just as it was lifting off.

The blades sliced through Sukhanov's attacker in a sickening whirl of red mist.

Sukhanov was covered in blood and as he wiped away the thick red liquid from his eyes, he saw Verity smiling and standing over him. She smiled then punched him hard knocking him to the ground, then she used some cable ties to tie Sukhanov's hands behind his back.

Max stood on the skid of the big chopper and reached up for a rope handle which was flapping in the doorway. His shoes were slippery from the snow and the skids were covered in a light layer of ice. He was holding on with all his strength as the helicopter climbed into the air. The remaining A&A solider climbed over into the rear with Lyadova and started punching and pushing Max, trying to get him to fall from the aircraft.

Max was fighting him with one hand as the chopper climbed higher and moved in over the greenhouses.

Max grabbed the guard's belt and reefed him through the door. Lyadova's final guard fell, screaming the whole way down until he smashed through the glass roof of the greenhouse and was engulfed by the flames below.

As the screaming airman sailed passed, Max's foot slipped off the skid and he was struggling to pull himself back up. Lyadova smiled watching him flapping about, but her smile faded when he regained his footing.

Lyadova undid her seatbelt and stomped over. She drew back her right hand, then threw a punch.

Max caught her fist and her eyes went wide in fear, thinking she was about to follow the guard out the door.

Max pushed her back and she fell into the cabin and scrambled across the floor away from him.

"Call off the attacks!" Max yelled over the sound of the chopper blades.

"It is too late," Lyadova said. "The missiles are almost at their first destinations."

Max grabbed Lyadova by the throat and dragged her up onto the chair. He looked around and found the tablet on the opposite seat.

"Are you going to kill me?" Lyadova asked.

"You deserve to die," Max said, "but contrary to what you or others may believe I don't need or want to kill you. I have spent most of my life killing people, people like you, but I don't want to do it anymore. I've lost loved ones and I've been running for so long. I have been shot and stabbed, and I have bled. You are going to unlock this tablet and stop the attacks, then I'm going to place you under arrest and personally deliver you to The Hague. You are my final mission. You and your dear old dad."

Max stepped over to the other seat and picked up the tablet.

As he turned back, Lyadova was out of her seat and running for the door.

She jumped.

Max dived and caught her wrist, but her momentum dragged him with her. His feet slid in under the seats and they jolted to a stop.

Lyadova smiled up at Max. Max reached back behind himself. His fingers danced around on the metal floor until he found what he was looking for.

"It's too late! I'm not going to let you stop me from getting my revenge and destroying him!" Lyadova yelled up, feeling his grip slipping on her wrist. "All that matters is that he loses. You have failed your final mission, Agent Shaw. Enjoy the chaos that follows."

"I haven't failed yet," Max said, reaching out with his other hand and dragging her up and pressing her hand to the tablet.

Lyadova's eyes widened in realisation.

The tablet unlocked as Max lost his grip on Lyadova's wrist. She fell, eyes wide in fear and in failure, but she did not scream.

Max watched as she fell. She didn't make a sound or flail about, she just accepted her fate.

Her back slammed into the thick layer of ice on a pond on the palace grounds and it shattered. She paused on the surface for a few seconds, before sinking between the ice shards into the cold black pond and into the darkness below the surface. There was no way she could have survived.

Max pulled himself back into the helicopter and climbed over into the cockpit.

"Take us back and land the helicopter," Max said to the pilot.

"I'm not taking you anywhere," the pilot said.

Max turned to the pilot and grabbed his head and threw it into the glass. Once, twice, three times. He reached over, opened the pilot's door.

The pilot punched and lashed out as the helicopter started swinging wildly in the air. Max elbowed the pilot, then unclipped his seatbelt and pushed him out. The Pilot grabbed on tight, but Max punched his fingers, and he lost his grip and he dropped from the door.

Max took the controls and levelled the helicopter, as the pilot fell to his death, piercing through the ice covered lake not far from where Lyadova had hit.

Max opened the Apollo app on the tablet and sent the abort command to the missiles closest to their targets, then set about aborting the remaining missiles.

As Max brought the helicopter in to land, the missiles were splashing down in the ocean or dropping harmlessly to the ground around the world.

Verity and Sukhanov were waiting. Verity pushed Sukhanov into the rear of the aircraft and took a seat beside him.

Max took off and headed for the airport.

Verity took control of Apollo as she held the Russian leader at gunpoint.

"Mister Vice President," Max said into his headset as Blake connected the call. "This is Agent Max Shaw of the Australian Intelligence Service. The threat is over. My colleague Agent Verity Humphries from MI6 has aborted the cyber-attack and I aborted the Russian missiles."

"They still fired them," Moore said. *"The missiles splashed down, in more than one case, only metres from some of our bases and ships."*

"It wasn't the Russians, sir. It was Lyadova."

"How can we be sure?"

"Let me put Sukhanov on the phone."

"He is with you now?"

"Yes, sir."

"How?"

"I will let him fill you in."

Max turned back to Sukhanov.

"Now is your chance, Mister President," Max said. "Time to do the right thing."

Sukhanov explained what Lyadova had done and gave assurances that the Russian military had been told to stand down. He promised to work with the allies over the next few hours to take their respective militaries off high alert and bring them back to a normal footing.

Moore had cautiously agreed with a warning of catastrophic consequences if Sukhanov was lying.

"The Americans and their allies have agreed to terms," Sukhanov said. "Where do we go from here?"

"We're going to the airport," Max said. "You'll clear our flight out of Russia and then we'll discuss what happens next."

"I will make sure you are both thanked and honoured for what you did today," Sukhanov said to Max and Verity, almost begging for forgiveness. "You saved our countries from a war neither side could ever have won. I will ensure your records are clear with my country and that you are honoured here for your efforts."

Max and Verity just nodded unsure how to respond. Sukhanov seemed to think he might be in the clear and was happy with himself.

"So, what do we do now?" Verity asked, breaking the awkward silence.

"I've got to make a few calls and you need to get back to work," Max said. "And, MI6 is going to need to take Birmingham into custody."

"Can't we just go somewhere warm and drink cocktails on the beach? I'm sick of the snow and the fighting."

"Tell me about it."

Max landed at the airport where they found Gabriel's plane and left Russia.

Epilogue

Max flew back to The Hague and turned himself over to van den Berg and presented his prisoner, Sukhanov.

Van den Berg and Blake had been sharing information, and the officer was quick to agree a lot of what had happened since Max's escape hadn't made sense. He knew when Max escaped the farm in France something wasn't right. Max had stopped to check if he was all right after the car crashed into the lake. Hardly the actions of a terrorist.

Van den Berg took Max back to International Criminal Court and gave evidence in support of Max's actions.

"Mister Shaw," the new Chief Justice of the International Criminal Court said, "this court and the world owes you a debt of gratitude. Following the statement from the President of the Russian Federation, who accompanied you here, he has been placed in custody until a full inquiry can be held. The court has heard the evidence presented by the Australian Intelligence Service that you recorded in Moscow, and thanks to Commander van den Berg, a series of arrests have been made. The former Prime Minister and Attorney-General of the United Kingdom have been arrested and are en route, here to The Hague, as we speak. The former Chief Justice of this court was also arrested for accepting bribes to influence cases. A&A Enterprises has been taken over by the American Government and the Apollo program has been dismantled, along with its servers."

"Given the overwhelming evidence and the acknowledgement of your role in stopping what could have escalated into World War III – a war the world may never have recovered from – all charges have been dropped and I am pleased to say you are free to go. Is there anything you would like to say?"

"Thank you, Madam Chief Justice," Max said. "I don't have anything to add other than to thank the court and say I look forward to my early retirement."

"We wish you well. The court is adjourned."

"Thank you," Max said, standing as the justices left the room.

Max met Verity at the back of the courtroom.

"How's the leg?" Verity asked.

"It'll heal," Max said. "I've had worse."

"I'm sure you have. So, are you really retiring?"

"Yes. I finally have the chance to return home to be with the man I love after so many years of loneliness and death and heartache. I'm sick of running and I'm sick of not having a life. And, as you said on the chopper, I'm sick of fighting. I have given everything and now it is time for me to take some time for myself."

"It's well deserved, Max."

"What are you going to do?"

"The acting Prime Minister has abandoned plans to abolish MI6, so when I fully recover, I will be going back to work, but for now, I'm thinking of heading to Hawaii or somewhere for those cocktails on the beach."

"Well, I'm glad someone as tough and ruthless as you will be on the job, when you get back from the beach. I'll retire easier knowing that someone is out there looking after the world."

"We all owe you, Max. I owe you for saving my life."

"You saved mine too. Thank you."

"Good luck, Max," Verity said, hugging Max.

"Same to you," Max said as Verity walked away.

Max walked out of the court and climbed into his waiting car which took him to the airport.

He climbed the steps of the gleaming white, unmarked converted Dreamliner owned by the Australian Intelligence Service.

"Retiring, hey?" Blake asked as Max walked into the main suite.

"It's time for me to finally have a life," Max said smiling, "and I'm hoping you will be a big part of it."

"I would love to be a part of it, on one condition."

"What's that?" Max asked as Blake walked over and took Max's hands.

"That you play a big part in my life too."

"It's a deal," Max said as they kissed passionately.

"Admiral Smyth," the pilot said, walking into the room, "Agent Shaw, I apologise for the interruption. Are you ready to take off?"

"Yes, thank you, Jack," Blake said. "Take us home."

"Yes, sir," the pilot said, turning to leave, but he stopped in the doorway and turned back. "Agent Shaw, that item you requested is in the top drawer."

"Thanks, Jack," Max said, walking over to the cabinet as the pilot left.

"What item?" Blake asked, genuinely shocked someone had put something on the plane without him knowing it.

Max opened the drawer and pulled out the item.

"Since the day I met you all those years ago at the Wool Shed," Max said, turning around again to face Blake, "I knew there was something special about you. We have been friends ever since and you have been there for me through the highest of highs and the lowest of lows. I have thought of nothing more than having you in my life and being with you for years. You mean the world to me and I want to make it official."

Max got down on one knee and opened the small box he had retrieved from the drawer.

"I love you, Blake," Max said, taking out the platinum ring with its five small square diamonds. "Will you marry me?"

Blake walked over to his desk and pulled out a small box. He walked back over to Max and took a knee in front of him.

He opened his own small box.

"I love you too, Max," Blake said, taking out a similar platinum ring with square cut diamonds. "Of course I will marry you. I want to spend the rest of our lives together. You mean the world to me too. We've waited so long and I don't want to wait a minute longer."

"Me either," Max said as the couple exchanged rings and kissed passionately again.

"You're such a romantic," Blake said, smiling.

"That I am guilty of," Max said, looking down at his own engagement ring and smiling, "but so are you."

"Please be seated for take-off," the pilot said over the intercom as the engines whirled to life.

Max and Blake got to their feet.

Blake took his seat as Max walked over and grabbed a bottle of wine and two glasses.

He took his seat beside Blake, poured the wine and they held hands and sipped their wine as the plane climbed into the sky and banked for home.

The End.

Max Shaw will return in *Shaw Salvation*.

www.jwpublishing.com.au